THE WEEKEND ESCAPE

RAKIE BENNETT

One More Chapter
a division of HarperCollins*Publishers*
1 London Bridge Street
London SE1 9GF
www.harpercollins.co.uk

HarperCollins*Publishers*
1st Floor, Watermarque Building, Ringsend Road
Dublin 4, Ireland

1

This paperback edition 2022
First published in Great Britain in ebook format
by HarperCollins*Publishers* 2021

A catalogue record of this book is available from the British Library

ISBN: 978-0-00-848696-9

Printed and bound in the UK using 100% Renewable Electricity
by CPI Group (UK) Ltd

For my mum-in-law, Helen

Prologue

SUNDAY 25TH AUGUST 2019

9:15am

Furness General Hospital, Barrow-in-Furness

When the police officers came to speak to her, less than twelve hours after she'd been brought to the hospital, Lyndsey had told them she'd just woken up. She wanted an excuse for her muddled thinking. The truth was she'd been awake for hours. Despite her exhaustion, she was sure she'd never sleep right again.

'Do you know where you are?'

The police officer had introduced herself, but Lyndsey had immediately forgotten the name. It was difficult to retain information. Her mind felt like it was full of wet cotton.

'Hospital,' Lyndsey answered. She was grateful for an easy question. 'I'm pretty sure this is a hospital. I mean, if it's not, I've got queries … about the catheter, in particular.'

The officer gave her a look. It was the wrong time for making jokes.

Lyndsey scrunched the edge of the blanket between her fingers. *Why would I say something so flippant? What's wrong with me?* But she knew why. Her brain was trying to protect her. She didn't want to think about the past two days. She would've given anything to erase them from her memory.

'Do you remember why you're here?' the officer asked. Her tone was gentle, like she was trying to coax Lyndsey down from a ledge.

'I drowned,' Lyndsey said, then amended, 'I *almost* drowned. They're worried I've got water in my lungs. Also, shock. They tell me I'm in shock, from … everything.' She made a half-hearted gesture towards the clumpy bandage covering half of her face.

'Can you tell us how it happened?'

Lyndsey looked away. The bright lights on the monitor at her bedside were blurry. She realised she was crying.

The police officer put a comforting hand on Lyndsey's arm, just below where the cannula was taped down. 'It'll be all right. Just take it slow.'

Lyndsey couldn't blink away the tears. 'My friends are dead.' Her voice cracked on the words. 'They're *dead*. Please don't tell me it's going to be all right.'

Chapter One

FRIDAY 23RD AUGUST 2019

11am

Shell Island

'Remind me again why we agreed to this?' Lyndsey asked. She tried to keep her words light, but they came out too thin and high. She heard the tremor in her own voice.

'Because we promised,' Amanda said from a safe distance away. 'Look how happy Juliet is. Just look at her face.'

Lyndsey was stood at the very edge with her back to the drop. She had no intention of twisting round to look down at Juliet, a hundred and fifty feet below her. Over the constant bluster of the wind, she heard Juliet shout something that was probably encouragement.

Instead of looking down, Lyndsey glanced at her other four friends, who stood in the main rotunda of the gallery deck, well away from the sheer drop. Bobbie looked ill. Val was leaning against a wall to rest. Amanda smiled and gave Lyndsey a thumbs-up. Sonia, with a playful roll of her eyes, said, 'C'mon, Lynds. You're holding up traffic.'

Taking a deep breath, Lyndsey stepped backwards off the concrete ledge.

There was a sickening moment – a moment long enough for her to be horribly certain something had gone wrong and she would plummet to her death – before the harness around her waist caught her weight. The blue rope, which she gripped tightly in her gloved hands, ran through the figure-of-eight descender attached to the harness; a red safety rope was tied around her middle as a fail-safe. In theory, she was safer in this harness than in a car. As Val had helpfully pointed out, the gear was tested to hold the weight of an elephant. The safety line was looped up through an anchor point above her, on the gallery deck of the old lighthouse, the loose end trailing down past Lyndsey to where Juliet, at the base of the lighthouse, held it slung around her hips, letting out a measure at a time. If anything went wrong with the blue rope, the red rope would stop Lyndsey from falling.

And yet, Lyndsey couldn't calm her racing pulse. The ropes looked barely strong enough to hold up a brick, let alone a whole person.

It didn't help that, because of the overhang of the

concrete balcony, Lyndsey now hung a few feet away from the sheer wall. A gust of wind pushed her into a gentle spin that made her want to scream.

'How're you doing?' Sonia called from above.

Lyndsey didn't dare look up. Her attention was fixed on the blue rope. Her left hand held it above the descender, her right hand below it. Gingerly, she relaxed her grip a little and the rope slid through the metal loops, enough to lower her a few inches. At the same time, Juliet gave out some slack to the safety line.

'That's it,' Sonia called encouragingly. 'Just a *little* bit faster. Y'know, if you want to reach the ground sometime today.'

Lyndsey wished she had a hand free to make a rude gesture at her. She gritted her teeth and lowered herself a bit more. *Come on*, she told herself, *you've done this before...* Just not since she was a teenager. Somehow, she'd managed to forget, in the intervening ten years, just how terrifying an abseil could be.

Another few feet and she could set her feet against the concrete wall of the lighthouse. Now, even though the wind still buffeted her, she didn't feel like she'd be plucked off and flung into the sea at any moment. She focused on her breathing.

The cold bit at her exposed face and forearms. A jacket would've kept off the wind but it would've restricted her movement too much. Everyone had taken off their outer layers and left them in a pile at the base of the lighthouse, along with their rucksacks. Despite the chill, Lyndsey was sweating hard.

The worst bit is over, she told herself. Now it was just a slow backwards walk to the bottom. Easy, so long as she didn't look down … or up. Looking up would make her just as dizzy. Off to her left was the coast, and beyond that, the wild, empty stretch of the ruffled Irish Sea. There was nothing to block the wind, save for the lighthouse itself.

If she'd twisted all the way round, she might've been able to spot the rolling hills of the mainland. Shell Island sat just a couple of miles off the coast of northwest England. But Lyndsey kept her eyes on the rope. Right at that moment, she didn't want to be reminded of how far she was from home.

The lighthouse was almost two hundred feet high and had been disused since the 1970s. Somehow, Juliet had used her contacts to get access to the building. A previous climbing group had installed an anchor point on the gallery deck at the top, where Lyndsey's friends were now waiting their turn. Lyndsey tried not to wonder how long it'd been since anyone had used the anchor point.

Even if the main rope gives way, Juliet's got you on the safety line. She won't let you fall.

A blast of wind caught her. Her feet scooted sideways across the concrete as she fought to keep from going into another spin. She hunched her shoulders and gripped tightly onto the rope. As the gust subsided, she let herself swing gently back to beneath the balcony.

'You're doing great,' Juliet called from below. She still sounded far away, but at least Lyndsey could hear her now over the wind.

The gust had scared Lyndsey. She forced herself to breathe steadily. Then she kept moving.

Once Lyndsey found her rhythm, it was a lot easier: keeping a steady grip on the rope, letting it slide through the metal ring on her harness, walking her feet down the concrete, one step at a time. Remaining braced against the wind. It was surprising how quickly the moves came back to her. It was hard to believe it was ten years since she'd last abseiled.

She wondered how the rest of the group would manage. Amanda would be fine because, from what she'd said when they were on their way here, she'd kept going on climbing trips almost every weekend, even after she left high school and moved away. But as for the others…

'You're there, you're there!' Juliet said. 'Put your legs down!'

Lyndsey had been moving on autopilot. She glanced over her shoulder. The ground was no more than ten feet below her.

She shoved off from the wall and let out the rope. Her intention was to get her feet below her and land sort-of gracefully, but she misjudged and came down in an awkward crouch. She struggled to keep her balance. Juliet came to help.

'How was it?' Juliet asked with a grin.

'Relatively awful.' Lyndsey tried to unfasten her harness. After two failed attempts, she realised her hands were shaking. She had to let Juliet disentangle the ropes.

Once Lyndsey was unclipped, Juliet stepped back and

shouted up, 'Clear!' to the group at the top. On the balcony above, Amanda hauled up the blue rope.

Juliet pulled Lyndsey into a hug. 'You did great,' Juliet said. 'You didn't really hate it, did you?'

'No, of course not. Just the bit at the start. And the middle. Also the end – that wasn't great.' Despite everything, Lyndsey laughed. 'No, it wasn't terrible.'

'We used to do this all the time.' Juliet's tone was wistful.

'Yeah, when we were kids. We felt like we were—' Lyndsey bit her tongue. *Invincible*, she was about to say. 'It didn't seem so scary back then,' she said instead. 'And I didn't used to get winded climbing up a few stairs.'

They were sheltered at the base of the lighthouse. A high stone wall encircled a small square courtyard and blocked the worst of the wind. The scrubby grass had been clipped short by rabbits, and there was a rough path leading around to the lighthouse entrance, but the edges of the courtyard were overgrown with thick nests of gorse and ragwort. Although it was only the end of August, a few of the bramble bushes already had blackberries ripening.

High above them, someone else shuffled backwards to the edge of the concrete balcony. Lyndsey could see curls of red hair escaping from under the climbing helmet. *Bobbie*. It was standard for Bobbie to go in the middle of the group – not first or last, but comfortably mid-league, to give her time to steel her nerves. She was always the most moderate of them.

'Here she goes,' Juliet said. She slung the loops of the

safety rope around her hips, and braced her legs, ready. 'Go for it, Bobs!'

Lyndsey watched Bobbie lean back over the drop. Looking up like that, with the grey clouds scudding past overhead, made it seem like the lighthouse was about to topple on top of them. Lyndsey had to drop her gaze.

'I knew she could do it!' Juliet said. She was grinning proudly up at Bobbie.

'How did you convince her, in the end?' Lyndsey asked. Reflexively she lowered her voice, even though there was zero chance Bobbie could overhear.

'What d'you mean? There was no convincing necessary. She signed up for this weekend before I'd even asked the rest of you.'

'Really?' Lyndsey couldn't keep the surprise from her voice. 'You told Sonia she'd bailed out.'

'I didn't want to jinx things.' Juliet shrugged it off. 'You know what she's like. Sometimes the slightest thing can make her change her mind.'

Lyndsey had to admit it'd been a lovely surprise to see Bobbie arrive that morning. The group had all met up in a pub near the train station in Ravenswater before walking down to the harbour, and when Bobbie had appeared, it'd been a surprise for everyone. Sonia in particular had looked stunned and speechless – a real rarity for her. Lyndsey had just felt relieved. Bobbie was one of her best friends, and had always been a stabilising element in the group. Hers was the voice of reason. When she'd walked into the pub that morning, Lyndsey's shoulders had relaxed a touch.

This weekend will be fun, Lyndsey had repeated to herself

– a private mantra that had stopped her from backing out, weeks ago. *You're going to enjoy yourself.*

'Bobbie turned so sensible after she got married,' Lyndsey said. 'Does she still hang out with you? I've hardly heard from her before this year.'

Juliet started to answer, but broke off as Bobbie stepped off the ledge. 'Atta girl!' Juliet called. 'You can do it!' She let the safety line play out through her gloved hands.

At a cautious, steady pace, Bobbie descended towards them. Her entire attention was focused on her hands. Even the wind couldn't rattle her. She kept her feet planted firmly against the concrete all the way to the bottom.

As soon as she touched down, Juliet rushed over for a high five, but Bobbie fended her off, hurrying to unclip herself, then staggered away to be noisily sick in the gorse.

'Are you okay?' Juliet asked. Bobbie nodded and waved her away.

'Give her some space.' Lyndsey took Juliet's arm. No one liked having people hovering over them while they were ill. Lyndsey was just glad Bobbie had held it in till she got off the climb.

Juliet returned to her position with the safety line as Val came down next. Lyndsey could see someone, presumably Sonia, assisting Val as the harness took her weight. Once she was swinging free, Val moved easier. She kept her legs ramrod straight as she descended, not so much walking down as dragging her feet along the wall.

Sonia came next, fast and jerky, like she wanted it to be over as quickly as possible. She reached the bottom almost before the others were ready. Lyndsey got there first, putting a steadying hand on Sonia's back.

'I think I remember why I quit doing this stuff,' Sonia said. She looked relieved to be on solid ground. 'Is it possible to develop spontaneous vertigo?'

'Don't see why not,' Lyndsey said. 'It's kinda sensible to be scared of falling from heights.'

Sonia looked over her shoulder. 'Is Bobbie all right?'

'Sure. Just a touch of nerves.'

Val said, 'I don't blame her at all. Give me a minute, I might join her in the bushes.' She lowered herself to sit on the damp grass with her legs sticking out in front of her like a toddler. With a grimace, she bent one knee then the other. Even before she'd left high school, she'd started having trouble with her joints. Apparently, it'd got worse in the past ten years.

High above them, Amanda, the last one left at the top of the lighthouse, pulled up the loose end of the blue rope. A minute later, she shouted down to say she was ready, and Juliet responded. There was a practised ease in the way they called back and forth. It had a soothing effect on Lyndsey's nerves, reminding her of better times, when adventures like this were normal. Every weekend – or as often as they could manage – during their Sixth Form years at high school, the group of friends would go out scrambling, or orienteering, or hillwalking … whatever they fancied. A few times they'd gone sea kayaking, although Bobbie had avoided that, because just looking at the ocean made her nauseous.

That was another reason why Lyndsey was surprised Bobbie had agreed to coming on this weekend retreat.

They'd travelled to the island from Ravenswater via the smallest, oldest fishing boat Lyndsey had ever seen, with an engine that smoked and sputtered and sounded like it was on the verge of conking out. Bobbie had turned green before they'd even left the harbour on the mainland. The journey was only supposed to take twenty minutes, out of the estuary mouth then down the curve of the coast to Shell Island, but because of the choppy state of the sea, it had taken more than thirty. It was no wonder she was still feeling ill.

Lyndsey's own stomach wasn't too settled either. She'd been too nervous to eat breakfast and, even though it was now lunchtime, she wasn't thinking about food. The two pints of bitter she'd had at the pub, while waiting for the rest of the group to arrive on their various trains, hadn't helped like she'd hoped they would.

The wind was definitely picking up. Lyndsey shielded her eyes as she watched Amanda step off the ledge. The clouds were a thick, dark grey, threatening rain at any moment. She hoped it would hold off until they reached the bunkhouse, which was apparently half a mile further inland. The group had gone straight to the lighthouse for their first abseil, since it was close to the tiny landing stage at the south of the island where the fishing boat had dropped them off. Lyndsey was sure she wasn't the only one looking forward to discovering where they'd be spending the night. Out of the group, only Juliet had visited the island before, and that'd been eighteen years ago, when she was eleven, on a family camping trip. The place was bound to have changed since then.

A particularly strong gust of wind hit Amanda full force. She was shoved away from the wall like a spider on a thread. The wind twisted her and, as she swung back, she thumped her shoulder against the concrete.

'Are you okay?' Lyndsey called.

Awkwardly, Amanda managed to get her feet back onto the wall. She waited till she was steady before shouting to say she was all right.

'You're doing great,' Juliet said, letting out a little more safety rope. It was doubtful that Amanda had heard her over the wind.

Not that Amanda needed encouragement. As soon as she got her feet in place, she started bounding down the wall in a series of smooth glides. Her experience made it look effortless.

'Glad those two are having fun,' Sonia said with a nod towards Juliet and Amanda. 'Makes you happy you changed your mind, huh?'

'Changed my mind about what?' Lyndsey asked.

'About coming with us.' Sonia lifted her gaze to watch the scudding clouds. 'Last we heard, you were dead against the idea.'

Lyndsey gave her an irritated look. 'I wasn't dead against anything. I just got put off when Juliet sent through the kit list last month.'

Sonia snorted. 'Tell me about it. A full page of equipment for three days of climbing? Get in the sea.'

Juliet glanced away from the ropes for long enough to give her a mock-irritated look, which made Sonia laugh.

'Still, nice to get away,' Sonia said. 'Reconnect with old

friends and new places.' She made a gesture towards the rest of the small island. 'Feels like we're at the edge of the world here, doesn't it?'

'Don't be dramatic. We can't be more than fifty miles in a straight line from your house.'

'Yeah, but there's a couple of miles of seawater in the way right now. That kinda makes me feel ... hemmed in, y'know?'

Lyndsey hadn't thought about it that way at all. If anything, she felt too exposed on this tiny chunk of rock in the middle of the sea, with nothing but the grey bowl of sky above them. Looking up at the clouds gave her pangs of agoraphobia.

'Can't believe Amanda's here,' Sonia said then. 'I thought I'd misheard when Juliet said she was coming. When was the last time any of us—?'

A sudden shout grabbed their attention. Lyndsey spun round in time to see Amanda fall.

She must've been at least twenty feet up when the blue rope gave way. The safety line snapped taut under Amanda's full weight, yanking Juliet off balance. Juliet lost her grip for a vital half-second. That was all the time it took. Amanda landed hard on her back on the grass.

'Look out!' Lyndsey yelled.

The blue rope must've come untethered at the top, because it was unravelling fast, right behind Amanda. Amanda had the presence of mind to roll sideways. The heavy coils of rope thudded down, right where she'd landed.

Everyone rushed to her. Juliet reached her first.

'Amanda! Are you okay?'

From the back of the group, Bobbie asked, 'What happened? Is she all right?'

For a second, Amanda was silent, and Lyndsey's stomach lurched. Twenty feet was a long way. You could be badly injured from falling even half that height.

Then Amanda sucked in a painful breath. The scrubby grass hadn't done much to cushion her landing. She gasped for breath like she was badly winded.

'My leg,' she moaned. 'My leg hurts.'

Her left leg was tucked underneath her right one. She must've tried to put her feet down at the last instant.

'Don't move,' Val ordered. 'You're okay, just don't try to move. Does anything hurt apart from your leg?'

'Winded.' Amanda scrunched up her face in pain. 'Give me a sec.'

Sonia was waving her phone around, trying to get a signal. 'I've got no reception,' she said, then looked up at the lighthouse. 'I'll see if it works higher up.'

No one stopped her as she raced around the lighthouse to the entrance. Everyone was too concerned about Amanda.

'Do your hands hurt?' Val was asking. 'Any tingling? What about your feet? Can you feel your toes?'

'What happened?' Bobbie asked again.

'The rope.' Lyndsey picked up the coils of blue climbing rope. 'It must've come untied…'

Even as she said it, she knew that couldn't be true. Amanda and Juliet were both experienced climbers. There was no way they would've cocked up tying the rope at the top. Lyndsey had watched them do it. She'd even checked it herself.

'I'm so sorry,' Juliet said. 'I thought I had a tight hold of the safety line.' She opened her hands to reveal the scuffed palms of her climbing gloves. When the main rope gave way, all of Amanda's weight had fallen onto the red safety line. If Juliet hadn't been wearing gloves, her hands would've been torn open. 'I'm so sorry.'

Gently, Val prodded Amanda's knee and lower leg. 'Can you flex your toes?' she asked.

Amanda nodded. Her face had gone ashen. 'It's not so bad. Maybe it's okay.'

'Here, I'll hold this leg while you try and straighten your knee. All right?'

The movement made Amanda suck in her breath, but she was able to slowly straighten her left leg.

'If you can move it, it's probably not broken,' Val said. 'Don't try and get up. You might've hurt your back.'

Lyndsey followed the blue rope until she found where it came to an end in a mass of frayed, twisted cords.

'The rope—' she started to say, then had to swallow, hard. 'Your rope snapped,' she finished.

There was a silence, filled only by the noise of the wind. 'No.' said Juliet. A simple denial. 'There's no way. It's a new rope. I've only used it a few times.'

'See for yourself.'

Juliet snatched the frayed end of the rope and held it close to her face, as if that might disprove anything.

Lyndsey looked up at the balcony they'd abseiled from.

She tried to spot the dangling end of the rope but couldn't see it. It must've broken very high up.

'We need to get the coastguard,' Val said.

Amanda immediately objected. 'No, we don't. I'm fine. Just winded.'

'You might've seriously damaged yourself. We should get you taken to a hospital.'

'Are you kidding? You want to call the coastguard for *this?*'

'You fell off a lighthouse.'

'I did not. I fell like ten feet. And I'm fine.'

'Please quit trying to sit up. Don't make me forcibly restrain you.'

If Amanda could argue, Lyndsey reasoned, she couldn't be too badly hurt. But still, the very fact the accident had happened made Lyndsey's hands shake. Thank God the rope hadn't snapped when Amanda had been higher up. Or when any of the others were descending.

The thought made Lyndsey's stomach clench. It could've happened to any of them. She hated herself for the sudden relief she felt. *It could've been me.*

She left Val and Juliet in charge of Amanda and went into the lighthouse. They'd entered through the heavy wooden door at the bottom, where a padlock hung from a bolt. Juliet had been entrusted by National Heritage with the only key, but she'd left the padlock open while they were abseiling.

There was very little light inside. Lyndsey switched on the headtorch attached to her climbing helmet. The yellowy beam fell on the mess of brick dust and bird droppings that covered the floor. She tilted her head towards the stone stairs, which snaked up in a lazy spiral around the inside of the lighthouse, leaving the centre empty. She lifted her light up … and up … and up…

Right at the very top, a square of daylight was visible. It was so far away, Lyndsey got a twinge of vertigo.

'Sonia?' she called. Her voice echoed. 'Are you up there?'

Sonia must've gone all the way to the gallery deck to try and get a signal. Lyndsey had no idea if that would work. Did phone signal really get stronger the higher up you were, or was that a myth? On this isolated island, miles from home, she doubted any amount of altitude would help.

Lyndsey set off up the stairs for the second time that day. The first section wasn't too bad, but as she climbed higher, she became increasingly aware of the sheer drop on her right-hand side. All that protected her was a narrow metal handrail, sticking up on rusted spindles. Time and neglect had corroded away whole sections. When she leaned her hand on it, it wobbled. Flecks of rust fluttered off towards the distant floor.

She had to pause to steady her nerves. Normally, Lyndsey didn't have a problem with heights. She was used to going up and down cliffs – or at least she *had* been, as a teenager. But something about this place gave her the jitters. Perhaps it was the shape of the lighthouse interior, which narrowed as it got higher, so she felt like the walls were pushing her towards the drop with each step.

Or perhaps it was the thought of Amanda falling from this height.

'Sonia?' she called again.

As she approached the top, Lyndsey heard the wind howling. It sounded strong enough to make the whole building tremble. One hand clutched onto the rail with a death-grip, the other pressed flat against the wall, and she swore she could feel the stone shuddering with each gust.

By that point, she was out of breath and winded. Her first climb up the steps had brought home how much her fitness had slipped over the past couple of years. When was the last time she'd done any serious cardio? That was one of the main reasons why she'd agreed to this trip – she'd hoped it would rekindle her urge to exercise.

At the top of the stairs, a doorway led into the rotunda which had once housed the mechanical heart of the lighthouse. The machinery had been stripped out years ago, and the bits and pieces that remained – a few metal brackets and screws on the concrete floor – were surrounded by discoloured halos of rust. Wind shrieked through the cracked panes of glass on all sides. Several of the windows had been broken over the years, and the floor was littered with shards of glass, some of them as big as her hand.

A second open doorway led outside to the wide balcony. Beyond it, the sea stretched away, furrowed into wind-tossed waves. It seemed like an age ago that Lyndsey had stepped backwards off that ledge to abseil down. Another thin railing protected against the drop on the other side. The scariest part of the descent had been climbing over that railing in order to begin the abseil.

She expected Sonia to be outside on the balcony, seeking phone reception, but instead the woman was inside the rotunda, crouched to look at something on the floor.

'Sonia? What's wrong?' Lyndsey's voice was hoarse and breathless. Her heart pounded from exertion.

'Come and look at this,' Sonia said. She was near the steel bracket that protruded from the middle of the concrete floor. It'd been put there a decade earlier, Juliet said, by that other bunch of climbers, so everyone could use it as a safe belay point. Solid steel bolts secured it to the floor.

'What're you doing? Did you call the coastguard?'

Sonia shook her head. 'No reception. Look.'

She was holding the tattered end of the rope. It had snapped no more than two feet from the anchor point. That surprised Lyndsey. If it was going to break anywhere, she would've expected it to be at the lip of the balcony, where the rope would've rubbed against the rough concrete edge.

She got another surprise when she looked closer. The top edge of the cut was clean and sharp as if someone had cut halfway through the rope before it snapped under Amanda's weight.

Chapter Two

FRIDAY

11:35am

S onia led the way down the spiralling stairs. She moved fast, apparently uncaring of the drop to their left, which to Lyndsey looked a lot worse now she was going downstairs.

'Sonia, slow down. You'll fall.'

It was maybe the wrong choice of words. Sonia paused long enough to glare up at her. Her face was tight and angry in the light from Lyndsey's headtorch. But she slowed her pace a little, and kept a reassuring hand on the railing. Lyndsey followed her as fast as she dared.

When they at last reached the bottom, they found Amanda was upright, leaning heavily against Juliet. She'd taken off her climbing helmet, and strands of her flyaway blonde hair had come loose from her ponytail. Her face was pinched and pale, which made her eyes look particularly large and vulnerable. Lyndsey was again struck by how frail she looked, even though Amanda was probably the most physically fit of them all.

'She wouldn't listen to me,' Val complained as soon as she caught sight of Sonia and Lyndsey. 'I told her to stay lying down. Please tell me the coastguard are on their way.'

Sonia shook her head tersely. 'Couldn't get through. And we've got bigger problems.'

She flung the short length of rope onto the ground. She'd insisted on untying it and bringing it down so everyone could see.

'The rope didn't snap,' Sonia said. 'Someone cut through it.'

'What?'

Juliet stared at the piece of rope like it was a snake. Val nudged it with her foot. They could all clearly see the clean, sharp edge of the cut next to the frayed strands that'd twisted and snapped.

The main coil of the blue rope was lying on the ground nearby. Sonia snatched it up and held out the broken end. Now Lyndsey knew what she was looking for, it was obvious, although the cut there was less clearly defined.

'That – that can't be right,' Juliet said. She looked like she wanted to take the rope from Sonia, but her arms were occupied keeping Amanda upright. 'It was fine when I tied it. You were all there. Amanda, you checked it yourself. Didn't you?'

Amanda couldn't stop staring at the cut rope. Her

complexion had paled further. 'I didn't check,' she said. 'I mean, I saw you tying the belay, but ... you knew what you were doing so I didn't...' She trailed off, shaking her head.

Juliet looked at the others in distress. 'It wasn't like that when I tied it,' she insisted. 'We would've noticed.'

Lyndsey nodded, because she wanted to agree, but inside she was wondering if maybe they *had* all overlooked it. A neat little cut in the rope ... it wouldn't necessarily have been visible unless they'd really examined it. And none of them had, not closely enough.

'You're sure it wasn't like that before?' Sonia asked, looking at Juliet.

'What're you saying? Yes, I'm sure. You think I'd miss something like that?'

'Okay.' Sonia narrowed her eyes. 'In that case, someone must've done it while we were descending.'

There was silence, apart from the whistle of the wind.

It was Bobbie who spoke first. She was standing some distance away, hands wrapped around the purple water bottle she always carried. 'No one would've done that,' she said. Her voice was faint. 'It was an accident.'

'She's right,' Amanda said. 'There must've been a – a scratch or a fault in the rope. Something we just – we just didn't notice. It happens. Right?'

Lyndsey found herself nodding. It had to be an accident. Because the alternative didn't bear thinking about.

'We need to contact the coastguard,' Juliet said. She raised her chin. 'That's what we should be worried about. Amanda needs medical attention.'

This time, Amanda didn't argue. Her thin face was pale

and drawn, and she was worrying her lower lip between her teeth.

'How're we going to contact anyone?' Val asked. 'Our phones aren't working.'

'There's a radio at the bunkhouse. The warden can help us.' Juliet straightened up with her arm still tucked around Amanda to help keep her upright. 'All right. Sonia, can you run on ahead and raise the alarm? We'll get Amanda to the bunkhouse.'

'We shouldn't be moving her,' Val grumbled. 'It'd be smarter to keep her here.'

'Yeah? For how long?' Juliet asked. 'It could be hours waiting for rescue.'

'I'd rather not wait out here,' Amanda said with a weak smile. 'Let's get to the bunkhouse, yeah? I can walk that far.'

'We'll take it slow, okay?' Juliet said. 'Leave your bags here. We'll come back for them later. Sonia, leave your bag too; you'll go faster without it.'

Sonia looked like she still wanted to argue, but swallowed it back. 'See you there,' she said shortly. Then she started off at a jog out of the courtyard and away from the lighthouse.

Lyndsey unclipped her harness and grabbed her rucksack, as well as the water-resistant bag containing the spare climbing kit. Val was sorting through the pile of jackets. She picked up two identical grey coats and held them up for size comparison, before passing the smaller one to Amanda. 'We must've visited the same sale rail,' Val commented. 'I knew I should've sewn names into my stuff.'

They left Sonia's backpack, along with Juliet's and

Amanda's, in the shelter of the wall. Lyndsey opened her mouth to ask whether it was safe to leave the bags unguarded, then realised how daft the question was. There was no one on the island to steal their stuff.

With Juliet's help, Amanda could limp at a slow pace. Bobbie walked alongside them, taking small, continuous sips from her water bottle, as if still battling nausea. Her face was creased with worry.

The island was only small, less than a mile wide. Most of the land was given over to scrubby grass, gorse, and bracken, with a few hardy trees braving the salt air. The island had once been used, many years ago, for cow and sheep farming. Dry stone walls, many of them tumbledown, separated the old fields and grazing paddocks. A track led up from the southern harbour to the bunkhouse, passing close to the old lighthouse.

Their pace was necessarily slow, because of Amanda's injured leg. Lyndsey lifted her face and felt the first drops of rain. *Typical.* She hoped it would hold off until they reached shelter.

Val came to walk next to Lyndsey. She'd unfastened her climbing helmet, but still wore it perched atop her head, since it was the easiest way to carry it. She took it off briefly to rub a hand over her cropped hair. Every time Lyndsey saw her, there was more grey in Val's hair. Val had always been an old soul, making a big deal of the fact that she was a year older than the rest of them, but over the last few years she'd really leaned into her old-lady aesthetic. She'd used the excuse of turning thirty to cheerfully quit buying any clothes or shoes that weren't designed solely for comfort.

'It would've been difficult for any of us to cut the rope,' Val said, conversationally.

'What?'

'We were all up at the top of the lighthouse together. None of us could've done it without the rest noticing.'

'No one cut the rope.' Lyndsey glanced around. Juliet, Amanda, and Bobbie were a little way behind them. She lowered her voice. 'It snapped, all right?'

'Sure, but what if it didn't?'

'None of us would've done it. For one thing, we were all using the same rope. It could've given way on any of us.'

'That's true.' Val didn't seem fazed by the conversation. She had a familiar tilt to her head which meant she was puzzling something, in the oddly detached manner Lyndsey remembered from school. *Professor Val*, they'd called her. Always picking away at everything to discover how it worked. On more than one occasion, she'd been sent out of class for arguing with their teacher.

Right at that moment, Lyndsey didn't want to think of this as a puzzle to be solved. She wanted to forget the whole nasty incident.

'Of course, we weren't paying attention,' Val said then. 'We were watching each other, not the belay point. It's possible someone could've damaged the rope without the rest of us noticing.'

'Stop it, Val. None of us did it. None of us would want to risk hurting someone.'

'No, of course not.' Why was there a sceptical note in her voice? 'But who else is there?'

'No one.' Lyndsey was losing patience. 'No one else was there. There's no one on this island but us.' Even as she said it, she knew it wasn't completely true: according to Juliet, there was a warden who lived in the bird observatory on the island, right next to the bunkhouse where the group would be staying. But Lyndsey said it anyway, hoping Val would drop the matter.

No such luck. 'Amanda was the last to come down,' Val said. 'The rope didn't snap until she was nearly at the bottom. So, perhaps it wasn't damaged until she started descending.'

'We were all on the ground by then,' Lyndsey said. 'No one was in the lighthouse.'

'None of *us*, no.' Val turned to look at Lyndsey with her pale eyes. 'But someone else could've been.'

The words sent a chill through Lyndsey. 'There's no one here but us,' she said again.

'We don't know that. Someone could've come into the lighthouse without us noticing. The door's on the other side to where we were abseiling. They could've slipped in, waited until Amanda started coming down the rope, then– '

From behind them, Juliet asked, 'What're you two talking about?'

Lyndsey gave Val a warning glare. 'Nothing,' she said. 'Just wondering if it's starting to rain.'

Mercifully, Val didn't say anything.

The rain started a few minutes before the bunkhouse came into view. The track passed through a gap in the drystone wall. Beyond it, to the left, was a sweep of stunted grass, kept short by rabbits, since there were no sheep on the island anymore. A few tenacious trees clung to the edges of the field. Lyndsey ran a gloved finger along the wet stones of the wall. When she touched it to her lips, it tasted of salt. The spray from the sea must reach every corner of this island.

Off to her right, on the other side of a large, flat field, were the bird observatory and, next door, the bunkhouse.

The bunkhouse looked bleaker and more exposed than it'd appeared on the National Heritage website. The stone building had been there for so long it'd begun to blend into the background. Moss and lichen climbed its walls. Its windows were dingy and a few slates were missing from its roof. Next door, the observatory looked like it was in a similar condition, but it at least appeared inhabited. The enclosed gardens in front were strewn with wooden pallets and netting.

Lyndsey glanced back at her friends. Juliet and Amanda weren't too far behind, although neither of them had spoken for a while. There was an identical look of concentration on their faces. Behind them, Bobbie brought up the rear. She looked worse than any of them. Her face was ghostly and her gaze was fixed on the ground at her feet. She didn't look like she could focus on anything except putting one foot in front of the other. The bright blue of her jacket washed the colour from her complexion.

I should check on her. Lyndsey started to go back, but at that moment she heard a shout.

She turned and spotted Sonia next to the bunkhouse, waving. Lyndsey waved back.

Sonia shouted something else. Her waving was more frantic.

'Something's wrong,' Lyndsey said.

She broke into a run. Within a dozen steps she realised her backpack and climbing bag were too heavy. She shrugged them off mid-step and kept going.

Sonia came out through the gate at the end of the overgrown garden. Her expression was pissed-off.

'No one's here,' Sonia called as soon as Lyndsey was within earshot.

'What?'

Sonia lifted her hands in exasperation. 'No one's here. I can't find the bloody warden.'

Lyndsey jogged to a halt, one hand pressed to her chest. 'Christ, I thought someone had died or something. Don't panic me like that.'

'I think we're entitled to panic.' Sonia glared at the blank windows of the bird observatory. 'The warden's supposed to be here. We were told they'd be here. Now we've got a proper emergency and we can't get in to use the goddamn radio.'

Lyndsey put her hands on her knees while she caught her breath. When she'd seen Sonia waving, she'd thought … well, she had no idea what she'd thought. Her nerves were stretched as tight as wire.

Belatedly, she remembered to signal to the others. 'It's okay,' she called. 'Don't panic.' She didn't want any of them busting a gut to run across the field like she'd just done.

'I'm considering whether to break a window,' Sonia said. 'I can see the radio – at least, I think I can. There's something boxy and radio-ish on the workbench in the warden's front room. Do you think I could get away with smashing a window? This is an emergency, after all.'

'Just … hold off on the window-smashing for a minute, okay?' Lyndsey looked at the two buildings – which were really just one building that'd been partitioned into two, sharing a common wall. At some point in the past, it looked like it'd been a decent-sized house with a barn or stable attached. 'What about the bunkhouse?' she asked. 'Can we get in there?'

'Yeah.' Sonia held up a key. 'It was taped to the front door. No note or anything, just the key. Very high security.'

'I guess casual burglary isn't a major issue out here.' Lyndsey glanced at the others, who were approaching at Amanda's limping pace. Even though they were some distance away, Lyndsey dropped her voice. 'Listen, we don't know how badly Amanda is hurt. I think the best thing we can do is get her into the bunkhouse and settled down. As soon as we find the warden, we'll call the coastguard.'

'All right, but the option of smashing a window is still right there. Just saying.'

Lyndsey went to the others to tell them the situation, then jogged back to pick up her bags from where she'd ditched them on the grass. Bobbie had waited for her by the bags.

'I would've carried them for you,' Bobbie said, 'but, y'know, your backpack is unnecessarily heavy.'

'I brought a couple of bottles of something nice for us all.' Lyndsey shouldered her rucksack. 'I thought we'd deserve a treat by this evening.' Now, she was thinking they would need a lunchtime drink just to fix their nerves. 'How're you feeling now?'

'Urgh, moderate to terrible.' Bobbie gave a flimsy smile. 'I don't know why, but somehow I forgot we'd need to get on a boat to get here. I hate boats. If I close my eyes, it still feels like the ground is boggling.'

The rain had progressed to a constant drizzle, which looked soft but was collecting on Lyndsey's climbing helmet, then running down to drip onto her face and down her neck.

'You'll feel better with a cup of tea and a rest,' Lyndsey said. 'And maybe a drop of something stronger.'

Bobbie wrinkled her nose, but didn't reply.

Chapter Three

FRIDAY

12:10pm

S onia had unlocked the front door to the bunkhouse and stepped inside by the time the others got there. 'Home sweet home,' she said sourly.

Lyndsey had expected the accommodation to be basic. It'd been advertised as a bothy, providing 'a base for up to eight adventurous people'. Whilst preparing for the trip, Juliet had warned the group to bring sleeping bags, a pillow, and food and water for the full three days. So, Lyndsey had known not to expect luxury.

Still, she was taken aback. The first thing she noticed was the damp, fusty smell, like the place hadn't been aired out in a long time. It was cold too. Lyndsey had been praying for central heating or maybe a nice wood-burning stove. Anything to take off the chill that'd been settling into her bones since she'd stepped onto the boat that morning.

Sonia found a light switch and clicked it on and off. Nothing happened. 'Great,' she muttered.

There were only three rooms in the single-story building. The largest, to Lyndsey's right, was the bunkroom. In the dim light filtering through the two grimy windows, Lyndsey could see two rows of four bunkbeds. It looked uncomfortably like a prison cell. The mattresses on the bunks were thin and had obviously seen a lot of use. To her left was a small kitchen – or rather, a food preparation area, since there was no fridge or cooker, just a counter with some cupboards underneath, and a sink. An old table with a peeling Formica top took up a fair chunk of the room, with its three mismatched chairs. *We'll have to eat in shifts,* Lyndsey thought, irrationally.

The third door stood partially open, revealing the tiny bathroom, which had just enough room for a toilet, sink, and shower unit. The floors throughout the building were unfinished concrete. Lyndsey shuddered at the thought of putting her bare feet on the floor when stepping out of the shower or off her bunk. There were nibble marks in the skirting boards and along the bottoms of the kitchen cabinets. Lyndsey really hoped the marks had been made a long time ago, by rodents who would be long gone.

'Juliet,' Val said as she surveyed the rooms, 'what exactly have you got us into this time?'

'Shift out of the way, will you?' Juliet was attempting to bundle Amanda through the door to the bunkroom. Val moved aside.

With Juliet's help, Amanda limped to the nearest bunk and dropped heavily onto the thin mattress with a groan that was either relief or despair.

'There.' Juliet straightened up and looked at their accommodation properly for the first time. 'Hmm. Okay. The lights aren't working?'

'Nope.' Sonia tried the switches in the kitchen and bathroom as well, to zero effect. 'No light, no heat, no warden, no access to the radio—'

'The warden can't have gone far. She probably wasn't expecting us to arrive this early.' Juliet checked her watch. 'See, it's just past midday. I gave her an ETA of mid-afternoon. She's probably out doing her ... warden stuff.'

'There's nothing to cook on,' Sonia added. She turned the tap in the kitchen. It clonked and gurgled and produced a thin stream of peat-coloured water. 'What the hell, Jules? You said this place was okay.'

'Well, *obviously* I've not stayed in this building myself,' Juliet snapped. 'Last time I was here, they were busy converting it from a barn.'

'And that was, when? Nearly twenty years ago? The place looks like it's not been touched since then.'

'I just went by the description on the webpage. It looked fine. A bit rough and ready, sure, but what were you expecting? The *Hilton*?'

'I was expecting somewhere with lights that worked and at least a token attempt at central heating.' Sonia put a hand on the radiator in the bunkroom. 'It's freezing! How're we meant to stay here?'

'We've roughed it before. Don't tell me you're going soft.'

Sonia glared at her. 'I knew this was a mistake. I never should've let you talk us into coming here.'

'Can you quit complaining for two minutes? No one forced you to come. And we've got other things to worry about right now, thank you very much.' Juliet helped Amanda unlace her walking boots. 'How're you feeling, sweetie?' she asked her.

'Could be worse. Still sore.' Amanda winced as she stretched her narrow shoulders. 'My ribs hurt a bit as well. I thought I'd just winded myself, but maybe...'

Val said, 'Bet you wished you'd stayed lying on that comfortable ground now, huh?' She opened the side pocket of her rucksack. 'Here, I've got some decent painkillers. They'll take the edge off it.'

'We should wait till the rescue team gets here,' Juliet said. 'She shouldn't take anything until then.'

'No, that's not how it works. If you're in pain now, you take meds now. The first question the medics will ask is whether you've taken any painkillers, the second question will be why not.' Val sorted through a number of cardboard packets. 'Let's see what we've got here.'

'Aren't there rules about sharing prescription drugs?' Sonia muttered.

Amanda raised her eyebrows. 'Right now, I'm happy to take whatever's on offer. Don't judge me, Doctor Death.'

Sonia gave a surprised half-laugh. *Doctor Death*. Another nickname from high school. Lyndsey remembered it with a lurch. Sonia had always been the one to bring a bottle of sambuca or absinthe or something equally lethal to every party.

It was crass of Amanda to remind them of that. Amanda must've realised, because she reddened and dropped her gaze.

While they were talking, Lyndsey did a quick search of the rooms. There was one radiator per room, none of which were working. Same with the lights. But if there were radiators and lightbulbs, there had to be a way to turn them on. Maybe a master switch somewhere. She searched the building but couldn't find anything that looked like an electrical box.

'I'm gonna look outside,' Lyndsey said. 'See if I can figure out the electricity.'

Juliet snapped her fingers. 'The website bumf said there are solar panels and a generator.'

The solar panels wouldn't be doing much right then. It'd been days since the sun had last put in an appearance. 'I'll look for the generator,' Lyndsey said. She took off her climbing helmet and tossed it onto a bunk, grabbing a beanie hat from her pocket instead. 'Shouldn't be difficult to find. They're usually pretty obvious, right?'

'I'll come with you,' Sonia offered. She looked keen to get out of the room.

Outside, the wind threw spatters of rain into their faces. Lyndsey pulled her hat down over her eyebrows. The clouds were gathering low and heavy over the island, and the air had a close, thunderous look. Lyndsey breathed deeply. How come the air smelled so clean? Was it just her imagination? Every breath felt purer, less tainted with pollution. It was like she could feel the toxins being leached out of her. She wished she could appreciate it properly, but right at that moment, they had other things to focus on.

'I knew this was a mistake,' Sonia said. The hat she'd put on had two oversized black bobbles on top, which looked rather frivolous in comparison to her expression. 'Every instinct told me not to come. Why the hell didn't I listen to my gut?'

'Because your gut's full of shit.' Lyndsey trudged out of the small garden and followed a vague path around the side of the building. 'Besides, we couldn't say no. Juliet's going through a rough time.'

Sonia rolled her eyes. 'And doesn't she like to remind us of it. How long do we have to keep humouring her?'

'Don't be awful. It's only been a month. You can't expect her to bounce back that quickly from a break-up. Especially after what he put her through.'

Sonia hunched her shoulders. 'Yeah. You're right. I'm sorry. I just…' She sighed heavily. 'I've got a lot going on at home. Stuff I should be there for.'

'Oh?'

Sonia shook her head. 'Never mind. Point is, you're right. I shouldn't take it out on Juliet. I owe her more than that. Even if it *is* her fault we're weekending in an unheated shack.'

At the back of the building were several ramshackle stone structures, which had originally been designed as sheds or outhouses. Two had no roofs. A third had collapsed in on itself, its remains tangled with brambles and gorse. Two other stone sheds, up against the back wall of the bunkhouse, looked more intact, although their roofs had lost several slates. A creeping vine of some kind had grown thickly around one corner. These two buildings had their wooden doors more or less intact.

'In here, do you think?' Lyndsey asked. She tried the latch of the first door. It wasn't locked, but the hinges stuck. With a bit of force, she got it open.

Inside was a disordered mess of old tins of whitewash, rolls of netting, some very rusty gardening tools, shelves of mouldering packets and boxes with worn labels, and a pervasive smell of neglect. There was nothing that looked remotely like a generator.

Sonia was having a go at getting into the second shed, but the door was in even worse shape than the first. No amount of pushing and shoving could get it to budge.

'This is stupid,' Sonia complained. 'It'd be easier to kick a hole in it.'

'Why is that your go-to option?' Lyndsey took a step back and looked at the shed roof. 'I don't think the generator can be in here. Look at the state of the roof. It's probably been leaking for years. If you were going to put an important electrical item somewhere, it wouldn't be in here.'

Sonia stuck her head through the open door of the first shed. 'Urgh, I knew it,' she said. 'They've got a rodent problem. I smelled it as soon as we walked in.' She indicated the boxes that lined the shelves. Although most of the labels were faded, the skull-and-crossbones warning sign was still visible on a bunch of them.

A voice behind Lyndsey said, 'Something I can help you with?'

Lyndsey spun around. A woman had appeared at the boundary wall into the next field. She was bundled up in a sensible waterproof jacket, cargo pants, and wellies, all a uniform drab green in colour. Her hat and scarf hid her face.

'Who're you?' Sonia demanded.

'My name's Marne,' the woman said. She tugged down the scarf to reveal a tanned, freckled face. 'I'm the bird warden here. You must be my visitors for the weekend.' She came around the wall to reach them. 'Found the key all right, did you? Sorry I wasn't here to let you in myself.'

There was the edge of a Scouse accent to her voice. She offered her hand to shake. Lyndsey automatically took it. The woman had a firm grip to match her no-nonsense smile. She wasn't at all what Lyndsey had pictured when Juliet had said there was a bird warden who lived on the island for six months of the year. For a start, she looked too young – certainly no more than early thirties, just a few years older than Lyndsey herself.

'Where have you been?' Sonia wanted to know.

The warden, Marne, was taken aback by her tone. 'I had to take down the blinds on the hill. Took me all morning.'

'Blinds?'

'Bird traps. Not the way you're thinking,' Marne added quickly as she saw the look on Lyndsey's face. 'We string up nets to catch the migrating birds, then we bag and tag them, and let them go. It doesn't hurt them.'

Lyndsey thought of the nets strewn across the garden. She'd vaguely assumed they were for fishing.

'We don't leave the blinds up when bad weather's coming in,' Marne said. 'For starters, the wind could carry them away. Plus, I don't know for definite that I'll be able to get out tomorrow to check the nets. I wouldn't want a bunch of birds left tangled up for that long in rough weather.'

'Look, never mind that,' Sonia said. 'We need to use your radio.'

'The radio? What for?'

'Our friend had a fall,' Lyndsey said. 'She's hurt her leg, and maybe her ribs. We need to radio the mainland and get the coastguard.'

'Where is she?' Marne asked with concern.

'We got her to the bunkhouse. I know we shouldn't have moved her, but—'

'It's probably sensible, with the weather coming down.' Marne nodded, relieved. 'I'd hate to think of anybody getting stuck outside. Do you want me to take a look at her? When I'm not here on the island, I work in a hospital, so I've got a bit of training.'

'Can we use your radio?' Sonia pressed. 'It's an emergency.'

'We can give it a go.' All of a sudden, Marne looked evasive. 'It's in the observatory.'

She led the way back around the building. The wind buffeted all three of them, and shook the tops of the trees. The rain was increasing from the earlier damp drizzle. Lyndsey quickened her step, eager to be indoors.

'What were you looking for in the sheds?' Marne asked.

'Oh. We couldn't figure out how to turn on the

electricity,' Lyndsey said. 'We thought there might be a generator?'

'There is, yes. It's in a bunker at the side of the house. There are a set of switches to get it working, but you would've needed the key to get access. Sorry, I meant to do it earlier. Get the place warmed up for you. But I was out on the hills for longer than expected.'

'Are you the only person who lives here?'

'Usually there are two research assistants as well. They both had to leave early this season, though. Personal reasons. Shame for them.'

'Don't you mind being here alone?'

'Can't say it's too onerous. I do my best work when I'm solo.' Marne reached the door of the building next to the bunkhouse and unlocked it. 'Although it's a pain when I need more than one pair of hands. But I can manage for a few months at a time. I go back home for the winter months anyway. My contract's only for the season, when the birds are migrating and nesting.'

Inside, there was a strange combination of smells – oil and wood-glue and burnt electrics and, for some reason, patchouli. It brought back sharp memories of the Design and Technology classrooms at school.

The downstairs level of Marne's home was smaller than the bunkhouse, and significantly more disordered. The main room, off to their right, was cramped with tables and workbenches, all piled with papers, books, and equipment. More rolls of netting were stacked in the corners. Directly in front of the front door, narrow stairs led up to the second floor. It was slightly warmer than the bunkhouse, but not by much.

Marne led them through a doorway to the left, into what looked like a workroom. There was more clutter here, but one workbench was neat and tidy, with a variety of instruments used for delicate weighing and measuring. A roll of tiny metal tags, like the ones Lyndsey had sometimes seen around the ankles of seabirds, hung from a hook above the bench.

The lights were off in there as well, so Marne quickly lit a hurricane lamp, adding the sharp smell of paraffin to the air. She took off her hat and scarf, revealing mousy brown hair worn in a short, functional plait. Her freckles extended down to the rolled neck of her jumper.

'Now, the thing is,' Marne said, 'we don't usually have cause to use the radio much. We're supposed to check in with the mainland once a week, but—'

Lyndsey spotted a large, square object by the window that could've been a radio. It resembled something a switchboard operator from the 1950s would use. Its front was covered in knobs and dials and switches. It looked intimidating and unintuitive.

Sonia went straight to the radio. 'How do you switch it on?' She tapped a light on the front, labelled POWER, which was dark.

'There's a switch on the side. But—'

Sonia flipped the switch, waited, then tried it a couple more times. Nothing obvious happened. 'Is it because the electricity's not on?' she asked.

'No, it's got a back-up battery. The thing is—' Marne

looked sheepish. 'It's been playing up these past few weeks,' she admitted. 'Sometimes it's a little slow to warm up. And other times…'

'Other times what?'

'Sometimes it doesn't turn on at all.' Marne lifted her hands in a weak shrug.

'What does that mean?' Sonia demanded.

'I-I've been tinkering with it.' Marne made a half-hearted gesture towards the workbench next to the radio. A number of unidentifiable electronic parts were laid out on a sheet of newspaper. 'Don't know what's wrong with the stupid thing. I've taken it apart and cleaned it – that usually does the trick – but no joy so far.'

'Why would you take it apart?'

'It comes and goes,' Marne said defensively. 'Sometimes it's right as rain; sometimes it claps out for no reason. It's the same with everything here. There isn't a piece of equipment in this house that I haven't had to take apart at some point or another. Anyway, I've ordered a replacement part from the mainland for the radio, and usually I can botch it back into working order, if it's an emergency.'

'This is definitely an emergency,' Sonia said.

Lyndsey asked Marne, 'What back-up do you have, if the radio isn't working?'

'Back-up?'

'Yeah, you have like a–a failsafe or something, right? Some other way to contact the mainland?'

'Well … no.'

'No?' Sonia's eyes widened, incredulously. 'None at all?'

'We're only a mile and a half offshore. I'm usually the

only one here. What's likely to happen that'd be *that* big of an emergency?'

Sonia stalked towards her. 'Our friend pitched off the lighthouse. She needs to get to the hospital. Not in two days, not in five hours, *now*. Do you understand?'

Marne blinked at the force of the words. Then she seemed to break out of her stupor. 'I'll get the radio working,' she said.

Chapter Four

FRIDAY

12:35pm

Before she started on the radio, Marne quickly showed Lyndsey the waterproof box affixed to the side wall of the bunkhouse, where the master switches for the electricity and heating were housed. Lyndsey had walked right past it earlier and paid it no attention, because it was obviously too small to house a generator. Marne unlocked the box with a key from a bundle she carried in her pocket.

'The generator's over there,' Marne said, with a nod of her head towards a wooden bunker set a little way apart from the building, with a tarpaulin thrown over it. 'You'll definitely hear it when it starts up, even if you're inside the bunkhouse. It's set to turn itself on automatically, for an hour in the morning and two hours in the evening. There'll be enough charge in the storage batteries to keep you going the rest of the time, but don't be wasteful, yeah? Don't leave lights on if you don't need to.'

Sonia kept her distance during this exchange. She huddled near the back wall with her hand cupped around a cigarette, a thunderous expression on her face. The collar of her red jacket was pulled up around her chin.

When Marne flipped the master switches, the generator, hidden in its wooden bunker, rumbled into life. There was an audible cheer from inside the bunkhouse.

'There.' Marne closed and latched the waterproof box. 'Place should start to warm up nicely. You get yourself inside. Weather's going to turn a tad breezy this afternoon.'

Lyndsey looked at the grey sky. 'It won't get that bad, will it? The forecast said—'

'The forecast says lots of things.' Marne smiled, showing uneven front teeth. 'Trust me, if you live here for any amount of time, you learn to read the weather better than anyone. It's going to get a bit wild for the next couple of days.'

Lyndsey frowned. 'How wild?'

'Ah, y'know,' Marne said with a shrug. 'Nothing we can't cope with. But you'll probably want to wrap up well if you're venturing out. And maybe stay away from the clifftops. It can get interesting up there.' She flashed another smile. 'Don't worry. I'm sure the boat wouldn't have brought you here if they weren't confident they could fetch you back on Sunday.' She clapped Lyndsey on the shoulder. 'Go look after your friend. I'll give you a shout when I have any luck with the radio.'

Juliet greeted Lyndsey and Sonia with a relieved smile. 'Well done, you!' Juliet said. 'This place looks more welcoming already, don't you think?'

As far as Lyndsey could tell, even with the lights on, the rooms were still fairly bleak. If anything, the harsh strip lighting accentuated the rough walls and patches of damp on the ceiling and under the windows. But at least she heard a few reassuring *clonks* from the central heating system as it switched on.

Juliet was in the kitchen, setting up a camping stove on the counter. 'I thought we all could use a cup of tea,' she said. 'Did you find the warden?'

'Yeah, she's next door in the bird observatory.' Lyndsey peeled off her jacket and hung it up with the others on the pegs by the door. She was very grateful that Bobbie had found her a good, sturdy jacket at a discount price. It might not have been a posh brand name, like Sonia's or Juliet's, but it was the most waterproof item Lyndsey had owed in years. 'There's a problem with the radio, though.'

'What problem?'

'It's not working right now.' Lyndsey glanced at Sonia for back-up, but Sonia had disappeared into the bathroom, slamming the flimsy door behind her. 'Apparently, it's quite temperamental.'

Juliet stopped fiddling with the stove and looked at her in alarm. 'But we can still call the coastguard, right?'

'Not at this exact moment. The warden's trying to fix it. We don't know how long it'll take.'

'But this is an emergency!'

'Believe it or not, we told her that. It doesn't make the radio any less broken.'

Juliet swore under her breath. It looked like she was debating whether to grab her coat and storm over to the warden's house herself. Lyndsey wouldn't have stopped her. In the end though, Juliet turned back to the stove. She slotted two of its pieces together with deliberate calm.

'All right,' she said. 'What's the plan if we can't radio for help?'

'Beats me.' Lyndsey was fairly sure it was a rhetorical question. Juliet liked to speak her questions aloud; she said it helped her formulate answers. Lyndsey suspected it was a tactic Juliet used in her management job – if you asked something out loud, someone would likely answer it for you.

In the bunkroom, Amanda was laid out on a bed with a blanket tucked up around her. Some of the colour had returned to her face. Her eyelids were heavy and she was obviously only half awake.

'Is she okay?' Lyndsey asked Val, who was perched on the edge of her own bunk.

'Difficult to say. The painkillers might knock her out.'

Amanda murmured, 'I can still hear you, y'know.'

'Thought as much. Go to sleep, will you? We don't know how long it'll be for rescue to get here.'

The rooms were small enough that everyone had heard Lyndsey saying the radio was broken. She was grateful to Val for not arguing with her. Lyndsey sat down on the bed next to Amanda's. At the far end of the room, Bobbie had laid down on a bunk as well, curled up on her side like a child, her purple water bottle tucked into the crook of her arm. Val looked like she was keeping an eye on both Amanda and Bobbie, although she'd also taken her slimline laptop from her bag and was studying a page of text.

'Why'd you bring your laptop?' Lyndsey asked. 'You won't be able to charge it.'

'You lot brought your phones, even though you can't charge them and there's no reception,' Val said. 'I can manage eight hours of battery life on this if I'm careful. I promised the missus I'd get some work done while we're here.'

One of Val's hobbies was writing. At present – and for the last three years – she'd been working laboriously and loudly on a Victorian murder mystery, although the majority was research. Every now and again, Lyndsey would bump into Val in one of the coffee shops they both frequented, where Val would always be ensconced at a table with her granny jumper and her bottomless pot of tea, working away on her project.

Without more than a glance at the laptop, Lyndsey knew the current page would be one of Val's various research documents. Each contained all the minutiae anyone could possibly want about Victorians, their lives, and the various ways to murder them.

'What're you looking up?' Lyndsey asked. 'Is it the central heating system? Because I know it's old, but I don't think it's *that* old.'

'I'm brushing up on my first aid skills.' Val angled the screen so Lyndsey could see the text. 'Granted, none of my notes cover this *exact* situation, but I figured it couldn't hurt to refresh my knowhow.'

'You're brushing up on Victorian first aid?'

'I researched contemporary techniques too.' Val sniffed. 'Can't know what people did wrong till you know how it's done right.'

Lyndsey looked over at Bobbie. 'How about you? How're you feeling?'

'I'm okay.' Bobbie gave a weak smile. 'A bit more settled now.'

From the kitchen, Juliet called, 'We'll all feel better once we've had a cup of tea.' She'd finally got the camping stove lit. The smell of gas tinged the air.

'Open a window,' Val shouted. 'You'll suffocate us all.'

'Don't open a window,' Bobbie said. 'We'll never get warm.'

'It's fine,' Juliet said, annoyed. 'Everything's going to be fine.'

Lyndsey didn't know what she was basing that on. She glanced at Amanda, who'd lapsed into a doze. Things were going wrong so quickly. Not for the first time, Lyndsey wished she'd had the heart to tell Juliet no when she'd suggested this stupid adventure.

You wanted to be here, she reminded herself. After being antisocial and ducking her friends for so long, she'd been grateful just for an invitation. *You missed your friends. You missed being part of a group, missed having a purpose.*

Lyndsey looked around the dingy bunkhouse. This was certainly an adventure. Just not the one she'd been hoping for.

Chapter Five

FRIDAY

2:00pm

Despite assorted grumblings, Juliet made a hot drink for everyone, on the basis that, even if it didn't improve the situation, it wouldn't make it any worse.

Lyndsey climbed up onto a top bunk and cradled the tin mug between her palms. Since there were only four bunkbeds, she and Sonia had opted to take two of the top bunks, leaving the lower ones for the others. Val in particular hated climbing ladders. 'I'm okay with stairs,' she said, 'but ladders were designed by people with no concept of how hips work.' Being on the top bunk was kinda fun, Lyndsey thought. She'd never been in one before. It was a novelty, and it made her feel like a kid again.

Hauling her rucksack up onto her bunk had been less

fun. She dumped the heavy bag at the end of the mattress and sat cross-legged, holding her coffee in one hand while she dragged stuff out of her bag with the other. All her borrowed climbing gear was packed at the top, because for some reason rucksacks were easier to carry if they were lighter at the bottom, but it meant she had to make a pile of ropes on her bed before she could get out her sleeping bag.

Under normal circumstances, they would've already found a place to stash all the climbing gear, keeping it ready for when they went out again that afternoon. But, with Amanda's accident, they weren't going anywhere. Lyndsey looked at the big heap of ropes and harnesses on her bed – all of which she'd had to borrow, along with her sleeping bag, since there was no way she could've afforded to buy it all, even at the discount prices that Bobbie had found for her. Lyndsey had had to borrow money just to get a decent jacket and walking boots suitable for that weekend. And now, just like that, all the gear was pointless. They wouldn't get a chance to use even half of it.

With a grunt of annoyance, she pulled a bottle out of her bag. Each one was wrapped in a protective T-shirt. It took her a couple of tries to find the bottle of Baileys. She'd brought only one mug, and it was currently filled with strong black coffee. After only a moment's thought, she broke the seal of the bottle and tipped a decent measure into her hot drink. *Irish coffee for lunch, how civilised.*

The weather grew steadily worse. By now, fat raindrops bounced off the windows like sprays of machine-gun fire, and the wind rattled the front door. Despite this, Sonia went out every half hour to check how the warden was getting on with the radio. Lyndsey wasn't sure if Sonia volunteered for this because she hated being cooped up, or because she was using her time outside to stress-smoke without anyone hassling her.

Juliet was equally on edge. After she'd made and drunk her cup of herbal tea, she and Sonia went back to the lighthouse to pick up the bags they'd left there, and to make sure the door to the lighthouse was padlocked and secure. When they returned, with nothing else to occupy her time, Juliet sat at the table in the kitchen, poring over a folded A4 sheet of paper she'd taken from her pocket. Even without looking, Lyndsey knew what it was – the itinerary that Juliet had emailed to them all last week. It was a breakdown of all the activities they were scheduled to do on this three-day weekend adventure. Abseiling, climbing, coasteering, more climbing … practically every hour was accounted for. Juliet chewed her lower lip as she read and reread the typed words. Lyndsey knew she was stewing over the time they were losing.

Lyndsey didn't know and didn't care exactly what activity they were missing that afternoon. She hadn't bothered to print out the itinerary … which would've necessitated a trip to the public library, because who on earth owned their own printer? In fact, she'd barely glanced at it at all. She knew Juliet would've spent days or even weeks planning the perfect use of their time. She was never the sort to leave hours unfilled. The last time Lyndsey had gone away with her was for Juliet's hen do, and that'd been micromanaged to death as well.

Don't mention that holiday, Lyndsey reminded herself.

Like everything else associated with Juliet's marriage, which had imploded so spectacularly last month, the hen party was a tainted memory, and Juliet wouldn't thank her for bringing it up.

Poor thing. Juliet had had a rotten year so far, and now this trip – which she'd spent so long planning – had gone wrong really fast. She'd always talked about bringing the group here to Shell Island, but every year something got in the way. For some reason, she'd been particularly strident about it this year, and finally she'd got everyone to commit to the three-day trip … only to see it fall apart on the very first morning.

The worst of it was, there was nothing any of them could do. Their only option was to look after Amanda and pray the radio would be fixed soon.

Lyndsey's eyes wandered to Amanda. *Talk about bad luck.* Lyndsey hadn't seen Amanda in person for ten years, since the summer they'd finished Sixth Form together. Amanda's family had moved away not long afterwards. It'd been a real shock to hear she was coming this weekend, especially given that she hadn't attended any of the other major events, like Juliet's wedding or hen weekend. Lyndsey wondered what exactly Juliet had said to finally bring Amanda back into the group.

It felt like the worst possible luck for them all to be reunited, only for this to happen. Lyndsey had really been looking forward to a chance to chat with Amanda. Maybe find out what she'd been up to in the last decade. Now it looked like they wouldn't get that chance, not this weekend.

At least Amanda was sleeping. Whatever tablets Val had

given her had done the trick. Maybe Amanda would be lucky, and wake up with bruises and nothing more. Lyndsey studied her sleeping face. Amanda had always been thin, but it'd become more pronounced over the years. She had the sort of delicate bone structure you'd see in magazine photos of supermodels.

In her head, Lyndsey replayed the sickening moment when Amanda had hit the ground. It was pure luck Amanda hadn't been seriously injured, or worse. The rope could've snapped at any time. What if it'd broken as soon as she'd put her weight on it, when she was 150 feet up in the air?

Or, what if it had snapped when she, herself, was climbing down? She tried not to think about that. It gave her a horrible sense of … relief, which was an awful thing to think because it was tantamount to admitting she was happy it'd happened to Amanda instead of her.

Will the police need to get involved?

The thought hadn't occurred to her. But if Sonia was right, if someone had tampered with the rope…

'Do you hear that?' Bobbie asked suddenly.

Lyndsey looked over the edge of her bunk. She'd thought Bobbie was napping, but she was half sitting up, her eyes wide as she listened.

'Hear what?' Lyndsey asked.

'It sounds like … someone screaming.'

The hairs rose on Lyndsey's neck. She tilted her head to listen. 'It's just the wind, Bobs.'

'No, I can hear…' Bobbie's forehead scrunched into a

frown. 'No. Maybe not. Sorry.' She shook her head and lay back down on her bunk.

Val, who was sitting at the kitchen table, tapping away at her laptop, stretched her back and said, 'Right, sun's past the yardarm, or at least I assume it is, wherever it's hiding behind the clouds. Shall we have a drink?'

'I'm not sure that's a good idea,' Juliet said.

'Why not? It's not like any of us are a designated driver today.'

Juliet chewed her lip and glanced at the itinerary in her hands. 'But what if—?'

'I'm not suggesting we get too trolleyed to talk to the rescue crew when they turn up. Just a little dram to ease our nerves. God knows we need it.'

Juliet looked unhappy, but she couldn't think of any sensible objection. There was no way the group was doing any climbing that afternoon. Regardless of what the itinerary said.

Val went to her bunk and opened her rucksack. After a brief rummage, she came up with a bottle of gin and another of tonic.

'Here we go,' she said. 'A touch of civilisation.'

Lyndsey had been keeping her mug topped up. It'd stopped being Irish coffee some time ago and started just being Irish. When she shoogled the bottle, it sounded about two-thirds full.

Lyndsey smiled down at Bobbie. 'Hey, I brought Baileys,' she said. 'You fancy a drink?'

After a moment's thought, Bobbie smiled. 'Go on then. Just a small one. Thank you.'

Lyndsey reached down, and Bobbie passed up her mug. None of them had bothered to bring actual drinking glasses, and there weren't any in the kitchen. Lyndsey poured a rough measure of alcohol into Bobbie's mug, then a far more substantial slug into her own. Bobbie sat up and drained her water bottle before accepting the drink.

A few minutes later, Sonia returned from her latest visit to the warden's house. 'Radio's still fucked,' she announced as she shrugged off her damp jacket. 'Hey, did you start drinking without me?'

'Not at all,' Val said, topping up her glass. 'It's your imagination.'

Sonia grunted. 'Get my imagination to pour me a decent drink, will you?' She pulled off her double-bobble hat. Her black hair was worn in a cute, trim bob, which looked great on her but didn't seem very practical for a climbing trip, in Lyndsey's opinion. Either very short or slightly longer hair, which could be tied up out of the way, was better. 'And a towel.'

From the kitchen, Juliet said, 'I'm making food. Pasta and red sauce.'

'Peachy.' Sonia grabbed the towel that Lyndsey flung at her from the top bunk. 'What're you drinking, Lynds?'

'Baileys.'

'Urgh. Creamy nonsense.' Sonia wrapped the towel around her head. 'Let me see what I've got in my magic bag.'

Lyndsey smiled. She was glad everyone had stopped sniping at each other. There'd been a lot of tension in the bunkhouse. Maybe once they had all had a proper drink, they'd start to unwind. Lyndsey was already feeling less stressed. She topped up her drink. Normally she didn't drink Baileys either, but she'd packed it because it was Bobbie's favourite. After all the help Bobbie had given her to prepare for this trip, Lyndsey was keen to repay her in any way she could.

Should've brought something cheaper. Lyndsey glanced down at Bobbie, who'd taken only the smallest sip of her drink, and felt a brief flare of irritation. It wasn't like Lyndsey could afford to waste money on brand-name booze. For the price of this one bottle of Baileys, she could've bought three reasonable bottles of wine, or a decent one of vodka. But no, she'd gone for the pricey option, to score points with Bobbie.

Money had always been an issue for Lyndsey. Even before the start of this year, it'd been bad. When they went out as a group – usually her, Bobbie, and Juliet, sometimes with Val as well – she was the one who drank beer instead of cocktails, who insisted on paying her dinner bill separately so she could budget exactly. It annoyed her that she couldn't keep up with the others, who always had cash on hand. Juliet, in particular, had scored a promotion last year and always had money to burn. Lyndsey guessed it was easy to get promoted when your dad ran the company.

Even though this weekend was a budget-option for the rest of the group, it'd still cost more than Lyndsey could sensibly afford, especially when she factored in the hidden costs, like those pricey walking boots. There's no way she could've come if Bobbie hadn't stepped in. Bobbie's husband owned an online store that sold outdoor sportswear, and Bobbie worked for him as an administrative assistant, so she'd been able to source a load of end-of-line clothing and equipment at cut prices.

When it'd become clear that Lyndsey's budget still wouldn't cover even half the stuff, Bobbie had offered to lend her the money. They'd both promised to keep quiet about the arrangement. Lyndsey wasn't keen for her other friends to think she was a scrounger; Bobbie was happy for her husband to stay unaware of the loan. Apparently, he kept a tight hold of the purse-strings in their house.

Since then, Bobbie had gone back and forth on whether she was definitely coming on this weekend or not. She was always adamant, however, that Lyndsey should go, regardless. Lyndsey had agreed to that promise easily enough. After all, she'd spent so much cash on the deposit, the equipment, the train ticket to Ravenswater – all non-refundable – that it caused Lyndsey almost physical pain to think of cancelling and wasting all that money. She'd been too invested *not* to go.

Lyndsey took a swig of her drink. Her mood had soured. Right at that moment, she had no idea how she was going to pay Bobbie back. It was money Lyndsey simply didn't have. And she'd squandered it on this trip, to come to this dreary island and sit around in a damp, poorly heated bunkhouse, with a bunch of people she'd not spent any significant amount of time with in years. Everyone was being weird with each other because, if she was being honest, none of them properly knew each other anymore.

'I don't suppose anyone brought a knife, did they?' Juliet asked from the kitchen.

'Um, no?' Sonia said.

Val said, 'Left mine in my other pants, sorry.'

'I can't find a single decent blade in this kitchen.' Juliet pulled out the cutlery drawer and rifled through the contents. 'I don't know how they expect us to – aha!' She snatched up a black-handled knife from the back of the drawer. 'Right, we have one sharp knife. Huzzah.'

'Why're you even cooking right now?' Sonia asked. 'It's the middle of the afternoon.'

'And none of us had lunch. Plus – ' She threw a look at the others. 'It's apparently gin-o'clock, so we need something to line our stomachs.'

'In my defence,' Val said, 'it's always gin-o'clock somewhere.'

Sonia hauled herself up onto her top bunk, lugging her rucksack with her. None of the group had properly unpacked yet. It was like they were in limbo, waiting to find out what would happen with the coastguard. Lyndsey had mentally written off the weekend already. When the coastguard took Amanda to hospital, Lyndsey figured that the rest of them would go with her. An all-expenses-paid helicopter ride back to the mainland, perhaps.

But now, watching Sonia wrestle her sleeping bag out of her rucksack, Lyndsey suddenly wondered if she'd get out of this weekend so easily.

'Is the warden any closer to getting the radio fixed?' Lyndsey asked Sonia.

'Honestly? I don't have a clue. She keeps talking about transistors and receptors and doppleganger-fruitloops or some other made-up thing. As far as I can see, the damn thing's getting more broken, not less.'

'So, we might be stuck here till tomorrow?'

'We're not stuck here,' Juliet said from the kitchen. It was impossible to have a conversation in that building without everyone hearing. 'We've booked and paid for this place. You should be happy we've got a roof over our heads.'

As if in response, more pellets of rain struck the windows. The sky had gone an ugly, thunderous colour.

'But what if we can't contact the mainland?' Lyndsey asked. Her gaze strayed to Amanda who was sleeping restlessly. 'What'll we do then?'

'We'll think of something.' Juliet tipped two tins of chopped tomatoes into the sauce mix. The smell of frying onion and garlic awoke Lyndsey's stomach. 'It's not like we're on the moon, for goodness' sake. We're barely two kilometres offshore. In an absolute pinch, we could probably shout loud enough for folks to hear us.' She paused to brush her bangs out of her face. 'Anyway, maybe we won't need to call the coastguard. Amanda's ankle might just be bruised. When she wakes up, we'll see how she's feeling. It might not be that bad after all.'

'And it might be worse,' Sonia muttered, but she said it so quietly that only Lyndsey heard her.

Chapter Six

FRIDAY

3:40pm

'Should we wake Amanda?'

Juliet shook her head. 'Let her sleep. The longer she's resting and pain-free, the better she'll feel. We'll save her some food.'

She set the plates down on the kitchen table. Val, Bobbie, and Lyndsey had taken the seats. Juliet insisted she was fine to eat off her lap, sitting perched on the edge of her bunk. Sonia, still cocooned in a nest of blankets up on her bunk and busy putting a dent into the bottle of vodka she'd brought, was making a slow move to join them for dinner. She had, therefore, forfeited her chance to sit on an actual chair.

The meal that Juliet had cooked – pasta with tomato-ish

sauce – was passable, although kind of bland. Juliet was perpetually on some kind of health kick, refusing to add seasoning to her cooking, and using wholewheat pasta, which had taken ages to cook on the double-hob camping stove. She'd already made some pointed remarks about everyone else's diets. Lyndsey couldn't comment though, since her own supply of food that she'd brought was mostly crisps and biscuits, with some instant noodles thrown in for variety.

None of the group complained either. It was comforting to have a hot meal. And, although no one admitted it, it did feel good to line their stomachs. Lyndsey already felt fuzzier than she should've. She made a mental note to space out her drinks better. Usually, she kept a better eye on everyone else, and paced her drinks to theirs.

'This is like Brownie Guides, isn't it?' Val said, as she speared pasta onto her fork. 'We ought to have a singsong or tell ghost stories.'

'My mum would never let me go camping with the Girl Guides,' Bobbie said. She was toying with her food, and hadn't eaten more than a few mouthfuls. After the one glass of Baileys, she'd switched back to water, refilling her bottle from the stash of mineral water they'd all brought. 'All my friends went, but I wasn't allowed. I don't even know why I kicked up a fuss. I would've hated sleeping on the ground, and sharing a tent with people, and all that other stuff.'

'Well, you're here now, Bobs.' Juliet smiled at her. 'Our adventure group was better than the Girl Guides, anyway.'

Sonia was at last coming down the ladder from her bunk. She drained her glass then topped it off from the bottle before wandering into the kitchen. 'I got kicked out of my Brownie troop,' she said.

'Of course you did.' Lyndsey chuckled. 'That's incredibly on-brand for you.'

Sonia shrugged, but she was hiding a smile. 'It all felt a bit sinister, anyway. Getting kids dressed up in uniform and making them swear oaths... It gave me the heebie-jeebies.'

'Again, exactly what we'd expect from you,' Lyndsey said. 'Reading evil intentions into benign institutions.'

'They weren't benign, they tried to make me sing.' Sonia stifled a yawn as she picked up her plate from the counter. 'This one mine? Cool.'

'You're welcome,' Juliet said. 'Hey, if we wanna tell ghost stories, I reckon I can remember the ones we used to tell.'

Val hooted with laughter. 'You can't.'

'Of course I can. We must've heard you tell that daft tale about the haunted cellar a dozen times.'

'That wasn't a story; it genuinely happened.'

Lyndsey was laughing as well now. 'And it got more and more exaggerated every time you told it,' she remembered. 'By the end there was ... what was it, a ghost dog? And pools of blood on the floor?'

'True story,' Val insisted. 'Every word of it.'

Then Bobbie said, 'There's someone at the window.'

Everyone looked up. From where Lyndsey was sitting, she had a clear view through the window. She could see nothing more than the fields, the trees, and the iron-grey sky.

'Where?' Lyndsey asked. She hopped to her feet and

peered right and left through the grubby panes at the empty garden. 'I can't see anyone.'

Juliet opened the front door. A gust of frigid air blew through the bunkhouse. 'Nope,' she reported, 'no one.'

'Who did you see, Bobs?' Lyndsey asked.

Bobbie had gone quiet. She was chewing her lip.

'Bobs?'

Slowly, Bobbie shook her head. 'I must've imagined it,' she said. 'Sorry.'

Juliet shut the door. As an afterthought, she locked it.

'Maybe it was Marne,' Sonia suggested. 'She looks the type to go creeping around, peering into windows.'

'What're you basing that on?' Lyndsey asked. It'd always annoyed her when Sonia made snap decisions about people.

'She voluntarily lives on a tiny island by herself,' Sonia said with a shrug. Her words were slightly slurred. How much had she drunk? 'Textbook weirdo.'

Bobbie shook her head. 'It wasn't her.'

'How do you know?' Sonia asked. 'You've not met Marne. You don't know what she looks like.'

'It was... For a second, I thought...' Bobbie trailed off. She shook her head again. 'Never mind. I already sound crazy.'

'No crazier than normal,' Juliet said with a smile that was meant to be affectionate but looked distracted.

There were no curtains in the bunkhouse; no way to cover the windows. The fact hadn't bothered Lyndsey before. After all, it wasn't like there were bright streetlights outside, or nosy neighbours. Now, from the corners of her eyes, Lyndsey kept imagining faces pressed against the glass.

'What time is it?' Sonia asked.

'Almost four o'clock,' Juliet said, then muttered, 'Waste of a whole bloody day.'

Sonia gave her a look. 'What would you rather we were doing?'

'Ideally? Any of the activities on our itinerary. That would've been good.'

'You and your bloody itinerary. I bet you're really upset at us for disrupting your plans.'

'I'm not upset.' Juliet picked up her plate and took it to the sink. 'You asked me what I'd prefer to be doing, and I answered. I put a lot of effort into organising this weekend. You have no idea how difficult it was to get all of us here.'

'Shall I wake Amanda up so she can apologise for falling off a lighthouse?' There was a look in Sonia's eyes that everyone recognised. Lyndsey felt a familiar sense of foreboding rising in her stomach. Sonia had drunk too much too quickly on an empty stomach, and now she wanted a fight. Apparently, that much hadn't changed.

'There's no need to shout at me.' Juliet gave her plate a quick rinse in the copper-coloured tap water. 'I know the situation can't be helped. I just wish things were different, that's all. I really wanted this weekend to work out.'

Sonia shook her head in disgust. 'It's a write-off. Accept it. You'll just have to try it again some other time.'

'That's the point though, isn't it? We'll never get another chance.' Juliet grabbed a tea towel to dry her plate. She kept her voice calm and level. 'As soon as National Heritage find out what happened, they'll close off the lighthouse. They might close the whole island to climbers.'

'Good.' Sonia folded her arms. 'They absolutely should. This might've escaped your notice, but Amanda could've died.'

'It was an accident.'

'It fucking wasn't.' Sonia took a step towards Juliet. 'That rope was cut. We all saw it. And now we're sitting around, eating and drinking and chatting, pretending nothing happened.'

'What do you suggest we do differently?' Juliet turned to face her at last. 'We can't contact the police until the radio is fixed. The absolute best thing we can do is stay calm and not start these petty arguments with each other. If you can think of something more productive, go ahead and do it.'

Sonia held Juliet's gaze for a moment longer, then looked away. She muttered something inaudible.

'Out of interest,' Val said then, 'did anyone ask the bird warden whether she was near the lighthouse this afternoon?'

Lyndsey frowned, although she was grateful for the interruption. 'What's that got to do with it?'

'Just an idea.' Val was still eating, chewing each mouthful thoughtfully. 'If Sonia's right and someone did cut Amanda's rope, it was either one of us lot—'

'It wasn't.' Juliet's tone was sharp. 'Don't even suggest that.'

'*Or* it was someone else,' Val finished. 'And there's only one "someone else" on this island. Our resident bird warden.'

Juliet was already shaking her head. 'No one cut the rope. It was an accident.'

Sonia opened her mouth to reply, but Lyndsey spoke over her, before another argument could start. 'Why on earth would Marne do something like that?'

'Why not? Some people are crazy.' Val gestured with her fork. 'Could be she likes being here by herself and resents tourists like us intruding on her peace. Wouldn't she benefit if the island got cordoned off, like Juliet suggested? She'd have the place to herself.'

'We don't know her well enough to assume anything,' Lyndsey said.

'That's kind of the point, isn't it? She could be anyone.' Val was warming to her topic. 'Who knows how she feels about us being here?'

Sonia grabbed her red coat from the pegs by the door. 'I'm gonna go ask her,' she said.

'Are you sure that's a smart idea?' Juliet asked.

'Why the hell not? There's no sense cowering in here, asking ourselves stupid questions, when we could get to the heart of the matter.'

She just wants to start a fight with someone else, Lyndsey knew. *We should stop her.* But she made no move to get up from the table.

Juliet must've guessed Sonia's intentions as well, because she pulled a face. 'I'll come with you.'

'Yippee.' Sonia pulled on her double-bobble hat, tucking her bobbed hair behind her ears. 'Let's go, then.'

'What about the rest of us?' Lyndsey asked.

'Stay here and keep an eye on Amanda,' Juliet

instructed. 'And lock the door behind us.' To Bobbie, she said, 'It'll be okay.'

Bobbie nodded but said nothing. She was chewing her lower lip again, and her eyes kept straying to the windows. Again, Lyndsey wished there were curtains to block out the view and give them some privacy.

Lyndsey went to the window so she could watch Juliet and Sonia head towards the warden's house. Even though it wasn't yet dinner time, the afternoon light was already fading. The two women were grey shadows against a monochrome background. Juliet had taken her headtorch with her, just in case it got darker while they were out. *Always prepared.* Through the glass, Lyndsey thought she heard Sonia aim another barbed comment at Juliet.

Irrationally, Lyndsey wanted to call them back inside and make them talk things through properly. Why had that argument even started between Juliet and Sonia? Couldn't it have waited till they got home?

But Lyndsey knew the fight had been brewing all afternoon. The accident and the weather and the broken radio had put them all on edge. It'd only been a matter of time before Sonia said something.

Maybe if we hadn't started drinking so early...

It felt wrong to lock the door with her friends outside, but Lyndsey did so anyway. 'They won't be long,' she said, as much to herself as anyone else.

'What'll we do till they get back?' Bobbie asked.

'Take a nap,' Val suggested. 'I find that's the answer to most problems in life.' She stretched her arms. Her shoulders and back made a series of unpleasant clicking noises. 'Do you reckon the weather's going to improve overnight?'

'I don't know,' Lyndsey said. She watched Juliet pause outside the door of the observatory. 'Marne said the weather was going to get worse before it got better.'

'Eh, that's usually what weather does.'

Bobbie tore her gaze away from the windows. 'What if the boat can't get to us on Sunday?'

It was a question Lyndsey had been stewing over as well. She hadn't wanted to raise it in front of Juliet, who would get defensive.

'They'll send a coastguard helicopter if they have to,' Val said. 'They won't leave us stranded here.'

'What if it gets so bad the helicopter can't fly?'

'Don't worry. They've got a Sikorsky based in Anglesey.'

'A Skir—?'

'Sikorsky. It's a big bugger of a rescue helicopter. If you're interested, I've got a photo on my laptop.'

'Of course you do.'

'That beast can fly in anything short of a hurricane.' Val looked around for her laptop. 'We're not due a hurricane. The weather report would've said so.'

Lyndsey resolutely turned her back to the dark windows. 'What *did* the forecast say?'

'I don't know,' Val said. 'I didn't check.'

'You didn't?'

'Well, no. Did you?'

Lyndsey gave a half-hearted laugh. 'I guess I took Juliet's word for it. But you're the research queen. When we went to Krakow for Juliet's hen do, you knew everything about the city, down to the bus timetables. Didn't you look into this place in the same way?'

Val made a face. 'I did all my research four months ago, when we first booked this holiday. I didn't think to update it.'

'If there'd been a serious weather warning,' Bobbie said, 'Juliet would've told us. Right?'

'What if—?' Lyndsey hesitated, then asked, 'What if she *knew* the weather was going to be bad, and she didn't tell us?'

Val raised her eyebrows. 'She would've said something. There's no way she'd risk screwing up this weekend.'

Bobbie nodded slowly. 'That's true. It's been her dream for years. Ever since she came here as a kid, she's wanted to come back and *share* it with us.' There was the faintest edge of bitterness in her voice. 'It's sometimes felt like we were doomed never to come here. Something's always stopped us in the past.'

'Sure,' Lyndsey said, and let the matter drop.

But it still niggled her. Even if Juliet had known about the incoming storm, she might've decided to risk going ahead with the trip anyway. Juliet was always inclined to gamble. It'd been drummed into her by years of working in the financial sector. The rest of the group were more cautious. Certainly, if Lyndsey had known there was the slightest chance the weather might strand them on the island … well, it would've been the perfect excuse not to come. Some of the others might've felt the same.

I wish we hadn't come, Lyndsey thought bitterly. She'd known from the outset that she should've refused. It would've been tough to argue with Juliet, especially given everything she'd been through recently, but Lyndsey should've tried harder. Reunions were always a terrible idea. What sort of person found it fun to relieve their teenage years? They'd all changed. None of them hung out regularly anymore. In fact, none of them would've had the slightest inclination to hang out if Juliet hadn't pestered them, year on year, about doing this reunion trip.

Maybe the group had been best friends back at school, and maybe they'd shared a common interest in climbing up and down things, but why were they pretending nothing had changed between them?

Why do we pretend it's fine that there are only six people in the group now, when there should still be seven?

Chapter Seven

FRIDAY

6:00pm

'S he says she was nowhere near the lighthouse this afternoon,' Sonia said, slamming the door behind her with enough force to startle Lyndsey out of her doze.

'You're welcome,' Val muttered. She'd been keeping an eye out through the kitchen window, and had got up to unlock the door for Sonia and Juliet. She grimaced and stepped out of the way as Sonia stomped the mud from her boots.

Lyndsey sat up. She'd climbed onto her bunk and burrowed into her sleeping bag while waiting for Sonia and Juliet to return. It'd given her a chance to be alone with her thoughts. And to refill her drink a couple of times. She'd given up on the Baileys and instead dug a bottle of vodka out of her backpack. She'd offered it round but no one had taken up her offer.

The bunkhouse had been nice and quiet. Amanda was asleep again, and Bobbie had curled up on her bunk, either asleep or just needing some peace. The only noise came from the steady tap-tap-tap of Val working away on her laptop at the kitchen table.

For a while, Lyndsey was annoyed about being stuck there, unable to do anything more than count the hours until rescue would arrive. But the more she thought about it, the less it bothered her. If she'd stayed at home that weekend, would she have been doing anything other than sitting alone, drinking? At least here, she couldn't torment herself by doom-scrolling through social media, reading status updates of people living a better life than her.

There's nowhere else you could be right now, she told herself, *so you might as well enjoy it as best you can. You're warm, you're dry, and you're surrounded by friends. Things could be worse.*

Val seemed to have come to the same conclusion. She looked happy enough, working away on her laptop, occasionally frowning or pouting at her screen. She was visibly annoyed when Sonia and Juliet made their noisy entrance.

'According to the warden, there's no reason for her to go to the south of the island,' Juliet said. She shrugged off her black jacket. Rainwater dripped from her sleeves, even though she'd only been outside for a short while. 'All her bird traps are up on the hills to the north and east.'

Val lifted her eyebrows. 'And do we believe her?' she asked.

'Why wouldn't we?' Juliet asked.

'I can think of a bunch of reasons,' Sonia said, sourly. 'She's still procrastinating about the radio, for a start.'

'She's doing her best,' Juliet said. 'We can't ask anything more than that.'

Sonia clumped around the bunkroom in a foul temper, lifting her bag then flinging it back onto her bunk, muttering to herself. Juliet was doing something similar in the kitchen, noisily lighting the camping stove to make another cup of tea.

When Juliet came into the bunkroom, Lyndsey asked her, 'What did you think of the warden?'

'How d'you mean?'

'Just interested in your impression of her. We thought she was a bit odd, didn't we?'

Sonia grunted. 'Odd is certainly one word for her,' she muttered.

'I think she's telling the truth though,' Juliet said firmly. 'We hung around for a while because I wanted to keep her talking. She had no reason to go near the lighthouse today. It's obvious she just wants to get on with her work.'

Lyndsey pulled her sleeping bag up around her shoulders so she could settle into it like a nest. She refilled her mug from the bottle. As Sonia went past, Lyndsey waved the bottle at her, and Sonia gratefully accepted. Juliet wrinkled her nose like Lyndsey was offering around a cup of poison.

Whenever something goes wrong, Juliet always takes it out on whoever's closest. Lyndsey had somehow forgotten that about her. Really, she wanted to ask Juliet about the weather forecast, and if there actually was a storm incoming, but she didn't have the energy to start another argument. She especially didn't want to get Juliet and Sonia sniping at each other again.

With a yawn, Val got up from her chair. 'I need to pee,' she announced. 'Can everyone sing loudly so you can't hear me?' They'd discovered that, as well as being cramped and drafty, the bathroom was poorly soundproofed.

'We should make a rota for the morning,' Juliet said. 'Otherwise, we'll all be trying to shower at the same time.'

'I'm not into group showers,' Val said as she disappeared into the bathroom.

'There's a stream at the top of the field,' Sonia suggested. 'Why don't we really rough it and have a rousing fresh-water morning wash?'

'Sure, why not?' Juliet said. 'It's August. The water won't be *that* cold.'

Lyndsey pulled the hood of her sleeping bag up over her head. It certainly didn't feel like August, with the wind whistling through the gaps in the windows, and flurries of rain splattering the panes. It felt like the depths of winter.

Bloody typical. They'd planned this trip for this time of year specifically because the weather should've been better than if they'd left it till September. Lyndsey was being reminded the hard way that the weather should never be taken for granted.

But somehow, despite everything, it was almost comforting to be there, warm and cosy, in a room with her best friends. The soft murmur of voices reminded her of better times.

The thought made her pause. Were these women really her best friends? Maybe once, years ago, she would've said so, but now? How well did she really know any of them anymore? When they'd all met up in the pub that morning, Lyndsey had experienced a moment of panic that she'd signed up to a weekend retreat with a bunch of complete strangers.

The low sounds of conversation merged with the steady howl of wind and rain outside. It lulled Lyndsey into a doze. She tried, idly, to think of the last time she'd slept in a room with so many other people. It must've been high school, she concluded. Back in Sixth Form, when sleepovers were still cool. When it was completely normal to have all your friends round to your house to sleep on the floor. Although never at Lyndsey's house, of course. It would've been tricky to find enough space for six people in the cramped flat where Lyndsey had grown up.

Even then, she'd been aware that her circumstances weren't like those of her friends. Other families didn't live in tiny flats in the centre of town. They didn't have mismatched furniture that'd come from the charity shop warehouse or – more often – the tip. The few times she'd tried inviting friends home, it had opened her eyes. To this day, she still hated letting people see where she lived. Somehow, despite her best intentions, she'd ended up living in a flat that could be the double of her childhood home.

No, when they were kids, the group had usually gone to Juliet's house, or Amanda's. Juliet's was the nicer house, to be honest, spacious and grand, but Amanda's parents were tolerant, and always let the girls stay up half the night, shrieking at horror movies. If it hadn't been for those sleepovers, the group probably wouldn't have made friends with Cherry, Amanda's elder sister. They wouldn't have discovered they all shared the same urge for climbing and abseiling. They wouldn't have decided, almost on a whim, to form their adventure group.

Their first year of Sixth Form was when it had all come together for them. Lyndsey could clearly remember coming into the common room to find Juliet holding court as usual. Up until that point, Lyndsey had felt like she was on the periphery of Juliet's expansive social group. Lyndsey and Sonia were the outsiders, a two-person clique who'd been friends since before they could remember. Even Val, who'd been somehow drawn into the group despite being in the year above them, fitted in better than they did.

But, for some reason, they'd all fallen in together. Maybe it was simply because there were fewer people in the Sixth Form, fewer places to hide, and more circumstances pushing them into proximity. Whatever it was, the adventure group truly started the moment when Juliet saw Lyndsey and Sonia coming into the common room and shouted, 'Sonia, you know how to climb, right? D'you think it's possible to get up the back wall of C Block?'

Juliet's grand plan that day – which had involved climbing onto the school roof and pinning up a massive protest banner in support of whichever cause she was passionate about that week – never took off. But the group did discover, over the course of a few practice climbs, that they really liked the fun of climbing together. More than that, they liked *each other*. It'd helped that Cherry, who was two years older than her sister Amanda and was busy doing a foundation course at the local polytechnic in preparation for university the following September, was also into climbing. Her skill, expertise, and ability to scrounge up enough equipment for all seven of them meant that the group was able to go out almost every weekend. Those had been some of the best days of Lyndsey's life.

Things had changed after high school. After everything, Lyndsey was surprised they hadn't gone their separate ways at the first opportunity. And, honestly, some of their extended group of friends *had* left – like Tracy, who'd moved to Singapore and married an extremely attractive flight attendant; or Ollie, who was somewhere in Scotland, living off-grid … although not so far off-grid that they didn't regularly update their Facebook page with photos of pre-dawn swims in the lochs or campfire suppers beneath the stars.

If Lyndsey put her mind to it, she could think of a half-dozen friends – good friends, the sort who swore they'd always stay in touch – who'd drifted out of her life as they grew older. This group here in the bunkhouse were the remnants of her friendship circle. The core. Or the dregs.

She kicked out that last thought as soon as it occurred to her. Her subconscious could be such a bitch sometimes.

It was something of a miracle that Lyndsey hadn't lost contact with these five friends too. Bobbie and Sonia had gone away to university but wound up coming home afterwards; Sonia to take up a junior position at the local law firm, and Bobbie to get married. Val had deferred her university place to go travelling, then, after realising she hated travel, met her partner and discovered that a stable, steady relationship was the best kind of inertia for her. Juliet had scored a great job in finance straight out of high school, courtesy of her dad, and had steadily worked her way upwards. It'd seemed like she'd been set for life, with a good job and a loving husband, until the break-up knocked her for six. Lyndsey couldn't remember ever seeing Juliet's confidence being so shaken. It was a wonder she was handling it this well.

Amanda ... well, it was no surprise that Amanda and her family had moved away as soon as they could. Since then, Lyndsey could count on the fingers of one hand the number of times she'd communicated with Amanda, and those had all been via social media, never in person. Their conversations had been stilted and awkward. Always skirting around the unspoken. This weekend should've been a welcome chance to catch up.

As for Lyndsey herself ... obviously she'd always wanted to leave her hometown. Travel. Get an education. Make new and interesting friends. Figure out her life. But somehow it'd never happened. She'd drifted into a catering job after school, figuring she'd make a quick bit of money before deciding what to do. Ten years later she still didn't know. All she had to look back on was a string of lousy jobs that never paid quite enough for her to start a savings account. And now she didn't even have the tenuous security of a job.

Lyndsey frowned. She'd hoped she could've left her worries back on the mainland. As soon as she set foot back there, she'd have to deal with the fact that she was broke, apparently unemployable, and about to be homeless, unless she could figure out a solution to pay off her rent arrears.

With a sigh, she rolled onto her side and closed her eyes. *Nothing you can do about it now,* she thought again. The eerie noise of the wind was like a protective barrier between her and her problems. For the moment at least, she was safe.

Without meaning to, Lyndsey drifted off to sleep, only to wake up fast when Bobbie started screaming.

'He's outside!' Bobbie yelled. 'He's outside!'

'What? What's going on?' Juliet's voice rang out.

Lyndsey sat up too fast and almost cracked her head on the ceiling. Someone had switched off the lights, and it was dark. The only light came from the kitchen.

She twisted round and saw Bobbie trying to fight her way out of her sleeping bag.

'He's screaming,' Bobbie wailed. 'Can't you hear it?'

'That's you,' Sonia shouted back. '*You're* screaming.'

The overhead lights stuttered to life, quickly enough to make Lyndsey shield her eyes.

Juliet stood by the door with her hand on the light switch. Val and Sonia, who'd been seated at the kitchen table, were halfway out of their seats. Bobbie blinked at them all, as if the light had snapped her back to her senses.

'What the hell, Bobbie?' Sonia asked. 'What're you doing?'

'I—' Bobbie opened and closed her mouth. She looked as surprised as everyone else. 'I heard – I can hear—'

Juliet passed a hand over her face. 'You had a nightmare, sweetie. It's all right.'

'No, I wasn't asleep,' Bobbie insisted. 'I was just dozing. I thought—'

'It's all right,' Juliet said, her voice gentle. 'These things happen.'

Bobbie hesitated, then nodded.

The brief silence was broken by a faint noise outside.

It was distant, faint, distorted by the wind. But it did sound like a scream.

'What is that?' Lyndsey whispered. A chill went up her back. It sounded unearthly. Inhuman.

Juliet unlocked the front door.

'Wait,' Lyndsey said, but too quietly to stop Juliet from throwing open the door.

Cold air flooded in. The chill was enough to make Lyndsey gasp.

Before anyone could stop her, Juliet went outside.

The scream – or whatever it was – came again. It was almost too faint to hear.

'It's a long way off,' Val said.

'What d'you think it is?' Lyndsey asked. She pulled her sleeping bag pulled up to her ears against the cold draft.

Juliet came back in and closed the door. 'It must be a seagull or something,' she said. 'Or an animal. Something that's hurt. Could be a rabbit. Rabbits scream like that when they're injured.'

She locked the door. 'Juliet…' Bobbie said.

'What? There's nothing we can do, Bobs. If it's an injured animal, we'll never find it. It's already pretty dark out there.'

From her perch on the top bunk, Lyndsey couldn't see

much of the outside world through the low windows, but it was clear the light had gone out from the sky. She was surprised to realise she must've been asleep for a few hours. A glance at her phone showed her it was half past nine.

A voice drifted up from the lower bunk. 'What's going on?' Amanda asked groggily. 'What's the shouting for?'

'Nothing, it's fine,' Juliet reassured her. 'Nothing's wrong.'

'Oh.' Amanda let her head fall back to the pillow. She had barely opened her eyes. 'Thought it might be the helicopter. Is it on the way?'

'We'll let you know. Don't worry.'

Lyndsey raised her eyebrows at the lie, but Juliet just shrugged. Maybe she figured there was no sense in waking Amanda up properly to tell her the full story.

Juliet went back into the kitchen. 'I'll put the kettle back on,' she said. 'Do you want a cup of tea, Bobs? I've got camomile.'

Slowly, Bobbie disentangled herself from her sleeping bag. Her eyes were still a little too wide. Every few seconds, her gaze would dart anxiously to the window. She moistened her dry lips with the tip of her tongue.

'What about you, Lyndsey?' Juliet asked. 'You wanna come join us for a bit? Have a cup of tea to rehydrate yourself?'

Lyndsey's mouth felt gummy from sleep and residual alcohol. She very much wanted to go back to the blissful, dreamless sleep she'd been enjoying. But now her nerves felt shot to pieces. She wasn't sure she could go back to sleep, not quickly, not easily. So instead, she nodded.

'Come on,' she said to Bobbie as she groped for the ladder. 'Let's have a nightcap, yeah? Settle our heads.' She retrieved her vodka bottle, ignoring the look Juliet gave her.

Bobbie nodded, but still her attention drifted to the windows. Lyndsey wished again there was some way she could've covered them up. More than ever, the black rectangles looked ominous, as if anyone or anything could be peering in at them. Outside, the night was black as pitch, without the slightest glimmer of light. No moon, no stars, no streetlights. It was unnerving. Like they were on the edge of the world.

Stop it, she told herself. *You're too old for ghost stories. There's nobody here but us.*

But the more she repeated it, the less true it felt.

Chapter Eight

SATURDAY 24TH AUGUST

8:05am

D espite everyone's concerns, the bathroom rota more or less sorted itself out in the morning.

Sonia was up first, in and out of the shower room before any of the others had stirred. Lyndsey only woke up when she heard the quiet clunk of the front door closing. She rolled over and peered out of the window, in time to see Sonia wandering to the end of the garden, the wind tossing her damp hair. When she reached the garden wall, Sonia stood contemplating the empty field and the ruffled trees.

The sky was gunmetal grey, but at least it wasn't actively raining. The wind continued to whine through the gaps in the brickwork of the building, just as it'd done all night.

Lyndsey's sleep – when she'd finally found sleep – had been unsettled and broken, punctuated by nonsensical dreams.

Val was up next, beating Juliet to the kitchen to put on the kettle and set a huge pan of bacon on to cook. The smell soon filled the building. They'd only been able to bring a certain amount of fresh food to the island. Once it was gone, it was gone. Peeking out from her nest of blankets and her sleeping bag, Lyndsey suspected Val had cooked the entire weekend supply of bacon. It smelled amazing. She ducked her head back into the sleeping bag but couldn't keep her mouth from watering.

Juliet, who'd been taking her shower when Val started cooking, immediately came out of the bathroom wearing only a towel. 'I thought I was handling the food this weekend,' Juliet objected.

'I'm helping,' Val said. 'I'm not much of a hot shot when it comes to cooking, but I make a mean bacon sarnie. I do it every Saturday as a special treat for my missus.'

'I was hoping we might try eating healthier this weekend.'

'You can do what you like. No one's stopping you.'

'Yes, but … I mean, I've been reading up on early onset rheumatoid arthritis, and it sounds like diet could really make a difference in your case. If you made a few little changes—'

'You know what else makes a big difference? Minding your own damn business. Now, go get dressed. There'll be no naked bacon-eating on my watch.'

On the lower bunks, Bobbie was wrapped up so tightly not even a wisp of hair was showing. Amanda was still asleep, her bad leg cushioned with pillows. At some point during the night, Val had got up to give her some more painkillers – Lyndsey remembered a torch being waved around, and the murmur of voices. Of course, her sleep had been so ragged, she couldn't be sure it'd happened at all, let alone what time it'd been.

Eventually, Lyndsey gave in to the temptation of bacon. She pulled on her jeans and a clean hoodie, then crammed into the kitchen. She took one of the bacon sandwiches that Val offered, with a grateful smile.

Juliet had – with a certain amount of sulking – got dressed in what looked like yoga gear, a skimpy crop top and matching leggings, both of which had neon highlights and a Swedish brand name. Her wet hair was pinned on top of her head to stop it from going curly. She must've been missing her straightening tongs, which she'd had to leave at home.

'How're you feeling?' Juliet asked Lyndsey.

'Fine. Why?'

'I just thought you looked a bit … delicate this morning, that's all.' Juliet tossed her head. 'Help yourself to tea or coffee. Kettle's just boiled. The tap water's running clearer this morning, so Val used that. It's still a bit peat-coloured but it tastes fine.' She was pointedly nursing a cup of herbal tea.

'Lyndsey, you didn't move my laptop, did you?' Val asked. She was concentrating on shoving bacon around the pan, but had obviously clocked the empty space on the table where her laptop should've been.

'Didn't you put it away last night?' Juliet asked.

'What am I supposed to do?' Val squashed the bacon in the pan with a spatula to make it crispier. 'Shove it under my mattress?'

'Just a question. I thought you might've put it somewhere safe.'

'It should've been safe on the table. Who moved it?'

Lyndsey had a clear memory of pushing the laptop aside last night so there was room for her to stand at the table with Bobbie, Sonia, and Juliet to have a drink, after Bobbie woke everyone up. Lyndsey and Sonia had been the only two actually drinking, and Juliet had gone to bed once it was clear they intended to make a night of it. They'd sat up for a while, trying to talk out their fears, but each and every one of them had been listening; straining their ears. The shrill cry of the injured animal – or whatever it was – hadn't come again. Lyndsey wondered who'd be the first to suggest they should go out and look, now it was daylight.

'Your laptop won't have gone far,' Juliet said. 'We'll have a good rummage for it after breakfast. Lyndsey, could you see if Bobbie and Amanda want any food?'

It seemed to Lyndsey like the best thing they could do for those two would be to let them sleep. She didn't think any of the group had slept well. Her own brain had felt too full of everything that'd happened. That, coupled with the noise of the wind, and the absolute pitch black of the bunkhouse once the lights were out... It was a wonder she'd got any rest at all.

Lyndsey passed by Amanda without waking her. Unless things had changed a lot over the past decade, Amanda wouldn't want to come to the breakfast table. She'd always hated eating in front of people. If someone was ever rude enough to comment on what she was having for lunch, she would immediately stop eating and leave the remainder of her food. Everyone except Juliet had caught on to that pretty quickly at school.

'Bobs?' Lyndsey asked as she approached her bunk. 'You awake?'

There was no response. Lyndsey reached down and gave Bobbie's shoulder a gentle shake.

The sleeping bag squashed flat beneath her palm.

Lyndsey flung back the blanket. The pile of pillows and blankets had disguised the fact that, although the sleeping bag still held the vague shape of a sleeping person, it was empty.

'Bobbie's not here!' Lyndsey cried.

'What?'

Lyndsey dragged the sleeping bag off the bunk, as if Bobbie might somehow have been concealed underneath. 'She's gone. She's not here.' Irrationally, she ducked down to check under the bunk.

Juliet came hurrying over. 'Well, where is she?'

'How should I know?' Lyndsey went to check the shower room, even though the door was open and they all could see the tiny room was empty.

'She didn't go out this morning,' Val said. She switched the heat off under the pan. 'I've been awake since seven and I didn't see her.'

Juliet opened the front door and ran outside barefoot. Lyndsey shoved on her boots but didn't bother tying the laces as she hurried to follow Juliet.

'What's going on?' Sonia demanded from the end of the garden. She'd had to step out of the way as Juliet barrelled past her. 'What the hell's the matter? Is the kitchen on fire?'

'Bobbie's gone,' Lyndsey told her. 'She's not in her bunk.'

Juliet ran along the lane to the highpoint in the road. 'Bobbie!' she yelled. 'Bobbie!'

'She might be next door,' Sonia said. She threw away the lit cigarette she'd been hiding in her hand. 'I'll go check.'

Lyndsey jogged round to the back of the buildings. There was no sign of Bobbie there either. The wet grass showed no footprints. From the front of the buildings, she heard Sonia banging on the door of the bird observatory.

By the time Lyndsey came back round to the front door, Sonia had returned. 'Marne isn't there,' Sonia said. She looked furious. 'The observatory's all locked.'

'Maybe she's in bed still.'

'I hammered on the door. Trust me, if she was there, she would've heard me.'

Juliet came striding back towards them, uncaring of the wet stones of the path beneath her bare feet. 'Marne's not there?' she asked.

'No.' Sonia flung her hands up in anger. 'Where the fuck has she gone now? She's meant to be fixing that radio for us, not gallivanting off doing bird warden stuff.'

'You don't think they've gone somewhere together, do you? Marne and Bobbie?'

'We don't know anything yet,' Juliet said. 'Sonia, you were the first one outside today. Was the door locked?'

Sonia blinked. 'I don't – no, it wasn't locked. I didn't have to unlock it when I went out.'

'And you didn't think to mention that?'

'No, of course I didn't. For all I knew, you'd been up before me to greet the sun or whatever.'

'Bobbie must've unlocked it.' Juliet wrung her hands. 'She must've gone out sometime during the night. While we were all asleep.'

From the open door of the bunkhouse, Val called, 'Folks? Come look at this.'

They hurried back in. Val was rifling through the jackets hanging by the door.

'She took her coat,' Val said. 'It's not here. Her boots are gone too.'

'What time did everyone go to bed last night?' Juliet asked. 'I was asleep earlier than you lot. What time did you stay up till?

Lyndsey and Sonia looked at each other. 'We were awake till about one o'clock,' Sonia said. 'Bobbie went to bed a while before that, not long after you did. I was the last one up.'

'And no one heard her get out of bed?'

They all shook their heads. Lyndsey silently cursed herself. How could she not have noticed Bobbie getting up and leaving the bunkhouse? It wasn't like any of them had been sleeping soundly. 'Val, did you hear anything?' she asked. 'You got up to check on Amanda, didn't you?'

Val nodded slowly. 'Amanda woke me. That was about … it'd be four o'clock. She got up to use the bathroom, then she said she couldn't sleep, so I gave her some more painkillers. I checked the time to make sure it was long enough since her last dose.'

'Was Bobbie still in her bunk then?' Juliet asked.

Val lifted her arms in a shrug. 'I didn't check. I was trying not to wake anyone else.'

With a glance at her watch, Juliet made a quick calculation. 'It's half eight now. She's been outside for at least a couple of hours. Possibly more.'

'Why the hell would she go wandering off?' Sonia asked.

The question hung in the air. 'She was upset,' Lyndsey said. 'Something freaked her out.'

'That was just a bad dream,' Juliet said.

'Are you sure? She seemed properly worked up. Before that as well.'

'She always sleeps badly when she's away from home. You know what she's like.' Juliet rummaged in her bag until she found her phone.

'There's no reception,' Lyndsey reminded her.

'Shh.' Juliet tried anyway. She held the phone to her ear for several long seconds before shaking her head. 'No, you're right, no reception.'

'She can't have gone far,' Sonia said. She stood with her hands on her hips as she looked out of the kitchen window. 'There's no place to go on this stupid island.'

She was right. There was nothing on the island to drag Bobbie out of the safety of the bunkhouse, and no rational reason for her to wander off into the darkness. Would a bad dream really have made her go outside in the rain? At least she'd been sensible enough to take her shoes and coat. Even so, it would be freezing out there.

'Let's go,' Juliet said. She grabbed her boots from under her bed.

'Go where?' Val asked.

'We've got to look for her.' Juliet pursed her lips. 'Actually, Val, you should stay here, in case she comes back and wonders where the hell we've all gone.'

Val didn't object. Juliet sat down at the table to tie her bootlaces. Her hands shook very slightly.

'She's probably gone for a walk or something,' Sonia said. 'Probably wanted some fresh air. Nothing more than that.'

'Good.' Juliet finished lacing her boots. 'In that case, she'll be easy to find and we can be back before our cups of tea go cold. Let's get moving.'

Lyndsey held down her complaints as she shrugged on her big coat. There was a sick niggle of worry in the pit of her stomach. Where had Bobbie gone? Why would she sneak out?

A blast of wind caught them all as soon as Juliet opened the door. Sonia visibly shuddered. Val picked up her comforter from the chair and wrapped it tightly around her shoulders.

Lyndsey yanked up her hood and stepped out into the cold. Why would Bobbie come out here? The weather was horrible.

'Hopefully she hasn't wandered too far,' Juliet said. 'I'll go west. There're some little beaches she might've gone to look at. Lyndsey, Sonia…'

'We'll head south,' Lyndsey said. 'There's a path that goes along the coast and down past the lighthouse. We'll check there.'

Juliet nodded. 'Meet back here in an hour. She'll probably have come home by then. If there's no sign of her ... Val, keep your eye out for the warden, okay? We really need that radio.'

No one suggested there was anything sinister about Bobbie's disappearance. Lyndsey wanted desperately to believe Bobbie had gone for an early morning walk and lost track of time. Or even that she and Marne had gone out somewhere together for some unknown reason. But Bobbie had been so distressed last night. So absolutely convinced someone was outside the bunkhouse, looking in. Someone she recognised.

'Everyone take care,' Lyndsey said.

Juliet nodded again. 'See you in an hour.'

Chapter Nine

SATURDAY

9:00am

The trail wound in and out through the bracken and the heather. Within five minutes, Lyndsey and Sonia had crested a small hill and could no longer see the bunkhouse. Ahead of them was nothing but wild, empty landscape and, beyond that, the sea. It looked just as rough as yesterday. Off near the horizon, a tanker was battling its way south.

'Boot prints,' Sonia said, snagging Lyndsey's attention. Sonia pointed out the marks in the muddy track. The rain had softened their edges and dimpled them with water.

'They might not be Bobbie's,' Lyndsey said. 'Marne said she was out yesterday. They could be hers.'

'Yeah, she also said she had no reason to go to the south

of the island. All her bird traps are north of here, apparently.'

'Or they could be your own prints – you walked along here yesterday afternoon, when you and Juliet went back to the lighthouse to get the other bags.' The prints were too vague to be certain who they belonged to.

The wind was picking up again. Spots of rain hit Lyndsey's face. Lifting her head, she could see over the rest of the island and out to sea. The clouds looked blacker and more ominous out there, and were heading towards the island. She shuddered at the thought of being caught in the open in a storm.

What if Bobbie can't find shelter?

The niggle of fear in her stomach wouldn't go away. It wasn't at all like Bobbie to wander off. If it'd been any of the others, Lyndsey wouldn't have been so worried. Juliet and Sonia were *exactly* the sort to take off before dawn without telling anyone. But Bobbie was smart and cautious. She would shake her head with a smile if anyone suggested anything too crazy. She was the sort to bring a jacket *and* an umbrella.

Sonia paused in her stride to fish out a packet of cigarettes from her pocket. Her face looked pale and pinched that morning. It took Lyndsey a moment to realise Sonia hadn't bothered to put on makeup that day. It was a shock to see her without her immaculate eyeliner.

'I thought you'd quit smoking,' Lyndsey said.

'This is not the time to be judgemental.' There was no rancour in Sonia's voice. She shielded her face to light her cigarette. 'I wish we'd never come here.'

'You and me both. Honestly, I was surprised when Juliet said you were coming. I didn't think you'd want to spend three days trapped on an island with us.'

'Yeah, I guess I didn't fully think it through, did I?' Again, there was no anger or malice in Sonia's voice. No matter how abrasive her words were, it was seldom reflected in her tone – at least, when she was sober. 'It's no one's fault. Just mine. My brain's not good at coping with close quarters.'

'So … why *did* you come?'

'Spite.'

'Really? That's so unlike you.'

Sonia barked a laugh. 'I know, right? No, it's because … I've been getting a lot of grief off my family recently. Christmas last year was a particular highlight. They wanted to know why I'd not invited Paul for Christmas dinner.'

'Who the hell is Paul?'

'Exactly. I went on, like, two dates with him in December, and suddenly I should be inviting him for lunch on Christmas Day with my ridiculous family? Give over. And then my mum started hassling me about her cousin's wedding this year – was I going, was I bringing *someone special*, and if not why not; after all, I'm nearly thirty now, practically in the winter of my life… So, when Juliet asked me if I fancied a weekend away, I said yeah. So long as it could be on a particular date in August.'

'Let me guess. The cousin's wedding is this weekend.'

'In about four hours' time, yep.' Sonia smiled.

'That's a lot of effort to go to. Couldn't you just make something up? Hide in bed for a couple of days?'

'You know what my family's like. If they thought I was at home, they would've busted the front door down. Much better to be on a remote island, where, coincidentally, there's no phone reception and no wifi, so they can't even message me.' Sonia grimaced. 'Of course, if I'd known then what I know now, I probably would've sucked it up and gone to the damn wedding. Having twenty-five different relatives ask why I don't have a *nice boyfriend* would still be better than this.' Sonia finished her cigarette, hesitated, then lit another. 'I came here to avoid drama, not find more of it. I swear, when Bobbie came walking into the pub yesterday morning, I knew right then I should've abandoned ship.'

Lyndsey frowned. 'What's your beef with Bobbie? I know you two had a bust-up, but that was months ago, wasn't it?'

After a hesitation, Sonia said, 'We never exactly made up. You know how it goes. I'm almost certain Juliet wanted to use this weekend to force us to talk out our problems, become best friends again, hug, all that. It'd explain why she let me think Bobbie wasn't going to be here. That bloody woman is such a meddler. Was she always this bad, or have I become less tolerant?'

'Be nice. Her heart's in the right place, and she's always looked out for us. Even if we didn't ask her to.'

From the top of the next rise, they had a clear view out to the southern coast of the small island. Ahead of them, the abandoned lighthouse jutted up like an accusing finger. Lyndsey looked up at the high balcony where they'd started their abseil yesterday, and shuddered. It was a frightening distance from the balcony to the ground. Tatters of mist were caught around the old lightning rod at the very top of the structure.

Beyond the lighthouse, the craggy rocks led down to the sea, which was whipped into a frenzy by the wind. White caps dotted the tops of the waves all the way out to the horizon. Half a mile offshore there stood a newer lighthouse, built on an outcrop named Chicken Rock. It'd been constructed as an automated replacement for the old lighthouse. Right now, the waves were breaking high over its foundations. It looked fragile against the vastness of the ocean. The noise of the waves was a constant wall of sound.

There was still no sign of Bobbie.

'Let's check the lighthouse,' Lyndsey said.

Sonia stubbed out her cigarette on a nearby rock. 'You really think she's there?'

'She's got to be *somewhere*.'

Sonia grunted. 'Can't believe she wandered off without telling anyone. D'you reckon she got sick of the sight of us?'

'That doesn't sound like Bobbie.'

'No? If I were her, I would've leapt at the chance to get out of that bunkhouse.'

'Yes, but you're a strident antisocial person.'

It was meant as a joke, but Sonia's mouth twisted. 'I'm a lousy friend, is that what you mean.'

'What? No. No, of course I don't mean that. Why would you think you're not a good friend? Is it the spite thing?'

They hurried down the sloping path towards the lighthouse. The track led between empty fields and swathes of bracken. Lyndsey kept her head on a swivel. Still no sign of Bobbie. Where the hell had she gone?

'If I were a proper friend, I would've stayed at home,' Sonia said then.

'What?'

Sonia let out a breath. 'One of my mates called me the other night,' she said. 'She thinks she's pregnant.'

'Oh.' Lyndsey resisted the urge to ask who it was. If it was any of Lyndsey's business, Sonia would've already told her.

'She doesn't know what to do,' Sonia said. 'I told her to take a test. That's common sense, right? You get a scare, you take a test, *before* you start calling people at stupid-o'clock in the morning. But, y'know. Sometimes common sense isn't that common.'

'Is she okay?'

'No. She's in a right state. And I'm not there for her.' Sonia shielded her eyes against the drizzling rain. 'She told me I should still come here this weekend. Like, she didn't want to be responsible for me missing this, on top of all her other dumb problems.'

What's she going to do? Lyndsey wanted to ask, but it wasn't her place. 'Nothing's going to happen until you get back,' she said. 'Your friend won't be able to get a doctor's appointment or … or anything else, not until after the weekend.'

'I know. Like, intellectually, I know I'd be no use to her. But – you need to be with your friends at a time like that, don't you?'

'What about her boyfriend? Can she talk to him?'

'I doubt it. He's probably busy with his wife.'

Lyndsey bit her tongue for a second time. At moments

like that, she was grateful to be single and off the dating scene. Everything about relationships was a drama. It never seemed to be just two people hooking up and having fun, *no*, of course there had to be infidelity and heartbreak and a failure of contraception as well. She often wondered why people bothered. By the time she'd turned twenty, she'd had enough of it. If she had one wish, it'd be that she could turn back time and skip the terrible dating experiences that'd marred her teenage years. It made her shudder to think of the idiotic mistakes she'd made.

'If you're really worried,' Lyndsey said, 'we could get a message to her. When the radio is fixed, I mean.'

'Yeah, forgive me if I don't fancy telling my friend's business to the bird warden. Besides, we've no idea when or if that radio's ever going to start working.'

Lyndsey didn't want to consider that. 'Your friend will be all right,' she said. 'I mean, obviously, she won't be *all right*. But she'll survive. And she'll be grateful she's got you to help her through this.'

Sonia grunted. She didn't look convinced. 'What would *you* do?'

'Huh?'

'My friend's gonna want advice.' Sonia looked at Lyndsey from the edges of her eyes, as if she didn't want to risk full eye contact. 'What would you say?'

'Good lord. That's a hell of a question.'

'Yeah. Isn't it just?' Without waiting for an answer, Sonia strode away.

Lyndsey had to hurry to catch up. She couldn't think of

anything that would make the situation any better, so she kept quiet.

As they approached the abandoned lighthouse, Lyndsey couldn't help but draw back. She hadn't wanted to return to this place. Certainly not so soon after Amanda's accident. But Sonia went into the walled courtyard around the base of the lighthouse without hesitation. Reluctantly, Lyndsey followed.

It would've been easy for someone to hide in the tangle of gorse, brambles, and nettles that had flourished, sheltered from the harsh wind, inside the courtyard. Lyndsey crouched to peer into the heart of a couple of gorse bushes. The mass of prickles and stingers convinced her that no one in their right mind would go in there, no matter how desperate they were for shelter.

The access door to the lighthouse was closed and padlocked. Juliet had done that when she came to pick up the bags they'd left. Sonia gave the padlock a tug to make sure it was secure.

'She's not been here,' Sonia said.

Hope was leaking out of Lyndsey with every passing moment. Had she really believed Bobbie would've come back to the lighthouse? Maybe not, but Lyndsey had clung to that idea anyway, because she needed to believe Bobbie was somewhere safe and dry and unhurt.

Together, Lyndsey and Sonia left the lighthouse and followed the path up along the clifftops, heading east. With nothing to block the wind, the cold cut into them. The rain increased from a drizzle. Off to their right was the harbour, where they'd arrived yesterday. The waves were breaking over the concrete dock.

Lyndsey glanced back at the abandoned lighthouse. From this angle, she could see the outer wall of the courtyard that faced the sea. She remembered the old story Juliet had told them, from the days when both this lighthouse and the one offshore on Chicken Rock were still occupied. The lighthouse keeper's wife gave birth during a storm, but there was no way to contact the mainland, so the keeper wrote the word BABY in five-foot-high letters on the courtyard wall, so the other lighthouse would see it and radio for help. The word was still just about visible, white against the grey stone wall, but only if you knew to look for it. Lyndsey opted not to point it out to Sonia right then.

'Hell of a lonely place to live,' Sonia said. She had to raise her voice above the wind. 'Don't know how Marne deals with it.'

'If someone was paying me, I think I could learn to cope. Right now, I'd accept a position as caretaker of the moon, if there was a steady wage.'

Sonia squinted at her. 'What's wrong with your current job?'

The only person who knew the full extent of Lyndsey's situation was Bobbie, and Lyndsey had been reluctant to tell even her. 'It's non-existent,' she admitted. 'I got fired.'

'What? When?'

'February.'

'*February*? Why the hell didn't you say anything?'

'I've not seen you since then.' That was true. Lyndsey had used every excuse in the book to avoid going out with her friends that year. 'And I didn't put it on Facebook in case my mum saw.'

'You haven't told your mum?'

'I've hardly told anyone. It's not the sort of thing I want to broadcast, y'know?' Lyndsey had always been fiercely independent. Ever since she'd lied about her age to get a paper round job, just so she could afford trainers that weren't falling apart, she'd supported herself. She hated to even admit when she was struggling, let alone ask anyone for help. Bobbie had found out more or less by accident, when she'd spotted Lyndsey coming out of the job centre.

'So...' Sonia asked, 'if you've not been working, what the hell have you been doing?'

Lyndsey didn't have an answer. How could she describe the weight that'd settled onto her shoulders over the last few months? 'Nothing, I guess,' she muttered at last.

'You should've said. We could've helped you find something. What about bar work? The pubs are always looking for casual staff.'

'I can't. I've got a Pub Watch ban.'

Sonia turned to her, incredulous. 'Oh, hell. What did you do?'

'Does it matter?' Lyndsey really didn't want to get into this. 'There was an incident at the Rovers. The door staff told me to leave and I argued the toss. I know I should've kept my mouth shut. Anyway, they barred me. And, y'know, all the landlords are friends, so if you get barred from one place you get barred from them all...'

'Wow. That's rough.'

'So, I can't work on any licensed premises at the moment, and that apparently includes Tescos and Marksies and just about every other shop you can think of…' Lyndsey trailed off, then added, 'Don't you dare tell Juliet. I don't need her berating me. She's only just stopped lecturing me about how I wasted my life by not going to university.'

'All right, but in return you can't tell her I'm only here because I wanted to duck out of a godawful wedding.'

'Deal.'

The path led them up onto the clifftops. Each gust of wind tried to shove them off their feet. Above their heads, gulls screeched and circled. Sonia flinched away as one bird wheeled close past her head.

'Is it nesting season?' Sonia asked. 'Should we even be here?'

'I think they nest in spring. And the warden would've warned us if there were places we should keep away from.' Still, Lyndsey eyed the circling seabirds cautiously. She had no wish to be divebombed by an angry gull. 'They're definitely mad about something, aren't they?' Their shrieking sounded almost human.

'Seagulls are always mad. It's their default setting. I saw one kill a pigeon once. Speared it right out of the sky. They're nature's sociopaths.'

'That's unfair. I'm sure some of them are nice.'

'And some of them are jerks. What's your point?'

The path petered out into a wide patch of scrubby grass. Lyndsey and Sonia tracked their way down to the edge of the field, where the grass gave way to ragged stone. The cliffs dropped off sharply down to the sea. Here, the noise of the surf was a constant, booming roar.

A little way offshore, a natural column of rock rose, unsupported, for almost two hundred feet. This was the Bear Post, one of the main reasons why the island was a top destination for climbers. Chiselled away from the limestone cliffs by millennia of tidal action, it was a formidable but attainable challenge. The group had seen it from the fishing boat yesterday, and Lyndsey had immediately recognised it from a handful of travel documentaries. It'd also featured in at least one movie. In person, it looked a lot more dramatic. If events hadn't conspired against them, the group would've been climbing the Bear Post on Sunday morning, the last adventure of the weekend before the boat picked them up. Part of the challenge would've been getting there at exactly the right time, when the tide was low enough to walk out to the tower, then returning before the tide turned and cut them off. More than one previous group of climbers had mistimed it and had to be rescued by boat.

At present, there was only a narrow, treacherous strip of rock leading to the Bear Post. Once the tide came in, even that would vanish. Lyndsey walked a little closer to the edge so she could see the waves washing over the slick rocks.

If Bobbie had been wearing a darker jacket, Lyndsey might've never spotted her. They were picking their way along the rocky slope at the clifftop, trying to watch their footing and the gulls and everything else all at once. Lyndsey leaned out over the cliff edge again, and her attention was snagged by a flutter of something bright blue that didn't fit with the grey-black rock. It was on a shelf of stone that jutted out from the cliff-face, some six feet below the grassy edge where Lyndsey stood. At first, she thought it was a piece of plastic tarp caught under a rock. It was only when she leaned out a little further she saw the familiar, sickening outline of a person.

'Oh my God,' she said. 'There.'

Without even pausing, Sonia pushed past her and scrambled down to the ledge.

'Be careful!'

The rock was wet and Lyndsey almost lost her footing as she followed Sonia. She had to pick her way down. The shelf itself was at least ten feet wide, but Lyndsey was still keenly aware that if she slipped off it, there was nothing to catch her except more rocks and – if she fell far enough – the ocean. Sonia stepped along the shelf with the agility of a mountain goat. A seagull startled and took flight with a cry of annoyance.

Sonia dropped to her knees next to the fallen figure. *Bobbie.* It was definitely Bobbie. Lyndsey's heart stuttered in her chest. She ran the last few feet to reach her.

Bobbie lay on her side. Her hands were clutched like claws against her chest. The rain had flattened the red curls of her hair against her skull. Her eyes were open, staring at nothing.

'Bobbie?' Lyndsey's voice came out as a whisper. Like she was afraid to rouse the woman. She put a hand on Bobbie's shoulder. There was a sheen of water on her jacket. 'Bobbie?'

Despite the pressure of Lyndsey's hand, Bobbie didn't

move. It was like she was frozen in place. With hesitant fingers, Lyndsey reached down and touched Bobbie's face, brushing aside a wet curl of hair. Bobbie's skin was like ice. Her lips were drawn back in a rictus to show clenched teeth. There was white foam on her lips and around her mouth, although the drizzle that morning was already washing it away.

'Get her onto her back,' Lyndsey said. In her panicked mind, she was trying to remember the CPR techniques she'd been taught in the First Aid at Work course, two years ago. *Roll the casualty onto their back.* That was the first step. She remembered that, at least.

'Lyndsey—' Sonia said.

Lyndsey refused to listen. All the helpful advice and acronyms of the first aid course had gone out of her mind. *Check her breathing. Tilt her head back. Chest compressions. Yell for help.* Where the hell was Val and her encyclopaedic knowledge when they needed her?

Grabbing Bobbie's shoulders, Lyndsey attempted to roll her. Bobbie moved like a plank of wood. Her hands remained clutched tight against her chest. When Lyndsey tried to tilt the woman's head back to open the airway, the jaw refused to move. It was like she'd been left in a freezer overnight. The thought made a sob build in Lyndsey's chest.

'She's dead,' Sonia said, dully. 'Lyndsey, she's been dead for hours.'

Lyndsey put her ear down close to Bobbie's blue lips, listening in vain for a breath, watching the stationary chest in case it spontaneously hitched. Nothing. She put her fingers on Bobbie's neck, in search of a pulse, and felt nothing but the unyielding solidness of dead flesh.

Her mind freewheeled for several moments. *Check her breathing, tilt her head back...* She'd done those things, to no avail... *Yell for help...*

'Help!' Her voice was swallowed by the drizzle. Lyndsey kept yelling until her voice cracked. Then she doubled over as grief choked her.

Sonia had barely moved, as if she too were frozen. Her hands were pressed tightly together like she couldn't bear the thought of accidentally touching the body. 'What the hell happened to her?' she asked. Her voice was flat. 'Did she fall?'

The ledge Bobbie lay on was less than six feet below the edge of the rocky slope. If she'd fallen, she couldn't have fallen far. There were no rips or scuffs on her jacket to suggest she'd rolled down the slope. But it didn't have to be a big fall. Just a few feet could break a skull... Lyndsey shuddered, remembering Amanda's accident yesterday. If Bobbie had landed badly, she might've twisted an ankle or even broken her leg, then she'd be stuck here, exposed to the elements. Waiting for a rescue that never came.

'Try your phone,' Lyndsey said. She was already fumbling in her pocket for her own. Maybe by some miracle, one of them could get reception...

Neither of them could. Sonia kept trying, her fingers hitting each contact in her phone numbly, like she was on autopilot. Lyndsey didn't know much about the effects of shock, but she could tell Sonia wasn't in a position to think rationally.

'We have to get help,' Lyndsey said.

That seemed to get Sonia's attention. 'Our phones are useless.'

'I mean the others. We have to get Juliet. She'll—' Lyndsey wanted to say, *she'll know what to do*, but how true was that really? Would Juliet have any idea how to handle this awful situation?

Sonia's gaze slipped back to Bobbie. 'What happened to her?' she asked again. 'Why is she out here?'

Lyndsey closed her eyes. If Bobbie really had left the bunkhouse well before seven o'clock that morning, like they suspected, she could've been lying here for three hours, or even more. That was a long time to be outside in the bitter cold. Had Bobbie shouted for help? Had she laid here, shivering, hoping in vain for her friends to notice she was missing?

Lyndsey wiped her eyes with the backs of her hands. She couldn't stop looking at poor Bobbie, those hands curled up like claws, teeth bared like an animal. She'd died in pain, that much was obvious. In pain and alone. There were crescents of dirt underneath her fingernails.

'Come on.' Lyndsey staggered to her feet. The world tilted for an instant. 'We need to get the others.'

'One of us should stay with her.'

'There's nothing we can do, Sonia.'

Slowly, Sonia raised her gaze to the sky. A number of seagulls wheeled overhead, adding their angry cries to the noise of the sea. 'We need to keep the birds away,' she said.

With a sickening lurch, Lyndsey realised she was right. She remembered the gull that'd taken flight just as they'd arrived. How long would it be before the rest of the flock got enough courage to take advantage of the body? She thought of Sonia's comment earlier, about how vicious the birds could be when they were hungry, and shuddered again.

'I'll stay with her,' Lyndsey said. The idea of sitting on that exposed ledge next to the body of her dead friend horrified her, but she'd rather do it herself than ask Sonia to.

To her surprise, Sonia shook her head. 'I'll stay,' she said. 'You fetch the others. Juliet should be heading back to the bunkhouse soon.'

Lyndsey nodded. She couldn't find the words to argue. And, a guilty part of her realised, she was relieved not to stay. She couldn't cope with staring at Bobbie's slack face for a moment longer.

So, with barely a backwards glance, Lyndsey heaved herself up the rocks and set off at a run back to the bunkhouse.

Chapter Ten

SATURDAY

9:45am

By the time she got back, Lyndsey was dishevelled and distraught. She'd tried to run all the way, but a debilitating stitch in her side had slowed her down. The last stretch had been completed at a hobbling limp. Her breath hitched in her chest.

She reached the bunkhouse and shoved open the door.

'Lyndsey! What's wrong with you?'

It was Val who came bustling up from her chair in the kitchen to catch Lyndsey in her arms. Lyndsey clung to the big woman, unable to stop crying. She realised she didn't have the slightest clue how to tell the others what'd happened.

'Here, sit down,' Val said. She pulled a chair out from the table. 'Tell me what the problem is.'

In between gulping sobs, Lyndsey got out the whole story.

There was a stunned silence when she'd finished.

'That—' Val swallowed; tried again to speak. 'That's not possible. You must be wrong.'

'I'm not. I'm sorry.' Lyndsey didn't know why she was apologising. But she couldn't help it. She wiped her face with the neckline of her hoodie. 'I know what I saw.'

Val passed her a wadded square of kitchen roll that she'd grabbed from somewhere. 'She can't be dead,' she said, stubbornly. 'Did you check?'

'Of course we did,' Lyndsey snapped. 'D'you think I'd chase all the way back here if I wasn't sure?'

'No. No, of course not.' Val sat back down. The news had stunned her, like a sharp blow to the head. 'I can't believe Bobbie snuck past us all,' she said then. 'What the hell was she thinking?'

'I need to talk to Marne,' Lyndsey said. 'The radio—' She stood up too quickly and almost fell. She had to catch herself against the edge of the table.

'Let me check if she's back yet,' Val said. 'I haven't seen her come home, but she might've got past me. You stay here.'

There was a sour taste in Lyndsey's mouth as she slumped into her seat. What would they do if the radio was still broken? The thought pinballed around her head and made her feel sick. 'I should go and look for Juliet...' she started to say.

'No. Definitely not.' Val picked up a grey jacket from the hooks, then put it back when she realised it was Amanda's. She grabbed her own and started pulling it on. 'If you go out looking for her, chances are we'll end up with folk separated across the island, all searching for each other. Much better to stay put. She'll be back soon.'

Lyndsey tried to think of an argument, but her thoughts were scattered. She remembered Sonia's blank face as she stared at Bobbie. That was how Lyndsey felt now. Like the shock had just caught up with her.

As Val disappeared outside, closing the front door behind her, Lyndsey glanced around the silent bunkhouse. In her bed, Amanda was still dozing. She hadn't so much as stirred when Lyndsey came in. For an irrational moment, Lyndsey was jealous. She wanted nothing more than the blissful ignorance of deep sleep.

With that thought in mind, Lyndsey went to her bunk and dug one of the bottles out of her bag. She couldn't remember if they'd finished off the first bottle last night, so she grabbed a new one instead. In the kitchen, she rinsed out her mug, then poured a large measure of vodka and drank it in one. Her hands barely shook as she poured a second.

She wished she'd thought to ask Val for something stronger. Who knew what else Val had in her bag of tricks? There had to be something to take away the sick feeling of horror that filled Lyndsey's chest and stomach.

The urge sent her into the bunkroom before she could think twice about it. Val's bag was sitting in the middle of the lower bunk. Lyndsey patted the side pockets until she found one that crinkled. Unzipping it revealed a tightly-packed wodge of medication packets. It shocked Lyndsey to see how many there were. Val often joked about her body rattling from all the tablets she had to take for her arthritis, but did she really need this many for a single weekend?

Lyndsey pulled out a cardboard packet at random and peered at the label. To her surprise, it wasn't Val's name on the printed label. The tablets were prescribed to Josephine Miller, whoever the hell that was.

Why on earth would Val have someone else's tablets?

The door of the bunkhouse banged open. Lyndsey hastily shoved the medication back into Val's bag and zipped up the pocket.

'Anyone here?' Juliet asked as she stuck her head around the door. When she spotted Lyndsey she opened her mouth, then noticed the blotchiness around Lyndsey's eyes, and the mug in her hand.

'We found her,' Lyndsey managed to say.

'Where?'

'On the cliffs, just around the corner from the old lighthouse. Near the Bear Post. I left Sonia there with her.'

'Is she hurt?'

Lyndsey shook her head. She realised now why Sonia had opted to stay with Bobbie – because, however awful that task was, it wasn't as bad as breaking the news to their friends, one by one.

'She's dead,' Lyndsey said. Her voice sounded weird and flat, like it was someone else who'd spoken.

Juliet went very still. For a moment, Lyndsey thought the shock had made her mind shut down, like Sonia's had.

Either that, or Juliet was gearing up to tell Lyndsey she was mistaken, like Val. But then Juliet's face crumpled and she started to cry.

'I knew it,' Juliet said in a broken voice. 'I knew something terrible had happened. Why else wouldn't she have come back by now?'

'We don't know what happened.' It seemed important to stress that. 'It's not clear if she fell or … or…'

'She's on the cliffs, did you say?'

Lyndsey nodded. 'I'm trying to figure out a way to carry her back here.' The idea had been floating around, unformed, in her head, but she was a long way from figuring out a solution. It seemed important to think about logistics. If she concentrated on the next thing she had to do, she wouldn't have to look at the bigger picture, which involved one of her best friends lying dead on an isolated rock face.

'Good. Good idea.' With a nod, Juliet straightened her back and wiped her eyes. Lyndsey felt relieved. This was more like Juliet. No matter how awful the situation, Juliet would cope. If Juliet had fallen apart right then, Lyndsey wasn't sure what she would've done. 'What've you come up with?'

That was the issue. Lyndsey had no ideas. There were no bedsheets in the bunkhouse. No blankets. Nothing to use as poles for a stretcher. Her eyes wandered the bedroom from one end to the other and found zero answers.

Juliet was blinking fast, holding back tears, her pragmatic façade already threatening to crack. 'Grab her sleeping bag,' she said. 'Then show me where she is.'

Chapter Eleven

SATURDAY

10:05am

It took them ten minutes to reach the coast. Juliet raged ahead with her long-legged stride. Lyndsey struggled to keep up. The pace was too fast to allow for any conversation. Or maybe they just didn't want to talk. When she needed to give directions, Lyndsey would wordlessly point to where they were going. Under her arm, she carried Bobbie's sleeping bag, rolled up into a day bag to keep it dry.

Lyndsey was half-afraid she wouldn't be able to find the place where Bobbie lay. Her memories were scattered and unreliable. What if she'd been wrong about what she'd seen? Maybe Bobbie had only been injured after all. Maybe she'd got up after Lyndsey left and was right now chatting to Sonia and —

Lyndsey shook the thought away. She knew what she'd seen. There was no denying it.

They followed the path back to the rocky grassland that sloped down to the cliffs. In the distance, Lyndsey caught sight of Sonia's red windbreaker. The woman was sitting above the ledge, angled towards the sea, but her face was turned to the sky. As Lyndsey and June approached, Sonia flapped her hands at a seagull that was circling too close.

'Sonia!' Lyndsey called.

Her voice startled two more seagulls who'd been perching on the cliff face lower down. They took off with a flurry of wings. Sonia looked around and raised a hand as a weak greeting.

'Are you okay?' Lyndsey asked as she hurried over.

Sonia shook her head. 'I'm glad you're back. Those flying sea-vermin are getting cockier by the minute. I was worried they'd start taking bites out of me.'

Juliet walked to the edge of the ledge and peered over. There she stood, frozen, unable to look away.

Lyndsey knew how she felt. Even though she'd braced herself, it was a jarring shock to see Bobbie again, lying on her back, her eyes staring unseeing at the sky.

'That's how we found her,' Lyndsey said. Her voice sounded too loud. The wind tried to tear her words away. 'Except she was lying on her side. I moved her. To see if she was—'

She couldn't complete the sentence.

Sonia let Lyndsey and Juliet climb down first to the rocky shelf, then followed them. With all three of them, plus Bobbie, on the ledge, there wasn't a lot of room. Lyndsey was uncomfortably aware of the steep drop next to them. If one of them put a foot wrong, they would bounce and tumble all the way to the sea.

Juliet crouched down at Bobbie's side and touched the dead woman's face. A lot of the foam around Bobbie's mouth had been washed away by the rain. There was still some on the underside of her cheek.

'What the hell happened?' Juliet asked. There was a raw edge to her voice, like something in her chest had ripped open.

'I don't know,' Lyndsey said. 'We don't think she fell.'

'She wasn't well.' Sonia looked at her with haunted eyes. 'She kept telling us all yesterday that she felt ill. We didn't listen.'

'She wasn't that sick,' Juliet said. 'She always gets ill when we travel.' She was still crouching next to Bobbie. Her eyes took in everything Lyndsey had already catalogued – the bared teeth, the foam around the mouth, the claw-like hands, the dark crescents under the fingernails. 'Anyway, no matter how ill she felt, she wouldn't have gone walking out here in the night for no reason.'

'Are you sure? Maybe she went out for some fresh air and wandered too far from the bunkhouse...' Lyndsey remembered the night before, and the darkness outside the windows. The landscape had been utterly dark and featureless. It'd felt like the bunkhouse was the only point of light for a thousand miles. 'It'd be easily done. If she walked away from the bunkhouse, for whatever reason, she could've got disorientated and not found her way back. There aren't any points of reference in the dark.'

'She's always had a lousy sense of direction,' Sonia agreed. 'Remember when—' But she broke off and pressed her lips together tight. It wasn't the right moment to share memories.

'We should bring her back to the bunkhouse,' Lyndsey said, to break the silence. 'We've brought her sleeping bag. I guess we can put her in that and carry her.'

Sonia nodded slowly. 'It won't be dignified, but it'll probably work.'

'I think we have to leave her here,' Juliet said.

'What? No.' Sonia shook her head. 'We can't do that.'

'I think we have to.' Juliet gestured at Bobbie. 'The police will need to see this. They'll have to take photographs. Gather evidence. If we move her … what if we destroy something important? What if it means the police can't figure out what happened to her?'

Lyndsey looked at the sky. 'We can't leave her here. The weather might get worse.'

'Listen, I don't like it either. But once the radio is fixed and we contact the mainland, they'll have a rescue helicopter here within an hour. It'll have to fly over from Wales, but it'll get here. We should wait until then.'

'So, what?' Sonia asked. 'We're supposed to just leave Bobbie here? With these jerks?' She waved an arm at the circling seagulls. Lyndsey shuddered again. How long would it be before more wildlife found the body?

'It's the best way,' Juliet insisted. 'We want the police to know what happened to her.'

'Leaving her out here in the rain won't do much to preserve evidence,' Sonia said. 'Plus, those seagulls. Chances are, if we leave her here, by the time we come back she'll be in bits. I don't think the authorities will be super happy about that either.'

The constant references to the police were making Lyndsey edgy. 'Why would the police need to take photographs?' she asked.

Juliet wouldn't meet her gaze. 'None of us know what happened to her. We won't find out for sure until the police get here.' She stood up. 'We'll put her in her sleeping bag. That'll protect her, at least a little.'

The idea of leaving Bobbie out there in the open disturbed Lyndsey a lot. But in her heart, she knew Juliet was right. If they moved Bobbie, they'd have to explain it to the police later. She just didn't want to admit it because...

Because if the police are involved, that means it was more than just an accident.

'Come on,' Juliet said. 'We have to work together.'

Getting Bobbie into the bag was traumatic. None of them wanted to be the first to touch her. Beneath her wet clothes, her flesh had taken on a cold, hard aspect. Her legs had begun to seize up. It was like trying to put a mannequin into a sack.

They'd just got Bobbie's feet into the sleeping bag when Juliet said, 'Wait, wait.' She stooped and retrieved something that was about to fall out of Bobbie's jacket pocket. Her mobile phone. Juliet slipped it into her own pocket.

Together, they pulled the sleeping bag up to Bobbie's shoulders. Sonia smoothed down Bobbie's wet hair while Juliet drew the hood up over her head. It was only once they pulled the drawstrings tight, so Bobbie was completely enveloped, that Lyndsey realised how much it resembled a body bag.

Once they were finished, the three women straightened up. Lyndsey was aware they were standing around the body like this was a burial. Bobbie did in fact look ready to be buried at sea. Lyndsey had the sudden urge to say a few words of farewell.

'Why on earth would she go off in the middle of the night like that?' Sonia asked quietly.

'Beats the hell out of me,' Juliet said. She cradled Bobbie's phone in her gloved hands.

'She was irrational when she woke up,' Sonia said. 'She obviously wasn't thinking straight.'

'Yeah, but what if it was more than that?' Lyndsey asked. 'She saw someone. Outside the window. Remember?'

'She *said* she saw someone,' Sonia said. 'We all went to look. There was nothing there.'

You didn't go to look, Lyndsey thought. *Only Juliet went outside.* But she held her tongue.

Juliet unlocked Bobbie's phone. There was a passcode, but all three of them knew it. Bobbie had a habit of saying it out loud each time she unlocked her phone, like there was a prize for guessing it correctly.

Tears burned the backs of Lyndsey's eyes. It seemed impossible that she'd never see Bobbie do any of those daft, endearing things again.

'She sent a text,' Juliet said with surprise. 'It went through at five twenty-two this morning.'

'It went through?' Sonia asked with equal surprise. 'How?'

Juliet lifted the phone high above her head, searching for a signal. 'Some kind of fluke, I guess. Must've picked up just enough signal.'

'At least that gives us an idea what time she left the bunkhouse,' Lyndsey said. *For all the good it does us.*

'The message might've sat on her phone for a while, waiting for signal,' Sonia said. 'There's no guarantee she definitely pressed send at exactly five twenty-two. What does the message say?'

Juliet held out the phone for them to see. On the screen, in clear white letters, it read, WHERE ARE YOU?

'It was sent to her husband,' Juliet said.

'God, the poor thing,' Sonia muttered. 'She must've been more confused than we thought. Maybe she didn't even realise she was still out here on the island.'

'There's a bunch of attempted phone calls as well,' Juliet said, scrolling through the phone. 'Between half past four and ten to five this morning. All to him. None of them connected.'

'She was calling him all that time,' Sonia said. 'How fucking awful.'

The three of them stared down at their friend's body. Each, in their own way, tried to imagine what it must've been like for Bobbie out there, alone, freezing cold, desperate for help. Lyndsey thought the phone records made a twisted sort of sense. If Bobbie had been ill and disorientated, it figured that she would try to reach the one person she knew would help her.

Except...

'When she woke us up, she thought she saw a man outside the window,' Lyndsey said. 'She said, "*He's* outside."'

'So?' Juliet asked.

'So, what if she saw ... what if she *thought* she saw her husband out there?'

Sonia looked disturbed. 'C'mon, now. Why would she think that?'

'I don't know.' Some part of Lyndsey was worried she *did* know. 'But the way she was acting, the way she spoke ... it had to be someone she recognised.'

Sonia lifted her hands in exasperation. 'Okay, so, she was so freaked out she thought she saw her husband. There was obviously something very much the matter with her. A lot more than travel nerves or sea sickness.'

'Come on,' Juliet said, pocketing the phone. 'We shouldn't be talking this way in front of her. It's disrespectful.'

Neither Lyndsey nor Sonia disagreed. It did indeed feel wrong to be discussing Bobbie's mental health over her literal dead body.

They climbed back up onto the grass. Lyndsey glanced back once.

What she hadn't said – what she couldn't help thinking, but didn't want to say aloud because she was scared it'd make her sound crazy – was that she thought Bobbie had been telling the truth. Bobbie really had seen someone she recognised outside the window during the night.

Chapter Twelve

SATURDAY

10:20am

The whole way back to the bunkhouse, Lyndsey couldn't shake the feeling they were being watched. She had to stop herself from constantly looking around to check the horizon. It was crazy, she knew. There had to be a rational reason for the itch at the nape of her neck. But still, the idea ate at her nerves until she had to say something.

'Hey, what if Bobbie did see someone outside last night?' Lyndsey asked as they tramped back along the path. The rain was heavier now, bouncing off the stones and creating a constant *shush*ing noise as it hit the bracken.

'She didn't.' Juliet immediately dismissed the idea. 'There's no one here but us.'

'Well, we don't know that for definite, do we?' Sonia

said. 'This is all public land. If someone hopped on a fishing boat, or even a canoe, they could get here easily enough. And we'd be none the wiser.'

'We've got the only shelter on the island. There're no other buildings that're habitable.' Juliet frowned as she said it. 'Anyway, Marne would've told us if anyone else was staying on the island.'

'Unless she didn't think it was important,' Lyndsey said. 'Like how she didn't think the broken radio was a big deal. Maybe she knows other people sometimes come here, but didn't think to mention it to us.'

Like Sonia said, it wasn't difficult to get to the island, at least when the weather was calm. There was another harbour, at the north of the island where the distance between the island and the mainland was at its narrowest, although landing there was harder because of the currents that tore through the narrow channel. When they'd booked this trip, the owner of the fishing boat had given the group the option of landing at the north harbour, which was a shorter journey but would be far more dependent on the tides. The channel was all but impassable at any time except during slack tide, when the sea was at its highest or lowest.

As far as Lyndsey knew no one monitored who came and went to the island. And there were always dozens of fishing boats pottering around the mainland coast. Maybe fewer in this weather, but still. It wouldn't be beyond the realms of possibility for someone to sail out here and make landfall without anyone being aware.

Juliet chewed the thought over. 'Why would anyone go to that much effort to come here in this weather?' she asked.

Sonia gave her a hard look. 'Why indeed.'

It was a good point though. A person would have to be very determined to risk the currents and the high winds to sail out to the island. Lyndsey couldn't think of anyone who hated Bobbie enough to go to that effort.

Lyndsey drew her jacket tighter. At some point in the last hour, her thinking had changed. At first, she'd wondered what kind of awful accident had befallen Bobbie. But, the more she thought about it, the less it seemed like an accident.

Lyndsey hated to think someone would've deliberately hurt Bobbie. Especially since the only people in the vicinity were their group of friends … and the bird warden.

Yeah … mustn't forget Marne.

As they walked, Juliet took out her phone and started texting.

'There's no signal,' Lyndsey reminded her, as gently as she could. She was worried that the stress of the situation might've made Juliet forget.

'Bobbie's managed to get a text message to go through. It might've sat in her phone's outbox for an hour or two while she was wandering out here, but it sent eventually. That means there must be at least one pocket of signal somewhere on this island. If we all do the same – if we send out a bunch of text messages – then maybe we'll get lucky as well, if we happen to pass through one of those pockets.'

Sonia shook her head. 'My phone doesn't do that. If it doesn't deliver the message straight away, it bounces back to me. It won't keep trying to send it.'

'Well, mine does. I'm going to try anyway,' Juliet said. 'It's got to be worth a shot.'

Lyndsey took out her own phone. It was the cheapest one she could get away with, although she'd had to pay a bit more than she'd wanted, because she needed to get on the internet to access the job centre. She paused with her thumb over the keys. Who would she text? It'd have to be her mum. Which would be awkward, since they hadn't spoken for the better part of two months. What would her mum think, if she got a text out of the blue, saying her daughter was in trouble?

Get over yourself. Lyndsey's personal feelings didn't matter at that moment. It was an emergency. They had to raise the alarm.

'Who're you sending yours to?' Lyndsey asked Juliet.

'Gary.'

'Your husband? I thought you weren't, y'know—'

Juliet closed her eyes briefly. 'Shit. I didn't—' She let out an explosive breath. 'It's just instinctive. Soon as something goes wrong, he's the first person I think of calling. That's really something, isn't it?' She hesitated, then deleted the message. 'Fuck it. I can't have him thinking I might run back to him as soon as there's a crisis. I'll text some people from work instead.'

Lyndsey nodded. She pressed SEND on the message to her mum, then locked the screen and put her phone away. She wasn't sure she could deal with watching the symbol circling below the message as it searched in vain for a signal.

Although none of them discussed it, they all headed for

the observatory rather than the bunkhouse. Juliet hammered on the front door. When she didn't get an answer straight away, she pushed open the door and stepped inside regardless.

She almost ran into Val, who was coming out of the workroom.

'Radio's still broken,' Val said, in lieu of a greeting. 'I figured I should stay here and supervise. Maybe things will get done quicker.'

'Where's Marne?'

'Here.' Marne was coming down the stairs, holding a towel against her cheek. She frowned at the three women who'd come rushing into her home unannounced. 'I told you, I'll let you know as soon as the radio's fixed. You can't keep hassling me.'

Juliet looked at Val. 'Did you tell her what's happened?'

'She's only just shown up,' Val said, annoyed. 'Apparently, it was more important for her to go out checking her bird nets this morning, rather than working on the radio.'

'This is my job,' Marne said. She took the towel away from her cheek, revealing two deep scratches, both leaking blood. The towel was spotted red. 'It's not something I can put on hold.'

'What happened to your face?' Lyndsey asked.

Marne winced. 'I got scratched by a polecat.'

'A polecat?'

'Yeah, like a ferret? It was—'

'We don't have polecats here,' Sonia said.

'You should tell that to the nest of them living in the

field behind us. Every now and again I catch one, but there's always a couple more to take their place. Had to go after this one though. It's been killing fledglings. Horrible.'

Lyndsey remembered the screaming that'd woken Bobbie up the night before. It had sounded like an animal in pain. Could it have been a polecat attacking a seabird? Lyndsey had no idea what that would sound like.

While she was thinking, she also remembered Bobbie's hands, clutched into claws, with what looked like dirt under the nails.

'Look, we don't have time for this,' Juliet said. 'We need the radio.'

'I'm quite aware of that,' Marne said, examining her bloodied towel. 'I'm—'

'We need to raise the alarm. Our friend's been hurt.'

'Yes, I know.'

'You—?'

'She hurt her ankle when you lot were abseiling at the lighthouse, you said. Why? Is she worse today?'

'Not her,' Juliet said with exasperation. 'Our other friend. Bobbie.'

Marne raised her eyebrows. 'Someone else is hurt? How bad? I can take a look if you want. I've got a bit of training.'

'You can't help her,' Lyndsey snapped, then regretted her tone. 'Sorry. But you can't.'

Juliet took a breath. 'She's dead. We just found her. On the cliffs over at the east of the island.'

Marne blinked at each of them in turn. She opened her mouth, then shut it again.

'She wandered out of the bunkhouse during the night,' Lyndsey said. 'She was probably outside for hours.'

'So, we need to get the rescue helicopter here now,' Juliet said. She stepped towards Marne to emphasise her words. 'It's more important than your job, or some bloody polecats. You need to fix the radio.'

It was an echo of what they'd said yesterday, back when Amanda's accident was the most urgent thing in the world. Marne nodded and, without a word, went back to the workbench, the towel still pressed to her bleeding face.

Val came over to the front door so she could talk quietly with her friends. 'Where's Bobbie?' she asked. 'Did you manage to carry her?'

'We had to leave her,' Juliet said.

It wasn't the full truth, but it wasn't a complete lie. Val nodded. She looked exhausted.

'Val, I'll stay here with you,' Juliet said. 'We'll keep an eye on things.' By *things*, it was obvious she meant Marne. 'Lyndsey, you and Sonia look after Amanda. I don't want her to wake up and think we've abandoned her.'

What with one thing and another, Lyndsey had all but forgotten Amanda. She wondered if the woman was still asleep; if she'd somehow remained oblivious to everything. Lyndsey didn't relish having to tell her what'd happened to Bobbie.

Together, Lyndsey and Sonia returned to the bunkhouse. Lyndsey went to check on Amanda, who was dozing. *We should tell her*, Lyndsey thought, before guiltily deciding to let her sleep.

'Should I put the kettle on?' Sonia asked. She was

standing in the middle of the kitchen, looking lost. Her hands were clutched together so tightly that the knuckles had turned white. On the table sat the remains of their abandoned breakfast. The bacon sandwiches had congealed and the cups of tea were cold.

'What for?'

Sonia didn't seem to have an answer. 'It's what Juliet would do,' she said at last.

'Go ahead, if it keeps you happy.' Lyndsey's gaze went to her bottle of vodka, which she'd left at the foot of her bunk. The alcohol she'd drunk earlier had been burnt straight out of her system by adrenaline, leaving her headachy and sore. Part of that feeling must be due to stress. She wanted to keep drinking until she passed out. Maybe when she woke up, things would look better.

Sonia picked up the kettle and filled it from the squeaky tap. 'Juliet doesn't trust Marne either,' she said. 'She doesn't think we should leave her unsupervised.'

'Val was keeping an eye on Marne already.'

Sonia fiddled with the camping stove. It took her three attempts to get it lit. 'It's probably safer if more than one of us stays with her,' she said. 'Just in case.'

'In case of what?'

Setting the kettle on the stove, Sonia turned to face her. 'Because of what happened to Bobbie.'

Lyndsey took a seat at the table. Even though they'd been thinking the same thing, it was different to hear it spoken aloud. 'You don't trust Marne,' she said.

'No. Not at all. Those scratches on her face... D'you honestly believe her story about a polecat?'

Lyndsey thought of Bobbie's hands, curled into claws. 'No,' she admitted.

'And this whole business with the radio. It just happens to break, right before we arrive, just when it turns out we need it? Bullshit.'

'You think she broke it herself?'

That made Sonia pause. 'I don't know. I don't want to think that, because it'd mean ... well, it'd mean she'd trapped us here on purpose. That's a pretty fucked-up thing to consider.'

'Why would she do something like that? She doesn't know any of us.'

'She's obviously a weirdo. No one in their right mind would choose to live out here alone on an isolated rock. She traps *birds* for a living. That's weird.'

'She just weighs them and puts those little rings on their feet, then lets them go. It's perfectly normal. People have been doing it for centuries.'

'If you reckon so.'

Lyndsey watched the kettle as it slowly heated up. 'We shouldn't speculate,' she said. 'It won't do us any good. We should wait for the police.'

'Yeah, except they're not here yet, and we don't know how long it'll take. It could be hours. What if the weather gets worse? What if they can't get here at all?'

Her words sent a chill down Lyndsey's spine. There had to be emergency procedures to get them back to the mainland in the event of catastrophic weather. Didn't there?

Sonia grimaced. 'This just feels like more than terrible timing to me. The radio breaks – and Marne doesn't tell anyone about it – right before Bobbie gets hurt, when the boat isn't due to come pick us up for at least another twenty-four hours. And don't forget what happened to Amanda.'

Lyndsey glanced at Amanda's sleeping form. *That was an accident,* Lyndsey wanted to say, but the words stuck in her throat. She was no longer sure she believed that.

'Either this is all a string of coincidences,' Sonia said, 'or someone's out to get us. And there aren't a lot of suspects here.'

Lyndsey didn't want to agree, but – 'Maybe we shouldn't have left Val and Juliet alone with her.'

'Juliet can handle herself,' Sonia said, dismissively. 'And Val – wait, that's a thought.'

She went into the bunkroom, moving quietly to avoid waking Amanda. Reaching up to her own bunk, she slipped a laptop out from underneath her sleeping bag and brought it to the table.

'That's Val's laptop,' Lyndsey said. 'What're you doing with it?'

'I want to check something.'

'She was looking for it this morning. Why on earth did you take it?'

Sonia didn't answer. She sat down at the table, opened the laptop and, as soon as it woke up, started clicking through files.

'That's not yours,' Lyndsey said, although Sonia obviously knew that. 'What're you looking for?'

'Val's the research queen. She always goes overboard on research for that novel she's eternally writing. Remember when she spent an hour telling us the difference between salt-water drowning and freshwater drowning? Then she didn't even use it in her story, after all that.'

'Yeah, so?'

'She also never deletes anything. Hangs onto every piece of research she's ever done. It's disturbing how much information she's amassed. Did you know she's also got a document full of character details about everyone in this group? She must be planning to crowbar us into one of her stories some time.'

'Really, what is your point?'

'This.' Sonia turned the screen around so Lyndsey could see the word document she'd found.

Lyndsey's eyes skimmed the page. At a glance, it looked to be a fairly exhaustive list of different types of poison that could be found at any particular time period, along with their symptoms and where an average person might conceivably obtain them. Val, as Sonia said, was nothing if not thorough.

'I don't get it,' Lyndsey said. 'Val researched poisons last year. So what?'

'Something struck a bell with me while I was sitting out on that ledge, waiting for you to get back. I remembered Val talking about different poisoning symptoms when we all met up for coffee one time. Look at this.'

Her finger hovered over the paragraph about arsenic poisoning. Lyndsey's eyes immediately went to certain words. *Convulsions, muscle spasms, foaming at the mouth…* She thought of Bobbie's clawed hands and rictus grin.

'Sounds familiar, doesn't it,' Sonia said grimly.

Chapter Thirteen

SATURDAY

10:50am

'W here're you going?' Sonia asked. Lyndsey had got up from the table and grabbed her coat.

'The sheds,' Lyndsey said. 'The shelves there are full of poisons.'

Sonia jumped up from her seat. Quickly, she turned the kettle off, which was still only halfway to boiling, then shut down Val's laptop and put it back in the bunkroom. She grabbed her coat as well.

'One of us should stay with Amanda,' Lyndsey said.

'Balls to that.' Sonia zipped her red jacket up to her chin. 'She's fine. Doing better than any of us. Anyway, this is more important.'

Together, they went out, tracking left around the

bunkhouse to avoid walking past the observatory. They didn't want to alert Marne to what they were doing.

Lyndsey's thoughts were in turmoil. Was Marne really capable of killing Bobbie? The woman seemed harmless enough; a little socially awkward, sure, but so were most people. It was difficult to imagine her as a murderer. Lyndsey didn't even want to consider it.

At the back of the bunkhouse, the full force of the wind hit them, driving the rain into their faces. It felt like pellets of ice against them. She told herself she was mistaken – it couldn't be hailing in August, could it? It must just be extremely cold rain. In the distance she heard the boom of waves hitting the shore, loud as thunder.

Lyndsey reached the shed that they'd looked into the day before. When she wrenched open the door, there was a brief flurry of movement near her feet as a fat, furry body scurried for cover. Sonia made a strangled noise of disgust. Cautiously, Lyndsey stepped into the shed, trying not to picture how many rodents might be sheltering within the walls.

She clicked on her headtorch, which she'd unclipped from her climbing helmet before she came out, and swept the beam across the shelf of boxes and bottles.

She reached to pick up a packet and Sonia hissed at her, 'Don't touch anything! It might be evidence.'

Lyndsey snatched her hand back. *Evidence.* At some point in the future, the police would stand in this exact spot and catalogue every box of poison. The thought made her stomach turn. What if she'd disturbed some vital piece of evidence just by opening the shed door and stepping inside? She glanced down at the wet boot prints she'd left on the concrete floor.

'Most of these packets haven't been moved in years,' Lyndsey said. She shone her torch onto each in turn. Layers of cobwebs, dust, and dead insects festooned the boxes. She tilted her head so she could read the side of one bottle. 'This one's out of date by three years. Would that make it more or less poisonous?'

'Something's been moved,' Sonia said. 'Here.' She pointed to a conspicuously clean rectangle in the dust on the shelf, where a box had been removed. 'Was that one missing yesterday?'

Lyndsey racked her brains but couldn't remember. It felt like a very long time ago. And they'd been looking for the generator at the time, so her priority hadn't been the ancient, mouldering packets on the old shelves.

'It doesn't make sense,' Lyndsey said. 'Even if Marne had wanted to poison Bobbie, how would she have done it? We brought our own food.'

Sonia frowned, but then her eyes widened. 'What about water? Where does the water supply for the bunkhouse come from?'

'I've no idea. There must be a water tank somewhere, I guess. Juliet might know.'

'And Marne.' Sonia's gaze hardened. 'She'd have access to it as well, right?'

'I guess … but we've not been drinking the tap water. We've been using bottled water.'

'Except when we boiled the kettle. Val filled it straight

from the tap this morning. Boiling it would get rid of germs, but not toxins.'

Lyndsey's mind shied away from what she was suggesting. 'But if Marne poisoned the water tank... I mean, we've all—'

'She wasn't necessary targeting Bobbie,' Sonia said. 'She was targeting all of us.'

The idea shocked Lyndsey. Automatically, she wanted to shake her head, to deny even the possibility. *Who would do something like that?* 'Why was Bobbie the only one affected?' she asked.

'I don't know.' Sonia's frown returned. 'Maybe she drank more cups of tea than us. Or maybe it affected her quicker.'

'Quicker? What—?'

'C'mon. We've gotta tell Juliet.'

As Sonia hurried away, Lyndsey stumbled after her. Her brain spun in circles. *The water supply is poisoned. She didn't care how many of us she killed.* And, on top of that, another realisation – they'd all drunk from the water supply. Some of them more than others, sure, but it meant they all had an amount of poison in their system.

How much is a fatal dose?

Are we all going to die?

How long will it take before we know?

Lyndsey remembered Bobbie from last night; her disorientation and confusion, the distress on her face when she woke in the night. Would that happen to them all?

We have to get off this island.

When they reached the front of the observatory, Lyndsey

held out a hand to stop Sonia. 'How're we going to do this?' she asked in a whisper.

'I can tell you how I'd *like* to do it,' Sonia said. 'I'd like to tie Marne up and throw her in the sea.'

'Okay, we can't do that. We still need her to fix the radio.'

Sonia blew air through her lips. 'But she's *not* fixing the radio. For all we know, she's making it more broken. I say confront her. Call her out.'

Lyndsey hesitated, unsure.

Sonia took advantage of her dithering. She shoved open the door and strode into the observatory.

In the workroom, Marne was bent over the dismantled radio. It looked like the machine was in more pieces than before. Val was supervising from a nearby chair. She'd found a blanket from somewhere to put over her knees.

'Where's Juliet?' Lyndsey asked, but Sonia was already racing for the kitchen.

'Stop!' Sonia yelled.

Lyndsey went to the kitchen door. Inside, Juliet was standing next to the stove, with a steam kettle in her hand and an expression of surprise on her face. On the counter there were two cups.

'What're you doing?' Sonia demanded.

Juliet blinked at the force of her words. 'I'm making tea.'

'Can't we leave you unsupervised for ten minutes?' Sonia went to snatch the kettle out of her hand.

'Careful, it's hot! I'm putting it down, look, there, it's down. What the hell are you so worked up about?'

Lyndsey's gaze fell on the two cups on the counter. 'Who

were you making tea for?' she asked. 'You and Val?' Without waiting for an answer, she turned to glare at Marne. 'Let me guess – you said you weren't thirsty?'

'I'm not.' Marne looked at her in confusion. 'What's wrong with that?'

'Come over here.'

'But – I'm working on—'

'This is more important. Come here.'

Grumbling, Marne got up from her chair. 'I wish you'd make up your mind. First you say the radio's the most important thing in the world, now—'

'Sit there. On the stairs.' Lyndsey didn't know where else to put her. For the moment, she just wanted to keep Marne away from the radio.

Sonia came out of the kitchen, dragging Juliet by the arm. 'We've found out some stuff,' she said.

'We *suspect* some stuff,' Lyndsey amended. After all, there was no proof. She still wasn't sure they had enough to confront Marne with, but there was no stopping Sonia now.

'Bobbie was poisoned,' Sonia said.

Several people objected at once. 'Hang on,' Juliet said, 'how can you be sure of that?'

'Think about the symptoms. She got confused, distressed; she was hallucinating. When we found her – Juliet, you remember how she looked.'

Slowly, Juliet nodded. It was unlikely any of them would forget the sight.

'What sort of poison?' Val asked.

'We don't know exactly,' Lyndsey said. 'We can only guess.'

'I can look on my laptop.' Val started to stand. 'I've done a bunch of research on—'

'Yeah,' Sonia said. 'We know.'

'So, I can go check.' Val paused. 'Wait, I couldn't find my laptop this morning. It'd gone missing.'

Impatient, Lyndsey said, 'It's on Sonia's bunk.'

Val blinked. 'Why's it there?'

'Look, that's not important right now,' Sonia said. 'What matters is that Bobbie's dead, she was poisoned, and there's a box of rat poison missing from the shed.'

Marne's head came up. She'd been listening with a frown, but now sat upright, startled. 'Why were you going into the shed?' she asked. 'That's my property, not yours.'

'Exactly.' Sonia glared at her with undisguised hostility. 'It was you who took the box. You put it into our water supply.'

For a moment, Marne was speechless. 'How on earth—?' she started to say.

Sonia jumped on that as an admission. 'What else did you do? Was it you who was sneaking around during the night, peering into windows?'

'What? No. Why would—?'

'You scared poor Bobbie so much that she went outside during the night. Then what? Did you lead her to the cliffs? Did she try to get away? Is that how you got those scratches on your face?'

Marne automatically touched a hand to her cheek, where the two scratches had crusted over. 'I told you, that was—'

'A polecat. Yeah, you said. Excuse us if we don't believe you.'

'Sonia.' Juliet touched a hand to her arm. 'Let her speak.' Turning to Marne, who was still perched, stunned, on the stairs, she asked, 'Well? Is any of this true?'

Sonia rolled her eyes and muttered, 'She's hardly likely to admit it, is she?'

Marne's hands were shaking as she held them out, defensively, in front of her. 'I haven't done anything,' she said. 'How on earth would I get poison into the water tank, even if I wanted to? It's all sealed up.'

'But you've got access to it, right? For maintenance purposes, if nothing else.'

Marne shook her head quickly. 'I've got no reason to go tinkering with it. If something goes wrong, we get a maintenance bod over from the mainland to fix it. It's way past my paygrade to mess around with the water supply.'

'Could anyone else have tampered with it?' Lyndsey asked.

'I don't see how. It's a sealed system. I don't even have a key to get near it.'

'Whereabouts is the water tank?' Lyndsey hadn't seen anything near the bunkhouse which looked like it was used for storing water.

'It's up on the hill, over that way.' Marne gestured with her head.

Sonia raised an eyebrow. 'Isn't that where you were yesterday before we arrived?' she asked. 'You said you'd been out on the hills all day, sorting out your bird traps.'

'This morning too,' Val put in. 'When I came to find her this morning, she was out.'

Marne looked from one face to the next. There was a slow panic dawning behind her eyes. 'Why would I even want to poison the water?' she asked, her voice rising. 'It supplies my house as well. I'd be poisoning myself.'

'You've got plenty of bottled water,' Sonia said. 'There's a five-litre bottle, right there on the counter.' They could see it from where they were standing.

'Well, yes, but that's only sensible. They don't recommend we drink the tap water unless we boil it first. And things are temperamental here. You've seen that for yourself. Sometimes the supply breaks down.'

Juliet's mouth had set into a thin line as she processed everything. Lyndsey knew what she was thinking – *if the poison's in the water, it could've been any of us who died. It could've been* all *of us.*

'What about the radio?' Juliet asked in a faint voice. 'Is it really broken? Or are you just stopping us from calling the police?'

The question hung in the air. Marne opened her mouth, then closed it again. Her shoulders slumped. 'I've been trying to fix it,' she said. 'I swear. If you reckon you can do better, go right ahead.'

'I think we will.' Juliet turned to her friends. She was visibly holding her composure together with difficulty. 'Who wants to have a go at it? Lyndsey?'

Lyndsey grimaced. 'I'm no good with electrics. I can't even change a plug.'

'I'll have a go,' Sonia said. 'It's not like I can break it more than it's already broken, can I?'

'All right. You and Val stay here.' Juliet grabbed her coat from the peg by the door. 'Lyndsey, you come with me.'

'Where're we going?'

'I want to look at the water tank.'

Marne started to her feet. 'I can show you where it is,' she started to say.

'I think we should go alone. Give us your keys.'

'But I don't have a key for—'

'So you say. How about we find out for ourselves?'

Juliet kept her hand held out until, reluctantly, Marne fished the bundle of keys out of her pocket and handed them over. Then Juliet turned away. Her jaw was clenched as if she was holding back from saying something she'd regret.

She caught Lyndsey's arm. 'Let's go.'

Chapter Fourteen

SATURDAY

11:05am

The trees on the slope of the hill didn't provide as much of a windbreak as Lyndsey had hoped. The trunks were thin, stunted, battered by the weather since they were saplings. Their leaves drooped under the constant pattering of the rain.

Lyndsey and Juliet followed a narrow path that cut straight up the side of the hill. Unlike most of the other paths on the island, which looked like they followed old sheep-trails, this one had been made with a purpose. Even so, it was overgrown on both sides with bracken that swiped at Lyndsey's legs at every step. Within minutes, her jeans were soaked through. She wished she'd put on her waterproof trousers before she'd come out.

'I came past this way this morning,' Juliet said. She was leading the way, as always. Underneath her jacket, she still wore her yoga outfit, as if cold weather was something that only affected other people. 'When I was out looking for … for Bobbie, this is the track I took. I saw something that might be the water tank.'

'Okay.' Personally, Lyndsey thought they should've got some better directions from Marne. If the water tank was hidden in any way, they could walk right past it. It might take them hours to find it. She didn't want to be outside any longer than was necessary.

Her fears turned out to be unfounded. As they reached the top of the hill, Lyndsey spotted a mound of grass-topped earth, too regular in shape to be a natural formation. It poked up a couple of feet above the top of the bracken. The straight path took a right-angled turn to reach it.

'Guess this is it,' Juliet said.

There was a waist-high fence around the rectangular mound, although much of the fence had been swamped by gorse bushes. A metal gate stood open, held in place by the thick, tufty grass that'd grown up around it. There were several prominent warning signs attached to the gate, declaring this was private property and not to be tampered with.

'Doesn't look like anyone's been here in a while,' Juliet said.

Lyndsey glanced behind them. Their own progress through the wet grass had left a distinctive trail of footprints. Ahead of them, there were none. It didn't look like anyone could've walked to the water tank without leaving a track.

'Maybe she came here yesterday, or the day before,' Lyndsey said. She wasn't ready to discard this theory just yet. 'Or some time before that, even. It could've been a week ago that she put the poison in.'

Juliet pursed her lips but didn't reply. She waded through the ankle-high grass to the mound. It was a smooth, regular shape, without any obvious access point. All of the important workings were probably underground.

'Where does the water come from anyway?' Lyndsey asked. 'Rainfall?'

'I don't know. There must be a natural spring or something. Probably the same one that feeds the stream at the top of the field.'

'I'm surprised you didn't check that before we came here.'

'Yes, well, I didn't realise it would be relevant, did I? I put all my time into looking up the best climbing routes, the nicest beaches to scramble down to, the stretch of coastline where we could do some coasteering…' Juliet shook her head. 'All for nothing. I should never have bothered.' She pressed the heel of her hand to her forehead as if forcibly suppressing her tears.

Tracking around the side of the mound, Juliet found a set of steps leading down to a sturdy metal door. There were more warning signs here. Most obvious was the DANGER OF DEATH sign, right in the middle. Juliet tried the door but it was locked. She put her ear to the door to listen.

'Does it sound like poisoned water?' Lyndsey couldn't help but ask.

Juliet gave her an annoyed look. 'I can hear machinery in there. I guess there must be pumps and stuff. I thought maybe it'd be a simpler set-up here. Like, I don't know, like one of those big plastic tanks people have in their garden.'

She started searching through Marne's bundle of keys, trying each one in the door lock.

Lyndsey wandered back up the steps. She climbed onto the top of the mound, feeling the wet grass slide beneath her feet with every step. From the top, she had quite a good view out over the north of the island. Past the trees, the land sloped downhill to the rocky northern shore. Beyond that was the stretch of water known as the Sound, which separated the island from the mainland. Even though the Sound was only a couple of kilometres wide, it was daunting. At most times of the day, except during the highest and lowest points of the tide, the tidal difference caused currents to sweep through it at frightening speed. From where she stood, Lyndsey could see the dark swirls and lighter white-caps on the surface as they zipped past.

She raised her eyes to look at the mainland.

The sheets of rain made it seem as distant as the moon. The land rose in dark lumps. If she squinted, Lyndsey could just make out the lights of a building, directly opposite the northern harbour of the island. She remembered the café and visitor centre there, which mostly catered to the ramblers and birdwatchers who found their way along the costal path. The single-track road leading to the café was a ribbon of grey against the dark hillside. There were no other houses or farms that Lyndsey could see, although admittedly her eyesight wasn't fantastic. She'd been putting off an eye test for quite a while now. But, as far as she remembered, most of the area around this stretch of the mainland coast was a wildlife preserve.

She wondered if there would be any visitors in the café on a day like this.

'We're not really that far from land,' Lyndsey called down to Juliet. 'Do you think they'd hear us if we shouted?'

'What?' Juliet's voice was muffled. She was still bent over her task with the keys.

Lyndsey strained her eyes towards the distant café. Realistically speaking, it was only a couple of miles away, in a straight line. *There must be some way to attract their attention. Maybe if we—*

'No bloody use,' Juliet said, loudly enough to make Lyndsey jump. She'd come back up the steps with a scowl on her face. 'None of these keys works. I guess maybe Marne was telling the truth.'

'Not necessarily. She might have other keys that she keeps separate.'

'I don't know.' Juliet weighed the bundle of keys in her hand, frowning. 'I thought the water tank would be easier to access. But this looks like a proper professional set-up. I doubt there's any way to get into the system unless you're an authorised engineer. Even then, I expect it's designed to make it difficult for someone to purposefully dump poison into it.'

'We still can't rule it out completely,' Lyndsey said,

stubbornly. 'If it wasn't the water supply, how else would Marne have poisoned Bobbie?'

'I don't know if she did.' Juliet's face was serious. 'I've been turning it over in my mind. I just can't make it fit.'

'She had access to the whole bunkhouse before we got there. Maybe the poison wasn't in the water, but somewhere else. And what about those scratches on her face?'

Juliet let out a breath. 'I know what you're thinking,' she said, 'but it can't have been Bobbie who caused those scratches. Marne came back to the observatory just after Val went there to look for her, right? So about ten o'clock this morning. Bobbie had been lying out there for hours at that point. If she'd inflicted the scratches … well, they would've scabbed over by then. They certainly wouldn't have been still bleeding several hours later.'

Lyndsey hadn't thought of that. 'Then why else were Bobbie's nails so dirty?'

'Honestly? It could've been anything. She could've fallen and put out her hands to stop herself. She could've tried to climb back up from that ledge.' Juliet held up her hands. 'I've washed my hands four times since I woke up this morning, and I've still got dirty nails.'

It was true. Lyndsey glanced at her own fingers. There were slivers of mud under her nails, except for the thumbnails, which she had a habit of chewing down to the quick. She couldn't even remember when she'd got her hands dirty. It just seemed to happen naturally when she was outdoors.

But still… 'I don't think we should trust Marne,' she said.

'Of course not.' Juliet climbed up onto the top of the mound to stand next to Lyndsey. 'We shouldn't trust anyone.'

'Except each other, right?' Lyndsey said it jokingly, but Juliet's expression was grim. 'Right? We need to trust everyone in our group, don't we?'

Juliet didn't answer. She was standing next to Lyndsey, but looking off in a different direction, towards the west. 'Let me show you something,' she said then.

She climbed down from the mound. Puzzled, Lyndsey followed. 'Show me what?'

'I found something else while I was looking for Bobbie. It's over this way.'

Past the turn-off for the water tank, the path became a narrow, wiggly line that pushed its way through the wet bracken. Juliet moved with a purpose. She obviously knew exactly where she was going. As always, Lyndsey could only tag along after her. It seemed like Lyndsey had been shadowing Juliet's footsteps for as long as she could remember.

'I think this is the area where we camped last time I was here,' Juliet said over her shoulder. 'It's difficult to be sure after all this time, but this looks familiar. I think we camped in the shelter of those rocks. That was back when wild camping was allowed on the island.'

That family holiday, all those years ago, had obviously made a fast impression on Juliet, more so than any of the dozens of other camping holidays her parents took her on. 'Has it changed much?' Lyndsey asked as she waded through the bracken.

'I don't know. It's all so unfamiliar.' Juliet lifted her head to look around as she walked. Overhead, a hawk of some kind was hovering, despite the buffeting winds, its sharp gaze fixed on the ground. 'I thought I remembered every inch of the place, but apparently not. I remember the bunkhouse, but it was in the process of being converted. My parents were so excited to come back here once it was completed. But then … well, I suppose it dropped off the cards, what with their divorce and everything. No more family holidays after that. I've waited eighteen years to get back here… I was so keen to show it to you all. And then, when I saw the state of the bunkhouse…' She shook her head. 'You can't imagine.'

Lyndsey said nothing. She suspected Juliet was only talking because she didn't want to think about Bobbie, or the poisoned water.

After a few minutes of walking, the path led them out onto grassy heathland again. Lyndsey was glad to be in the open. The wet bracken fronds that'd constantly slapped her legs and soaked through her jeans had left her thighs clammy and cold. She wanted to go back to the bunkhouse. Without even the thin protection of the stunted trees, the wind and rain seemed to pounce on them, whipping into Lyndsey's face and trying to snatch the hood off her head. Grimly, she put her head down and kept walking.

They were close to the coast again. It was impossible to walk for any distance without coming up against the edge of the sea. Lyndsey felt a twinge of claustrophobia, and realised what Sonia had meant the day before, when she talked about how hemmed in she felt. Despite the rolling emptiness of the waves and sky, Lyndsey was trapped. The island was effectively a prison, like a police cell.

Lyndsey spotted a patch of greyish-white feathers scattered across an area of grass. In the middle were the remains of a seabird. It lay with its wings spread, its thorax ripped open, the wind ruffling its stray feathers. Its head was missing. Under other circumstances, she would've guessed it'd been attacked by a cat, but there weren't any on the island.

Polecats, she remembered. Again, she wondered about the scream they'd heard the night before. The seabird certainly looked like it'd been killed quite recently.

'Over here,' Juliet said. She'd stepped off the path – which had more or less disappeared now anyway – and was heading to an outcrop of rock that jutted up from the ground like a broken tooth.

From there, the land sloped down at a careless angle until it met the sea. The coastline here was a lacework of jutting promontories and intricate coves, carved out of the limestone. Somewhere along here was an impressive natural arch which Juliet had intended to make them climb down to that weekend. Lyndsey remembered Juliet saying that there were a number of pretty beaches along that stretch of coast as well, but it couldn't be proved right then. The waves were smashing themselves to pieces right up against the rocks.

Juliet walked around the jutting stone in the middle of the field. In the leeward side, out of the full force of the wind and rain, there was a gap in the rock, about three feet high. It looked like there was a small, dry space inside.

'This is what I found. Look.' Juliet pointed out a darkened circle on the grass next to the rock. 'Someone made a fire here.'

Even the pelting rain couldn't eliminate the evidence of a small campfire. Someone had cleared an area of grass, building up the edges with stones. The ground in the centre was scorched and blackened.

'Do you think it's recent?' Lyndsey asked.

'Not a clue. It can't have been from today or last night; it's been too wet to make a fire.'

Lyndsey's stomach rolled at the suggestion that the fire could've been set so recently. 'It could be from a month ago,' she said. 'It doesn't mean anyone's been here this week.'

'But it *does* mean people come here.'

'We knew that already. It wouldn't take a lot of effort to kayak across the water.' Although, looking at the sea right then, the thought made Lyndsey quail. A person would have to be crazy to brave those waves.

Juliet took her headtorch out from her pocket. 'There's a shelter of sorts in there,' she said, nodding to the gap in the rocks. 'It goes back further than you'd expect. I might not have thought it was anything at all, if not for this firepit outside. I didn't check it out properly this morning. I just put my head in to make sure Bobbie wasn't there.'

Lyndsey nodded. *Maybe if Bobbie had come this way, she would've found this shelter… She would've been safe and dry… Maybe it would've been enough to keep her alive till we found her.* She shook the thought away. There was no telling what might've made a difference.

'Let me take a look,' Lyndsey said. She took the headtorch from Juliet and shone it inside.

As Juliet had indicated, the shelter was larger than the entrance made it seem. Lyndsey had to crouch to get inside. The ground was cold beneath her palm but, once she moved further inside, it wasn't damp. It wasn't a bad little shelter. It reminded Lyndsey of the dens they'd used to make in the woods.

The memory had sharp edges. Seven teenage girls, crowded into the dubious shelter of overhanging rocks or roots, giggling as they attempted to toast marshmallows on a campfire that threatened to sputter and die at any moment. The smell of woodsmoke and damp earth. A moment in time when everything was ideal. Strange, to look back at it that way – because at the time, it'd definitely been chilly and uncomfortable and very little gain for the effort they put in. Also, there had almost always been far more spiders and crawling insects in those dens than Lyndsey would've liked. But, in retrospect, it was one of the best times Lyndsey could remember. A tiny oasis before things fell apart, when there were still seven of them instead of six, before Cherry was gone from their lives.

The cold ground beneath Lyndsey's fingers brought her back to the present. She swept the beam of the torch around the interior of the shelter. There wasn't much to see. A space just big enough for her to stand up, if she kept her head ducked. Bare stone walls. Certainly nothing to suggest when the shelter had last been used. The air was cold and damp.

Her searching hand struck something hard that rolled

away from her. When she turned her torch on it, she saw a glass bottle. Although the label was faded and tattered, she recognised the logo of a Stolichnaya vodka. Instinctively, she flinched. Another reminder of a bad memory, doubly unnerving for appearing so close on the heels of the first memory. That particular brand of vodka was the one Cherry had been drinking on the night she died.

Lyndsey turned, flashing the light into all the corners of the shelter. Tucked into another wide crack in the rock, something reflected back at her.

Lyndsey crouched to check it out. It was a thick orange bivvy bag, wedged tightly into the crack, streaked with condensation. She pulled it out, surprised by its weight. It felt like it was full of rocks.

Cautiously, she opened the bag and shone the light into it. Inside were a dozen cans of food. Beans, tinned meat, spaghetti hoops – all things that could be reheated easily or, if necessary, eaten cold. There was also another bag underneath, wrapped tightly around something.

'There's a cache of food in here,' Lyndsey called to Juliet. She reversed out of the shelter, dragging the bags behind her.

'Where the hell was that?' Juliet asked. 'I didn't see it when I was here.'

'It was shoved into a crack. It just looked like an old plastic bag.'

Juliet picked out a can and peered at the label. 'It's in date. Someone must've put it here quite recently.'

Recently was a relative term, of course. The food could've been left there a week ago, a month ago, or longer.

Lyndsey dug down to the bottom of the big bag and tried to lift out the plastic-wrapped item in the bottom. It was bigger and heavier than expected, at least three feet long, narrow and tapering at one end.

'I guess it could've been a kayaker,' Juliet said. 'Someone who likes coming over here, having some time alone, making a campfire… It's probably nothing more sinister than that. I mean, it's quite nice, in a way. Your own private island hideout.'

Lyndsey didn't answer, because she'd unwrapped the heavy item from its plastic covering. The glint of metal made her stomach contract. She pulled the plastic away, unwilling to touch the item itself.

It was an air rifle.

'Oh, heck,' Juliet said.

The plastic bag had done a good job of protecting the metal from the elements. The air rifle was obviously old, and much used, but it'd been looked after over the years. In the bottom of the plastic wrapping was a round tub of metal pellets, which rattled when Lyndsey shook it.

'Don't touch it,' Juliet said. She sounded breathless.

It occurred to Lyndsey that Juliet had mistaken it for an actual firearm. 'It's an air rifle,' she told her. 'Look. It's cranked up by operating the lever here. That increases the air pressure so it can be fired.'

'Are you sure? It looks real.'

'My uncle in Glasgow had one. He used to let us put holes in the trees in his back garden with it.' Lyndsey unscrewed the lid from the tub of pellets. 'It fires these. They're just metal. No explosives. You could probably kill a rabbit, or put someone's eye out with it.' She remembered reading a news story about someone who'd accidentally killed themself with their father's air pistol, but she opted not to mention that.

'Why would someone bring it here?'

'Probably because it's not legal. You used to be able to buy these as toys, but I think they're better regulated now. Whoever set up this shelter … well, maybe they brought it here because it might've been confiscated if they'd kept it at home. Or, I guess, maybe they wanted to take potshots at rabbits.'

Juliet shuddered. 'Horrible. What're you doing?'

Lyndsey had started to wrap the weapon up. 'I'm putting it back where we found it.'

'You can't leave it here.'

'It's not ours. It belongs to someone.'

'*Who* does it belong to? Huh? Someone put it here, and maybe they're just a random person who likes sea-kayaking and animal cruelty, but what if—' Juliet had to take a breath before she could continue. 'What if they're here *now?*'

In all the drama about the water tank, Lyndsey had forgotten her early certainty that someone other than themselves was on the island. She glanced at the shelter. 'This wouldn't be a very comfortable place to bivouac,' she said.

'But it's evidence that people *do* come here, and *have* been here recently. Someone *could* have used it yesterday.'

Lyndsey raised her gaze to the sea. With the waves as they were at that moment, it looked impossible to land a boat on this side of the island. But she knew that was deceptive. In calmer weather, someone could've brought a boat or a kayak all the way into the little coves on the coast here, and walked up to the shelter. An experienced sea-goer might even risk it now. There were probably places on the coast where it was safe to make landfall in any weather.

'They would've needed to drag the boat up from the shore,' Lyndsey said aloud. 'If they'd left it down on the beach, it would've been smashed to pieces by now.'

'There are a dozen places they could've hidden it though. Down by the sea, in one of the sea caves … or up here on the land. All they would've had to do is drag it into the bracken or throw a tarp over it, and we'd walk right past without knowing it was there.'

'Who would do that?'

Again, the question hung in the air. The simple fact, the one Lyndsey couldn't get past, was that no one hated Bobbie enough to go to so much effort to hurt her.

'I can think of one person,' Juliet said. 'Her husband.'

Chapter Fifteen

SATURDAY

11:40am

Lyndsey shook her head. 'Her husband loves her,' she said. 'He wouldn't do anything to hurt her.'

As she said it, she realised that Bobbie's husband had no idea what had happened. *He doesn't know she's dead.* The thought punched her hard in the stomach.

'Her marriage wasn't as great as she let on,' Juliet said.

Lyndsey wrapped the air rifle back in its plastic covering, mostly to give her something to concentrate on. 'Oh?' she asked.

'She said – well, you know how it is. Sometimes it's not what people say, it's what they *don't* say. Bobbie's marriage wasn't great. That's all I know.'

'Are you sure you're not projecting?' Lyndsey asked without thinking.

Juliet's expression froze. 'What d'you mean by that?'

'Just … you've had a really tough time of it this year. But, I mean, just because your husband was a complete jerk, that doesn't mean everyone's as bad as him…' Lyndsey trailed off, her cheeks burning. She wished she'd kept her stupid mouth shut.

Juliet stared at her for a moment longer, her lips thin, then abruptly turned away. 'Let's get back to the bunkhouse,' she said.

Lyndsey bundled up the bag of tins and took it back into the shelter. On the off-chance the cache did belong to some innocent visitor to the island, she didn't want to steal their food. The air rifle was a different matter. Juliet's words had rattled her, and now she wasn't sure at all about leaving the weapon where she'd found it. Unsure what else to do, she rewrapped it in the plastic bag and tucked it under her arm. It was an uncomfortable weight.

Then she hurried to catch up with Juliet, who was striding away up the hill. Lyndsey quietly cursed herself. She knew better than to mention Juliet's break-up. It was still an extremely sore point. And now, because of a few poorly chosen words, Lyndsey had offended her friend.

She let the silence stretch until they reached the brow of the hill. 'I always thought Bobbie's home life was okay,' Lyndsey said at last, in as conversational a tone as she could manage. 'She never said anything different to me.'

'She also didn't talk to you very often.'

Lyndsey winced. Juliet's tone had been intended to

sting. 'No, I guess not. But I saw her quite a few times this year. I went round to her house when she – she helped me pick out what climbing gear I needed for this trip. She never gave me the impression that things weren't fine between her and Darren.'

'Are you sure? Perhaps she dropped plenty of hints, but you didn't pick up on them. It wouldn't be the first time.'

'Hey, that's not—'

'Yes, it *is* true. Like how everyone except *you* knew things were going south between me and Gary. You're the only one who was surprised when we broke up. You've always been too wrapped up in your own stuff.'

Lyndsey shifted the plastic-wrapped package to her other arm. It was heavy and awkward to carry. *She's upset and angry. She doesn't mean to be personal.* 'Look, you know I'm not great with relationships. They're just weird and confusing and I don't understand them at all. But that doesn't mean I don't listen. If you'd told me what was going on, I would've listened. And I would've listened to Bobbie as well.'

It hurt that Bobbie hadn't confided in her. Lyndsey had thought they were good friends – and this year in particular, Bobbie was the one person Lyndsey had felt closest to. Lyndsey had poured out her troubles to her, about losing her job and falling into debt, and how she was going to get evicted if she couldn't turn things around. It'd felt like they could talk about anything. But, looking back, Bobbie hadn't shared much in return. Lyndsey had assumed it was because Bobbie's life was going fine.

She probably did tell you things weren't great. More than likely, you weren't listening.

Juliet laughed, but it was soft. Her annoyance was already melting away. She could never maintain a bad temper for long. It would flare up then die away just as fast. 'If she'd spoken to you about it, you would've just told her to dump her husband. That's always your advice.'

Lyndsey threw her free hand up in exasperation. 'That's because it's good advice. And I only ever suggest it if the person isn't happy with how things are. If you're *that* unhappy, leave. I genuinely don't get why people are so scared of it. It beats the crap out of staying with someone who's lousy for your mental health. I mean, look at Sonia and—' She bit her tongue before she could spill anyone's secrets. 'Sonia's got a terrible track record when it comes to dating,' she finished instead. That at least wasn't a secret. '*Everyone's* advice to her was always to dump them.'

Juliet smiled. She slowed down so Lyndsey wasn't having to speed-walk to keep up. 'To be honest, I wish I could've given Bobbie the same advice,' Juliet said. 'I never liked Darren. Do you remember how he tried to stop her coming on my hen weekend with us?'

'He did? I never heard about that.'

'Yeah, that was when he had that nebulous ill-health thing. Every time she wanted to go out, he suffered a sudden relapse – nothing serious enough to call a doctor or anything, of course, just bad enough that she had to stay home with him and couldn't possibly go out with us. He played that card all the time. For my hen weekend, he flat-out told her she couldn't possibly go away; he needed her at home to look after him.'

'Then she went anyway.' Lyndsey had trouble picturing Bobbie putting her foot down like that. She'd always been so easy-going.

'That's why she made us promise not to tell him anything that happened while we were on the hen do.'

Lyndsey half-laughed. 'The worst that happened was when Bobbie was so hungover she threw up on the metro, and that guy made her take his seat because he assumed she was pregnant.'

'Exactly. Bobbie didn't want her husband to know she'd drunk that much.'

'What, really? She was worried he'd be mad at her for getting wasted, on a *hen weekend?* That's literally the point.'

Juliet spread her hands. 'That's what I mean. Things weren't great in her marriage. It's why she hardly ever came out with us after that. Her stupid husband kept insisting he needed her to stay home with him.'

Lyndsey did remember that happening a few times, but she hadn't given it much weight. Bobbie had always been a bit flaky when it came to making plans. It felt dishonest to think that about her now, but it was true. She'd often used ill-health – either her own or her husband's – as an excuse not to go out with her friends. Lyndsey had never really thought about it. She figured sometimes people just wanted to stay home and be antisocial. Lyndsey had used it as an excuse herself, plenty of times.

'He *really* didn't want her to come on this weekend with us,' Juliet said. 'He's been giving her grief about it for months. I kept expecting her to give in to him, to be honest. She changed her mind so many times. Even yesterday, I wasn't completely certain she'd turn up for the boat. I guess, in the end, she really wanted to do this trip.'

'We all did.' Lyndsey said it automatically. She still didn't want to admit to Juliet that they'd all had second thoughts.

To her surprise, Juliet's eyes filled with tears. 'It's all my fault,' she said. 'If I hadn't pushed so hard for us all to come here…' She sniffed. 'It just felt like … I *so* wanted to show you this place. There was an article in the *Guardian* last summer about the top climbing spots in the UK, with a big section about Shell Island. It reminded me… How long ago were we first planning this trip? Eight years ago?'

'Ten.' It was originally supposed to be a weekend away to celebrate finishing their A-levels. Juliet surely couldn't have forgotten that, could she?

'Exactly. And if we didn't do it this year, it would never happen.'

'We could've postponed. What would another year matter?'

Juliet scrunched her nose, but she didn't answer the question. 'I just wanted this to be the perfect reunion,' she said. 'It's all my fault.'

Lyndsey hesitated before saying, 'You weren't to know what would happen. You didn't know the weather would change like this. Right?'

Juliet shook her head, blinking away tears. It wasn't as strong a denial as Lyndsey would've liked. Lyndsey was still worried Juliet had seen the weather forecast and just ignored it. 'When we found Bobbie,' Juliet said instead, 'you said you thought perhaps she was right. Perhaps she *did* see someone outside the window last night. I shouldn't have dismissed that out of hand. What if you're correct?'

Lyndsey glanced around. They were back amongst the trees, with the wet bracken pressing at their legs. Within another few minutes the bunkhouse would be in sight. They were alone out there ... but Lyndsey couldn't shake the feeling that they were being watched. She'd had the feeling all day – a prickling on the back of her neck that she'd been trying to ignore or dismiss.

'Do you really think Bobbie's husband would come here?' Lyndsey asked. She'd turned the idea over in her head, but saying it out loud made it somehow solid and real. 'Do you think he'd want to hurt her like that?'

'Honestly, I don't know. And that kinda scares me. I mean, I know he was weird and jealous and manipulative. He could get really possessive sometimes. I've always thought he was controlling. I tried to talk to Bobbie about it, but ... well, no one likes to hear you badmouth the love of their life, do they?' Juliet's mouth twisted. 'Like with Gary. Plenty of people warned me about him, but did I listen? Of course I didn't.'

Lyndsey nodded, but didn't comment. Her most abiding memory of Juliet's soon-to-be-ex-husband was at their wedding, when he'd teared up during the speeches. Later, he'd blamed it on too much alcohol on an empty stomach, but at the time, Lyndsey had been struck by how lovely it was to see someone so genuinely emotional on their wedding day. It'd made her shelve any misgivings she'd had about him. He'd loved Juliet, that much was clear, and that should've been enough.

Although she would never admit it aloud, Lyndsey was privately angry at him – not so much for cheating on Juliet, although obviously that was a big part of it, but because Lyndsey had thought of him as a decent, caring person. He'd lied to all of them, not just Juliet.

As for Bobbie's husband, Darren … Lyndsey barely knew him. The wedding had been a private affair on a beach in Cyprus, family only, so none of Bobbie's friends had gone, not even Juliet. Lyndsey had met him a few times, of course, and she vaguely remembered him being at their school, back when he'd been a couple of years above them and Bobbie had had a desperate, unrequited crush on him. He'd seemed all right. Once they'd finally got together, Bobbie had seemed happy.

You are a lousy judge of character, Lyndsey reminded herself, with a grimace.

'But,' Juliet said then, 'do we really think Darren would hire a boat and come out here in this weather? Do I think he's capable of murder? I don't know. I don't think I want to believe it.'

Lyndsey understood how she felt. It was a horrible thing to consider. And yet… 'It would give him the perfect alibi,' she said. 'We're all here on an island, while he's safely at home. There's no way anyone would suspect him.' She pursed her lips in thought. 'If he planned it right … he could've come here yesterday evening and been gone before sunrise this morning. He'd be out of the house for less than ten hours. Chances are, no one would've noticed he was missing.'

'He might be home already,' Juliet said, continuing the thought.

'Unless the bad weather caught him out as well. Maybe he planned to leave here before it got light, but if the weather was rougher than expected—' *He could still be here.* Lyndsey fought the urge to glance around again. The feeling of being watched was stronger. She gripped the plastic-wrapped air rifle tight to her side.

'Or perhaps he drowned.' Juliet's gaze lifted at the idea. 'He doesn't know anything about sailing or kayaking. Perhaps the idiot tried to get home in this weather and capsized.'

It would've been justice of a sort, Lyndsey reflected. But then she shook her head. There were too many *ifs* to consider. *If* Bobbie's husband came here. *If* he killed her. *If* he tried to kayak back to the mainland.

'Does this mean we should apologise to Marne?' Lyndsey asked. 'We kinda accused her of murder. Do you think we were too hard on her?'

Juliet's expression turned stony again. 'No. We still shouldn't trust her. Until we get off this island and speak to the police, we have to suspect everyone.'

'Everyone?' Lyndsey was almost afraid to ask. 'Who else do you suspect?'

Juliet didn't answer.

Chapter Sixteen

SATURDAY

12:10pm

'What should I do with this?' Lyndsey asked as they approached the bunkhouse. She was still carrying the air rifle, and she still had no idea what to do with it. The thought of bringing it into the bunkhouse made her baulk. Everyone needed to know about it, she guessed, but still...

'Put it in the bunkroom for now,' Juliet said. 'We need to figure out a way to talk to everyone in private, without Marne. Except someone will need to stay with Marne, to keep an eye on her. Let me think.'

Lyndsey pushed open the door to the bunkhouse. The warmth of being indoors was so sudden it made her sneeze. She hadn't quite realised how cold and wet she'd got. At that moment, she wanted nothing more than to bundle herself up in a warm blanket and sit next to a log fire until she'd burned the gnawing ache out of her bones.

A noise in the kitchen startled her. She turned to see Amanda, leaning heavily on the kitchen counter. The door to the food cupboard stood open.

'What's going on?' Amanda asked, her voice bleary with residual sleep. 'Where is everyone?'

Lyndsey opened her mouth and closed it again. 'Bobbie's been hurt,' she blurted.

'What?'

Juliet had followed Lyndsey into the bunkhouse. 'Amanda, you're up! Are you okay? What're you doing?'

'I was hungry. I didn't know where you'd all gone.' Amanda swayed a little. It looked like she might've fallen if she hadn't been gripping the edge of the counter. 'What's happened to Bobbie? Is she okay?'

'Here, sit down.' Juliet guided her into a chair at the table. Amanda leaned on her, unable or unwilling to put weight on her bad leg. Her blonde hair hung in straggles around her face. A tissue was gripped tightly in her left hand.

Juliet sat down opposite and, with gentle words, tried to explain what had happened to Bobbie. Lyndsey went into the bunkroom. She wasn't sure she could bear seeing Amanda's face when they broke the news.

Not knowing what else to do with the air rifle, Lyndsey stood it in a corner. She wanted to hide it under a blanket, but the plastic wrapping was dripping rainwater, so she couldn't put it on a bunk. There was no reason to hide it anyway, she told herself. She couldn't wish it out of existence.

A sob came from the kitchen. Lyndsey grabbed the bottle of vodka from her bunk and brought it to the table.

Amanda let out another sob, which turned into a coughing fit. She held the tissue to her mouth until it passed. Lyndsey found a mug and gave it a quick rinse out so she could pour a drink for Amanda.

'Make sure you dry that mug before you use it,' Juliet said. Lyndsey frowned, and Juliet made a pointed nod towards the tap.

Lyndsey's stomach knotted. *The water supply.* She hadn't even thought before she rinsed the cup. It was such a natural, instinctive thing to do. How many times had each of them used the taps here to clean their mugs, their plates, to brush their teeth, to rinse out their mouths? All with potentially tainted water. Lyndsey hadn't had time to use the shower that morning, but some of her friends had.

Her hands shook as she used the tea towel to carefully dry the mug.

'I don't understand how this could've happened to Bobbie,' Amanda said. Her cheeks were wet with tears.

'We don't understand either,' Juliet said. She moved aside the discarded remains of everyone's breakfasts so she could reach across the table and take Amanda's hands in hers. 'Not fully. We're still trying to figure it all out. For the moment, everyone's gathered in the observatory. We thought it best to stick together.'

Amanda nodded. She took a steadying breath, then winced.

'Do your ribs still hurt?' Lyndsey asked.

'A little. It's worse since I made the mistake of standing up.'

Lyndsey poured out a measure of vodka for her and set it down on the table. As she did so, she noticed that the tissue in Amanda's hand was spotted with blood.

'Amanda, are you coughing up blood?'

Amanda startled, then gave a weak smile. 'No, no. This is just... Well, there was a little blood when I first woke up. But I probably just bit my lip or something. I wouldn't worry.'

Lyndsey and Juliet exchanged a glance. That *definitely* sounded like something to worry about.

'Do you feel up to coming next door?' Juliet asked her. 'I'd feel better if we were all in the same building.'

'I don't know.' Amanda blinked away fresh tears. 'I-I ought to get dressed first.' She wrinkled her nose. 'These are the same clothes I wore yesterday. I'm sure I meant to get undressed before I fell asleep, but...'

'You needed to sleep. Do you want me to ask Val for some more painkillers?'

Amanda hesitated, then nodded. 'That would be good. I think I'm more sore today than I was yesterday. But it's just bruises. I'll be fine.'

It sounded like she was trying to convince herself as much as anyone. Juliet caught Lyndsey's eye again. 'Can you go and check in on the others, Lynds?' she asked. 'I'll stay here with Amanda. Ask Val about some more tablets, yeah?'

Amanda's face crumpled again. 'I can't believe Bobbie's dead,' she said. 'It doesn't sound possible.'

Juliet put a comforting arm around her shoulders. Lyndsey took the opportunity to slip outside, closing the door quietly behind her. In her heart, she knew she should've stayed to help look after Amanda. But seeing the woman's distress was too much for her. It made her realise her own heart was broken as well.

Juliet will look after her. She's always looked after us. Lyndsey wasn't sure why Juliet felt like she needed to be responsible for everyone in the group. It'd just always been that way.

Pushing down her feelings of guilt, Lyndsey walked towards the observatory.

A faint, melodious sound, almost drowned out by the noise of the wind and the distant surf, stopped her in her tracks. Lyndsey cocked her head. She could hear music.

The radio!

She ran for the observatory door. *The radio's working, I can hear it. We're going to be okay, we're going to get out of here…*

She burst in through the front door, startling everyone inside. Immediately, she glanced into the workroom. Sonia was sitting at the workbench. The radio was still in pieces.

'But—' Lyndsey started to say. She could hear music – tinny and distorted, but a recognisable song, something poppy and innocuous that she vaguely recognised from hearing it on the radio at home.

'Sorry,' Marne said from behind her. 'Didn't mean to get your hopes up.'

Lyndsey spun around. Marne was sitting in the other room with a small transistor radio on the table in front of her. She twiddled a dial and the music disappeared into a hiss of static.

'Oh.' Lyndsey's hope drained out of her. 'I thought—'

'Sorry,' Marne said again. 'I remembered I had this old radio in the cupboard. I use it sometimes to get the shipping forecast. Or listen to the Six Nations. That's the only time of year I regret not having a TV.'

'Don't see what bloody good that radio is,' Val complained. She'd moved into the sitting room so she could keep an eye on Marne. She looked very settled in her armchair, with the blanket tucked around her knees, like she was ninety years old instead of thirty. 'We can't use it to transmit a message. And we can barely hear it anyway, there's so much static.'

'It's because you keep talking,' Marne said. 'Listen.'

She'd tuned it to a different station, and now a voice came through in gentle waves, interspersed with static. ' – Severe weather warning affecting the whole region, in particular the south – gale force – likely chance of coastal overtopping – yellow weather warning – '

'We're sunk,' Val said. 'You hear that? That's not just a bit of a breeze; it's a proper storm blowing in. This is just the start of it.'

'All the ferry services from Fleetwood have been cancelled,' Sonia said. She glared at the portable radio as if she could guilt-trip it into giving some good news. 'Not just the passenger service, the freight as well.'

Val threw her hands up. 'So that's it, isn't it? There's no

way that tiny fishing boat will be able to get here tomorrow. We're stuck.'

'Not necessarily,' Marne said. 'The little boats sometimes fare better than the bigger ones. They'll go out in rough seas if they need to. Ferries won't take those chances. And the fella who dropped you off – he knows you're here. He won't leave you stranded.'

She sounded so sure that for a moment Lyndsey was reassured.

'Did you look at the water tank?' Marne asked then.

Her gaze was steady enough to make Lyndsey hesitate. 'Yeah,' she admitted. 'It's all locked up behind a door. We couldn't get access to it.'

Marne nodded, satisfied. 'Told you so. Can I have my keys back now?'

'Juliet's got them. She's next door with Amanda.'

Val said, 'So, there's no way anyone could've got to the water tank?'

'Not as far as we could see, unless they've got a key. And I suspect the Water Board is kinda cautious with who has access.'

Marne nodded again. 'I'm pretty sure I told you that.'

'If we're ruling out the water tank,' Val said, thoughtfully, 'where does that leave us?'

'Beats me.' Suddenly, Lyndsey felt very tired. A sick headache was developing behind her eyes. She very much wanted to get changed out of her damp clothes. She wished she hadn't left her vodka in the bunkhouse kitchen.

'Have you considered accidental poisoning?' Val asked.

'The plumbing here is probably pretty old. It could be seepage from old lead pipes.'

'Don't look at me,' Marne said. 'I've got no idea about the pipes. It's not something I think about very often.'

'From memory, lead poisoning tends to be due to chronic build-up rather than acute poisoning, so we might be able to rule it out anyway. I'd have to check my notes.'

Marne frowned. 'Why do you have notes about lead poisoning?'

'I've got notes about every kind of poisoning. It's one of my interests.'

Marne's eyes widened. 'You've got an interest in poisoning people?'

'Of course not. It's just hypothetical.'

Marne turned her startled gaze to Lyndsey. 'Excuse me for saying, but I don't think it's fair that you immediately accused me of putting something in the water supply. Your friend here is apparently an expert about these things.'

Val snorted. 'If I wanted to poison someone, I'd find a much more efficient way of doing it than tainting the entire water supply.'

Lyndsey pinched the bridge of her nose. 'Val, could you go talk to Juliet for a minute, please?' she asked. 'Amanda's woken up and she's asking if you've got any more painkillers.'

'Fine.' Val heaved herself up out of her chair. 'While I'm at it, I can check my research documents, since my laptop has apparently made a miraculous appearance.'

Without looking up, Sonia scowled. 'Don't start that again. I said I was sorry, didn't I?'

'Yes, you did. But I'm still waiting for an explanation of why you took it in the first place.'

'Val—' Lyndsey said, with a sigh.

'I'm going. Quit hassling me.' Val took her time gathering up her coat and putting her shoes back on.

Lyndsey waited until she had left, then sat down at the table opposite Marne. The shipping forecast droned on, fading in and out so only snatches of bad news could be heard at a time. The voice was calm and professional. Lyndsey suspected they could've been reporting the end of the world and they'd still sound unruffled.

'How bad is the storm likely to get?' Lyndsey asked.

Marne made a face. She'd obviously not forgotten the accusations they'd thrown at her just an hour ago. 'It's difficult to say,' she allowed. 'It won't be the worst we've ever seen, but it sounds like it'll be the worst we've had this season. That's just the way it happens sometimes. We were surprisingly lucky last year; barely got hit by anything.'

'This storm … has it come out of nowhere? I mean, did they know it was coming?'

'They've been issuing warnings for the last few days, but they do tend to hedge their bets. No one knows for certain what the weather will do from one day to the next. It could've blown itself out to nothing by now.'

'And I guess it'd depend which forecast you listened to as well?'

'Some of them do more hedging than others, sure.'

Lyndsey was still wondering which forecasts Juliet had checked before they came here, and what they'd said. It was something they'd have to discuss later. 'Have you ever been stranded out here before?' she asked instead.

Marne thought about it. 'Not so much stranded. That's a stretch. Last October, I was supposed to go home on a Tuesday and the boat had engine trouble so they couldn't get to me until Thursday. It chafed a bit, but I suppose it wasn't the end of the world. It just meant I had to sleep another couple of nights here, instead of at home.'

'Where do you live when you're not here on the island?'

'Chester, mostly. I've got some friends who own a nice big house, and they like to go travelling during the winter months, so it's almost like a time-share – I look after the place in winter, they get the house to themselves in summer. It works out nicely.' Marne gave a rare smile. 'I met them when I was at university. I was their first student tenant, and I like to think I gave them a skewed view, because they never looked for another.'

Lyndsey chewed her lower lip, trying to phrase the next question correctly. 'Marne, do you know if there's anyone else on the island right now, apart from us?'

'I don't see why there would be. It's not a great place for wild camping, even if the National Heritage allowed it. Soil's too thin, ground's too rocky. I've met a few folks who came over here under their own steam – birdwatchers and canoe enthusiasts, mostly – but they only stay for a few hours at a time. They usually have the sense to leave when the tide is right. I know most of the regulars by sight. If I spot them coming ashore, I'll make a point of wandering over to say hi. No harm in being friendly. Groups like yourselves, who've come for the climbing, tend to book the bunkhouse so they can do more than one day. It's a long way to come if you're not staying overnight.'

'So, if someone came here in their own transport, they'd have to know where they were going, right? I'm guessing you can't just land a boat anywhere on the coast.'

'You *can*. It just depends if you want your canoe to be in one piece afterwards. There are plenty of little coves where you can beach a boat, but not all of them are a safe bet. Some are too close to the currents in the Sound. Some don't have access to the rest of the island – they've got steep cliffs all around, without any paths leading up from the sea. Others have hidden rocks ... there's all sorts of things to watch out for. So, no, it's not as easy as it might look. Doesn't stop folk trying, of course.'

'Do you think someone who had no experience on the sea, who didn't really know what they were doing at all ... do you think they could land here?'

'I don't see why not.' Marne's smile had little humour in it. 'God favours the cataclysmically optimistic.'

Lyndsey drummed her fingers on the table. She'd hoped Marne could've said there was no way at all anyone else could've reached the island. 'Have you seen anyone this week?' she asked, as a last option. 'You were out and about yesterday morning. Did you see anyone apart from us arrive?'

'Not a soul. Mind you, there's no way I could monitor the whole island. That's too much of a job even for me. But no, I didn't see any traffic out on the sea apart from the fishing boat that brought you lot in. And I probably would've noticed. You tend to take notice of small boats that are out in stupid weather.' Marne thought about it for another moment, then shrugged. 'But I could've missed it, of course. I wasn't specifically looking out for anyone arriving.'

Lyndsey nodded. She wished it was possible to be sure about anything. All she had was the queasy sensation in her stomach, and the itch at the back of her neck that made her feel like someone had been spying on her all day.

She glanced at the clock on the wall. It was coming up to half past twelve in the afternoon. *Still twenty-seven hours till the boat gets here.* A gust of wind whistled around the observatory, making the whole building tremble. *If it gets here at all.*

She got up and wandered into the workroom, where Sonia was still fiddling with the dismantled radio. 'Any joy?' she asked.

'Of course not.' Sonia's tone was irritated. 'It's not like this thing came with an instruction manual. Or, if it did, it would've been written fifty years ago.'

Lyndsey picked up a piece that looked like an oversized fuse and turned it between her fingers. 'I had a thought,' she said, 'maybe there's some other way we can contact the mainland. Something old school.'

'More old school than a radio?'

'Much more. I was thinking, we don't need to get a complicated message out. All we need is to let people know we're in trouble. Then they'll scramble the helicopter.'

'How do you intend to get anyone's attention?' Sonia asked. 'Jump up and down and wave your arms?'

'If that helps.' Lyndsey set down the fuse on the

newspaper. 'We could make a sign. Like a bedsheet, with HELP written on it, for example. If we take it to the landing dock in the north, then hold it up or fix it to something, it might be seen from the Sound Café.'

Sonia frowned as she considered it. 'We don't have bedsheets,' she pointed out. 'Or bedding of any kind. A sleeping bag probably wouldn't work.'

'I've got bedsheets,' Marne said. She'd got up from the table and come to the doorway of the workroom. 'I'm not supposed to lend them out, because I guess the National Heritage folk don't want visitors thinking they can rock up here with nothing and borrow things from me. Like how I'm not supposed to tell you I've got access to a washer-dryer.' Her gaze fell onto the dismantled radio. If she had a comment to make about Sonia's repair work, she kept it to herself. 'But I think they can make an exception for one bedsheet, given the circumstances. And if not, they can bill me, frankly.'

Lyndsey blinked in surprise. 'That would be good of you. Thank you.'

'Happy to help.' Marne gave a rueful smile. 'The sooner the police get here and sort out this mess, the better.'

Lyndsey had to agree, although she was surprised to hear Marne voice that opinion. 'Now we just need something to write with.'

'And a way of keeping it fixed in place,' Marne added. 'That might be the kicker. There aren't a lot of trees or fence posts around Cow Harbour. There's the old boat store, but I don't know how you'd fix anything to the brickwork of that.'

'I guess if it comes to it, we can stand there and hold it up, for however long that takes.' Lyndsey looked at Sonia. 'Did you bring a marker pen?'

Sonia shook her heads. 'Nothing better than a biro. We won't get far with that.'

'There might be some paint in the shed,' Marne said. 'Year before last, a group of volunteers came out to repaint the window frames. There could be some left over from then. Want me to have a look?'

'I'll go,' Lyndsey said. 'Sonia, do you want to keep trying the radio?'

Sonia sat back in her chair with a heavy sigh. 'Listen, you know I hate to admit defeat, but I'm beginning to think this is beyond me. I've been at this for an hour, and I've only figured out where two pieces go.' She turned her gaze up to Lyndsey. Her eyes were red-rimmed, like she'd been quietly crying. 'I need a break.'

'I can take over,' Marne said. 'I know you folks are reluctant to trust me, but—'

'If we can raise the alarm with a bedsheet, then we won't need this stupid contraption anyway.' Sonia pushed away from the table with obvious relief. 'Do your worst.'

'Let me get that sheet for you first.' Marne's expression was hard as she turned away. 'Sooner you lot get out of here, the better,' she muttered.

Chapter Seventeen

SATURDAY

12:35pm

In amongst the tangle of old supplies in the shed, Lyndsey found bird nets, hessian sacks, old weighing scales, and lots of coils of wire, which she avoided because they looked like a sure route to tetanus. She also unearthed most of an ancient kitchen range, which looked like it had been dumped there a century ago and left to moulder.

Right at the back, she turned up a number of paint cans. Most were empty or nearly empty, or had dried up from lack of use. The only decent ones contained whitewash.

'That's no bloody good,' Sonia said. She was holding the door so the wind wouldn't slam it shut on them. 'It won't show up. Unless she's got black sheets we can use.'

Lyndsey tried not to look up at the shelf of poisons, just

above her, but it was constantly in her peripheral vision. Sonia held the torch while Lyndsey pried open the remaining cans of paint with a butterknife. Eventually she found an extremely rusty tin of gloss paint. It had once been dark green – Buckingham Green, according to the label – and was roughly the colour of the peeling paint on the bunkhouse window frames, but when she opened it, it more closely resembled tar. A layer of clear liquid had separated to the top. It was still the best she could find. She also uncovered a number of paint brushes, their bristles stiff with age.

'This'll do,' she said, passing it out to Sonia. 'Let's get going.' By now, the wind had picked up, and was flinging the rain at them. The sky was dark and thunderous.

They brought the paint and the bedsheet Marne had given them into the bunkhouse. Juliet and Val had needed no convincing about this idea, although the look of consternation on Juliet's face made it clear she wished she'd thought of it earlier. Amanda had gone back to her bunk again, unable or unwilling to face talking to anyone.

'What on earth are you giving her?' Lyndsey asked Val quietly, but Val just shrugged it off without a proper answer. Lyndsey hadn't pushed the matter. She knew that hearing the news about Bobbie had crushed Amanda. It was no wonder she wanted to be by herself.

Juliet had cleared the kitchen table. The remains of their breakfast were in a binbag, and the plates and cups had been washed and were now stacked neatly on the draining board to dry. The table still wasn't big enough to spread out the bedsheet, so they flattened the sheet out on the floor of the bunkroom.

'Shame it's not a double,' Juliet said. 'Still, we work with what we've got. We're lucky Marne was cooperative enough to give us this one.'

'I think she wants to see the back of us,' Lyndsey said.

'Who can blame her?' Val asked. 'We stomped in there and accused her of murder in her own home. If I were her, I'd want rid of us as well.'

'Maybe we were too hasty,' Lyndsey said carefully. 'She's doing her best with the radio. And she gave us this bedsheet, and told us where to find the paint.'

'None of those things has got us off this island yet,' Sonia pointed out. 'Once we're safely back home, then we can assess whether or not she did anything to help us. For now, I still say we shouldn't trust her. Did I tell you about the wires?'

'What wires?'

'When I was fiddling with the radio, I took the back off. You have no idea how many random wires there are in that thing. Anyway, some of them were scorched, like they'd overheated or caught fire or something. But a few others had been cut through. Like, snipped clean in half. I couldn't tell if it was recent or what, but it looked to me like a component or a clump of wires had been cut out of it.'

Juliet stared at her. 'Then why on earth did you leave her unsupervised with it again?'

'Because there's no way I can fix it. I wouldn't know where to start. And, as far as I can tell, the damn thing's not going to get *more* broken, no matter what else she does to it.

We may as well let Marne pretend to tinker. It'll make it seem like we don't suspect her.'

Lyndsey wasn't sure she agreed with that reasoning. But she couldn't think of a good argument. *If this banner works*, she told herself, *we won't need the radio anymore. It won't matter that it's broken.* She tried to cling onto that thought.

'Did Lyndsey tell you what we found over to the west of here?' Juliet asked then. 'A shelter, in amongst some rocks. There was a cache of food and an air rifle inside.'

Sonia's eyebrows went up. 'You think there's someone on the island apart from us?'

'We don't know that for sure. The cache could've been there for months.' Juliet cleared her throat. 'We brought the air rifle back here.'

'What? Why?'

'I didn't know what else to do with it,' Lyndsey said, defensively. 'It's over there, in the corner.'

'I did wonder what that object was,' Val said.

'Don't touch it,' Juliet said in her stern tone. 'It's here for safekeeping. I don't want anyone messing with it.'

Sonia smoothed down the bedsheet and carefully, using an eyebrow pencil, traced the outline of the word HELP. It didn't have to be neat; they just needed it to be visible at a distance.

They each took a paintbrush and got to work. Val had to excuse herself because her bad joints wouldn't let her kneel on the floor for any length of time. Instead, she sat on the edge of her bunk and supervised them.

The green paint was lumpy and awkward to work with. It took them the better part of an hour to squash enough paint onto the bedsheet to fill out the letters. Even then, the end result looked scrappy.

'It's legible,' Lyndsey said. 'That's as much as we need.'

That at least was true. The big letters stood out clearly against the white background. It would be readable from quite a long way away. At the very least, someone in the café on the other side of the water would hopefully see it, even if they couldn't make out the writing, and wonder what was going on. It wouldn't take much for someone to raise the alarm.

Juliet stood up and stretched her back. There were dark circles under her eyes. 'Good job everyone,' she said. 'Once it's dry, we'll take it down to the harbour and see who's paying attention.'

Lyndsey wandered into the kitchen and picked up a bottle of water. Marne's big ring of keys lay on the side, where Juliet had dumped them. Lyndsey's gaze lingered on the pile of plates on the draining board. It must've bugged Juliet, to see the plates sitting on the table, marked with bacon grease. Lyndsey picked up a plate and turned it over in her hands. Her stomach growled, reminding her of how long it'd been since she last ate. Food had been the last thing on her mind.

She glanced round and found Sonia watching her with an unreadable expression. Lyndsey put the plate down, hoping that her own thoughts didn't show on her face.

If it wasn't the water supply that was tainted, then the poison must've come from somewhere else.

She didn't want to think about what that might mean.

Chapter Eighteen

SATURDAY

2:00pm

The paint was still sticky on their makeshift sign, but no one felt like waiting another hour for it to finish drying. They were fed up, anxious and miserable.

'Let's go now,' Juliet decided. 'If we wait much longer, the café might be closed. I've no idea how long after lunch they stay open in summer. Val, you stay here with Amanda.'

'If you insist.' Val looked entirely comfortable where she was. She'd already taken off her shoes and was sitting on her bunk with her laptop open on her knees. Behind her, Amanda lay on her side on her own bunk, turned away from everyone with the blankets pulled up around her head like a protective shield.

When Lyndsey touched the paint on the bedsheet, she found it was still tacky.

'It'll have to do,' Juliet said from the doorway. She was holding the door open whilst attempting to tighten the hood of her jacket so it wouldn't blow off from her head.

Gingerly, Lyndsey and Sonia folded the banner, trying to stop the two sides sticking together. That worked for all of thirty seconds, until they got outside and the wind immediately tried to rip it out of their hands.

Flurries of rain beat at them as they set off towards the harbour at the north of the island. The wind howled and snatched at their clothes. At first, the three women tried to protect the banner from the worst of the elements, but that proved impossible. It was all they could do to stand upright under the force of the wind. The storm had come in fast and hard.

Lyndsey put her head down and concentrated on walking. The track was a lot muddier than it had been earlier that day. She couldn't help thinking of poor Bobbie, lying alone and abandoned on that ledge by the sea. *We shouldn't have left her there.* The ledge was far above the high tide mark, but Lyndsey didn't know how high the waves could break over the rocks. If the wind got too strong, it might roll her right off the ledge.

It wasn't too late to go back and get her. But if it'd been daunting to imagine carrying Bobbie's weight halfway across the island that morning, how much more difficult would it be in this storm? It was hard enough just to follow the track down to the north harbour with the wind constantly trying to snatch the banner out of their hands.

Neither option – leaving Bobbie where she was or going to fetch her – made Lyndsey happy. She couldn't think what would be the best thing to do.

Focus on what you're doing. Once we raise the alarm, then we can think about Bobbie again. She tried to squash the pang of guilt that needled her stomach.

The path down to the north harbour was steep and rocky. Juliet hurried ahead, as sure-footed as always, but Sonia and Lyndsey had to follow more slowly, taking their steps with care. The wind battered Lyndsey's exposed face. It made the plastic fabric of her hood smack against the sides of her head. Rain dripped from her fringe and her eyebrows into her eyes. She hadn't put on her gloves before she came outside, and she was deeply regretting that now. Her fingers felt half-frozen already.

At last, they reached the harbour. It was on a jagged inlet with steep, rocky sides, studded with barnacles and orange lichen. The harbour itself was just a concrete jetty that projected out into the sea. The boathouse Marne had mentioned turned out to be a tiny stone hut barely big enough for a dingy. A very elderly life ring hung from a hook by the padlocked door.

Here, the wind was even fiercer. Waves slapped at the rocks. The currents rushed through the Sound, swirling and eddying as they met in the centre of the channel. In the middle of the Sound was a rocky islet known as Kitterland, and, a little closer to the northern harbour, there was a ten-foot-high concrete tower with a light on top, built atop another outcrop to warn people not to try sailing through there. Lyndsey took one look and shuddered. The currents looked vicious enough to drag a person down within seconds. On the other side of the channel, barely a mile and a half away, was the mainland. When Lyndsey had viewed it from the top of the hill, it hadn't looked too far, but now it seemed an impossible distance.

She remembered visiting the Sound Café with Juliet on a balmy day in March, sitting with a hot cup of coffee in her hands, gazing out towards Shell Island, and thinking it wasn't really *that* isolated. This awful trip had all been hypothetical then. Juliet had driven her all the way out to the café to help convince Lyndsey how great it would be. What Lyndsey would've given to go back in time to that day and call it off before it ever began.

'There's nowhere to hang the banner,' Sonia said. She had to shout over the wind. 'If we lay it down on the rocks, no one will see it.'

Lyndsey glanced across the channel. The café was barely visible in the driving rain. From that angle, the rocks of Kitterland partially blocked the view. A few cars were parked in the car park, but no one would be lingering outside. Would anyone even see them? The huge windows along the front of the café gave a great view out over the Sound, but in the rain, they'd probably be misted up.

'We'll hold it,' Juliet said. 'C'mon, hurry up!'

'We can't stand out here holding it, not in this weather.'

Lyndsey agreed. She was already shaking from the cold and wet. But – 'We have to.'

She gave one corner of the banner to Sonia and attempted to unfold it. The sheet was soaked through. The paint had stuck it together. With a lot of difficulty, Lyndsey and Juliet managed to peel it open. The wind lifted the bottom and immediately stuck one of the loose corners to the middle again.

'Hold onto it!'

Lyndsey took two corners. Sonia took the other two. Juliet hung onto the top and attempted to keep the sheet spread wide.

'It's upside down,' Lyndsey shouted.

'For fuck's sake!' Sonia tried to lift the lower corner.

A huge gust of wind struck them. It was hard enough to stagger Lyndsey. It ripped one corner of the bedsheet out of her hand.

'Keep hold of it!' Juliet shouted.

The bedsheet flipped up like a sail. Lyndsey and Juliet fought to keep hold. It popped and twisted as if it were alive. Then the wet fabric was wrenched from Lyndsey's grasp.

The wind lifted the banner like a kite. It went soaring up and away from them, twisting and twirling. Lyndsey turned to follow it, with the desperate hope that maybe it would land on the rocks.

The sheet billowed, floated, and at last settled gracefully into the sea.

'For fuck's sake,' Sonia said again.

Juliet rounded on her. 'Why did you let go?' she asked, furious.

'What? I didn't. The wind took it.'

'Lyndsey and I managed to hang on.'

'You obviously didn't, otherwise it wouldn't be in the sea right now.'

'You let go. I saw you.'

Lyndsey watched the sheet as it was caught by a current. It went twisting away across the water. It was visible for a moment longer, a flash of white and green, before it was sucked down into the depths. She made herself look away.

Instead, she found herself staring at the Sound Café. Had anyone seen them? Even a glimpse might've been enough.

'You're the idiot who held it upside down,' Sonia said. 'How difficult is it to get a fucking bedsheet the right way up?'

'We would've been fine if you'd just kept hold of it!'

Lyndsey turned back towards them. From the look on Juliet's face, she clearly expected Lyndsey to weigh in, presumably on her side. But Lyndsey had no time or patience for their argument. Losing the bedsheet felt like a punch to the gut.

She stepped around her friends and set off up the path. She didn't particularly care if they followed her or not.

Chapter Nineteen

SATURDAY

2:30pm

At the top of the hill that led down to the bunkhouse, Juliet stopped. 'I can't do this,' she said.

'What?' Lyndsey asked. 'What can't you do?'

'I can't go back in there. Val and Amanda are going to ask how we got on and we … we'll have to tell them we screwed up.' There were tears in Juliet's eyes.

'Jules—'

'I should've had a better plan. This is all my fault.'

Lyndsey glanced back at Sonia, who was trailing some distance behind them, visibly pissed off. 'None of this is your fault, Jules.'

'It is. It was my stupid idea to come here in the first place. I've been pushing the plan for years. Why couldn't I have picked a different venue? Literally anywhere that didn't leave us stranded on a goddamn rock. My parents took me to loads of *safe* holiday spots when I was a kid. Why is this the one I got hung up on? We could've been, I don't know, camping in Wales right now, or halfway up the Cairngorms.'

Juliet wiped her face with the back of her hand. It was difficult to tell if she was crying or if the rain was running into her eyes.

'I'm meant to be in charge,' she said. Her voice wavered. 'I'm meant to be looking out for everyone. I can't believe I didn't even realise Bobbie was missing.'

Lyndsey nudged her to start walking again. She was just as upset as Juliet, but it was freezing cold out there and the rain was lashing at her face. They could talk about this when they weren't in the middle of a storm. 'No one put you in charge,' Lyndsey said. 'Why do you think you have to be responsible for us all the time?'

'A team needs a leader,' Juliet said stubbornly. 'I tried my best to be that person. In case you've forgotten, our group almost fell apart when Cherry went to university. We *need* someone who'll be responsible.'

'Maybe we did when we were seventeen. But we're all adults now. We don't need babysitting.'

'Is that so? If I hadn't needled you into coming on this weekend, what would you be doing instead? Sitting on the sofa, drinking?'

Lyndsey winced. That was, in fact, a fairly accurate summation of her usual weekend. 'I can live my life however I want,' she said, in a voice that sounded calmer than she felt.

'Even if it's killing you? I know about your drinking, Lyndsey. It's out of control.'

'Whoa, now. I'm not—'

'Your rucksack is full of bottles. It's a wonder you had room for spare socks. Why on earth did you think you'd need so much alcohol for one weekend?'

Lyndsey felt her ears going red. 'To be sociable. We always have a few drinks when we're together. I brought a couple of spare bottles in case anyone ran out.'

'That's just an excuse,' Juliet said. 'You've got a problem and you know it. This weekend should've been a real opportunity for you. You could've used it to tackle your issues. But no. You started drinking before we even got on the boat.'

Lyndsey threw her hands up. 'It was your idea to meet in the pub!'

'It was a hotel, and it was the closest place to the harbour that was open at that time of day. You're the one who decided you had to make a beeline for the bar.'

'And if I'd had any sense, I would've stayed there. If you'd told us about the forecast, none of us would've—'

'The forecast said it was going to be a bit rainy and a bit blustery. That's all.'

'Really?' Lyndsey stopped walking. 'Before we got on the boat, we asked if you'd checked the forecast. You told us it might be a bit grim, but that it wouldn't matter because none of us were made of sugar. Are you saying *no one* predicted this big incoming storm?'

'I didn't think it would get *this* bad,' Juliet said. It was her turn to get defensive. 'They said there was a chance we'd catch the tail end of the storms from Scotland, but that was only a *chance*, wasn't it? Last time they said it'd be a force eight storm we barely got enough breeze to shake the leaves.'

Lyndsey stared at her. 'You knew the weather would be awful, and you dragged us here anyway.'

'We've been climbing in bad weather before. I know it doesn't always make it the most fun, but we're tough. As long as it wasn't actually too dangerous to be out on the cliffs, I figured it'd be okay. It would be an adventure.'

Lyndsey could barely bring herself to ask, 'What about the boat skipper? What did he say about the weather?'

Juliet looked away. 'He was … concerned. He thought there was a low risk he might not get back here on Sunday. He suggested we cancel.'

'And you ignored him.'

Juliet let out a breath. 'If I'd cancelled, we never would've found another time to do this. You know that's true. I had to fight tooth and nail to get everyone here for this weekend. If it fell through, there'd never be another chance.'

'Yes, there would. We could've easily tried again next year, or the year after. Why was *this* summer so important to you?'

Juliet wouldn't meet her gaze. 'We're all getting older,' she said. 'In another couple of years, who knows whether we'd still be able to manage a trip like this?'

'What're you talking about? None of us are even thirty

yet. Except Val, and she's been about eighty years old in her head since she was a kid. We're not exactly decrepit.'

'By the time I'm thirty, I want to have more important commitments to worry about.'

'Like what?'

'Like children,' Juliet said bluntly. 'I don't want to leave it any later, the way my parents did. It – it caused a lot of arguments between Gary and me.' She lifted her head. 'So yes, I wanted one more adventure with my friends before I settle down. Is that so much to ask? If we'd cancelled this trip—'

Lyndsey's stomach felt like lead. 'If we'd cancelled, Bobbie would still be alive.'

'Yes.' Juliet didn't bother denying it. 'It's my fault. I should never have talked her into coming here.'

Sonia had caught up with them now. Lyndsey dug her frozen hands into her pockets and started walking again. Her thoughts were a mess. 'I thought you said she wanted to come,' Lyndsey said.

'She *did*. Of course, she did. But you know what Bobbie's like. She's a worrier. She absolutely wanted to do this weekend with us, but she had all those doubts and fears, and if I'd left her to it, she would've talked herself out of it eventually. Or she would've let her husband talk her out of it.'

From behind them, Sonia said, 'Bet you wish you'd listened to her, rather than pushing her into doing this for your own selfish reasons.'

'It wasn't selfish,' Juliet snapped. 'This weekend was meant to be a do-over for us all. A chance for us to work through the things that've come between us over the years.'

'Who the hell appointed you Camp Counsellor?' Sonia asked.

Juliet ignored her. 'We're supposed to be best friends, all of us. When was the last time we were able to go climbing together as a group? Not counting the via ferrata we did on my hen weekend. Before that, it must be seven years, at least.'

'If you're counting us as a full group, like you should, it'll be eleven years,' Sonia said. 'The last time was when we all went to the Bad Step, the summer before Cherry died.'

Lyndsey lowered her face so the wind wasn't stinging her eyes. She'd forgotten about that climbing trip. But, yeah, Sonia would be right, that must've been the last time they'd all gone out together. Over the years since then, Juliet had persuaded them to try other climbing trips, and had succeeded in dragging them out to a few places as a group. Four of them had gone to Snowdonia a few years ago. Three of them had done a camping trip to Scotland. But it'd never been the full group. It could never have been, because there were supposed to be seven in the group, not six.

Deep inside, something twinged; a tight ball of guilt that permanently sat in Lyndsey's chest. Most of the time she could breathe around it. Sometimes, like now, it felt like it expanded until it threatened to choke her. She could almost feel Cherry's restless spirit, keeping pace with her.

Juliet took a steadying breath. 'There's nothing else for it,' she said. 'I'm gonna try and swim across.'

'What?'

'I looked at the sea when we were down at the harbour. It's not that far from here to the mainland.'

'Are you kidding?' Lyndsey said. 'It's at least a mile.'

'Yes, but it's less than that to Kitterland. If I can get there, I can rest, and then it's only a few hundred yards to the mainland.'

'You won't make it,' Sonia said bluntly. 'It's suicide.'

Lyndsey had to agree. 'I don't know what you were looking at when we were at the harbour, but all I saw were waves and currents. You'd be swept away within a minute. Did you see what happened to the banner? An undertow caught it and sucked it right down.'

'I can use the life ring that was next to the boat hut.' Juliet's jaw was set. 'We can attach one of the climbing ropes to it. I'll use that as a lifeline. If I get into trouble you can haul me back in.'

Lyndsey hadn't looked properly at the life ring. It must've been there for years, and was probably an antique. She also doubted they had a mile of rope in the bunkhouse, even if they lashed more than one climbing rope together. 'It's a stupid idea,' she said.

'Can you think of anything better?'

'Well, sure. We keep trying the radio, and if—'

'The radio's a bust,' Sonia interrupted. 'It's never going to work.'

'All right, well, then we get another bedsheet from Marne and try again.'

'It'll take another hour to paint and dry another sign,' Juliet said. 'By then, the Sound Café will be starting to close.

And there's no telling how dark it'll be. The weather's only going to get worse.'

Lyndsey searched for another option. She came up blank. 'You're a rubbish swimmer,' she said at last. 'I'm not being mean, but you are. Remember when we went paddle-boarding and you fell off? We had to tow you back to shore. And that was with you wearing a life-jacket.'

'That was years ago,' Juliet said. 'I've practised since then.' But Lyndsey could hear the lie in her voice.

'If you've practised at all, it would've been in a nice, warm swimming pool.' Lyndsey attempted to temper her words so they didn't sound too harsh, but she was still smarting from Juliet's earlier comments. 'That's significantly different to wild swimming in the middle of a storm.'

Juliet didn't have an answer for that.

They trudged the rest of the way, sodden and defeated, back to the bunkhouse. 'I need to get changed,' Sonia announced. 'I'm soaked through.'

'Yeah, me too,' Juliet said.

Lyndsey was cold and shivering by that stage. Her wet jeans chafed her thighs. The headache that'd been blooming all afternoon was now a constant strain behind her eyes. Her stomach growled at her.

The group stumbled into the bunkhouse and slammed the door against the cold wind.

'That was fast,' Val said, eyebrows raised. She must've been feeling the cold, because she'd added another jumper on under her comforter, this one handknitted in the big, chunky stitches that her partner loved to make. 'What happened with the banner?'

'It blew away. We couldn't hold onto it.' Embarrassment and annoyance made Lyndsey's cheeks flush. 'It's in the sea now.'

'Oh. Did anyone see it? Before it went in the sea?'

'I don't know. Maybe.' Lyndsey peeled off her wet jacket. 'No, probably not.'

Val rubbed an exhausted hand over her face. 'Today's just an unending nightmare, isn't it?'

'The day's not over yet,' Juliet said. She'd gone to her bunk and was stripping off her wet clothes. Lyndsey looked elsewhere. 'I'm going to swim across the Sound.'

'You're kidding.' Val glanced at Sonia and Lyndsey. 'Tell me she's kidding.'

'It's the quickest way to raise the alarm. I can make it.'

Lyndsey went into the bunkroom. She tried not to look at Bobbie's empty bed, with the pillows still piled at one end. Instead, she sat down on Val's bunk and pulled off her boots. Her socks were damp around the cuffs, but at least her feet were dry. They were the only part of her that were.

Woken by the noise of everyone coming in, Amanda raised her head from her pillow. 'Cherry?' she asked in a blurry voice.

Lyndsey winced. 'No, it's me. Lyndsey.'

'Oh. Right, yeah. Sorry.' Amanda put her head back down. 'Sorry. I was just thinking … remembering.'

Lyndsey reached over to put a hand on Amanda's shoulder. She wasn't sure what she could offer, apart from vague reassurance. 'It's okay.'

'I was thinking about the funeral.' Amanda's eyes were half-closed. 'It's brought it all back, you know? Cherry's funeral was supposed to be the worst day of my life. I was never meant to have a worse day than that.'

'I know.'

'I wish … I wish there was someone we could scream at. Someone to blame. Like at the funeral.' Amanda was drifting off, her words blurred. 'I want to scream at someone.'

Lyndsey nodded, even though Amanda couldn't see it. She felt the same. She wanted to scream and cry and fling rocks at trees. Her emotions were fighting to find a way out.

All at once, she could picture Cherry's funeral, as clearly as the day it'd happened. Amanda had been so distant, so cold. Like she'd switched off everything inside her. While everyone had filed into the church, Amanda had stared at nothing. Some random people had shown up, claiming to be friends of Cherry's, and only then had Amanda snapped back to life, shouting and swearing at the outsiders until they retreated. It was like all of her rage and grief had been bottled up until that exact moment.

'I'm sorry,' Amanda murmured. 'I should be helping. Cherry needs me to…'

'It's okay.' Lyndsey patted her shoulder again, carefully. 'You need to rest.'

Amanda murmured something else that could've been an objection, but she made no move to get up.

The others exchanged worried glances. 'She's half-asleep,' Juliet said in a whisper. 'It's nothing.'

216

'Are you sure?' Lyndsey's mouth had gone dry. 'What if—?'

'It's nothing,' Juliet repeated, firmly. 'She's just woozy from the painkillers.'

Lyndsey lifted her gaze to meet Val's eyes. 'Val?'

'I mean, it's possible.' Val shrugged. 'Everyone reacts a little differently to tablets.'

'Maybe you should quit giving them to her, then.'

'She's in pain. I know what I'm doing.'

'It's not even your medication. The label on the box has someone else's name on it.'

Val's forehead creased into a frown. 'Has everyone been going through my property today?' she demanded. 'What the hell happened to privacy?'

'We don't have time for this,' Juliet said. She'd changed into a lightweight T-shirt and jogging shorts. 'I want to get across the Sound before it gets dark. Shit. I knew I should've brought my wetsuit. I even laid it out on the bed before I left, but I thought, no, we're not planning to go in the sea, so I won't need it.' She glowered to herself. 'I knew I should've brought it. I'm supposed to be *organised*.'

Lyndsey looked back at Amanda, who appeared to have dozed off again. It was as though that bad moment, when Amanda had called her by the wrong name, had never happened. 'What if this isn't a side-effect of the painkillers?' she asked. 'What if she's getting sick? Remember how Bobbie was acting? What if—'

'Then we need to get the helicopter here immediately. It's more urgent than ever.'

Sonia was busy towelling her hair dry. 'I still say it's

impossible. Have you ever heard of anyone swimming across the Sound?'

'They used to swim cattle across there,' Val said, helpfully. 'That's why the northern harbour is called Cow Harbour. The farmers would swim them over to graze here for the day, then swim them back again in the evening.'

'Yeah, but the farmers themselves didn't swim, did they?' Sonia asked. 'They were sensible enough to take a boat.'

'True. Humans aren't as hardy as cows. You can die just by jumping into the sea, if it's too cold. The saltwater floods your sinuses and can stop your heart.'

Lyndsey chewed her lower lip. Hearing Cherry's name, so soon after talking about the last time they'd all gone climbing together... It had unnerved her more than she wanted to say. All too well, she remembered how Bobbie had acted the night before. It'd started small, with a few little missteps and confusions, which they'd all discounted as nothing serious. It'd ended with her walking out into the darkness and never coming back.

What if Amanda has been poisoned too? Is this the start of it?

There wasn't enough room in Lyndsey's head for all this. She closed her eyes, feeling her thoughts churning like the currents in the Sound.

'I'll go,' she heard herself say.

'No,' Juliet answered. 'Don't be stupid.'

'I'm a much better swimmer than you. I'm probably the only one here who can make it that far, in this weather.'

Val pursed her lips. 'You've certainly got me beat. I'm buoyant but I'm not exactly speedy.'

'If anyone's got a chance, it's me,' Lyndsey said. She had to force the words out.

Juliet watched her, frowning. 'I can't ask you to do that. I got us into this mess, so I need to get us out.'

'All you'll do is get yourself killed, and frankly that's the last thing we need right now.' Lyndsey attempted to smile, but failed. 'Besides, I owe it to Bobbie. If she hadn't lent me the money to pay for this trip, I wouldn't have been able to come at all. The only way I can pay her back now is to go and raise the alarm.'

Chapter Twenty

SATURDAY

3:30pm

The waves rolled up over the shore, sending crests of spray into the air, before retreating sullenly, as if gathering their strength for the next assault. Lyndsey edged down onto the slick rocks. She shuddered. The bare stone was freezing cold beneath the soles of her feet. She could only imagine how cold it would be once she stepped into the water itself.

'Are you sure about this?' Sonia asked, for the seventh time. She had to raise her voice to be heard over the noise of the waves.

No. I'm not sure at all. Lyndsey bit her lip. The waves looked a lot bigger from close up. The distance between the harbour and the rocks that jutted up from the middle of the

Sound – Kitterland – might've been a hundred miles. The tide had been rising all afternoon, eating into the stretch of barnacle-encrusted rock that led up to the high-tide mark, but it was still a long way off slack tide. The water was choppy and dark with currents. A hundred yards offshore, the warning light atop the concrete obelisk blinked steadily, as if telling her not to be so stupid.

She had to try. If she could swim to the rocks around the concrete tower, then on to Kitterland, it was only a short distance to the mainland. Close enough that she'd definitely be spotted by anyone who was still at the Sound Café. As long as they were looking in the right direction, and the weather didn't completely obstruct the view.

Gritting her teeth, one hand holding onto the rock behind her and the other clutching the life ring around her waist, she gingerly stepped into the surf.

The shock made her gasp. Instinctively she wanted to draw her foot back. She made herself stand still, balanced with one foot in and one foot out, until she could bear the cold. Another wave rolled up, lifting around her ankle. It was like standing in ice.

Grimly, she placed her other foot in the water. She took a careful step forward. The next wave came up to her shins. She wished she'd had a drink to fortify her nerves before she'd come out, but Val had advised against it. Something about alcohol pushing the blood to your extremities and hastening hypothermia. Right then, Lyndsey wished she'd ignored her, even if Juliet's accusations about her drinking habits were still ringing in her ears.

'Give her some slack,' Juliet said behind her. The rope

tied around her waist loosened a touch, enough for Lyndsey to keep shuffling forwards into the surf.

Lyndsey didn't dare look back. It was difficult enough to keep her balance with the waves shoving at her feet. Behind her, she knew Juliet and Sonia were keeping a tight hold of the other end of the rope, and, behind them, Val waited with a waterproof bag full of dry towels and a flask of hot tea – boiled from bottled water – in case Lyndsey had to be hauled bodily out of the water. They'd left Amanda alone at the bunkhouse, but Juliet had made sure to leave some bottled water by her bunk. Nothing they'd said had been enough to convince Amanda to get up and come with them. Her grief over Bobbie was like a heavy blanket, weighing her down.

The rope attached to her waist wouldn't stretch all the way to Kitterland. Once Lyndsey was past halfway, she'd be on her own. *If I make it halfway, I'll know whether it's safe to keep going.*

Right now, she wasn't sure she would even get into the water. She'd known the sea would be cold, but she hadn't been prepared for exactly how bone-chilling it was. Even though she was barely up to her knees, she was trembling and gasping.

The wind, with nothing to block it, cut into her. Lyndsey had never felt so underdressed. There was no way she could've even attempted the swim while wearing proper clothes, but she'd baulked at the idea of going out there in just her underwear. Her compromise was her pyjama top and shorts. She'd left her boots, socks, jumper, and waterproofs on the shore.

She hoped her pyjamas were lightweight enough not to drag her down. The thought made her mouth go dry.

One step at a time. Slow and steady.

Lyndsey shuffled forwards. The rocks beneath her feet were hidden by swirling water. Her toes squished down on seaweed. She had to feel for the edge of the rock with her toes then gingerly search for the next step. Each movement took her further out from the shore.

The surging waves were past her knees now. It was increasingly difficult to stay upright. Lyndsey had to grip onto the life ring to keep it in place. It was heavier than expected, and its weight pulled her off balance. Juliet and Sonia were holding the rope too tight.

'I'm okay,' Lyndsey called back to them. 'Let out the rope a bit.'

The tension eased off. When the next wave came in, Lyndsey was able to brace against it.

She couldn't blame her friends for clinging so tightly to the rope. If it'd been her holding the rope, watching one of her friends scoot into the fast-flowing water, she would've been just as scared.

Lyndsey misjudged the edge of a rock and stepped into suddenly deeper water, up to mid-thigh. She teetered for a moment until she got her balance. The cold made her breath catch in her throat.

'You okay?' Juliet called from the shore.

Lyndsey nodded. She had no breath to reply. *The cold can stop your heart,* she remembered. Stupid Val and her unnecessary wealth of information. Why did she have to tell people things like that?

Lyndsey had to steel herself before she could take another step, which brought the water up to her waist. All her internal organs seemed to retreat from the freezing hand that clamped around her lower half. She couldn't help but let out a small shriek, which she hoped was drowned out by the wind.

She paused there to let herself adjust. Each wave lifted the water up to her ribcage. She couldn't seem to catch her breath.

You're past the worst of it now, she told herself, though she knew that wasn't true. The worst bit would be when her shoulders went under the surface. She remembered days of paddling on the beach at Bardsea, with her friends daring each other to go out further and further, each squealing at the cold, emerging goose-fleshed and shivering to be wrapped in sandy blankets. The sea had been a benign friend on those days. It'd been cold, sure, but not scary.

Now, Lyndsey was scared. The water dragged at her like a hundred insistent hands. It flared out her shorts and top around her body. She tugged down her shirt to stop it riding up past her waist. *You're worried about modesty at a time like this?*

Well, sure, she argued with herself. *What would your mother say?* Her mum had always taught her to wear matching bra and panties, in case she got hit by a bus. *What if you get swept out to sea and the coastguards have to fish your drowned body out of the water and you're wearing your Pikachu pyjama shorts and that's the photo everyone sees at the inquest?*

A laugh stuck in her throat and almost choked her.

Don't think about drowning, idiot.

Lyndsey took another small step, then another, then her foot encountered empty water instead of a rock. For an instant, she teetered off-balance.

She tried to twist around to grab the rope, but missed. A wave crashed into her and shoved her over.

Lyndsey gasped as the rocks disappeared from under her feet. The life ring around her middle was suddenly pushed up under her armpits. If it hadn't been there, she would've been dunked under the waves. She kicked frantically like a toddler dropped into the deep end for the first time.

'Hold on!' Juliet shouted from the shore.

A sharp undertow tried to drag Lyndsey out of the life ring. She clung on with both arms. As the rope went taut, the last of her breath was squeezed from her chest. She gasped. Panic prevented her from filling her lungs.

Ahead of her, the concrete tower with the light on top loomed up, as big as a lighthouse from that angle. She'd been dragged way off course already. It was terrifying how strong the current was. She couldn't even think about trying to swim to the tower. It took all of her effort just to stay above water, even with the help of the life ring.

'Pull her back!' someone yelled. The words were all but swallowed by the roar of the waves.

The current spun her around like a dance partner and dragged her legs out in front of her. Lyndsey struggled to pull herself up higher onto the life ring. Her hands could barely keep hold. She felt herself slipping. Her shoulders were below the waves now, the chill water surging up around her chin. She would've screamed if she'd had any breath.

She was pulled this way and that by the competing currents. It felt like they were squabbling over which of them would be first to drag her under.

Another wave battered her. Lyndsey's right hand slipped. The life ring tipped up vertically in the water. She managed a frantic gasp of air before she was pulled below the surface.

Under the waves was all confusion and noise. Lyndsey kicked out blindly, expecting to find solid rocks somewhere beneath her feet, but encountering nothing except empty water. Somehow, she'd kept hold of the life ring in her left hand.

Just as she managed to get her other hand back onto the float, she felt a jolt through her waist and she knew, she *knew* that the rope had snapped, just like the rope had snapped on Amanda the day before—

Or Juliet and Sonia have let go.

The current swept her away and Lyndsey had no choice but to be taken. She fought her way back to the surface, managing a single gasping breath before she went under again. In that instant she saw nothing but the grey-black clouds overhead. She couldn't see the shore. She didn't even know which direction she was supposed to swim in. As the waves battered her, she clung onto the life ring with both hands. A detached part of her brain knew that, once the tide swept her clear of the Sound and the rocks, she would need the life ring to stay afloat. All her other instincts were screaming at her to let go and use both arms to keep herself above the water.

Lyndsey grabbed another gasp of breath but she was pulled down again, further than before, so deep that she kicked a rock at the bottom of the channel. The impact jolted pain through her toes. But she got her other foot underneath herself and kicked off against the stone.

She popped to the surface like a cork, gasping, dragging the life ring tight to her chest. She kicked again and for the second time bruised her toes against something solid. There were rocks under her feet. Hastily, she fought to scramble up on top of them. Waves kept lifting her off. She coughed and spluttered as she tried to shake water out of her eyes.

In front of her was a dark mass of land. She hadn't been swept out to sea. Somehow, she'd made it back to the rocks. Lyndsey kicked herself closer to safety. She raised her head to try and guess where she was. Had she been pulled around the coast? If so, she was still in trouble, because the limestone cliffs there rose sheer and slick for a hundred feet up from the water. In her current state there was no way she could even think about scaling them.

Something on the headland snagged her vision. A flash of light green against the dark landscape. Lyndsey had only an instant to take it in before another wave shoved her sideways and she lost her precarious balance on the submerged rocks. Saltwater stung her eyes as she went under again.

When she resurfaced, she heard someone shouting. She couldn't make out the words, but she recognised Juliet's voice. Hope flared inside Lyndsey. Maybe she hadn't been swept too far away.

Another wave shoved her towards the shore. No, not a wave – she was being dragged forcibly to the rocks. She blinked saltwater out of her eyes. The rope attached to her waist was taut. At the far end of it, all three of her friends were hauling with all their strength. They hadn't let her go.

Lyndsey's knees banged against the unseen rocks. She was suddenly in much shallower water and could stagger upright.

'Heave!' Juliet was yelling. 'Heave!'

Lyndsey felt like a fish on the end of a line as she was hauled bodily onto the rocks. The surf sucked around her legs as if taunting her for her narrow escape.

As soon as she was able, she let go of the life ring and used her hands to scramble up over the rocks. Juliet let go of the rope and came bounding towards her, her boots skidding on patches of seaweed. She grabbed Lyndsey by both arms.

'Are you all right? Are you okay?'

Lyndsey tried to answer but found she couldn't speak. Cold and shock had robbed her of her words.

'We've got you,' Juliet said. 'You're all right.'

Lyndsey would've liked to collapse right there, face down in the seaweed, with her feet still in the freezing water. She was shaking almost too much to stand. Juliet supported her as she took the first stumbling steps back onto dry land.

Sonia ran to them and bundled Val's huge bath towel around Lyndsey's shoulders. The warm, dry fabric made

Lyndsey realised she was chilled through to the bone. Her whole body was shaking. She couldn't seem to catch her breath.

'Holy shit, you scared us,' Sonia said. 'When you went under like that...'

Lyndsey relived that moment of panic, when she'd been ducked beneath the surf and she'd thought for a terrible instant that her friends had let go of the rope. She lifted her head to blink away sudden tears. Her smarting eyes automatically went to the headland above the harbour, where she'd glimpsed that flash of green. Even during her panic, she'd been sure of what she was seeing – a person who was wearing a light green dress, with no regard to the freezing weather, standing on the rocks and watching as Lyndsey fought against the tide.

'Sit her down,' Juliet said. 'Somewhere sheltered, out of the wind.'

'We've got to get her back to the bunkhouse,' Sonia said. 'She's turning blue.'

'What do you propose we do? Carry her? She can't walk in this state.'

Lyndsey wanted to tell them to stop talking over her like she wasn't there, but a coughing fit overtook her. She let Juliet ease her down into a sitting position against the stone building next to the harbour. Lyndsey put her head down between her knees until she stopped coughing. Her mouth tasted thick with salt.

When she straightened up, Val put a plastic mug of hot tea into her hands. 'Don't spill it on yourself,' she warned. 'It's hot.'

'Thanks.' Lyndsey's voice was rough. It hurt her throat. She wasn't convinced her stomach would tolerate the hot tea, but she held the cup between her palms, grateful for the warmth that scorched her skin. Her fingertips were so numb she could feel nothing at all.

'Take your time,' Juliet said. 'As soon as you're feeling up to it, we'll go to the bunkhouse.'

Behind her, Sonia said, 'We never should've tried this. I told you it was a terrible idea.'

'Not helpful,' Juliet snapped.

'I saw someone,' Lyndsey said then. Despite everything that'd happened, despite nearly drowning, this felt important. 'Up on the headland. Over there.' She gestured with her head. 'Wearing something light green.' She held back from saying it was a green dress. She wanted to believe she'd been mistaken about that.

Her friends exchanged a look. 'When?' Juliet asked.

'When I was in the water. I looked up and saw them.'

'You've had a bad scare,' Sonia said. 'We all have. It's no surprise if—'

'I didn't imagine it.' Although, honestly, Lyndsey couldn't have said for certain what she did or didn't see. Her mind kept shying away from it. *That green dress.* But still she clung to her certainty just like she'd clung to the life ring.

Juliet stood and looked up at the headland. 'I'll check it out,' she said.

'Juliet, I don't think—' Sonia started, but Juliet cut her off.

'You folks get Lyndsey home. I'll run up there and look. All right?'

Lyndsey nodded. 'Thanks,' she said, glad Juliet was taking her seriously.

Val said to Juliet, 'You shouldn't go on your own.'

'I'll be quick,' Juliet said. 'Unless you're volunteering to come with me?'

Val pulled a face. 'You'll be faster on your own.'

As Juliet strode off up the rocks, Sonia wrapped another towel around Lyndsey's head and started drying her wet hair. 'How're you feeling?'

'Half-drowned,' Lyndsey said. 'Stupid. Freezing.'

'Why stupid?'

'It was never going to work, trying to swim across like that. I was dumb to even try.'

Val was watching Juliet climb up the rocks. 'When we get back home,' she said to Lyndsey, 'you should get yourself checked out by a doctor. If any water gets into your lungs you can die of secondary drowning. It can happen hours or even days later.'

Sonia glared, but Lyndsey somehow found herself laughing. 'Shut up, Val,' she said.

Chapter Twenty-One

SATURDAY

4:00pm

As much as she hated the idea, Lyndsey knew she couldn't walk back to the bunkhouse in her sodden pyjamas. She forced herself to get changed back into her dry clothes. Sonia had to untie the knot in the rope around Lyndsey's waist, because Lyndsey's fingers were still numb. The knot had pulled so tight it took Sonia a solid minute to unpick it. The rope had left bloodless scuff marks around Lyndsey's lowermost ribs. She suspected they would start to hurt once she warmed up.

Trying to keep the beach towel wrapped around as much of her body as she could, Lyndsey squirmed out of her pyjamas and pulled on her jogging bottoms and hoodie. Despite her best efforts to bundle them up inside her waterproof coat, rainwater had seeped in, and her clothes were clammy and damp. She dressed as quickly as she could.

'Right,' Sonia said. 'Let's move.'

Since Val couldn't walk very fast, she agreed to hang back and wait for Juliet, while Sonia rushed Lyndsey back to the bunkhouse. *We shouldn't separate,* Lyndsey thought, but by that point, her teeth were chattering too loudly to let her speak.

She focused on putting one booted foot in front of the other, not even raising her head until the bunkhouse was in sight. She tried not to think about the figure in the light green dress.

When they got to the bunkhouse, Sonia opened the door and hustled her inside. Lyndsey collapsed onto one of the lower bunks gratefully. Across the room, Amanda raised her head. Her face was puffy from crying. She took in Lyndsey's dishevelled appearance and dropped her gaze. There was no need for her to ask how the attempt had gone.

'Here.' Sonia stripped the sleeping bag off Lyndsey's bunk and threw it at her. 'Take off everything that's damp, or you'll never get warm.'

'Okay, don't look.'

Sonia rolled her eyes with a relieved smile. 'I'm glad you're well enough to start acting like a prude again,' she said as she turned her back.

'Get in the sea.'

'No thanks. It looked cold.'

For some reason, that set Lyndsey off giggling. *Hysteria and shock,* she figured, but that didn't mean she could stop.

She pulled off her damp clothes and wriggled down into the sleeping bag.

Sonia grabbed the nearly full vodka bottle from Lyndsey's bunk. 'I thought we finished this off last night,' she said as she passed it to Lyndsey.

'We did. That's the second bottle I brought.'

'Oh good, you came prepared.'

'Probably over-prepared.' Lyndsey snuggled down on the bunk. Although she did want a drink, her hands felt like two blocks of ice, and she didn't want to take them out of the warm, not yet. She tucked her hands under her thighs to try and get the blood back into them. 'I brought quite a lot of booze.'

Sonia reached up to Lyndsey's bunk and dragged the rucksack to her. Her eyes widened as she peeked inside. 'Wow. Yeah. You brought a *lot*. Were you worried that none of us would bring anything?'

'I think I expected to spend all weekend at least half-cut.' The admission flowed out of her. Earlier, Lyndsey might've made an excuse, but that didn't seem to matter so much now. 'I wasn't sure how well I was going to cope. It's been a while since I had to share my time and space with this many people. So, I figured, a bottle a day, plus a couple extra for sharing … wow, when you say it out loud, it does sound like a lot, doesn't it?'

Sonia perched on the edge of the bunk. 'Even if this weekend had gone to plan, it still would've been fraught. Three days with all of us lot shoved into one bunkroom together? What were we thinking?'

'I guess it sounded good at the time.'

'I think we've got rose-tinted glasses about our old adventure group. Sure, we had some good times, but we had some absolute epics as well. Do you remember when we got lost on Helvellyn? I thought we'd have to spend the night in those bivvy bags. Or that one time we tried orienteering.'

'I still think that was sabotage. Val made absolutely sure the coordinates led us out of the woods and straight to the tearooms.'

Sonia smiled ruefully. 'There was always something that went wrong. I can't remember any time when our outings went entirely to plan. I suppose—' She glanced at Amanda, but the woman had curled up in her blankets again, a pillow pulled over her head. Blocking them out. Sonia lowered her voice. 'I remember we used to blame Cherry, didn't we? I know it's wrong to speak ill of the dead, but she led us into some disasters.'

'Yeah.' Lyndsey didn't want to think about Cherry. If she'd closed her eyes, she could've pictured Cherry perfectly, on the last night they saw her, wearing her favourite dress. Her chiffony light green dress. 'But then Juliet tried to take charge and plan our own outings, and those weren't exactly disaster-free either.'

'Maybe we're just fuck-ups,' Sonia said. 'Everything we do gets fucked up in some way.' She rubbed a tired hand across her face. 'I wish I were home.'

'Me too. Are you still worried about your friend?'

For a moment, Sonia's expression was blank, uncomprehending. 'My friend?'

'Your friend who thinks she's pregnant. You were worried about how she's getting on.'

'Oh, right. Yeah. Yeah, sure.'

Lyndsey stared at her. Slow realisation dawned. 'It's not one of your friends, is it? It's *you*. You're—'

'All right, shush. Keep it down.'

'Seriously, Sonia? You think you might be?'

'I don't know.' Sonia's face tightened defensively. 'I brought a test with me, but I haven't done it yet.'

'Why not?'

'Because I don't want to know.' She looked at her hands, at the floor – anywhere except at Lyndsey. 'I wanted to just forget about it. For this one weekend at least. I wanted one more weekend before I deal with … with this problem.'

Lyndsey didn't know what to say. 'I'd offer you a hug, but I'm naked in a sleeping bag, and I don't think you want that.'

'You're right, I don't.' Sonia gave a tremulous smile. She was fighting to hold back tears. 'Just … don't say anything to the others, all right? I can't deal with that right now, on top of everything.'

At that moment, the front door of the bunkhouse banged open, making them both jump.

'Are you okay?' Juliet asked as she bustled inside.

'I'm fine.' Lyndsey settled down on the bunk and closed her eyes. 'Just trying to get warm.'

Val came in behind Juliet and immediately clocked the bottle of vodka in Sonia's hand. 'Don't give her that,' she warned. 'I told you, alcohol increases circulation to the extremities. All the cold blood in her hands and feet will go back to her chest.'

'Thank you, Professor Valerie,' Lyndsey said without opening her eyes. In all honesty, she wasn't sure she could stomach anything right then, not even alcohol. The taste of saltwater still coated the inside of her mouth, a constant reminder of how close she'd come to drowning.

'Did you find anything up on the rocks?' Sonia asked. 'Any sign of the person Lyndsey saw?'

'Nothing. Sorry.' Juliet's tone was careful. 'I climbed up to the place above where you were. There's a bit of an old tarp caught in a gully near there. I wasn't sure if that might be what you saw.'

Lyndsey frowned as she tried to recall. 'It definitely looked like a person.'

'Here, I took a photo.' Juliet took out her phone and brought it over to Lyndsey. 'I tried to get an angle from underneath it.'

Lyndsey made herself sit up so she could study the photo. The rocks didn't look the same at all when they were flattened out into a digital image. From the sea, they'd looked a hundred feet high, unscalable, with a figure standing near the top, watching Lyndsey. The photo, however, showed a sheer but easily climbable scramble of rocks, less than fifty feet high. In the centre was a faded piece of blue tarpaulin, which must've blown away from some ship and got caught on the rocks, maybe years ago.

'It's not the right colour,' Lyndsey said, cautiously. 'But I guess that could be what I saw.' She should've felt relief that she'd been mistaken. But part of her felt weirdly disappointed. 'I'm sorry. I sent you on a wild goose chase.'

Sonia leaned in so she could see the picture. 'It does look like a person,' she said. 'If you just caught it out of the corner of your eye, I can see how you'd think that.'

Juliet put her phone away. 'I'd rather it was a wild goose chase than anything else,' she said as she went into the kitchen.

'Do you still think there's someone else on the island apart from us?' Sonia asked Lyndsey.

'Yeah.' Lyndsey hunched her shoulders. It wasn't just the cold that continued to make her shiver. 'I can't stop thinking about it. This whole weekend, I've felt like someone's been watching us. Have you ever had that feeling? Like you just know someone's following you with their eyes. When me and Juliet went out to the water tank, I was absolutely convinced that—'

In the kitchen, Juliet had opened one of the food cupboards below the counter and pulled out a pan. She let out a thin cry.

'What's wrong?' Sonia asked.

Juliet crouched down and began pulling items out of the cupboard. 'Look,' she said.

Sonia and Val hurried into the kitchen. Lyndsey got up more slowly, still cocooned in her sleeping bag, and shuffled after them. Pins and needles prickled her toes.

Juliet had cleared enough of their food out of the cupboard that they could all see into it. At the back of the cupboard, hidden behind the pans, was a cardboard packet that Lyndsey didn't immediately recognise.

'Who put it there?' Juliet demanded. She rounded on her friends, face flushed. 'Who brought it in?'

Lyndsey shuffled a little closer. The table obscured her view. It was only when she got close enough to duck down and peer into the cupboard, that she recognised the packet. It wasn't part of the food supplies they'd brought along with them. It wasn't even food.

The faded skull-and-crossbones design on the side told her it was the missing carton of poison from the shed.

Chapter Twenty-Two

SATURDAY

4:30pm

'Who put it there?' Juliet demanded again. Her tone had gone dangerously quiet. Her eyes were alight with an anger Lyndsey had never seen before.

'Holy shit.' Sonia put her hand to her mouth. 'That's—'

'It wasn't there yesterday, when I put the food in the cupboard,' Juliet said. 'Someone's brought it in since then.'

'Don't look at me,' Val said.

'I'm looking at everyone. We're the only people who could've put it there.'

'Hey, hang on, that's not true,' Lyndsey said. She clutched the sleeping bag tightly around her shoulders so it wouldn't slip down. 'We've been in and out of the building all day. If someone wanted to, they could easily have come in while we weren't looking.'

'Amanda's been here. She would've noticed.'

Lyndsey glanced into the bunkroom. Amanda had sat up on her bunk and was peering at them, but she made no move to get up. As she brushed a strand of hair away from her face, Lyndsey saw her hand was trembling.

'Amanda's slept through a lot,' Lyndsey said, carefully. 'She might not have woken up if someone came in quietly.'

Juliet rolled her eyes. 'Maybe if Val hadn't drugged her up to the eyeballs…'

'Wait, why is this my fault?' Val asked. 'The woman was in pain; I gave her painkillers. That's literally all I did.'

'We should've locked the door,' Sonia said, almost to herself. 'We should've locked it every single time we went out.'

Lyndsey felt her eyes drawn back to the faded packet. She didn't want to think about what it meant. 'Marne has access to this bunkhouse,' she said aloud. 'I'll bet she's got a key.'

'I've still got her keyring,' Juliet said. 'I've not given it back yet.' It was lying on the counter in plain sight of them all.

Sonia crouched down, as if she might reach into the cupboard for the box of poison, but stopped herself in time. 'Was it here this morning?' she asked.

'Do you seriously think I wouldn't have mentioned it if I'd seen it this morning?' Juliet asked. 'No, it wasn't there.'

'Are you sure? It would've been hidden by these pans. Val only took out the frying pan to make breakfast.'

'I—' The surety in Juliet's eyes wavered. 'I don't know. I don't remember.'

'I didn't see it either,' Val said.

The poison was right next to all of their food. Lyndsey trembled at the thought. The box was elderly, its seams weakened. It could've leaked poisonous grains across their food, their cookware, everything.

'It wasn't in the water supply,' Lyndsey said. The thought had been gaining strength in her mind all afternoon. 'Someone poisoned us directly. They put it in our food … or our drink.'

Sonia looked at the bottle of vodka she still carried. Horror dawned in her eyes. She dropped the bottle and it exploded on the concrete floor. The stink of alcohol filled the room.

'It could've been put into anything,' Sonia said. She backed away from the spreading puddle of vodka as if it might burn her. 'We've all left our bottles and cups just lying around. It would've been so easy for someone to put a spoonful or two in.'

'Okay, stop.' Juliet held up her hands for peace. 'We don't know any of this for definite.'

'It could've been in our food.' Sonia raised her gaze from the puddle on the floor. A strange look passed through her eyes. 'Juliet, you've done all the food preparation this weekend. You've insisted on cooking every meal for us.'

'What the hell are you implying?' Juliet drew herself up to her full height. 'I only offered to cook because if I didn't, you lot would've lived off crisps and biscuits all weekend, like a bunch of toddlers.'

'And if we'd done that, we'd have been a lot safer.'

Val said, 'You got very shirty when I took over the kitchen this morning, Juliet. If I hadn't been so stubborn you would've chased me right out of there.'

'Excuse me for wanting us to eat a decent breakfast, rather than half a pound of pig fat. None of you care what you put into your bodies. Even if it's ruining your health.'

Sonia rolled her eyes. 'You always know what's best for everyone, don't you, Jules?'

'Hold on now,' Lyndsey said. She wanted to step between her friends before the argument escalated, but she could barely keep her balance standing up in the sleeping bag. 'No one's accusing anyone of anything. Literally anyone could've come in and left that box there. Maybe it was even here before we arrived.'

'It wasn't,' Juliet said. She hadn't taken her eyes off Sonia. 'I would've seen it when I put the food supplies in there.'

'Listen, I know we're all upset, but we can't start blaming each other like this. None of us would've deliberately hurt Bobbie. Or each other. We need to hang onto that. Right?'

'I loved Bobbie like a sister,' Juliet said. 'Of course I wouldn't have hurt her.'

Sonia snorted. 'No, but you conned her into coming here for this weekend, didn't you? Just like you conned all of us, with that sob story about your break-up.'

'Stop,' Lyndsey said, firmly. 'We don't need to argue.'

'You think so? Juliet made us all feel sorry for her, so we couldn't possibly say no to this stupid trip. But it was all a lie, wasn't it?' Sonia threw a contemptuous look at Juliet. 'You and your daft husband haven't broken up at all.'

For the first time in years, Juliet looked too stunned to speak. She opened her mouth but no sound came out.

'Bobbie called you out on it,' Sonia said. 'She saw you and your husband out somewhere together last week. She knew you'd been lying to us.'

'I didn't lie,' Juliet said. It sounded weak. 'Gary and I … we've been having problems. We're going through a bad patch.'

'Maybe, but nowhere near as bad as you let us all think. You told us he'd cheated on you, and you kicked him out of the house and changed the locks.'

'It was an exaggeration,' Juliet admitted. 'But not by much. We had a bad fight and—'

'You're still living together, you're still married, he never cheated on you, you're trying to make it work. You're trying for a *baby* together. Those were your exact words to Bobbie.' Sonia turned her furious gaze to Lyndsey. 'Juliet made us think her marriage had imploded, just so we would feel sorry for her. She knew we wouldn't be able to refuse her anything. We couldn't back out of the lovely weekend escape she'd planned for her *best friends*, to take her mind off the awful things that'd happened.'

Lyndsey couldn't look away from Juliet's face. 'You lied, just to make sure we'd come on holiday with you?' she asked.

'Bobbie sussed out the real story,' Sonia said, 'but Juliet begged her not to say anything to us. She promised to come clean to us this weekend. But I guess you haven't found a good time to do that yet, right?'

Now that Juliet's shock had worn off, a frown creased her forehead. 'I told Bobbie the truth, yeah,' she said. 'There wasn't a big break-up. Gary didn't cheat on me. He went to stay with his cousin for a few days after we had a falling out, but he's back home now. I told Bobbie all of that – in private.' She tilted her head at Sonia. 'How did *you* find out?'

'Does it matter?'

Juliet's eyes went wide. She searched in her jacket pocket for something. 'The text messages! I messaged Bobbie the other day about this, and—' She produced a mobile phone from her pocket. *Bobbie's* phone, Lyndsey realised. They'd all forgotten that Juliet had taken it from Bobbie when they found her. 'You read her messages,' Juliet said in amazement.

It was Sonia's turn to say nothing. She pressed her lips into a thin line.

'You sneaky little cow.' Juliet looked stunned. 'When you were alone with her body … you went into her pocket and looked through her phone.'

'I thought it might help us.'

'No, you didn't, otherwise you wouldn't have put it back in her pocket. You would've shown it to us as soon as we got there. What the hell were you looking for in her messages?'

'Nothing.' Sonia folded her arms defensively. 'I wanted to see if she'd tried calling anyone. I didn't—'

'What else did you do while you had access to it? Were

you deleting messages? Was there something you didn't want us to see?'

'You're the one who should be ashamed,' Sonia said. 'Not me. You lied to everyone to get us here. I hope you're happy with the way it worked out.'

Val came up to the kitchen table then. She'd been so quiet that the others had more or less forgotten her. Now she dragged a chair out from the table so she could sit down. 'I know what you were looking for on Bobbie's phone,' she said to Sonia.

'I wasn't looking for anything.'

'Sure, you were. The same thing you thought you might find on my computer.' Val nodded, as if settling something in her mind. 'You wanted to know if I'd been messaging Bobbie.'

'No.' It looked like Sonia wanted to say more, but she clamped her mouth shut on the simple denial.

'I've got a programme on my laptop that records any internal file searches,' Val said, almost apologetically. 'It helps me keep track of things. So, I could see that you'd been into my emails, looking for saved conversations between me and Bobbie. Hope you had fun searching through ten years of threads and back-up drafts, since I never delete anything and I refuse to use social media for messaging.'

Lyndsey looked from one friend to the other. 'Why did you care what they were saying to each other?' she asked.

'I didn't,' Sonia said. 'I don't.'

'It kinda sounds like you do.'

Sonia pushed past them towards the door. 'I'm out of here,' she muttered.

Lyndsey would've tried to stop her, but she had very limited movement in her sleeping bag. None of the others moved.

The front door slammed shut behind Sonia.

'I should go after her,' Juliet said.

'You really shouldn't.' Lyndsey shuffled to the window, in time to see Sonia heading right, in the direction of the bird observatory. At least she won't be outside in this weather. 'Let me get dressed, then I'll go talk to her.'

'You're not going anywhere until you warm up,' Juliet said. 'And you—' She rounded on Val. 'What were you talking to Bobbie about that was so damn important?'

Val raised an eyebrow at her. 'I don't see how that's anyone's business except mine and Bobbie's.'

'Sonia certainly thought it was her business.'

'Well, she's wrong too.' Val was unfazed by Juliet's tone. 'I didn't say a word to Bobbie about Sonia.'

Lyndsey leaned against the window frame, watching the swirling rain. 'Sonia seems to think you said *something*,' she said. 'Any idea what it might've been?'

'It's none of your business either,' Val said, her voice gentle but firm.

Chapter Twenty-Three

SATURDAY

4:55pm

The whole situation made Lyndsey feel sick. She should've realised Sonia was upset about something serious. *Why am I so bad at social interactions? Why can I never tell when my friends need help?*

Looking back, Lyndsey could see how Sonia's behaviour had been erratic all weekend. The woman had been drinking more than usual, and she'd taken up smoking again, after all the struggles she'd had quitting the first time. It maybe wasn't the way everyone would react to a pregnancy scare, but Lyndsey thought she understood. Right now, Sonia was heavily in denial. She wanted to pretend like nothing was wrong.

It was the same strategy Lyndsey had been taking with

her own problems. Lyndsey had tried to leave her anxiety over her financial situation on the mainland. There'd been nothing she could do about it till she got home, so why spend all her time here fretting? Everything could be put on hold until Sunday evening. Sonia must've felt the same way.

Sitting on the bunk again, with the sleeping bag pulled up to her ears and a nest of blankets piled around her, Lyndsey closed her eyes. She wondered what Sonia's possible pregnancy had to do with Val's laptop. Had Val found out? Was Sonia worried about the news getting out before she was ready? That made sense. It wasn't the sort of thing you'd want your friends discussing behind your back. Lyndsey cringed thinking about how Juliet would react to the news.

Sometimes it seemed like Juliet was just waiting for her friends to screw up, so she could jump on an excuse to interfere with their lives, under the guise of helping. Had she always been like that? Lyndsey tried to remember. It'd never felt so overtly like meddling, that was for sure. During Sixth Form, Juliet had gone to great lengths to help all of them, particularly Sonia, with their revision. It was one of the main reasons why Sonia had done so well in her exams and gone on to study law – and also one reason why Sonia had forever afterwards felt indebted to Juliet.

Back then, Juliet's help had been offered freely and without conditions. When had that changed?

Lyndsay exhaled. She was finally beginning to warm up. It'd taken a lot longer than she'd expected. Her hands and feet had stopped tingling with pins and needles. If she could stay in there for another couple of hours, maybe she'd start feeling human again.

But, sadly, that wasn't an option. She needed to talk to Sonia.

With a heavy sigh, Lyndsey got up off the bunk, still swaddled in the sleeping bag, and reached for her rucksack.

'I'm not accusing you of anything,' Val said from the kitchen. 'I'm just saying, I don't think we should be cooking at a time like this. That's not a crazy suggestion, is it?'

'We need to eat,' Juliet said. She was sweeping up the shards of broken bottle with a dustpan and brush she'd found under the sink. 'None of us have had anything significant to eat since this morning.'

'None of us will starve if we miss a meal. And we all brought biscuits and chocolate.'

'We can't live on sugar.'

'No, but we can *survive* on it for one day. Which we won't do if we eat something that turns out to be poisoned. Excuse me if I don't want to take the risk, just for the sake of a hot meal.'

Lyndsey dragged some dry clothes out of her rucksack. Previous experience had taught her to bring far more clothes than she needed, because inevitably she would end up getting wet or muddy. She was grateful for that now. She pulled on a clean T-shirt and the warmest of her jumpers, a huge double-knitted beast that she'd found on a sale rail in the charity shop. Everything in her bag smelled a little fusty from the climbing gear that'd been packed on top of it, but she could live with that. Dry was more important than fresh.

An hour ago, Lyndsey would've said the weather was as bad as it could get. But somehow it'd found new reserves of energy. Gusts of wind howled over the moorland to batter the bunkhouse. Rain rattled the windows in their frames. The heating was fighting a valiant battle against all the cracks and gaps in the old brickwork of the building.

As Lyndsey pulled her socks on, the lights flickered. She raised her head. The lights stuttered again, but the power stayed on. *A power cut, that'd be all we needed.*

She looked across the room and made eye contact with Amanda, who was lying on her bunk, awake, but still unwilling to get up. She too was listening to Val and Juliet bickering in the kitchen. It looked like every moment pained her. Lyndsey gave her a weak smile. Amanda blinked away silent tears.

Lyndsey checked her phone, which she'd stored in her bag for safety when she'd gone for her ill-advised dunk in the sea. The message to her mum was still in the unsent items box, with the symbol circling below it as her phone searched for signal. It'd been too much to hope that her rubbish phone might've found some elusive pocket of signal.

With a sigh, she put on her climbing gloves as well as an extra pair of socks for added warmth, then padded into the kitchen.

'I think you're being too paranoid,' Juliet said. She'd dumped the broken glass into a bin bag and mopped up the spill of vodka as best she could. The kitchen still smelled strongly of alcohol. Now, Juliet was holding a bag of instant mashed potato, examining it minutely for leaks or tears.

'And I think you're not paranoid enough,' Val said. 'If it turns out I've hurt your feelings for nothing, well, then I'll apologise. But if it's a choice between giving offence and potentially dying—'

Lyndsey picked up a bottle of mineral water from the counter. She made sure the seal was intact before opening it. 'I'm going to check on Sonia,' she said.

'You should just leave her be,' Juliet said. 'Give her time to cool down. What are you hoping to achieve?'

'She's our friend.'

'Well, she's doing a terrible job of showing it. Bobbie is *dead*, in case you've somehow forgotten, and Sonia's acting like her own stupid problems are the most important thing in the world. How can she *sulk*, at a time like this? She needs to get over herself.'

'She's upset. We all are.' Lyndsey met Juliet's eyes. 'None of us have forgotten what happened. But starting petty arguments won't solve anything. We need to stick together. By this time tomorrow, at the very latest, we'll be home.'

Val cleared her throat. 'We can't be sure of that.'

'Before we left, we all told people where we were going, and when we were coming back. The boat skipper, just for starters. Those people know we've got shelter and food for at least today and tomorrow. And if the boat can't get us home tomorrow, for whatever reason, they'll find a way to get a message to us.'

'How will they do that?'

'They'll figure something out,' Lyndsey said, with more

confidence than she felt. 'We're not stranded. This is all temporary. We have to hang onto that.'

She went back to her bunk to put her boots on. Behind her, she could hear Val grumbling, but she ignored her. *This time tomorrow,* she promised herself. *We can all hold out until then.* She kept that thought firmly in the front of her mind. She couldn't let herself dwell on what would happen afterwards. Getting home wouldn't end the nightmare, because no matter what they did, Bobbie would still be dead.

'I need a sit down,' Val said. 'This weather's playing havoc with my joints.'

Juliet said, 'I wish you'd told us how bad it'd got before we came here. When I raised the subject, you said you'd have no problem keeping up with the rest of us.'

'I've kept up fine, thank you very much. I was just as good at the abseil yesterday as I've ever been.'

Juliet clucked her tongue. 'You can't even climb a ladder to the top bunks. How did you expect to climb the Bear Post stack tomorrow?'

'Slowly and steadily. Like I do everything.'

'I just hate to see you not taking your illness seriously. What would your girlfriend say?'

'She'd say, *oh Val, these are your best friends, you'll regret it if you don't go on this holiday.*' Val did a good job of imitating her partner's soft, primary-school-teacher tone. '*Look at the accommodations they've made for you. They know you hate flying, so they've picked a location you can get to by boat and train. What good friends they are to you.*' Val blew out an irritated breath. 'If anything, *you* should be concerned about what she's gonna say when she finds out you used this weekend as an excuse to berate me about my fitness and diet. That's less than chum-like behaviour, don't you think?'

Lyndsey pulled her boots on, wincing at the clamminess inside them. From her backpack, she also dug out a couple of cereal bars, a little bit squashed now, and a small bottle of scotch which she'd shoved into a side pocket because it was a convenient shape. The seal around the lid was still intact. She put the bottle and the cereal bars into the front pocket of her hoodie, along with the water she'd taken from the kitchen.

She left Val and Juliet bickering in the kitchen, and went outside.

The rain and wind that slapped her face almost triggered a panic attack. Lyndsey remembered the freezing waves of the Sound as they'd dragged her down and tried to drown her. She had to steel herself before she could walk to the end of the path. The scream of the wind echoed through her bones. She gritted her teeth and forced her steps towards the bird observatory.

Lyndsey knocked at the front door. She wasn't sure if anyone would answer.

A few moments passed, then the door was unlocked, and Marne opened it just wide enough to peer out. 'Something I can help you with?' Marne asked.

'Can I come in?' Lyndsey asked.

'Any particular reason?'

'I'd like to talk to Sonia.'

Marne leaned past her to check there was no one else

outside. 'Come on, then,' she said. 'You're letting the heat out.'

'Thank you.' Lyndsey stepped gratefully inside.

Marne led her into the sitting room, then picked up a glass of wine from the table. 'No hitting each other,' she said as she took her drink into the workroom. A moment later, the staticky-voices of the shipping forecast rose from the portable radio. Marne was giving Lyndsey and Sonia as much privacy as she could.

Sonia was nestled in one of the armchairs, with a tumbler of wine held tightly between her palms. On the table in front of her was an open bottle of red wine.

'I checked the bottle hadn't been tampered with before I opened it,' Sonia said, following Lyndsey's gaze. 'I think Marne's as worried as any of us. She doesn't want to risk drinking the tap water either.'

'I wasn't—'

'Oh, so were you going to lecture me about drinking alcohol in my condition? Is that what that look is for?'

Lyndsey glanced over her shoulder. Marne had busied herself in the workroom, although the house was so small that she'd probably eavesdrop, whether she meant to or not. With a sigh, Lyndsey sat down in the spare armchair, opposite Sonia. A broken spring poked her hip.

'So, you and Marne are friends now?' Lyndsey asked.

'I apparently don't have any friends,' Sonia said. 'I figured this non-friend was better than my other non-friends in the bunkhouse. At least here no one's accusing me of anything.'

Lyndsey eyed the bottle of wine on the table. 'Do you have another glass?' she asked.

After a moment, Sonia sighed and pushed her own, half-full glass towards her. 'Here, we can share,' she said. 'I think cooties are the least of our worries right now.'

Lyndsey took a grateful swallow of wine. It warmed her stomach, while failing to touch the bone-deep chill that she still couldn't shake. 'How're you feeling?' she asked.

'Awful. You?'

'Yup, awful basically covers it.' Lyndsey hesitated. 'Do you want to talk about it?'

'What for?' Sonia asked. 'I'm sure Val's given you the grisly details already.'

'Juliet keeps asking her,' Lyndsey admitted. 'But Val's having none of it. She says it's no one's business but yours and hers.'

'Oh.' Surprise smoothed out Sonia's expression. 'That's … not what I expected.'

'Val's a good egg. She's lacking a few filters in her brain, but she's not a gossip. She's good with privacy.'

'I hadn't thought of it that way.' Sonia curled up tighter in her chair. 'I just assumed she'd been telling everyone.'

'Is that why you were looking at her messages?'

Sonia didn't answer straight away. Lyndsey topped up the wine glass and passed it to her. 'I wanted to make myself sure,' Sonia said quietly. 'It felt important. Even when I didn't find anything in her emails, I was convinced she'd told people some other way.'

'She hates instant messaging. Always has done. She's not a big fan of texting either.' Val had never said as much, but Lyndsey suspected that the aches in her finger joints made texting a pain.

'I should've remembered that.' Sonia gave a sour smile. 'It would've saved me from annoying her.'

'Really, you should've stayed away from her laptop. You know how protective she is about it.' Lyndsey studied Sonia's face. 'Why didn't you just talk to us, Sonia? You didn't have to sneak around behind our backs. If you'd talked to us about your situation, we would've understood.'

'It's more than just that. I couldn't let Bobbie find out.'

'Bobbie? Why?' That didn't make sense to Lyndsey. Out of everyone in their group, Bobbie was the least judgemental of them all. Personally, Lyndsey would've been more worried about Juliet finding out.

'You must've guessed,' Sonia said. 'Haven't you?'

Lyndsey could only shake her head.

Sonia sighed. 'The guy I've been seeing… It's Bobbie's husband. Darren.'

Chapter Twenty-Four

SATURDAY

5:10pm

'Why would you do that?' Lyndsey asked. There were a hundred questions in her head, but that one pushed itself to the front.

Sonia stared down into her half-empty glass. 'It was a stupid mistake. That's all.'

'Let me guess. You were drunk? It just kinda happened?'

'Yeah. The first time, that's what it was. All the clichés. We were at a party earlier this year. Some kind of work thing that my boss organised. I forget how he knows Darren. Anyway. Bobbie was there too, and … we had that argument. She took a taxi home. Darren made some excuse to stay.'

'What was the argument about?' Lyndsey knew it'd

happened, but she'd never found out what caused it. *Or maybe you never bothered to ask.*

'Funnily enough, it was about Darren.' Sonia smiled without humour. 'I let slip that I'd never liked him. When we were at school, and Bobbie was besotted with him, it never sat right, the way he treated her. Brushing her off because she was two years younger than him. I swear, even now, I'm sure he only asked Cherry out because he knew it would upset Bobbie.'

'Maybe.' All that drama felt like a very long time ago. 'I don't know what Cherry's excuse was for saying yes to him, in that case.'

'Who knows? Cherry always did whatever the hell she liked. At least she was smart enough to ditch him when she realised what he was like. Then he ran back to Bobbie like she'd been his Plan A all along. Urgh. Anyway. The party. After Bobbie left, I went over to Darren, planning to start a fight.'

'So unlike you.'

'Shut up. I fully intended to tell him off, but it … didn't work out that way. I guess somewhere along the line it turned into flirting. It wasn't serious, until suddenly it was.' Sonia's mouth twisted. 'Such a bullshit excuse. I wasn't even that drunk. Not drunk enough to do something *that* awful, anyway.'

'Was it just that one time?'

'No. The second time … I figured the damage was already done, y'know? No one was ever gonna talk to me again, regardless of whether I slept with him once or a dozen times. I'd already trashed my friendships. It was just a question of when everyone would find out. I couldn't go back and undo what I'd done.'

Lyndsey eyed the bottle of wine. She felt too sober to be having this conversation. 'Does he know about—?'

'He doesn't know I might be pregnant, no. You're the only person I've told.' Sonia half-smiled. 'Although, Marne could be listening in right now. I wouldn't put it past her.'

Automatically, Lyndsey checked over her shoulder, but there was no sign that Marne had come out of the workroom. 'What about Val?'

Sonia shook her head. 'I don't think so. But she knows I've been seeing Bobbie's husband. She found out, somehow. She let me know that she knew, and—' She raised one shoulder in a shrug. 'I guess she wanted me to think about what I'd done and, presumably, come clean to Bobbie. Then Val never mentioned it again. I've been worried that she would tell Bobbie, but I guess maybe she didn't.' She let out a breath. 'I hope Bobbie didn't know. I hope she never found out what I did.'

'It doesn't sound like Val told her. Maybe you should've talked to Bobbie yourself.'

'What good would that have done? It would've trashed her marriage and lost me all my friends. There were no upsides at all. Chances are she wouldn't even have believed me … or Darren would've convinced her I was lying.' Sonia's mouth set itself into a grim line. 'He can talk his way out of anything. Believe me.'

'I take it you don't want to be with him in the long run.'

'Of course not. I just… God, I don't know what was wrong with me. I don't even like the stupid bastard. But …

you know how it is, right? When you want someone so badly it's like you're not even thinking straight.' She shuddered. 'Every time he looked at me, I just wanted to rip his pants off there and then. You understand that, right?'

'Not really.'

'C'mon. You must've felt like that about someone. What about—?' Sonia snapped her fingers twice, trying to conjure the name. 'That guy. Whatshisface. With the hair and the nose. You had a proper crush on him.'

'No, I just told you I had a crush on him to shut you up. You lot kept calling me frigid.' *Amongst other things.* 'So, I fabricated some crushes.' Lyndsey's ears burned at the memory. 'At least then you were just laughing at me for having rubbish taste in men. That felt more normal.'

'I did wonder what you saw in that guy.'

'I wondered what you saw in *every* person you fancied.' Lyndsey shrugged. 'But, y'know, I figured it was what people did. They had crushes, they fell in love, they got drunk and slept with people. Like a social convention. I still don't fully understand it.'

Sonia shifted in her seat. 'Why does this feel like a personal attack?'

'Sorry. I'm just trying to say … I don't get why you slept with Bobbie's husband.' Lyndsey spread her hands. 'I can't imagine sabotaging a good friendship just for the sake of getting laid.'

'When you put it like that, it does sounds like a pretty shitty thing to do, huh?'

Lyndsey reached over and took the glass off her. 'People

have done worse,' she said. 'I'm certain they have.' She drank the wine then poured some more.

'Are you going to tell Juliet?'

The look in Sonia's eyes was so naked and exposed, Lyndsey had to look away. 'It's not my business,' Lyndsey said. That felt like a cop-out, so she added, 'It's not Juliet's business, either.'

'Juliet will feel differently, I'm sure.' Sonia hesitated. 'Have you considered what it means?'

'What?'

'If the police find out about the affair, they'll make a big deal of it.' Sonia's voice was quiet. She sounded very unlike herself. 'I was sleeping with Bobbie's husband. Now Bobbie's dead. When they're drawing up the list of suspects, I can bet I'll be somewhere on the list. Probably right near the top.'

Lyndsey's stomach turned over. She hadn't thought of that. 'Even if they do,' she said carefully, 'it'll come to nothing. Because you didn't do anything to hurt Bobbie. Physically, anyway. Right?'

Sonia was quiet for longer than Lyndsey liked. 'I didn't do anything to hurt her physically, no. But you can imagine what people are going to think. I look like the shittiest, most suspicious person in the world. Just think how Juliet would react if she knew all this.'

'Maybe your best bet is to come clean about the affair. Tell everyone everything.'

'That's a terrible idea.'

'Well, I'm kinda short on advice right now, apart from

drinking heavily, and I think we've already figured that one out. Can you think of anything else that might help?'

The ceiling lights went out.

It was sudden enough that Lyndsey let out a small shriek.

'It's okay!' Marne said. 'Don't panic!'

Without the electric lights, the only illumination came from the weak grey daylight, leaking through the windows at the front of the house. Lyndsey could barely see Sonia's outline in the chair opposite her. The portable radio in the other room continued to chatter and buzz quietly to itself.

'What happened?' Lyndsey asked. 'Is it the generator?'

'Sounds likely,' Marne said. She was pulling on her wellies. 'I only usually run it for an hour each morning and evening, but I put it on again this afternoon, since you folks were spending the day inside. Chances are, it's overheated or turned itself off. I can set it running again. Wait.' She patted down her pockets. 'I don't have my keys.'

'They're in the bunkhouse. I'll get them for you.' Lyndsey got up from her seat. 'I better tell the others what's happened too. We don't want them freaking out. Are you okay here on your own?' she asked Sonia.

'More than fine,' Sonia said. 'Drinking wine in the dark is my favourite thing to do.'

Marne lit the paraffin lamp and left it on the table for Sonia. Then she grabbed a toolbox from the workbench and hurried outside. Lyndsey followed.

When Lyndsey opened the door to the bunkhouse, Juliet was immediately there, demanding to know what'd happened.

'The generator's gone off,' Lyndsey said. 'Marne's gone to fix it.'

'What about the solar panels? I thought they were supposed to provide power when the generator wasn't running.'

Lyndsey had forgotten that. 'There's not been much sun this week,' she guessed. 'Maybe not enough to power them up.'

At the table, Val said, 'Did the website say anything about this when you were booking our accommodation, Juliet? As well as a temperamental emergency radio, it also has lights that spontaneously turn themselves off... What other delights does this place offer? Could you not have booked us a retreat in a demilitarised zone instead?'

'Don't start,' Juliet muttered.

'I just feel like this fun weekend has been severely mis-sold to me.'

Lyndsey didn't want to get involved in yet another argument. She grabbed the ring of keys from the countertop. 'I'll go and help Marne,' she offered. 'She sounded hopeful that it's an easy fix.'

Before Juliet could argue, Lyndsey went back outside. She hurried around to the side of the building. There, she found Marne waiting by the fuse box.

'Keys,' Lyndsey said as she tossed them to her.

'Thanks.' Marne unlocked the box and peered inside, with the help of a Maglite torch. 'You can wait inside where it's warm, if you like. I don't need a supervisor.'

Lyndsey's cheeks flushed. 'I know. I just thought you might like some help.'

Marne scrunched up her nose, but then passed the torch to Lyndsey. 'Hold this for me, please. It's useful to have both hands free.'

She flipped a few switches, pausing each time to listen. Lyndsey realised she couldn't hear the steady chug-chug-chug of the generator, which had been a reassuring background noise for most of the afternoon.

'Does this happen often?' Lyndsey asked.

'Every now and again. Probably no more often than in any public building. The difference is, if a fuse blows in an office somewhere, there'll be a caretaker or technician right on hand to sort it out. Most of the time, the office workers wouldn't even notice there's a problem. Out here, there's just me.'

Lyndsey watched her try the switches again. 'Where did you learn about electronics?'

'Self-taught. The first season I was out here – that'd be four years ago now – I realised I didn't have much in the way of practical knowledge. I could change a plug, and I arrogantly thought that'd be enough to get by.' Marne rolled her eyes at herself. 'The other wardens who were here that year taught me the bits and pieces that they knew. Over the following winter, I took a college course to fill in the gaps.'

She paused, listening. The only noise was the shriek of the wind and the distant boom of waves. Lyndsey shuddered. It sounded like the tide was attempting to swallow the whole island.

'Well, that's not working,' Marne said. She closed and locked the switch box. 'Looks like it's a problem with the generator itself.'

She turned her attention to the wooden lean-to that housed the generator. She unlocked it with another key from her bundle.

The smell of hot oil and kerosene wafted up. Lyndsey held the torch steady. 'Are you sure you can fix this?' she asked. 'What if it needs a part, like the radio?'

'Let me have a look at it before we jump to conclusions.' Marne propped the lid of the lean-to open so it created a shelter from the rain. 'Some things can be bodged. Others can't.'

'Like the radio.'

Marne gave her a serious look. 'The radio can't be bodged. I'm sorry. It's been broken for at least a week. Probably more like nine days, if I'm being honest. I figured out on about day two that I couldn't get it working by myself. That's why I sent a message on the next boat to request a spare part.'

'So, why the hell did you tell us you could fix it?'

'I didn't. I said I would try my best.' Marne reached into the dark innards of the generator. 'It looked like one of the relays in the radio has failed. Sometimes you can work around that with a bit of creative soldering, but not always. Since this is an emergency situation, I figured I'd give it another try.'

'What about those wires in the radio that'd been cut through?' Lyndsey said, remembering what Sonia had said. 'Why'd you do that?'

Marne's brows drew together for a moment. Then her expression cleared. 'Oh, right. Those wires used to be attached to the earthing circuit,' she said. 'Except there was something faulty with it. Half the time, when you switched it on, it would short out. I got rid of the troublesome circuit and it's run a lot better since then.'

She found a length of rubber tubing, attached at both ends to the machinery. In the middle was a bulge. Marne started to squeeze the tube in both hands. It produced *whoosh*ing noises as air or fuel was sucked through the pipe.

'When I first came here,' Marne said then, 'they told me this whole island was cursed. I suppose that's probably true of every island which has tidal currents and hidden rocks – after the first couple of shipwrecks, people start making up stories to explain a run of bad luck. And then, climbers can be pretty superstitious too. It doesn't take much for a place to get a reputation. People embellish stories. There was that diving tragedy, about twenty-five years ago, when those two young fellas died. One of the wardens told me you can still hear their ship's bell, on a particular night of the year, if the wind's right. Islands like this are full of ghosts, apparently.' Marne grimaced. 'Sorry. I shouldn't talk like that. Not after what's happened to your friend.'

Lyndsey moved a little closer to the bunker, where there was more shelter. Her hands were cold from holding the torch. Her gloves were cheap, bought from a charity shop last spring, and weren't nearly as warm as she would've liked. 'Bobbie always wanted to know the history of places,' she said. 'When we were at school, we would go out climbing almost every weekend, and she and Val would compete to find out the most gruesome ghost story. Do you know the slate mines up at Honister? On the other side of the hill, there's an old river tunnel that's still technically accessible. There's a tale there about a miner who was killed in a landslide and his ghost is trapped in the walls. If you whistle, he'll come out and drag you into the walls as well.'

'I think I've heard a variant of that one.'

'We went through that river tunnel once, when we were seventeen, and it was the single most terrifying experience of my life. Cherry accidentally knocked over an old wooden support, and I swear to God, I thought the whole ceiling was gonna come down on us.'

Marne frowned. 'Which one's Cherry? Is she here on this trip with you?'

'No. She died, about ten years ago.'

'Sorry to hear that. Was it a climbing accident?'

'No, no. It was … so much more everyday than that. She was in her first year of university and she came back to celebrate her birthday.' Lyndsey couldn't remember the last time she'd related this story to anyone. Even so, time hadn't shaved off any of the sharp edges. 'We were all out together for a pub crawl.' All of them except Amanda, who'd been a few weeks shy of turning eighteen, and therefore couldn't get into the nightclubs. She'd gone home early that night. 'We ended up on a beach. Cherry drank too much, passed out on her back, and asphyxiated. Just a dumb, stupid, tragic accident. We were—'

'Holy shit, Cherry Parkinson?'

Lyndsey's amazement was reflected on Marne's face. 'You knew her?'

'Yeah, sort of. She was at university in Chester, same time as me.' Marne gave the tube a couple more squeezes. 'I was in my third year when she started, so I don't think we ever met, not properly anyway. I only remember her because she died. And because of her name. I don't think I've ever met anyone called Cherry.'

'It was a nickname. Her real name was Cheryl, but she hated it.'

'We had a remembrance service for her at university. She was a really nice girl, by all accounts. Everyone had fond memories of her.'

'Yeah. Us too.' Lyndsey wasn't too surprised by the coincidence. The world was always smaller than she realised. 'She was the founding member of our climbing group. The rest of us got involved because we're friends with her younger sister, Amanda.' Something occurred to her. 'Did you ever meet her sister?'

'Not to my knowledge. Like I say, I didn't really know Cherry, except via other people. There.' Marne sat back on her heels. 'Pump's primed, let's see if we can manually fire it up.' She reached down under the generator. 'It was awful, what happened to Cherry. The university tried to use her as a poster girl for a while. The dangers of over-indulging in alcohol when—'

Marne broke off. She snatched her hand back as if it'd been burned.

In the wavering torchlight, Lyndsey saw the woman's hand was coated in fluid. The stink of kerosene grew stronger.

'Ah, bollocks,' Marne said. 'We've got a leak.'

'Can you fix it?'

'I certainly hope so. Otherwise, we're in for a cold, dark – hang on, shine the light here, would you?'

Lyndsey crouched, ignoring the dribble of cold water that'd snuck in at her collar. She directed the torch beam where Marne was pointing.

At first, she couldn't work out what she was seeing. It looked like a black tube, protruding out of a plastic tank at the bottom of the generator. Kerosene dripped out around the broken seal. It was only when Lyndsey shifted closer, and the light glinted off metal at the place where the black tube met the tank, that she realised what she was seeing. It was the handle of a kitchen knife. The blade had been speared into the fuel tank.

'Well, shit,' Marne said.

Chapter Twenty-Five

SATURDAY

5:30pm

'That's from our kitchen,' Lyndsey said. The front of her brain was stunned, like someone had punched her in the face, but some analytical part of her mind was still functioning. 'Juliet was using it yesterday.' *The only sharp knife in the drawer.*

Marne snatched the torch and leaned farther into the bunker. 'I think we can rule out an accident here,' she said.

'Yeah, no kidding.' Lyndsey felt sick. 'Who would do something like that?'

'Someone who wanted to make trouble, evidently.' Marne sat back on her heels. 'Listen, I don't want to point fingers, but one of your group has done this.'

'Us? But you've got the only key.' Lyndsey had just

watched Marne unlock the lean-to from her key bundle. 'None of us would've had access.'

'You've had my keys all damn afternoon, seeing how your friend took them off me when you went to look at the water tank.'

'Juliet? There's no way she would do this.'

'You're sure about that, are you?'

Lyndsey hesitated. Before today, she would've confidently said she knew Juliet well enough. But now … now she just wasn't sure. 'I don't see why she would sabotage the generator,' she said, stubbornly. 'I don't see why any of us would.'

'If you're going by that logic, there's no way I would do it either. All the power and heating for the observatory runs off this generator. Cutting it off means a cold, dark night for me as well.'

Lyndsey stared at her. 'Why would the heating go off? I thought—'

'It's got an electrical switch-on. If the power's off, the heating's off.' Marne angled the torch under the generator. Light reflected off the puddle of fuel on the bare ground. 'This is a disaster.'

'Can you fix it?'

'I shouldn't even go anywhere near it. We'll have to get an engineer to patch the tank and clean up the spill.'

'Couldn't you tape up the tank somehow? Just enough to refill it?'

'It wouldn't be safe. Just using the ignition now could be enough to start a fire. Or an explosion.' Marne lifted her gaze. 'I need to move those spare tanks away.' She was looking at a number of black plastic barrels, covered by a tarpaulin nearby. 'The whole place could go up.'

She closed the lid of the lean-to and locked it. The key bundle went back into her pocket. Lyndsey stayed where she was for a moment longer. In her mind, she could still see the kitchen knife, stabbed hard into the side of the tank.

'It must've been done recently, right?' she said, clutching at straws.

'*Recently* is a broad term.' Marne scratched her freckled chin. 'It could've taken a couple of hours for the tank to drain. It's not a fast leak. I'd guess the damage was done sometime this afternoon.'

Which put it squarely in the timeframe when Juliet had been in possession of the keys. Lyndsey tried to shake the thought from her head, but failed. Juliet had had the keys. She had had access to the knife in the cutlery drawer.

Behind that bad thought came another. *She also had access to all our food. She's the one who cooked all our meals.*

'We need to find out who did this,' Marne said. 'They probably didn't know what they were doing – otherwise they would've sawn through the fuel line instead of going for the priming tank – but they definitely meant to cut off our power.'

Lyndsey nodded, unhappy. There was no innocent explanation for this. One of her friends had done it.

They trudged back to the bunkhouse. Lyndsey had to steel herself before she went inside.

She was greeted by Juliet shining a torch in her face. Both Juliet and Val had put on their headtorches. The beams cut across the gloom of the bunkhouse.

'Well?' Juliet demanded.

Lyndsey didn't know where to start. 'We need to talk,' she said.

'Talk? About what? What's wrong with the generator?'

'Someone sabotaged it.'

Juliet's torch swept into Marne's face. 'What the hell did you do?' she demanded. 'Why do you keep doing these things to us?'

'I haven't done anything.' Marne glared right back at her, one hand held up to shield her eyes. 'You probably shouldn't be so quick to throw accusations around.'

'What do you mean by that?'

Lyndsey went to the cutlery drawer. She'd half hoped the one sharp knife would still be in there, but it wasn't. There was no sign of it on the draining board either.

'Can we sit down?' Lyndsey asked. 'Maybe talk about this like adults?'

Juliet folded her arms. 'Fine,' she said, but she didn't sit down.

'We went out to look at the generator,' Lyndsey started. 'Someone got there before us. They stabbed a hole in the fuel tank using the kitchen knife that they took from our cutlery drawer.'

Juliet's mouth made an O of surprise. 'Why?'

'Presumably to leave us sitting here in the dark.'

Val rubbed her face thoughtfully. She'd tilted her headtorch upwards so the beam pointed at the ceiling rather than into anyone's eyes. 'How d'you know the knife came from this kitchen?' she asked.

'There was only one sharp knife in the drawer yesterday,

and it's missing now.' Lyndsey looked at Juliet. 'Unless you know where it's gone?'

'I left it on the draining board.' Juliet's complexion had gone pale. 'Someone must've taken it while we were out of the building.'

It was a handy excuse. Except – 'The only way to get access to the generator is if you've got a key,' Lyndsey said. 'The only key is on Marne's bundle.'

Again, Juliet swung her torch towards Marne. 'So *you* did it.'

'Get that light out of my face.' Scowling, Marne held up a hand again. 'If you remember, you took my keys off me this afternoon. So, *you're* the only one who had access.'

The light from the headtorch meant that Juliet's expression was shadowed, and difficult to read. Even so, Lyndsey saw her eyes widen. 'I-I left the keys here after we checked the water tank,' Juliet said. 'They were heavy. I didn't want to be carrying them around everywhere with me, so I left them here.'

A silence followed her words. No one actively contradicted her. Lyndsey, for one, knew that the keys had definitely been on the kitchen counter for at least a portion of the afternoon. But none of them knew for certain what time the generator had been damaged. It could've been before the keys were left unattended. So, Lyndsey couldn't make herself speak up in Juliet's defence either.

'It's the truth,' Juliet said, her voice rising. 'I left them right here in the kitchen. Anyone could've taken them.'

'And put them back again after they'd visited the generator,' Lyndsey said. 'Right?'

'Right. That must be what happened.' Juliet looked from one face to the next. 'I didn't go anywhere near the generator. Why would I? I don't want to sit here in the dark all evening.'

'None of us do,' Val said. 'Yet apparently that's what's happening.'

Marne cleared her throat. 'The lights aren't the main problem,' she said. 'We've all got torches, and there're some lanterns in the observatory that I can lend to you. The bigger problem is the heating. You all are in for a cold night.'

'Is there no way—?'

'The central heating won't come on unless the generator's running, and that's not going to happen any time soon. You'd better put on some extra jumpers.' Marne turned towards the door.

'Wait,' Juliet said, 'where do you think you're going?'

'Well, I was going to look for my old paraffin lamp. It'll give you a bit of light this evening. Might even put out a bit of heat, if you're lucky.'

There was an angry light in Juliet's eyes as she stepped forward. 'I don't care what anyone thinks,' she said. 'I still say that you're the one who did this. You're determined to make us suffer.'

'Me?' For the first time since they'd met her, Marne raised her voice. 'You only arrived yesterday, and since then you've done nothing but badger me, make me doubt whether I can drink the water supply in my own home, and accuse me of everything under the sun. And now one of you idiots has broken the generator. It's not just you who's affected by that, y'know. I'm without heat and power too. God knows how long it'll take before anyone can come here and fix it. I'll probably have to leave the island until the repair work is done, and I might not get to come back before the end of the season. You understand that? You people have probably cost me my job this year. So, excuse me if I can't find a lot of sympathy for you.'

She turned to storm out. 'Our friend is dead,' Juliet said. 'How can you worry about your job at a time like this?'

With one hand on the door, Marne rounded on her. 'For all I know, *you're* the one who killed her,' she said. 'You or one of your so-called friends.'

She slammed the door hard on her way out.

Chapter Twenty-Six

SATURDAY

5:40pm

The silence in the bunkhouse felt as thick as treacle. Lyndsey closed her eyes. Outside, the wind roared and shrieked. She wished she could join in.

'She's wrong,' Juliet said at last. Her voice wavered. 'I didn't do anything to hurt Bobbie. And I didn't go near the generator. I don't even know where it is. Lyndsey and Sonia are the ones who went with Marne to switch it on yesterday.'

Lyndsey let out a breath. 'Just … stop, will you? There's no sense throwing accusations around.'

'You didn't have any objections when Marne was accusing me now, did you? I didn't see you rushing to my defence.'

Val said, 'That's because Marne's points were valid. Maybe not the way she expressed them, but if you look at it logically—'

'How can you say that?' Juliet's voice rose again. 'How can you suspect me of hurting Bobbie? I only did the cooking for you lot because if I hadn't, none of you would've eaten properly. You're like kids; you don't know how to take care of yourselves. And none of you complained at the time. It's not fair to throw accusations at me now.' She glared at Val. 'Anyway, you cooked breakfast today. I don't care if you say the packet of bacon was completely sealed before you opened it. *You're* the one with the encyclopaedic knowledge of poisons. Why shouldn't we point the finger at you?'

'You should. See, now you're thinking it through.' Val smiled, happy to have a problem to work with. 'None of us is above suspicion. If we take it as a starting point that any of us could've done these things, then we can—'

'I don't want to hear it.' Juliet stormed off into the bunkroom, taking her headtorch with her.

Tired and wrung out, Lyndsey sat down at the table. She couldn't tell how much of her shakiness was due to adrenaline and how much was the residual effects of nearly drowning.

'If you think about it,' Val said, continuing her train of thought even though Juliet was in the other room, 'we should rightfully be suspicious of everyone. We don't know for sure that there's someone else on the island with us. If there's not, that leaves Marne, and us.'

'That's not a fun thing to think about, Val,' Lyndsey said.

'No, of course it's not. There's a better than average chance that we're friends with a murderer.'

'You don't have to sound so cheerful about it.'

'I'm not cheerful, I'm sensible. The poison could've been meant for Bobbie, or it could've been meant for all of us. It could just be blind luck that she got a lethal dose and we didn't. That means we could still be in danger.' She squinted at the ceiling. 'In danger and in the dark. Not the best combination, I'll admit.'

Lyndsey glanced towards the bunkroom, where Juliet was speaking quietly to Amanda. 'None of us would've hurt Bobbie,' she said quietly. 'We all loved her.'

Val gave her a patient look. '*Someone* didn't.'

Sonia. Val knew about Sonia's affair with Bobbie's husband. It was just like Sonia had said: if everyone knew about it, they'd look at her as a suspect. Sonia really was the only one of them with a solid reason to want Bobbie out of the way. It pained Lyndsey just to consider it.

'All of us had either motive or opportunity,' Val went on, in her professor voice. 'We've all had access to the sheds out back, where you found those boxes of poison. Any of us could've brought a packet into this kitchen and used it to poison our food, or our drinks. The front door hasn't been locked, except during the night. We didn't even lock it while we were outside watching you try to drown yourself.'

'Thanks for the reminder.' Lyndsey put her cold hands into the pocket of her hoodie. The half-bottle of whisky and her bottle of water were still in there, a heavy weight that dragged at the fabric. She opted for the water bottle. 'You were alone here more than anyone,' she pointed out. If Val could play this game, so could she. 'We left you unsupervised for hours.'

'That's right, you did. The only person who was here more than me was Amanda. And she hasn't been outside since yesterday.'

Lyndsey tapped a finger on the table. 'Those tablets you've been giving her – where did you get them?'

'They're prescription.'

'I know that. *Whose* prescription?'

Val's expression became wary. 'That's not relevant right now.'

'It kinda feels relevant.' Lyndsey watched her face. 'One of the boxes in your bag was prescribed to Josephine Miller. Who's that?'

'She's a friend of my aunt's.' The words came unwillingly. 'I visit her every other week to make sure she's doing okay. She's on her own and she doesn't get out of the house much. We have a few things in common.' Val held up her hands and wiggled her stiff joints. 'She's on a lot of medication for various things, and she's very conscientious about filling her prescriptions, even if she hasn't used up the last batch of tablets yet. So she often has spare medication. Now and again, she'll give some of it to me, to see if it helps me at all.'

'You really shouldn't do that.'

Val huffed. 'I know what I'm doing. I don't take anything that might be dangerous for me, or would screw up my other medication.'

'How d'you know it wouldn't be dangerous for Amanda?'

'I just gave her painkillers. Nothing more serious than that.' Val's forehead crinkled. 'They shouldn't have made her as sleepy as they did, though. She must have a very low tolerance. It might be because there's a lot less of her than there is of me.'

'That's what I mean,' Lyndsey said. 'You don't know for sure how they would affect her because you're not a doctor. You shouldn't act like one.'

'None of you were worried about that yesterday. When Amanda got hurt, I was the first person you turned to. I don't see why you're angry now.'

From the doorway, Juliet said, 'She's angry because you don't care.' Her tone was sharp enough to make Lyndsey flinch. She hadn't heard Juliet coming to the kitchen. 'You were happy to give Amanda an experimental dose, without knowing how it'd affect her. What else are you happy to try? Did you want to see the practical application of all your research into poisons?'

'Of course not.'

'Why not?' Juliet advanced into the room. 'By your reasoning, everyone in our group is a suspect, but you're the only one who had *opportunity* and *motive*.' She sneered as she stressed the words. 'You've been here all day on your own. You were here when I left the bundle of keys on the counter. You've got a research document full of information about poisons, but the one thing you've never seen are the effects in person. Did you decide to take your research one step further? Did you look at us and see a perfect bunch of guinea pigs, all stuck here in a controlled environment, where you could monitor everything we ate and drank?'

Val said nothing. She sat silently and waited for Juliet to run out of steam.

Unfortunately, it looked like Juliet had plenty of steam left. 'I'm sick of you dressing up your accusations as just a logical thought-exercise,' she said. 'If you can't be civil to us, then why don't you get out of here? Go next door with Marne and Sonia. All the little conspirators together.'

From the other room, Amanda asked, 'What's going on? Why are you shouting?'

'It's all right, sweetie,' Juliet called. 'Everything's fine.' She glared at Val and Lyndsey, even though her own voice had been the loudest. To Val, she said, 'Do you want me to bring Amanda in here so you can tell her what you've been doing? I'm sure she'd love to know why you used her as a guinea pig.'

'Your theory's broken,' Val said at last. 'If I'd planned to use this weekend to run a poisoning experiment on you all, why would I have left it to chance that there'd be rodent poison conveniently available? If I were doing a test, I would've done it properly.'

'Yeah? How would you have done it?'

Val pursed her lips, as if she were considering nothing more important than a hypothetical. 'I'd have brought the poison with me,' she said. 'It'd be properly disguised, of course, since everyone seems quite content to go rifling in my bag when I'm not looking. I would've administered it early, probably on the same morning we arrived, so I could track the symptoms properly. Not all poisons work quickly.'

'Jesus.' Juliet drew back from her, aghast. 'You've really thought about this.'

'I'm thinking about it *now*, because you told me to. I'm trying to point out how unlikely your theory is. Do you have any other theories? Would you like to accuse Lyndsey as well, for example?'

Lyndsey quickly held up her hands. 'Don't look at me. I didn't do anything.'

'You were the one pouring drinks for Bobbie. You're the only person she accepted a drink from yesterday evening.'

With a sickening lurch, Lyndsey realised that was true. She remembered Bobbie's soft smile, the moment of connection over a tin mug with a splash of Baileys in it.

'*And* you said you'd borrowed money off Bobbie,' Juliet said. 'You told us earlier you'd gone to her for money, and couldn't pay it back.'

Lyndsey blinked. 'Yeah, but it was only a few hundred quid. C'mon. I wouldn't kill someone over that little money.'

Val raised an eyebrow. 'What's an acceptable figure for a murder?' she wondered. 'A thousand? Two, five, ten?'

'Knock it off, Val. It's not funny.'

'You raised the possibility. Now we're just haggling.'

'Hey, I risked my *life* this afternoon. I almost drowned trying to raise the alarm. Do you think I would've done that if I were guilty of anything?'

'Sure, maybe.' Val didn't seem fazed by the possibility. 'A guilty conscience is a terrible thing.'

A loud knock at the door made them all start. For a moment, they just looked at each other, then Juliet broke away to open the door.

Marne stood in the doorway. 'I found a spare lamp,' she

said. 'No luck with the heater though – the only one I've got needs to be connected to a chimney, otherwise you'll all suffocate. I brought some extra blankets instead.'

Her tone was grudging and borderline unfriendly, as if she'd only brought the supplies to them under duress. Lyndsey couldn't blame her. There was a lot of bad feeling flying around.

Lyndsey stayed sitting at the table while Juliet took the blankets and the lamp into the bunkroom. She knew she should speak to Marne, say something reassuring, or even just smile to let her know the world wasn't against her. But Lyndsey's thoughts were in turmoil.

Did her friends really think she'd killed Bobbie, just to get out of a debt? It sounded crazy. Impossible. Two days ago, Lyndsey would've laughed at the idea. But now, with everything that'd happened, she was suddenly scared her friends would take it seriously. They would look at her and wonder, *is she capable of murder?*

Lyndsey lifted her gaze briefly. Across the table from her, Val was frowning to herself, her gaze fixed on the middle distance, her head tilted to one side. Lyndsey could almost see the cogs whirring in her brain.

For an irrational moment, Lyndsey hated Val. *Why couldn't she keep her stupid thoughts to herself?*

Chapter Twenty-Seven

SATURDAY

6:00pm

'Come to join the loser party, have you?' Sonia asked with a humourless smile. 'Take a seat. Wrap a blanket round your knees like you're a spinster aunt from the nineteen-hundreds.'

Outside, it felt like it was getting dark already, even though it was only six o'clock. The thunderous clouds and constant driving rain cast a perpetual twilight. Or maybe it was just that there were no external sources of light out there. Lyndsey had never fully appreciated what an important part streetlamps played in her everyday life. Right now, it felt like the light was going out of the world.

Sonia hadn't moved from her comfy armchair in the front room of the observatory. She was wrapped up in a crocheted granny blanket. Looking at the bottle on the table, it seemed she'd been drinking steadily since the last time Lyndsey had seen her. Her face was pinched with exhaustion. Her eyes were dry, though. She'd given up crying for now.

Lyndsey flopped down into the spare armchair. Somewhere behind her, she heard Marne in the workroom, rummaging in a cupboard for something. A lamp on the table next to the wine bottle cast a warm, welcome light across the room. It hissed quietly to itself while filling the air with the not unpleasant smell of warm paraffin. The glass plates around the flame cast dancing shadows up the walls.

'How're things in the winners' party?' Sonia asked. 'Is everyone feeling nice and smug over there?'

Lyndsey picked up the wine bottle. There was less than a glassful left. She set it back down and instead took the half-bottle of whisky out of her hoodie pocket. 'Did Marne tell you what happened to the generator?' she asked.

Sonia's gaze slid away. 'Yeah. Do we know who did it?'

'No one's admitting to it, if that's what you mean.'

With a certain amount of effort, Sonia turned to face Lyndsey. 'Who do you *think* did it?' she asked.

'That's the big question, isn't it?' Lyndsey wondered if she should get a glass from the kitchen, but decided not to bother. She broke the seal on the whisky and drank straight from the bottle. 'Marne had the key to the generator, except when Juliet had it, *except* when *she* left it in our kitchen, where just about any idiot could've picked it up. So—' She took another swig. 'Essentially, anyone had access.

Including people outside our group. It sounds like anyone could've wandered in while we were out. It's possible Amanda wouldn't have noticed an intruder coming into the bunkhouse, if they did it quietly enough. After we broke the news to her about Bobbie, she just… It's like she's shut down. I'm worried about her.'

'We've fucked this all up, haven't we?' Sonia muttered. 'We should've just stayed inside and locked the doors. The boat will be here tomorrow. We should all … just stay in our own bunks and wait for someone to save us.'

'*If* the boat can get here tomorrow,' Lyndsey couldn't help but say.

'Urgh. Even if it can't… Look.' Sonia struggled to sit up. 'Look. We've been out of contact for more than twenty-four hours now. That might work in our favour.'

'What? How?'

'If the boat can't get here tomorrow, someone will try to contact us. And they'll fail because—' She gestured. 'Broken radio. When we don't respond, they'll raise the alarm. I've been thinking about this. For all we know, that's already happened. Someone's already tried to check in with us, got no reply, and has called the coastguard.'

Lyndsey tried to quash the leap of hope she felt. 'We shouldn't pin our hopes on that,' she said.

'No, of course not. But, I'm saying, maybe we shouldn't panic. We can just sit tight. Chances are, someone on the mainland will've already figured out there's a problem. They're not going to forget about us.'

Lyndsey had to smile. 'When did you become an optimist?'

'Ah, you know how it goes. Some of us are born optimistic. Some of us have optimism thrust upon us.' Sonia tried to smile, but her lip quivered. 'I've got to think that things will turn out all right. I've got to.'

The loss of the generator had rattled them all. It was more than just the unexpected darkness of the rooms, or the cold that Lyndsey could already feel pinching at her skin. It was the sense of vulnerability. Someone had cut off their power without anyone seeing who it was. They'd walked right up and done it. That was unnerving. Lyndsey couldn't help but worry about what else they might've tampered with when no one was looking.

'I think it was someone from our group who broke the generator,' Lyndsey said. Just saying it aloud made her shiver. It felt like a betrayal of all her friends. 'The more I think about it, the less likely it seems that an intruder would've been able to do it.'

'But you just said—'

'Yeah, I know. Someone *could* have taken the keys and the knife from our kitchen. But think about the risk that would involve. How could they be sure we were all going to be out of the bunkhouse for any length of time? For all they knew, we could've come back at any second and caught them in the act. And they couldn't have known Amanda would definitely be asleep or zoned out. Or that Marne wouldn't happen to spot them through the window. She's got a pretty good view from her workbench.'

Sonia nodded slowly, as if she didn't like this train of thought either. 'I don't think it was Marne who cut the power either,' she said. 'You saw how angry she is about this all. Plus, she's got plenty of knives of her own. Why risk sneaking into our bunkhouse and taking one from there?'

'Unless it was to make us suspect each other.'

'Sure, but what are the chances that we would recognise a basic kitchen knife? It's not the most memorable of items. Now, if one of us had brought a jewel-encrusted dagger, with a handle that only fit the palm of one person—'

'You're beginning to sound like Val. She's been concocting elaborate theories as well.'

Sonia winced. 'Am I still the most likely suspect?'

'Not necessarily,' Lyndsey said carefully. 'Val's making a list. I think we're all on it.'

'Pfft. Even you?'

Lyndsey didn't answer.

With an effort, Sonia made a grab for the wine bottle and emptied the last inch of liquid into her tumbler. 'I'd be surprised if you're more of a suspect than me,' she said, with an edge to her voice. 'I'm the one who was having an affair. What did anyone else do that's worse than that?'

Lyndsey didn't know how to answer that. She glanced over her shoulder. 'Have you talked to Marne about this?' she asked. Sonia wasn't exactly keeping her voice down.

'I gave her the bare-bones outline.' Sonia made a face. 'She was quite judgey about it as well, to be honest.'

'So, you two have been talking? Has she forgiven you for accusing her of murder this afternoon?'

'We were very emotional this afternoon. She understands that. But, yeah, I apologised. I shouldn't have accused her.' Sonia saw the sceptical look on Lyndsey's face.

'All right, I know,' she said in a much quieter voice. 'Maybe I'm wrong to trust her. I just really needed a friend to talk to. Someone who isn't emotionally invested in my mistakes.'

You could've talked to me, Lyndsey thought, but she wasn't sure how true that was. Like everyone else in the group, Lyndsey was sickened by the thought of Sonia having an affair with Bobbie's husband. It made her realise that maybe her friends *were* capable of terrible things. She didn't like that thought at all.

It also highlighted how little she knew about these people. At the start of the weekend, she'd worried that she'd drifted too far from her at-one-time best friends. They were different people with different lives now. Things would never be the same as they had been when they were teenagers. It was stupid to pretend otherwise.

Maybe Sonia was thinking the same thing, because she said, 'It's so weird, isn't it? I've got out of the habit of talking like this. I mean, obviously I talk to people, every minute of every day, but never with any *substance*, y'know? The guys I work with ... they don't know a thing about me. I've got no compulsion to open up to any of them.' She frowned to herself. 'Maybe it's just being here, in this fucked-up situation. Or maybe it's more than that. You and me ... we used to tell each other everything, right?'

'To the point of over-sharing. Sure.'

'It feels like we've taken a step back to that time. Friendships used to be easier, don't you think?' Sonia held up her glass so the lamplight refracted through the wine. 'Or maybe I'm just drunk and emotional.'

'Either or,' Lyndsey agreed.

'Anyway,' Sonia said, with a note of finality, 'I didn't murder Bobbie. That's the important thing here. I might be an awful friend, but that doesn't mean I'd do something like this. And I'm pretty sure you didn't either.'

'Thank you for the vote of confidence.'

'I mean, I'd like to say I'm a hundred per cent sure for you, but we can never say that about anyone other than ourselves, can we?' With a sour smile, Sonia raised her glass. 'Cheers.'

Lyndsey hesitated, then lifted the bottle. 'Cheers.'

'Here's to going home.'

They drank in silence for a minute. Outside, the wind drove pellets of rain against the windows.

'You know what the most annoying thing is?' Sonia said. 'We've got an object that's specifically designed for getting warning messages across the water.'

'What, the radio?'

'Bigger than that.' Sonia made a loose gesture with one hand. 'We have a whole lighthouse here on the island.'

'Yeah, but it's non-operational.'

'Obviously. I'm just saying it's frustrating. Me and Marne have been discussing it – whether there's any way to flash an SOS from the top of the lighthouse. If we had a strong enough light source, or even if we built a campfire up there ... I can guarantee that's the sort of thing people would notice. If a passing ship spots it, they'll definitely radio the coastguard.'

Lyndsey turned the idea over in her mind, looking for weak spots. There were a lot, not least the effort it would require to locate enough dry firewood, bring it to the lighthouse, and start a substantial blaze on the gallery deck, with the wind howling through there. It made her think of the word painted on the outer wall of the courtyard, from seventy years ago, when the lighthouse keeper needed to signal for help.

'It might work,' Lyndsey said. She kept her tone cautious, because she didn't want to let hope into her heart just yet. 'The offshore lighthouse is automated, so there's no one there who'd see the fire, so it'd depend on whether there are any passing boats. And whether they'd be able to see it in this weather.'

'Light travels better than you think. That's why they use it for signalling. A lit match in the dark can be seen from two miles away.'

'Wait,' Lyndsey said then. 'We don't need to go to the lighthouse to send a signal. We could do it from the north harbour.'

'We'll never be able to light a signal fire there. Not in this weather.'

'No, but we've got our headtorches. And this.' Lyndsey grabbed the paraffin lamp from the table. 'Even if it's not fully dark yet, it might be bright enough. We can signal to the mainland.'

'Do you think anyone will see it?'

Lyndsey checked the time. 'There might still be someone at the Sound Café. I don't know what time they close at the weekend. If they've got an evening event on, people might still be there. All we need is for one person to see us. They'll raise the alarm.'

It looked like Sonia might shoot down the idea. She was likely remembering the failure they'd had with the banner, and with Lyndsey attempting to swim across the Sound.

'It's worth a try,' Lyndsey said. She snatched up her half-bottle of whisky and stuffed it back into her hoodie pocket. 'We'll all go. More torches mean more chance of being seen. Right?'

Slowly, the light of hope dawned in Sonia's eyes. 'Right,' she agreed. 'We'll all go.'

Chapter Twenty-Eight

SATURDAY

6:15pm

Lyndsey left Sonia to get her boots on and hurried back to the bunkhouse. For the first time in hours, she felt optimism nudge her brain. They could do this. They could get a signal out to the mainland.

Outside, the icy wind cut into her immediately. She pulled her hood down over her forehead and tucked her scarf up around her mouth. She'd taken off her gloves while talking to Sonia, but now tugged them back on. Just the sensation of the cold closing around her hands gave her flashbacks to being in the sea. She couldn't bear to leave her skin exposed to the elements, not even for the thirty seconds it would take her to track up the path from the observatory and into the front garden of the bunkhouse.

The sun, still hidden behind the clouds, must've been heading for the horizon now. The whole island was etched in grey. Lyndsey thought she heard a rumble of thunder as she reached the front door of the bunkhouse.

The door was locked. Lyndsey tried the handle twice more. Through the kitchen window to her left she could see the glow of torchlight, so she knew people were still inside. She hammered on the door.

'Hey! Let me in!'

There was a clack of the lock, then the door opened. Juliet stood inside as if to bar her way.

'What's the big idea?' Lyndsey pushed past her. 'Let me in, it's freezing out there.'

'We didn't know who it was,' Juliet said. 'Don't blame us for being cautious.'

To Lyndsey's surprise, she found Amanda sitting at the table with Val, both of them wrapped up in the blankets Marne had provided. Another paraffin light sat on the table between them. They looked like they were on an Arctic expedition in November, not the northwest of England in August.

'We've had an idea,' Lyndsey told them. 'We're going to use the torches and the lamps to signal across the water. If we hurry, we might catch the café before it closes. I know our lights won't be as effective in the daylight, but I'm worried if we leave it any later there won't be anyone there to see us. We should—'

'We?' Juliet asked.

'All of us.' Lyndsey kept her tone firm. She didn't want any more arguments. 'The more of us there are with torches, the better it'll work. We want the best possible chance of someone spotting us.'

'I don't know if we *all* should go,' Juliet started to say, with a worried glance at Amanda. 'Maybe—'

'I want to help,' Amanda said. There were dark shadows beneath her eyes, but a determined set to her chin. 'I've been doing nothing all day. I owe it to … to you all. Besides, my ankle's a lot better today. I put weight on it just now, and it barely hurt at all.'

'You and I can bring up the rear,' Val said. 'I'm not going to be particularly speedy either. Slow and steady, remember?'

Through the kitchen window, Lyndsey saw Marne and Sonia leaving the observatory. 'You folks get wrapped up warm,' Lyndsey told the others. 'Catch up with us at the harbour. Make sure you bring as many lights as you can.'

She ran into the bunkroom to grab her spare torch from her backpack. In her haste, she kicked over a plastic bottle and sent it bouncing off the skirting board. She glanced down to see where it'd gone. Her headtorch shone on a purple plastic water bottle. With a lurch, Lyndsey recognised it as Bobbie's. Bobbie had always carried it everywhere with her, like a comfort object, as if terrified of spontaneous dehydration.

Lyndsey picked up the flask.

She was sipping from her water bottle all morning yesterday. Even when Juliet gave her a bottle of mineral water, she decanted it into her flask.

Lyndsey unscrewed the lid. There was an inch of water still inside. She sniffed the contents, but it just smelled of water, with maybe a hint of something sweet and almondy underneath.

Troubled, she put the lid back on and set the flask carefully onto Bobbie's bunk.

Grabbing her spare torch and checking it was definitely working, Lyndsey hurried to the door.

'Wait,' Juliet said. 'Are we *all* going? Even those two next door?'

'I told you, we need as many people as we can.' Lyndsey was losing her patience. 'That means everybody. Everybody, and all their torches. What part of that is difficult to understand?'

'Yes, but—'

'Jules, I don't have time to humour you right now. We have to work together. All of us.' She gave Juliet a steely look. 'Hurry up and get ready. And wrap up warm; the weather's horrible out there.'

Before Juliet could come up with any more arguments, Lyndsey left the bunkhouse.

On the track leading north, she spotted Sonia and Marne, on their way towards the harbour. Lyndsey broke into a jog so she could catch up with them.

Another rumble of thunder crossed the sky. Despite her best efforts to bundle up against the weather, the cold slapped at Lyndsey, reminding her that she still hadn't fully recovered from her near drowning. Before she was halfway up the first hill, her lungs were aching. Each inward gasp of cold air felt like ice crystals forming in her lungs.

As she reached the top of the rise, the wind and rain hit

her full force. It whipped at her body. Occasional gusts almost shoved her off her feet. The track was one long stretch of mud and water. In places, puddles stretched from one side of the path to the other. Lyndsey was glad of her waterproof boots. Even so, rain seeped into her collar and cuffs, and a chill, unpleasant dampness was spreading through her clothes. *When I get back to the bunkhouse, I'll need to get changed again.* How many changes of clothes had she got through already? She doubted she'd ever be warm again.

Not much further down the track, she caught up with Sonia and Marne. Sonia carried the paraffin lamp, which was currently unlit, as well as her headtorch. Marne had a satchel slung over her shoulder, and she also carried a heavy industrial flashlight with a battery pack the size of a brick.

'That looks useful,' Lyndsey said, having to raise her voice to be heard over the wind. 'Where did you find it?'

'One of the previous wardens left it,' Marne said. She hefted the weight of the flashlight. 'God knows what they were using it for. They must've been really scared of the dark. Anyway, it's been sitting under my sink for the last four years at least, so the batteries aren't as strong as they could be. I thought it might be handy anyways.'

'Good idea.' Lyndsey had checked the batteries in her own torches earlier in the week, and had decided they had enough life left in them. Now, she wished she'd invested in fresh batteries. It was too late to worry about it, though.

Marne led the way. She strode along as if this wasn't nearly the worst weather she'd ever seen. The dark skies overhead didn't seem to faze her. It was obvious she knew every inch of the pathways on this island.

As they rounded the next corner, the Sound came into view, and Lyndsey balked. She hadn't thought about how awful it would be to come back here. The wind pushed at her shoulders as if shoving her towards the water. The Sound was a black ribbon, flecked with the white crests of waves. Even from this far away, Lyndsey could see the churning currents that tore and reformed across the surface.

The taste of saltwater was on her lips again. It almost made her throw up.

'You okay?' Sonia had stopped to check on Lyndsey. 'C'mon. We're nearly there.'

Lyndsey took a steadying breath. Then she nodded, and forced herself to keep walking. She tried not to think about the way it'd felt to nearly drown. With every cold breath, she relived the awful moments when she'd been in the sea, with the waves pulling her down. The feeling of kicking out with her foot, expecting to strike the rocks below her, and instead finding nothing but empty water.

Her chest started to seize up.

You'll be fine, she told herself. *You can stand back from the harbour. There's no need for you to get too close to the water.*

Ahead of them, Marne abruptly took a left turn off the track. Lyndsey thought she was just going around a deep puddle, but no – she was striking off along a rabbit trail that wound through the heather.

'Hey!' Lyndsey called. 'Where're you going?'

'This way.'

'I thought we were going to the harbour.'

Marne shook her head. 'We've got more chance of being seen up on the headland.' She gestured with the big flashlight. 'Better elevation. And it's more open there. If we go down to the harbour, we'll be hemmed in by the cliffs on two sides. You'd have to practically stand in the sea to be seen. Even then, Kitterland will be in your way.'

It was a good point, one that Lyndsey hadn't really thought about. She lifted her gaze to look at the mainland. The curtains of rain hid much of the land. Off to the east, she thought she saw a glimmer of light, which could've come from the windows of an isolated farmhouse. Hope flared in her again. *If we can see them, they can see us.*

She set off up the rabbit trail with renewed determination. It made her feel better to know they wouldn't be right at the water's edge. She wanted to keep as much distance as possible between herself and the sea.

After a moment, however, she paused. 'Go on ahead,' she told Sonia. 'I'll need to wait here for the others. They think we're going to the harbour.'

Sonia nodded shortly without bothering to answer. The noise of wind and waves was so loud they would've both had to shout to be heard. Lyndsey stepped off the path to let her pass.

Lyndsey didn't have to wait as long as expected for the others. No less than a few minutes later, she saw two figures appear, further up the track. She waved, then hurried to meet them.

It was Juliet and Amanda. Lyndsey hid her surprise. She knew Amanda had said her leg wasn't hurting anymore, but still, Lyndsey would've expected her to take longer to get here. Juliet must've hurried her.

'What's wrong?' Juliet asked when they got close enough.

'We're up on the headland instead of at the harbour. We'll be seen better there. Where's Val?' There was no sign of her on the track behind.

'She told us to go on ahead,' Juliet said. 'She doesn't want to admit it, but I'm sure she's struggling. I wish she wouldn't keep pretending she's fine.'

Lyndsey nodded, although she was irritated. Couldn't Juliet just shelve her opinions for five minutes? Now, Lyndsey would have to come back down to the junction here again in order to lead Val up to the headland as well. 'Come on, then,' she said with bad grace. She turned to lead the way up the rabbit trail.

'Are you sure about this?' Amanda asked.

'Yeah.' Lyndsey wasn't in the mood to have another shouted conversation. 'The others are waiting for us.'

'That's what I mean.' Amanda glanced past her, but Sonia and Marne were out of sight. 'How d'you know we can trust them?'

Lyndsey glanced at Juliet. It was difficult to read her face, since it was mostly hidden behind her scarf and hat. 'What've you been saying to her?' Lyndsey asked Juliet.

'I just filled her in on what we've been discussing,' Juliet said. 'She needed to know.'

Amanda said, 'I don't like the idea of being out here with those two. I don't think we can trust them.'

'We have to get a signal to the mainland,' Lyndsey said.

'That's more important than everything else. We can do our petty squabbling when we're home.'

'I don't like it,' Amanda said again. 'We should stick to the plan, and go to the harbour.'

'You don't have to like anything; you just have to do it.' The last strand of Lyndsey's patience had worn through some time ago. She was sick of being outside in the freezing rain. All she wanted was to get this over with.

She stalked away up the rabbit trail without bothering to check whether the others were following. She clicked on her headtorch to see how strong the beam was. It reflected off puddles and wet stones. Apart from that, it didn't give a lot of illumination, since the sun was still above the horizon, even if it was hidden behind a thick blanket of clouds. Lyndsey hoped the torch was strong enough to be seen.

If it doesn't work, we can come back when it's fully dark. The idea made her stomach clench. By the time it got dark, the Sound Café would definitely be closed, and the chances of anyone seeing them would be greatly reduced. Also, she did not want to come back again. She wanted this to work first time.

Chapter Twenty-Nine

SATURDAY

6:45pm

The trail led them to the top of the bluff that overlooked the harbour. With a start, Lyndsey realised it must be very close to the place where she'd seen the blue tarpaulin, snagged on the rocks, when she'd been in the sea.

At the highest point on the bluff, Sonia and Marne were waiting for them. Sonia waved when she saw the others approaching. 'There are cars in the car park!' she called. 'We might be in time!'

Lyndsey shielded her face from the wind as she looked out over the channel. She found it difficult to raise her gaze from the eddies and whirlpools on the choppy surface of the sea. *That's where I went in,* she thought, looking down on the harbour. *That's where the currents caught me. And over here is where they hauled me out.* It didn't seem like a very long distance, not from that vantage point, but still it made her shudder. A hundred yards out from the shore, the warning light atop the concrete bollard fought bravely to be seen.

When she finally tore her gaze away from the sea, she saw the Sound Café, with a handful of cars still in its car park. The big picture-windows along the front of the café reflected the grey sky, so it was impossible to tell if the lights were still on or not.

'Can't see anyone outside,' Marne said. She was holding a pair of binoculars to her eyes. 'If people are there, they must be in the building, or the cars.'

Sonia had already switched on both her headtorch and the big industrial flashlight. The flashlight was heavy enough that she had to hold it with both hands to sweep it back and forth in the direction of the café.

Lyndsey forced herself to walk right to the edge of the bluff and peer down. There was a sheer drop of about fifty feet to the water. The tide had risen since the last time they were there, and dark water swirled around the base of the cliff. Lyndsey couldn't tell how deep it was, and had no desire to find out. Tendrils of seaweed rose and fell with each wave, like eager fingers reaching out for her.

She switched her gaze to the rocky cliff. Off to her left, maybe ten feet below the top of the cliff, she saw the length of blue plastic that Juliet had mentioned. It was battered and faded by the weather. As Juliet had said, it appeared to be wedged into a crack in the rockface. From this angle, it didn't look anything like a person, and it was the wrong colour for the shape Lyndsey had thought she'd seen from the water.

She must've been mistaken. Her frightened brain must've invented a person where none existed. She'd seen a streak of faded blue and mistaken it for a familiar light-green dress.

You almost died out there. It's no wonder you're seeing ghosts.

Marne lowered the binoculars. She turned to look at the others. 'Oh. Hello,' she said to Amanda, with a faint air of surprise. 'I didn't realise you were with this group.'

Juliet frowned in either dislike or suspicion. 'How do you know her?' she asked Marne.

'Marne was at university with Cherry,' Lyndsey supplied. She was fiddling with her handheld torch. The lens didn't fit quite right and had a habit of trying to pop out at inconvenient times.

Amanda took a step backwards. There was a look of confusion in her eyes. 'I know you,' she said.

'Yeah.' Marne nodded. 'We met when—'

'I know exactly when it was. You tried to come to my sister's funeral.'

Marne blinked. 'No, it was—'

'*Yes.* I remember.' Amanda's initial surprise was gone, replaced by the first flames of anger. 'You were one of the group that showed up unannounced at the funeral. Cherry's *friends.*' She spat the word.

Marne held up her free hand defensively. 'Whoa, now. I don't know who you think you've got me mixed up with, but—'

Juliet stepped in, placing a restraining hand on

Amanda's arm. 'You were friends with Cherry?' Juliet asked Marne.

'No, I didn't even know her. We were at university at the same time. That's it.'

'But you came to her funeral?'

'I bloody didn't. Why would I?'

Amanda was shaking with anger. She flicked a glance at Juliet. 'You remember, don't you, Jules? That group of girls who showed up to the funeral. We had to throw them out. Remember?'

Lyndsey frowned as she thought back to that day. She recalled the disruption at the funeral; Amanda screaming abuse at a trio of women. Had Marne been one of them? Lyndsey couldn't picture any of their faces. It had been ten years ago, and she'd been wrapped up in her own grief.

Juliet's gaze wavered. 'Marne?' she asked.

'I told you, I wasn't there,' Marne said, her face set.

'So how come you recognise Amanda?'

'We met in the spring.' Marne's eyes darted from one person to another, as if searching for allies. 'She landed her kayak on the beach at Kennaugh Bay, over to the west of here. I spotted her coming in and wandered down to say hi. It must've not been long after Easter, because I'd just arrived for the season.'

'You liar.' Amanda tried to shove away Juliet's restraining arm. 'Why would you make up a story like that? I've never been here before. The only reason you know who I am is because you pretended to be my sister's friend. You made her life a misery.' A look of fear crossed Amanda's face. 'Why are you here?' she demanded. 'Why are you targeting us?'

It was Sonia's turn to intervene. 'Amanda. I think you're mistaken.'

'How do you know? You weren't even at the funeral.'

Sonia winced. The jab had obviously scored a hit. 'I know. But Marne wasn't there either. I mean, yesterday, when we arrived, she didn't recognise any of us.'

'She *said* she didn't. What if she's been lying to us this whole time?'

The accusation hung in the air between them. Marne seemed at a loss for words. She opened her mouth and closed it again.

'Amanda,' Sonia said firmly. 'You're being irrational. We—'

'I don't want to hear it, Sonia,' Amanda said. 'You're always on someone else's side. You never cared about Cherry, and you don't care about any of us either. And I know *exactly* how you felt about Bobbie. It's no wonder you wanted her out of the way.'

Sonia visibly flinched. 'I don't know what you're talking about,' she said, but her words lacked any kind of conviction.

Lyndsey said, 'This isn't helpful right now. We need to signal the café before everyone leaves for the day. Otherwise, we'll be trapped here for another night. All of us.'

That seemed to get their attention. No one wanted to spend another hour in each other's company, let alone a full night.

Juliet nodded, although she didn't look happy. 'She's right,' she said. 'She's right, Amanda. Let's just get this done.' Lyndsey resolutely turned to aim her handheld torch in the direction of the café. In her peripheral vision, she watched her friends. Amanda was speaking to Juliet, her words urgent and barely audible. Juliet's lips were pressed tightly together. She kept shaking her head and stealing glances at Marne.

Were we wrong to trust Marne? Lyndsey felt sick to her stomach. *Has she really been lying to us since we arrived?* It was too much to think about. *We need to get a signal out. Then we can unpick everything else.* But she couldn't help but notice how her friends were now keeping their distance from Marne.

Lyndsey's torch beam felt weak and watery in the dim light. She had to check it was definitely switched on. With care, she flashed the beam three times quickly, three times slowly, three times quickly. *SOS.* It was the only piece of Morse code she'd ever learned.

Sonia caught on immediately. She started doing the same with the big flashlight. Next to her, Marne was struggling to light the paraffin lamp, sheltering the flame from the wind.

'Try to keep time with each other,' Lyndsey said. 'It'll be a more obvious signal if we're all doing it at the same time.'

Sonia nodded. 'Do you think anyone will see us?'

'I don't know. There could be too much daylight still.' Lyndsey had thought the almost-twilight of the storm would've been dark enough, but now she wasn't so sure. 'We should've tried this earlier.'

'It was *definitely* too light earlier.' Sonia squinted across the water. 'There's a car moving in the car park. Do you see it?'

Lyndsey didn't want to admit that her eyesight wasn't good enough to make out the individual cars. She kept flashing her torch.

Thunder rolled across the sky again. Sonia glanced upwards. 'This is a *terrific* place to be during a thunderstorm,' she mentioned. 'If I see one single bolt of lightning, I'm running for cover.'

Juliet came to take up her position at Lyndsey's side and switched on her own headtorch. It was a brand-new LED torch, with five different settings, including one that shone a red light, for some reason. She struggled to find a setting that would let her flash the light on and off at will, so instead she set it to the third setting, which was a constant flashing.

'Goddamn technology,' she said with an irritated roll of her eyes. 'It's so great when it makes life easier, isn't it?' She stooped to light the second paraffin lamp.

Across the water, a pair of headlights appeared on the road leading down to the Sound Café. They disappeared in and out of view as the car made its way down the twisting road.

'They're looking right at us,' Lyndsey said.

'Let's hope they're paying attention.' Sonia raised her voice. 'Come on, you idiot! Look over here!'

'I'm almost certain they can't hear you.'

'But there's a possibility *someone* will hear.' Sonia gave Lyndsey a grin. She looked wild and fierce with the wind blowing her short hair about her face. 'It's worth a shot, right?'

'Sure.' Lyndsey laughed, then she shouted as well. 'Hey! Over here! Hey, café! Look out of your windows! We're over here!'

The wind whipped their voices away. *There's no way anyone can hear us.* Lyndsey shook off the doubt. If there was even a tiny chance their voices might carry…

Besides, all that shouting was cathartic. She felt like she'd been needing to scream for hours. It felt good to finally let it out.

After a moment, Juliet joined in as well.

Lyndsey shuffled as close as she dared to the edge of the cliffs. Some of the water that struck her face was spray from the sea, she was sure of it. When she licked her lips, she tasted salt. It didn't freak her out as much as it had done earlier. Sonia stepped even further, right onto an outcropping that overhung the sea.

'Be careful,' Lyndsey warned. 'That's a hell of a drop.'

'We should've brought a safety line,' Juliet fretted.

The car that was coming down the road in the distance paused just before it reached the car park. It was angled towards the channel. The headlights dipped once in acknowledgement.

'Yes!' Sonia shouted. 'Yes, they've seen us!'

Lyndsey waved and yelled. Sonia, with steadier hands, trained the heavy flashlight on the car and sent the SOS message again.

Again, the car dipped its headlights.

'We've done it!' Lyndsey couldn't believe it. 'Someone saw us!'

Juliet raised both arms in triumph. 'That's it! They'll send help. We're saved. Oh my God, I didn't think it was going to work. I take back everything I've ever said about your planning skills. It worked!'

In that moment, Lyndsey was more than happy to forget all the suspicion and harsh words that'd passed between them that day. She threw her free arm around Juliet's shoulders and hugged her. Juliet was laughing and crying at the same time.

It made Lyndsey think of that fleeting moment the day before, at the base of the lighthouse, when Lyndsey had completed the abseil, and Juliet had been right there to congratulate her. If either of them had realised at the time what was to follow, they would've clung to that moment for much longer.

'We're saved,' Juliet said into Lyndsey's shoulder.

Right at that moment, Marne let out a cry. Lyndsey spun around. The light from her headtorch caught Sonia's face as she leaned out over the precipice. The wind whipped strands of her bobbed hair up and around like a halo. In that frozen moment, Sonia was grinning, exultant.

The next instant, she pitched forward. Marne's cry of alarm had come too late. Sonia flung out her arms, but she was already falling. Her face stretched into an O of surprise.

It all happened so suddenly that she didn't even have time to scream as she fell.

She missed the rockface by inches and plunged into the ocean.

'Sonia!' Lyndsey yelled.

The waves closed over Sonia's head. For the space of three seconds – which felt like a hell of a lot longer – Lyndsey held her breath. Then Sonia burst back up like a cork. Her arms flailed.

'Grab onto the rocks!' Lyndsey yelled down at her. Sonia was only a few feet from shore. *She can get back out – if she's fast, she can—*

Sonia gasped an implosive breath. Her heavy clothes dragged her below the surface again. This time she was down for longer. When she at last came back up, a current had caught hold of her legs and pulled her further from shore.

'Someone help her!'

Lyndsey's feet might as well have been nailed to the ground. She watched her friend get sucked under the water again, and she couldn't move. Nothing in the world could've made her jump into the freezing sea. Not even to save her friend's life.

'Don't!' Juliet yelled from somewhere behind her. Lyndsey tore her stare away from the sea, in time to see Marne kick off her wellies and jacket, then, without hesitation, leap from the top of the bluff. She fell as if in slow motion and hit the water with straight legs, arms by her sides. She was only under for a second before she popped back up. She shook her head to clear the water from her eyes then immediately struck out in Sonia's direction. Her headtorch, still fastened around her skull, sent light glinting off the waves.

Sonia was like a ragdoll caught by the riptides. They

pulled her one way then the other. She was fighting to get out of her jacket. If she didn't shed some weight, she would drown within seconds.

At the same time, Marne was trying to reach her. She was obviously a strong swimmer, but that didn't matter right now. For every foot she gained, the water shoved her two feet in a random direction. Twice she was pulled down beneath the surface and had to claw her way back.

She's not going to reach Sonia in time. Lyndsey realised it with sick certainty. And, even if she did, that just meant the two of them would drown together.

'We've got to help them,' Juliet said. She flung down the lamp and ran off in the direction of the harbour.

It was the fastest way down to the water, short of jumping straight in. Lyndsey knew that. She knew she had to move. Sonia and Marne were going to drown if someone didn't help them. Yet still her legs felt like concrete. She was hyperventilating and didn't know how to stop.

Sonia fell off the cliff – she was leaning too far out and she fell –

No, that wasn't what'd happened.

Someone pushed her.

Lyndsey's brain replayed the moment in fierce clarity. Sonia leaning out over the edge, her face split by a grin, her hair wild. Then, behind her –

Amanda pushed her.

Like a bad dream, Lyndsey looked behind her.

Amanda was backing away down the trail. Her eyes were wide and scared. Her headtorch had been knocked askew. She blinked once and met Lyndsey's gaze.

'It was her fault,' Amanda said, so quietly the words were almost lost to the wind. 'She killed her.'

Then she spun on her heel and sprinted off down the trail. Her gait was awkward, lopsided, as if the residual drugs in her system were still affecting her.

'Lyndsey!' Juliet yelled from somewhere below.

Lyndsey snapped out of her trance. She lurched to her feet and ran to help Juliet. There was no time to go after Amanda. Right now, they had to worry about saving Sonia and Marne.

With every step, she prayed they wouldn't be too late.

Chapter Thirty

SATURDAY

7:00pm

'Find something to throw to them!'

Juliet had sprinted out onto to the concrete jetty at the harbour that projected into the channel. The undertow was dragging Marne and Sonia off into the middle of the Sound. They were getting further out by the second.

'Here!' Lyndsey found the life ring that had earlier saved her life. It was lying discarded on the grass, exactly where they'd abandoned it. Either Juliet or Val had taken the rope back to the bunkhouse earlier.

She snatched up the life ring then immediately fumbled it to the ground again. The feel of the cold, wet plastic beneath her palms, even while wearing her gloves, triggered a sudden flashback. She had to force herself to keep hold of the ring and run with it to Juliet. It would've been less traumatic for her to carry a dead animal.

She almost slipped twice on her way out onto the concrete jetty. The surface was slick with sea water and seaweed. Breathing hard, she shoved the life ring into Juliet's grasp, then quickly bunched her hands into tight fists. The sea surrounded the dock on three sides. It surrounded Lyndsey.

'Where are they?' Lyndsey asked. Her voice sounded thin and breathless.

'There!'

Lyndsey followed Juliet's finger. She spotted one dark head above the surface. It had to be Marne, because she was swimming away from them. Further out – a lot further out, Lyndsey realised with fright – a second head fought to keep above the surface. Sonia's pale face was just visible above the waves.

Even as they watched, a hidden current caught hold of Sonia and made her vanish. One second she was there, the next she was gone.

'Sonia!'

Marne powered towards the spot where Sonia had disappeared. She sucked in a deep breath then dived beneath the surface.

Lyndsey held her breath. Neither woman came back up.

'We've gotta go in after them.' Juliet dropped the life ring and started tugging off her boots.

'Don't,' Lyndsey said. 'You'll drown as well.'

'I'll take the life ring.' Juliet stripped off her jacket.

'We don't have the rope! We took it back to the bunkhouse.'

Juliet swore as she remembered. 'I still need to go in. The life ring will keep me afloat.'

'You're a terrible swimmer.'

'I know.'

'You saw what happened when I went out there this afternoon. I almost died. And that was with a life ring and a safety line and three people to haul me in.'

'I know!' Juliet glared at her. 'I've got to do it anyway.'

Tell her she doesn't have to. Tell her you'll do it instead. Lyndsey couldn't force her mouth to open. *You're the better swimmer. If you let Juliet go out there, she'll die too.*

Numbly, Lyndsey stepped back to give Juliet space. She couldn't even find her voice to tell Juliet to be careful.

Juliet hurriedly stripped down to her T-shirt and pants, then stepped to the very end of the concrete jetty. The rolling waves slapped against the rock, sending spray over her legs. She was already visibly shivering.

Lyndsey looked past her, towards the water. From this angle, she could see nothing but the white caps of waves, or the streaks of hidden currents. Then, from the corner of her eye, something snagged her attention.

'There!' she shouted.

A head had appeared above the waves. The dark hair was the same colour as the water. Lyndsey had only seen it because, somehow, Sonia's headtorch was still securely attached and functioning, and now shone a wavering light straight upwards into the clouds. She was at least fifty feet away from the shore. The current was dragging her with ferocious speed, but she was still fighting, kicking and flailing against the riptide. None of her efforts could bring her close to land. If anything, she was moving further away.

Lyndsey swept her free hand across her eyes to clear them of stinging water. There were *two* heads out there, bobbing in the waves. Marne had managed to reach Sonia. They huddled together, Marne helping Sonia stay afloat.

Juliet sat down on the dock then dropped the short distance into the water. The cold made her gasp. Her shoulders hunched. The next wave brought the water level up to her thighs.

'Wait,' Lyndsey said. She'd realised what Marne was doing.

There was no chance of the two of them fighting their way back to the harbour, so instead Marne had let the current sweep them towards another point of possible safety – the rocks, a hundred yards offshore, where the concrete tower with its red warning light stood.

The tide had risen enough that waves rolled continuously over the rocks at its base. Bursts of spray broke against the bollard itself. But Marne didn't have a lot of options. They were a lot closer to the marker than they were to the shore, and the currents were pushing them towards it. With a strength that must be waning fast, she towed Sonia in the direction of the rocks. Sonia let herself be dragged. It looked like all her effort was taken up by just staying afloat. The beams of their two headtorches waved at the sky like desperate beacons.

Relief flooded through Lyndsey. 'They're gonna be okay,' she said. 'They can make it.'

Juliet was watching the two women as well, but she shook her head. 'Even if they do, they'll be trapped out there. We've got to go get them.'

Marne at last reached the rocks and started pulling herself up. It was exhausting work. Each wave tried to shove her back into the channel. After half a minute of struggling, she got her feet underneath her and was able to help Sonia scramble up to safety. Sonia had managed to shed her bright red jacket and her boots during those panicked moments while she was in the sea. The waning light of her headtorch danced across the slick rocks. She clung onto Marne as if she'd never let go.

'They're okay.' Lyndsey came up to the end of the harbour and reached down to grip Juliet's shoulder with relief. 'They're okay.'

Juliet let out an explosive breath. 'That absolute bloody idiot,' she said with feeling. 'We *told* Sonia to watch her footing on the bluff. She could've killed herself, falling in like that.'

Lyndsey blinked. *I'm the only one who saw.* 'She didn't fall,' she said.

'Yeah, she did. We were right there, Lynds. We all saw it happen.'

'No, I mean … she didn't fall. She was pushed. Amanda pushed her off the bluff.'

It was Juliet's turn to blink. Her mouth formed words but no sound came out. She was still standing on the rocks at the base of the harbour jetty, with water swirling up around her thighs, but for that instant the cold was forgotten.

'No,' Juliet said at last. 'That's not – that can't be—'

'I saw her. Amanda shoved Sonia. That's what made her fall. I think—' Lyndsey swallowed thickly. Her mouth tasted of salt. 'I think Amanda blames her for what happened to Bobbie. She said as much, before she ran off.'

Juliet looked quickly behind Lyndsey, as if just realising Amanda wasn't with them anymore. 'Why would she—?' she started to ask, but broke off, biting her tongue.

Because you told her all of your suspicions. Lyndsey's stomach twisted again. *You told her that you suspected Sonia. It's no wonder Amanda freaked out.*

Lyndsey looked across the water at Sonia and Marne. They were huddled together in the meagre shelter of the concrete marker. At that tidal time, the rocks at its base were only about twenty feet wide, at best, and every wave either washed over it or broke against the sides, showering them with spray. And the tide was still coming in. In another hour, even that small amount of safety would be lost. The concrete bollard itself was ten feet high, its sides pitted from exposure to the elements, but there was no real way for them to climb up it, and no room on top for them to perch.

'We have to get them off there,' Lyndsey said. 'They'll die of hypothermia.'

Juliet set her jaw. 'I'll go in and get them.'

'We don't have a safety line—'

'Then we'll run back to the bunkhouse and get one.' Juliet climbed back onto the dock. 'We need to hurry.'

Lyndsey glanced at the café across the water, only partially visible from this angle. 'Someone definitely saw us,' she said. 'That car flashed its lights. So the helicopter will be on its way here soon.'

'If it makes it here in time. How long do you think those two can hold out for?'

Lyndsey peered through the rain at the car park. She couldn't see the car that had flashed its lights at them. She cast around and eventually spotted it, heading back up the road, away from the car park, its headlights briefly visible in the gloom. *Where are they going?*

Her heart plummeted. The driver hadn't seen them. Or hadn't attached any significance to their torchlights. What they'd all mistaken for a flash of the headlights must just have been the car going over a bump in the road.

The realisation floored her. No one had seen them. No one was going to raise the alarm. That meant the helicopter wasn't on its way after all. They were still on their own.

She directed her headtorch in the direction of the café. For all the good that would do. There were only a few cars still left in the car park. Soon the lights in the café would be turned off and everyone would go home.

An answering flash of light caught her eye, and for a moment she dared to hope. But, when she turned, she saw the light was from Marne's headtorch. Marne was signalling them.

Lyndsey flashed the beam twice at her. It was all the reassurance she could give.

'Are you all right?' Juliet yelled, but the words were lost in the wind and the rain.

Marne sent a series of short and long flashes to them

from her torch. Juliet looked at Lyndsey. 'You know Morse code, right?' she asked.

Lyndsey shook her head. 'I know how to signal if you're in trouble. That's the full extent of my knowledge.'

'I bet Val knows,' Juliet said. 'I bet she's done ten pages of research into Morse code and its applications in murder mysteries.' She dropped the life ring on the dock and quickly pulled her warm clothes back on. 'Where the hell is Val anyway?'

Lyndsey didn't know. She should definitely have got to the harbour by now. 'I don't like the idea of you going into the sea,' she said. 'If you get swept away as well, you're one more person we have to rescue. And, I mean, there's a good chance you *will* get swept away. It's a lot harder to swim out there than it looks.'

Juliet hesitated, but she couldn't deny the sense in Lyndsey's words. 'What if we tried throwing the life ring?'

'We'd never be able to throw it that far.'

'We don't have to, necessarily. If we could catch the right current, it could drag the float near enough to their rock, with us holding onto the rope. Then we could haul the pair of them back to safety.' Juliet kicked one of the metal rings embedded in the concrete dock, which the fishing boats used to moor onto. 'If we tie the end onto one of these, then there's no risk of us accidentally letting go and losing them.'

It didn't sound to Lyndsey like there was a high chance of them successfully floating the life ring over to Marne and Sonia, but it was the best plan they currently had. 'I'll run and fetch a safety line.' Lyndsey turned and found herself looking at the small stone building next to the harbour. 'Wait. What's in there?'

'Buggered if I know.'

The wooden door was held shut by a sturdy lock. Lyndsey put her shoulder against the door and shoved. It didn't budge at inch.

'There might be something in here we can use,' she said.

'Like a boat?'

'Like anything. Ropes, life jackets, emergency flares … there has to be something that could help us.' Lyndsey steadied herself against the doorframe. She set her right foot against the door, just next to the lock. 'I've never done this before.'

She kicked the lock with her heel, timidly at first, then, when it was clear the door wouldn't magically pop open, with more strength. The door shuddered in its frame but didn't move. The rain had made the paintwork slick. Her foot kept sliding rather than making solid contact.

After half a dozen kicks, the wood around the lock splintered a little. Lyndsey paused to catch her breath. The wind continued to batter her. She felt exhausted and on the verge of tears. How could she fix this? What else could she do?

She kicked the door again. And again.

Three more solid kicks and at last the lock gave way. Lyndsey shoved it a couple of times with her shoulder. The door shuddered reluctantly open.

Lyndsey shone her torch inside. The interior of the storehouse was piled with nets and fishing gear. She let out a sob. There was nothing here that could help.

'There might be something,' Juliet said, as if reading Lyndsey's mind. She pushed past and started dragging aside the ancient, musty nets.

They quickly uncovered a collection of fishing buoys, a lot of tangled rope, and a crate of lead weights too heavy to move. Everything had obviously been lying untouched for years. It stank of damp and old fish.

'Do you think one of these might work?' Juliet asked, hefting a buoy in both hands. 'It looks like the rope's long enough.'

Lyndsey looked doubtful. She picked up the rope attached to the buoy. It was a quarter inch thick, but fraying and spotted with rot. 'What if it breaks?' she asked. 'I don't know if it'll hold. We're better off fetching one of ours from the bunkhouse.' Lyndsey cursed herself for wasting time by looking in the building. She could've been halfway back to the bunkhouse by now.

'Hang on,' Juliet said, 'Do you smell that?'

All Lyndsey could smell were the nets. She lifted her head. 'What?'

'Smoke.' Juliet stepped outside into the rain. 'I swore I... Maybe it's nothing.'

She ducked back through the doorway. Lyndsey pulled up her hood and risked taking a step outside. The wind flung raindrops at her as if anxious to make up for the time it'd lost while she'd been inside. She raised her face to take the brunt of the wind. All she could smell was the wet ground; mud and trampled ferns; the salt that coated everything here ... and beneath that...

She caught a whiff of some arid tang that could've been smoke.

The wind was blowing directly into her face, so the smell couldn't be coming from the mainland. It had to be coming from somewhere on the island.

Everything here is saturated. There's nothing here that'll burn. Except –

Cold dread curled in Lyndsey's stomach. 'I'm going to check it out,' she called to Juliet. 'Stay here. Keep signalling to Sonia and Marne. Don't let them think we've abandoned them.'

Juliet nodded. Her hands were full as she dragged another heavy length of rope out of the store.

Lyndsey glanced behind her once as she set off at a run up the track. Marne's torch was a tiny point of light in the growing darkness of the channel. From that distance, it looked like the sea could swallow them at any moment.

As soon as Lyndsey rounded the first corner, she lost sight of them.

Chapter Thirty-One

SATURDAY

7:20pm

Before she was even halfway back to the bunkhouse, Lyndsey had to slow her pace to a walk. A stitch burned in her side. Every breath ached. She felt exhaustion and hysteria nibbling at her mind. Only the dread in her stomach kept her moving as fast as she could, rather than collapsing. Her boots slid on the muddy ground. Rain pelted her face.

Overhead, thunder rumbled again. It grew in strength for several seconds, so loud it seemed like the sky would split open.

The smell of smoke grew stronger as she reached the top of the first hill. It came in gusts, carried by the temperamental wind. Sometimes it was so faint she could barely be sure it was there at all. She prayed she was mistaken.

She was almost there when she realised she still hadn't seen Val. Where the hell was she? Had she decided against coming to the harbour and instead gone back to the bunkhouse? Had Amanda run into her?

The very best scenario was that Val had met Amanda on the track, realised that the woman was upset, and taken her back to the bunkhouse to look after her.

Then where is the smell of smoke coming from?

Ignoring the stitch in her side, Lyndsey broke into a jog.

The next time she looked up, she saw the plume of smoke, visible only because it was two shades darker than the storm clouds. There was no doubt it was coming from the bunkhouse.

Please let it be a bonfire – let them have found something to burn as a signal fire or – or –

She didn't know what else she could hope for.

With the taste of bile in her mouth, Lyndsey sprinted to the top of the last hill.

As she reached the summit, winded and out of breath, she saw the bunkhouse. Thick smoke was pouring out through the open door. The light that shone out of the windows wasn't the steady glow of electric light, but instead the wild flicker of flames.

No... No, no, no...

Lyndsey pushed herself back into a run.

By the time she was halfway down the track, the smoke was agitating her throat. She pulled her scarf up over her nose and mouth.

They can't be inside. The door's wide open. They must've got out.

Then where the hell are Val and Amanda?

At the top of the garden, she had to stop. Her eyes were streaming. From there, she could see in through the windows of the bunkhouse. The seat of the fire was right in the middle of the bunkroom. She glimpsed the outlines of the thin mattresses, all pulled off the bunks and piled in the centre of the room. Tendrils of flame licked around the frames of the bunks. The paint was peeling from the walls.

As well as smoke, she could smell the chemical reek of kerosene. She took a few steps up the path and her foot kicked an empty plastic container. It was identical to the ones at the side of the house, near the generator.

'Val!' she yelled. 'Amanda!'

She couldn't be sure they weren't still in the building. She had to check.

Lyndsey pulled her scarf up as high as she could, and squinted her eyes against the smoke. A tickle was building in the back of her throat. She knew she couldn't stay there long before it'd turn into a full-blown coughing fit.

She got as close as she dared to the bunkroom windows. The fire was raging in there, so bright she could barely stand to look at it. The ceiling was washed by flame.

No one was in there. No one on the bunks, no one on the floor. If they were in that room, they'd be dead already. The heat was overwhelming. Lyndsey backed away, then ran to the kitchen window. A light flashed at her and made her jump. But it was the reflection of her own headtorch, bouncing back at her from the windowpane. She'd forgotten she was still wearing it, and that it was switched on.

The kitchen was choked with smoke. It filled the top half of the room. The air nearer the floor was a little clearer, but not by much. She cupped her hands around her eyes so she could peer in. The glass was warm beneath her hands.

On the floor, under the table, was a dark shape. A person. With the smoke swirling around it, Lyndsey couldn't tell who it was, but in the light from her headtorch, she glimpsed a grey jacket. One hand was fisted up by the head, with strands of blonde hair caught between the fingers. *Amanda.*

There was no time to figure out what'd happened. Lyndsey had to back away to grab a lungful of air. She pulled off her scarf and dunked it into a puddle, soaking the fabric as best she could. Then she rewrapped it around her face. With the cold, wet wool covering her nose, mouth, and eyes, it was difficult to breathe. Almost impossible to see. But that didn't matter – if she was inside the building for more than a minute, she was as good as dead anyway. She knew enough about smoke inhalation to know that.

She dropped to her knees and felt her way to the front door. Thin tendrils of smoke were already snaking through her makeshift mask. Once she was through the door, it was ten times worse, thick and choking, like a blanket pressed over her face. Even through her layers of soaked clothing, she felt the heat of the fire in the bunkroom. She could hear it too – it roared like a beast as it devoured the beds, the sleeping bags, their possessions. There was a pop of glass which was probably a bottle exploding in the heat.

With her eyes screwed shut behind her scarf, Lyndsey crawled into the kitchen. Her hand found the edge of the kitchen door. It was further away than she'd expected. Already, she felt disorientated, her chest locked with fear and panic. The thought of getting turned around and not being able to find her way out was terrifying.

In the kitchen, the smoke was thicker than she expected. She dropped to her belly and crawled awkwardly with her elbows and knees scraping the concrete.

Her searching fingers found something softer than the table. Amanda's leg. Lyndsey grabbed it and gave it a hard shake. She was rewarded by a muted groan from Amanda. *She's alive.*

Lyndsey filled her lungs as much as she could, then got to her knees so she could grab Amanda's legs. Bracing hard, she hauled her towards the door.

She managed three decent pulls before she felt so lightheaded she had to duck down again into the better air.

Amanda was a dead weight. Lyndsey got a good grip of her ankles and pulled with all her strength. With her eyes pinched shut, she couldn't even be certain she was making any headway. She let go briefly so she could flail around with her left hand. It struck the reassuring solidness of the door frame.

Nearly there, she told herself. But hard on the heels of that thought came another: *What if you've gone too far? What if that's the door to the bunkroom, not the kitchen? What if you're reversing right into the fire?*

The urge to rip off the scarf and get her bearings was overwhelming. If she did that though, she'd be doomed.

The smoke would overwhelm her and she'd die here with Amanda.

The heat of the fire behind her was scorching her through her jacket and trousers. Even the soles of her feet felt like they were blistering. What little rainwater had coated her clothes had already evaporated.

She grabbed Amanda's ankles again, and heaved.

Gauging the distance by feel, Lyndsey angled her body towards where the front door should be. She prayed she wasn't mistaken. With another pull, her foot bumped into something else solid. The frame of the front door. She was going in the right direction.

Her strength was leaching away fast. The muscles in her arms burned from lack of oxygen. Although she tried to breathe shallowly, still the smoke seeped into lungs, making her cough and splutter beneath the scarf.

Nearly there. Nearly there.

On the next pull, she felt resistance. Amanda's upper body had snagged on something, probably the kitchen door. Lyndsey adjusted her grip and tried again. Adrenaline had got her this far, but now she was exhausted, unable to breathe, unable to cope with the suffocating heat for a moment longer. In that instant, she seriously considered that she'd have to abandon Amanda there.

Instead, she wrapped her arms around Amanda's feet and stood up, lifting with all her strength, then staggered backwards as fast as she could.

The force was enough. Amanda unsnagged from the door frame and slid out into the hall. Lyndsey scooted back another three steps and they were clear of the building. Sudden, wonderful cold air swooped down on them.

She dragged Amanda for several more feet before her strength at last gave out and she collapsed, retching and gasping, to the ground. Lyndsey ripped the scarf off her face. Her eyes were streaming and her lungs felt seared. A coughing fit overtook her. She lay curled up on her knees, with her forehead pressed to the wet ground, until it ran its course. It felt like her chest was trying to turn itself inside out. When she at last could open her eyes, black spots danced across her vision.

They were still too close to the burning building. Heat radiated off it like from an oven. Lyndsey knew she had to get them further away.

She got to her knees, unable to trust her feet just yet, and shuffled over to Amanda.

Amanda lay on her front with her arms stretched out like a ragdoll. The hood of her jacket hid her head and face. She hadn't moved.

In panic, Lyndsey rolled her onto her back.

It wasn't Amanda. It was Val.

Val's face was slack and streaked with soot. There was a nasty graze up her left cheekbone, which could well have happened when Lyndsey unceremoniously dragged her across the kitchen floor. The side of her mouth was crusted with vomit. Her eyes were red and swollen, while her lips were an unhealthy shade of blue. It didn't look like she was breathing.

'Val! Val, wake up!'

In response, Val moaned. Her eyelids fluttered.

Oh, thank God. Lyndsey wanted to weep. 'Val, I've gotta move you,' she said. 'We're not safe here.' Each word was an effort, forced out through the razor blades in her throat.

There was no dignified way of doing this, so Lyndsey took hold of Val's legs and dragged her to the end of the path, then into the shelter of the garden wall. Once there, she rolled Val onto her side on the wet grass, in case she wasn't done vomiting.

As she did so, she saw Val's left hand, clutched into a fist. In its grip was a clump of long blonde hair, just like Lyndsey had seen through the window. *Amanda's hair.*

'Val?' Lyndsey moved round so she was in front of the woman. 'You still with us? Can you wake up?'

Val moaned again, but this time there were words underneath. It sounded like an attempt to say, *go away.* Lyndsey's heart leapt.

'Okay, good,' Lyndsey said. 'You just lie there and keep breathing. Don't stop.'

She had no idea how to treat smoke inhalation. Would fresh air be enough to clear Val's lungs? Did she need to do mouth-to-mouth?

If Val was properly awake, she could tell you. She'd give you a whole damn lecture about smoke inhalation and how to deal with it.

The stupidity of the thought made a laugh catch in her throat. 'I'm going to check if you're injured,' Lyndsey said. 'All right? I'll try not to hurt you. Stay still.'

Without waiting for a response, Lyndsey carefully pulled back the hood of Val's jacket. Immediately, she spotted blood. Her stomach lurched.

Using the tips of her fingers, Lyndsey parted Val's hair. On the back of the skull was a hefty bruise, the size of an egg. A cut in the centre oozed blood.

Lyndsey's immediate reaction was guilt. Had she caused that, when she'd hauled Val out of the building? But no, that couldn't be right. The lump had been inflicted with some force. It looked a lot like Val had been hit on the back of the head with something pretty heavy.

Val murmured something inaudible. Her breathing was slow and raspy, but her lips were no longer tinged blue. That had to be a good sign. But Lyndsey didn't know what to do about the head injury. Val could be dying of a brain haemorrhage or a fractured skull, and Lyndsey couldn't do a thing about it.

'Just stay still,' Lyndsey said. 'Help's on its way.'

The lie stung her throat. They'd failed to contact the mainland, failed to raise the alarm, failed to summon help. No one was coming to rescue them.

She raised her gaze to the bunkhouse. Flames belched from the open doorway. Even as she watched, a window shattered, burst by the heat. Lyndsey could feel the heat against her face. Despite everything, she closed her eyes and almost welcomed it. She felt like she'd been cold since the moment she'd arrived on the island.

'Cherry,' Val murmured.

'No, it's me. Lyndsey.' But Val's eyes were still closed; she was just muttering in her delirium.

Still, Lyndsey felt a chill. Cherry, the seventh member of their climbing party, the founding member who had been the oldest and the least risk-adverse. The one who had always been up for an adventure. It seemed impossible that Cherry had been the one to die so tragically young. Out of all of them, she should've been the one who was invincible.

In Lyndsey's memories, she always pictured Cherry not in her climbing gear or wearing that shapeless rainbow bobble hat she loved, but instead in a light dress that clung to her figure in the moonlight. If Lyndsey closed her eyes, she would always see Cherry on that beach, in that dress, swigging from the Stolichnaya bottle, her blonde hair coming loose from its ponytail and her laughing as the waves menaced her feet.

'I should be out with my friends, not you bunch of losers,' Cherry had laughed as she kicked off her shoes. Later, Lyndsey would see photos of those heels, lying discarded on the shingle like survivors from a shipwreck. 'What kind of person doesn't have any friends their own age? Why do I have to spend my birthday with my sister's school group?'

It was the first and last time they'd seen her that drunk, or that mean. Afterwards, Lyndsey could never work out if Cherry had meant those things she'd said. Maybe it was just the alcohol talking. Maybe it was all the stuff going on in her life; at the inquest, everyone had learned how Cherry was struggling in her first year at university, suffering from homesickness and isolation, unable to make friends as easily as she'd expected to, trying to keep a long-distance relationship going with a boyfriend she'd never wanted in the first place.

Or maybe everything she'd said was the truth. Maybe Cherry really had resented all the time she'd spent with her sister's friends instead of making her own.

Ten years, she's been gone. Lyndsey realised it with a start. Ten years, while her friends steadily forgot her.

Lyndsey rubbed tears from her sore eyes. When she opened them again, she saw that Val's eyes were open too.

Val blinked a couple of times, slowly. 'Juliet?' she asked.

'For goodness' sake. Lyndsey. It's Lyndsey.' She took hold of Val's cold hands, trying to massage warmth back into them.

Val moved her eyes without trying to sit up or move her head. She must've realised there was a good reason for her lying on the wet ground. 'My laptop?' she asked.

Lyndsey couldn't help but laugh. It hurt her throat. 'Sorry. I don't think your laptop made it.'

Val looked past her, at the smoke blackening the sky. 'Shit,' she murmured.

'Yeah.' A sudden fear struck Lyndsey. 'Val, can you move your fingers?'

Val frowned, but she flexed her hand in Lyndsey's grasp. 'There's a fire,' she said. Her voice rasped in her throat, an octave deeper than usual.

'Yeah.'

'Did I do that?'

Lyndsey shook her head. The movement made her brain rattle in her skull. 'I don't think so. Did you?'

'I don't know. Did I leave the stove burning?'

'No.' Lyndsey flinched as something else exploded in the bunkhouse. It occurred to her that they were still too close to the building, but she didn't want to move Val again, not with that head injury. 'Do you remember anything?'

Val started to shake her head, before remembering she was hurt. 'Cherry,' she said.

Oh, Christ. 'Cherry's not here,' Lyndsey said. 'She's dead.'

'I know that.' Val scrunched up her face in annoyance. 'We were talking about Cherry. That's the last thing I remember.'

'Who was talking about her?'

'Amanda.'

Lyndsey lifted her head in sudden dread. 'Where were you talking? In the bunkhouse? Val, is she still in there?'

'I don't know.'

Lyndsey let go of her hand and bounced to her feet. *I checked the bunkroom, there was no one in there* – but how well had she actually checked? She'd had the briefest possible look through the bunkroom windows, before the glare pushed her back.

She took a step towards the bunkhouse. At that moment, another window burst outwards in a spray of blackened glass. Lyndsey stumbled back, one hand thrown up to protect her face.

Amanda wasn't in there, Lyndsey thought, trying to convince herself it was definitely true. *I checked. She wasn't there.*

It was possible Amanda might've taken shelter in the observatory next door, although Lyndsey thought Marne would've probably locked the door after she'd left. The fire was contained to the bunkhouse at the moment. She didn't know whether it would spread to the adjoining building. If it did, there was very little she could do. But that left the question – where had Amanda gone?

Lyndsey crouched next to Val again so she could shelter from the heat. 'What happened, Val?' she asked. 'Who hit you?'

Val didn't answer. She looked like she was either thinking of an answer, or just conserving her strength. Her breathing was still regular, but it rattled in her throat, as if her lungs were full of mucus.

Lyndsey risked a glance over the top of the wall. How long would the fire keep burning? The thin mattresses had proved worryingly flammable, but eventually they would burn down to ashes and melted plastics. It was just a question of whether they'd do so before the rafters in the ceiling caught light. Judging by the amount of black smoke still pouring out of the windows, that could be some time.

Someone had attacked Val and set the bunkhouse on fire. There was no other explanation. Kerosene wasn't as good a fuel as petrol, but with a bit of encouragement, it could've easily been used to start a blaze in the bunkroom.

There were also very few possible suspects. It was either Amanda … or an unknown person, loose on the island with them.

Could Amanda really have done this? Could she have hit Val over the head hard enough to knock her out – hard enough to kill her, perhaps, if Val hadn't been so thick-skulled – then pulled all the mattresses into the centre of the room and doused them with kerosene? If *was* Amanda, she would've had to work fast. From the time she'd run off, at the top of the bluff, to the time Juliet first smelled smoke, it couldn't have been more than ten minutes.

She was confused. She's been confused all day, whenever she woke up. Lyndsey remembered the look on Amanda's face right after Sonia went into the water. Shock and fear had been etched into her expression. Had she even meant to do that? After everything that'd happened, after whatever drugs Amanda had been given, and after Juliet telling her whatever version of her suspicions … it was no wonder her head was a mess.

Had she been irrational enough to do all this?

Lyndsey couldn't make herself believe it. She didn't *want* to believe it.

Off in the distance, she heard a scream.

She looked up at once. The smoke distorted the noise, so for one awful second, she thought it'd come from inside the building. The scream came again, and Lyndsey whipped her head around. No, it'd definitely come from the south, from some distance away. She peered through the rain but her eyes were still streaming.

It'd sounded a lot like Amanda.

'Lyndsey!' someone yelled from behind her.

Juliet came running down the hill from the direction of the harbour. She had to slow as she got closer, shielding her face against the flames from the bunkhouse.

'What happened?' Juliet demanded. 'Are you okay?'

'I'm fine, but Val's hurt. Don't move her. She's got a head injury, and she inhaled a lot of smoke. Are Sonia and Marne—?'

'They're still out there. I couldn't get to them.' Juliet's

eyes were already red from the smoke. 'I tried lashing a couple of buoys together and flinging them into the sea, with the ropes tied to the dock, but the current pulled them the wrong way. I couldn't figure out how to solve it.' She started to cough. 'I was looking for you and I saw the smoke – Lynds, we can't stay here. We've got to go.'

'I don't want to move Val.'

'If the roof comes down, it's going to throw smoke and heat all over this area.'

On the grass, Val stirred. 'I can move,' she said. 'I feel less dizzy now.' She stretched out a hand. 'Help me, please.'

'We can carry you.'

'You're more likely to damage me that way. I can walk.' Val grabbed at her, insistent. 'Assistance, if you don't mind.'

Lyndsey didn't like the idea at all, but she knew they weren't safe. She took hold of Val's right arm. Juliet grabbed the other. Together, they gently lifted Val to her feet. She needed a moment to steady herself, but then was able to shuffle away from the garden wall, with the support of her friends. They assisted her into the shelter of a boundary wall in the next field, a good two hundred feet away from the bunkhouse, where the sturdy stones offered better protection.

As they were lowering Val into a sitting position, Lyndsey heard that scream again. It drew out into a lingering wail.

'Did you hear that?' she asked. 'Is that Amanda?'

Juliet shook her head, bending to check on Val's contused head. 'A seabird,' she said shortly. 'Like we heard the other night.'

Lyndsey didn't agree. She remembered the distant sounds they'd heard the night before – it seemed like a hundred years ago now – but these weren't the same. She was certain she recognised Amanda's voice.

'I think she's hurt,' Lyndsey said. 'I'll go check it out. She might have—'

'It's not her. And even if it is … what the hell does it matter?'

The sharpness of her tone was shocking. 'Jules, we've got to—'

'No, we don't. She tried to kill Sonia. She very nearly killed Val. Look!' Juliet flapped an angry hand at the bunkhouse. 'Look what she's done! If she's hurt, good. I'm sure it's far less than she deserves.'

Lyndsey blinked. 'What if it wasn't her that set the fire?'

'It was her,' Juliet said, fiercely. 'Who the hell else could it have been?'

'If someone else is on the island with us—'

'You need to stop that. There's no one else. It's just us. It always has been.' Juliet shook her head in contempt. 'Whatever Amanda's doing out there, leave her to it. It's no concern of ours.'

Lyndsey stood up. To the south, she could see nothing but the wind-tossed bracken and the spindly trees, everything in the landscape pummelled by the rain. If Amanda was out there, she could be anywhere.

She needs our help.

Lyndsey couldn't stop thinking about Bobbie, who'd wandered out there for hours during the night, alone and tormented, hallucinating people who weren't there. The poison in her blood had driven her to stumble across the island before she fell, hands scrabbling for purchase, onto the unforgiving stone ledge by the sea. If her friends had realised in time that she was missing, they could've gone after her. They might have been able to talk some sense into her. Maybe even bring her back to safety.

Throughout the night, Lyndsey's sleep had been disturbed. She'd heard Val get up to tend to Amanda. Had she also heard Bobbie get up, but then dismissed it as nothing? Perhaps if Lyndsey had been sober, she would've awakened fully, and realised in time that Bobbie had gone outside. She could've saved her.

Lyndsey took her coat off and wrapped it around Val to keep the rain off her. 'I'm going to find Amanda,' Lyndsey said to Juliet. 'Stay here and look after Val.'

Juliet shook her head in mute disgust, but she didn't try to talk her out of it again.

Chapter Thirty-Two

SATURDAY

7:40pm

As she set off across the field, heading south, Lyndsey could feel the warmth of the burning building on her cheek, even from such a distance away. Glowing sparks fluttered up into the sky, only to be extinguished by the rain. Smoke was leaking out from between the tiles of the roof. It wouldn't be long until the whole building collapsed.

Thin trails of smoke were finding their way out from the stonework of the observatory as well. Lyndsey had hoped the fire might stay contained to the bunkhouse. But without anyone to put out the blaze, there was no way to keep it confined. The observatory would burn as well. Lyndsey's heart broke for Marne, who was about to lose her home and everything in it, and who wasn't even there to prevent it, because she'd dived into the sea to save a woman she barely knew.

Lyndsey tried to push herself into a jog, but her lungs ached too much. Even walking too fast caused painful spasms in her chest. She'd almost drowned then almost suffocated. After so much trauma, it was a wonder she could breathe at all.

At the edge of the field, she stopped to listen, but all she heard was wind and waves and the continued roar of the fire. There was no sign of anyone.

'Amanda!' she yelled. The wind tore her words away from her.

Where would she go?

Lacking solid options, Lyndsey set off down the track that led to the southern harbour. Her steps felt like lead. The heat of the fire had left her face feeling scalded and raw, and, although at first she was grateful for the coolness of the rain, soon the residual warmth leached out of her again, and she was left shivering and unhappy. The rain soaked through her hoodie within minutes. She pulled the hood up over her head, on top of the head torch she still wore, shuddering at the touch of the chill fabric against her ears.

She was no longer sure she'd made the smart decision, leaving her waterproof jacket with Val. Val's need had been greater, she'd reasoned. Without the extra warmth, Val might go into shock. But now, with the cold needling her, Lyndsey regretted the action. It was a struggle just to keep walking. The front of her hoodie was heavy from the stuff she'd forgotten to take out of the pocket.

She lifted her head and saw a stone finger pointing up from the earth in the distance. *The old lighthouse.*

The courtyard around it would provide a shelter of sorts. Would Amanda go there, seeking safety from the weather? It would depend how confused her mind really was. She might've seen it as a beacon, drawing her back, even after her accident yesterday.

Lyndsey set off down the track as fast as she could, which wasn't much faster than a painful hobble. Pain sang through her chest.

When she next raised her head, she happened to look up at the top of the lighthouse, at exactly the right time to see a flash of light. She stopped. The flash came again. It was the beam of a torch, struggling to be seen through the rain.

Someone's up there on the gallery deck.

Lyndsey hurried down the path and followed the narrow trail that led to the lighthouse. The ground was slick and wet underfoot. More than once she almost fell. She looked up a couple more times but didn't see the torch at the top of the lighthouse again.

When she reached the outer wall, she ducked gratefully through the stone doorway into the relative shelter of the courtyard. The dark shadow of the lighthouse loomed over her. Here, protected from the brunt of the wind, Lyndsey stood for a moment, listening to the rain pattering off the gorse and brambles. The air smelled wild, full of soot and salt.

She made her way around to the lighthouse door. If someone had got inside, they would've had to smash the padlock, she figured. But when she got there, she found the padlock opened neatly, and the door standing ajar.

So whoever was up there had the key. Lyndsey had been led to believe that the only key was in Juliet's possession – but she didn't know for certain if that was true. It was possible someone else had a key. Marne, for example, might have had one on that big keyring of hers. Or Juliet could've left her copy lying around in the bunkhouse somewhere, like she'd done with the keyring.

Lyndsey pushed the door open. 'Amanda?' she called.

No answer. Lyndsey took a cautious step inside.

The interior was as dank and musty as she remembered. Now, it was also loud. She would've thought the thick walls would dampen the noise of the weather, but somehow it amplified the eerie moan of the wind. Lyndsey was still wearing her headtorch, so she shone the beam across the empty floor, then towards the stone steps.

There were wet footprints on the lowermost steps. The prints weren't clear enough to make out any details. They could've belonged to anyone. But they overlapped – which meant at least two sets of feet. Both leading upwards.

'Amanda?' Lyndsey called. 'It's me. Lyndsey. Are you up there?'

In response, she heard a woman's laugh. It was high and trilling, and the wind smothered it before Lyndsey could be certain she'd definitely heard it.

It froze her in place. It hadn't sounded like Amanda. It'd sounded like her sister, Cherry.

Lyndsey edged into the lighthouse. She lifted her torch beam. It struggled to reach the top of the stairs that wound their way up the inside wall of the lighthouse. The batteries were failing. Lyndsey could only hope they'd last long enough for her to—

At the very top of the stairs, in the doorway that led to the gallery deck, she caught a glimpse of something green. It was there and gone so quickly it could've been a trick of the eye. Or a reflection of something outside.

'Amanda,' Lyndsey said, but there was no strength behind the word, and her voice didn't carry.

She started up the stairs.

It felt like it was a lot longer than yesterday lunchtime when she'd last climbed these steps. She remembered the whole group ascending for their abseil, with Juliet in the lead and Val at the back, everyone strung together on a safety line because Juliet had worried about how sturdy the guard rail was. They'd laughed and joked with nervous energy, their voices bouncing off the interior walls of the lighthouse. Lyndsey had been in the middle then, with friends before her and after her. Now, she felt their absence all the more keenly. In her head, she heard the echo of their voices.

She wished she could've saved Bobbie's life. She wished she could've somehow stopped Sonia going into the sea, and Marne going after her. She wished she'd got Val out of the building quicker. There was a good chance that all three of those friends might die before rescue arrived. The thought made a sob build in Lyndsey's throat.

She didn't know if she'd be in time to save Amanda. But she had to try.

Lyndsey drew what little strength remained to her as she

mounted the stairs. She kept her torch beam stubbornly in front of her, pausing every twenty steps to catch her breath and glance upwards. There was no repeat of the eerie laugh, or the glimpse of green fabric. All she could hear was the wind. Even that was almost drowned out by the hammering of her heart.

As she neared the top, the sound of the weather changed, incorporating the surge and smash of waves against rock from the coastline far below. The roar of noise made Lyndsey dizzy. She forced herself not to look down.

At last, the doorway to the gallery deck was in front of her. Lyndsey hesitated. She had no idea who was up here. It might not even be Amanda. It could be someone else, luring her into a trap at the top of this desolate building.

What would she do if Amanda wasn't here? Or if it was someone else? Lyndsey was in no state to fight. Right at that moment, she wasn't even sure she could talk her way out of trouble, since she was so out of breath.

They know you're here. You've not exactly been stealthy. All you can do is walk in and see what's waiting for you.

Lyndsey steadied herself, then went up the last few steps to the doorway.

The storm was like a living presence up there. It rattled the old glass in its frames, and sent rain lashing against the concrete balcony where, just yesterday, Lyndsey and her friends had started their abseil. The wind blew flurries of rain into the gallery deck through the balcony door and every broken window. All across the floor were puddles of water, collecting in each imperfection in the concrete. If Lyndsey had really wanted to, she could've crossed to the balcony and seen the ocean tearing itself to pieces against the coastline below.

Off to her right were the rusty remains of the old machinery that'd operated this lighthouse. On the floor in front was the steel belay point. Shards of glass from the broken windows glinted in the light from her torch. To Lyndsey's left—

The shadows were darker over there, away from the windows and the open door. From memory, she couldn't think that there'd been anything interesting stored there. More dust and rusted bits of machinery. Her torchlight reflected back off more pieces of broken glass. And something else. A glimmer of light moss-coloured fabric, in the depths of the shadows.

A blast of cold air snaked through the gallery deck. It made the fabric move, like someone dancing. Lyndsey took a step closer.

'Who's there?' she asked. Her voice wasn't as loud or as strong as she'd hoped.

Her boots crunched on glass shards. The gallery deck was thick with the smell of salt and rusted metal. The same smell as blood, Lyndsey realised. Beneath that, Lyndsey could smell smoke – but she was certain that it was just the stink of her own clothes, or the singed hair in her sinuses. Everything would smell of smoke to her from that point onwards, possibly forever.

The green dress – she knew in her gut it was a dress – glimmered like a beacon in her torch light. Whoever wore it was right at the very back of the room, where the shadows were deepest. The hem of the dress stopped an inch short of the ground. Lyndsey couldn't see any shoes beneath it.

She kicked off her shoes so she could paddle in the surf.

Lyndsey shook her head. Cherry was dead; ten years dead. This wasn't her. It was just Lyndsey's over-stressed brain panicking and misfiring.

It's amazing what a guilty conscience can do.

Unwillingly, Lyndsey raised her head so the torch tracked up the dress to where the person's shoulders and head should've been.

There was nothing there. The dress hung empty. A piece of wire was attached to the shoulder straps and looped over an old brass hook in the ceiling. Every so often, a strong gust of wind would catch the fabric and make it move, giving the illusion that someone was wearing it.

Lyndsey swallowed her pulse. She made herself go up to the dress so she could see it clearly. More than anything, she hoped for reassurance that it wasn't a dress at all, but some other bit of fabric that her mind had misinterpreted. Another faded tarpaulin, perhaps. An old curtain. Anything.

As she got closer, her heart started to hammer again. The fabric was definitely a dress. Worse yet, she was almost certain it was *the* dress. The same one that Cherry had worn on the night she died. Lyndsey recognised the missing rhinestones from the neckline, and a tear at the hem where Val had accidentally trodden on it. In the photos at the inquest, the dress had been dirty and scuffed from Cherry lying on the beach all night, but the worst stains were gone now, although the fabric was still rumpled.

Lyndsey reached out to touch the skirt. She wanted the reassurance that it was definitely real, not just some trick of her brain.

There was a noise behind her. A crunch of someone putting their weight on the shards of glass underfoot.

Lyndsey turned to find Amanda behind her.

Chapter Thirty-Three

SATURDAY

8:00pm

'It was your fault,' Amanda said. The light from the doorway was behind her, hiding her features. 'You killed her.'

Lyndsey's brain stalled. She remembered Amanda saying the same thing, right after she pushed Sonia into the sea. 'Amanda—'

'All of you killed her. You were in on it together.'

'Amanda – I – I didn't kill Bobbie. None of us did. It's—'

'Not her.' Amanda lifted her head as if looking past Lyndsey. 'Cherry.'

Lyndsey resisted the urge to look at the dress behind her. She raised her failing torch beam so she could see Amanda's face. The woman flinched.

'Get that light out of my face,' Amanda said.

The edge in her voice made Lyndsey comply immediately. She snatched the torch off her head, holding it instead pointed at their feet. The reflected beam gave her just enough light to see Amanda. She was holding something cradled in her arms.

'Amanda,' Lyndsey said again, but then she faltered. What the hell could she say? 'What's going on? Are you okay?'

'You all forgot about her.'

This time, Lyndsey did look behind her. The green dress was still empty. But the way Amanda was staring had made Lyndsey think, just for a second, that it wasn't.

'We didn't forget Cherry,' Lyndsey said. 'We remember her all the time.'

'No, you don't. You never talk about her. To you, she's just a bad memory, something you don't want to be reminded of.'

'That's not true.'

'It was the anniversary this year. The tenth anniversary.'

Lyndsey winced. She'd remembered, but only an hour ago. The actual date had slipped past without her noticing. 'I know,' she said.

'Do you? Not one of you messaged or called to check in on me that day. My mum lit a candle, and that was it. That was all the remembering I was allowed to do. No one wants to talk about Cherry anymore.' Amanda shook her head in the darkness. 'And then, the very next day, Juliet texted me, to remind me I needed to pay her the deposit for this weekend retreat. *That's* what she contacted me for.'

'I'm sorry.' Lyndsey wracked her brain for the exact date of Cherry's death. It was in June sometime, she knew that. What had she been doing on the anniversary, when she should've been thinking of her friends? Probably nothing. Sitting alone, feeling sorry for herself, drinking. Counting the hours until she could go to sleep and then restart the whole process again.

Lyndsey would've expected at least one of her friends to remember, though. Juliet never forgot anyone's birthday, and Val probably had everyone's important dates written down in a word document somewhere. There must have been *something* on social media about it, from Cherry's university friends if no one else, but obviously Lyndsey hadn't bothered to check.

'I'm sorry,' she said again, knowing how inadequate it was. 'We should've been there for you.'

She took a step towards Amanda, one hand held out as a peace offering. Lyndsey knew she needed to tread carefully. She didn't know whether Amanda was thinking clearly right at that moment. It certainly didn't sound like it. But, if they could talk it out, then –

Amanda flinched away from her, and at the same time there was a loud *crack*, which sounded like she'd put her heel down on a large fragment of glass. Something poked Lyndsey hard in the stomach, like a disembodied finger from nowhere. It was so unexpected it made her stumble backwards.

Chill wetness flowed down her stomach and over the top of her thighs.

Lyndsey put a hand to the front of her hoodie; felt liquid soaking the fabric. She raised her shocked eyes to Amanda.

Too late, she recognised the bulky item that Amanda carried. Amanda had kept her arms around it, disguising the tell-tale glint of metal in the torchlight, but now she held it steady in both hands. It was the air rifle that Lyndsey had found in the rocky shelter that afternoon and stupidly brought back to the bunkhouse. Amanda must've taken it with her before the fire.

Lyndsey dropped her torch. She fell back another step and her left leg folded beneath her. As she collapsed, she flailed out with her hand, desperate for something to stop her fall. Her fingers tangled in the soft fabric of the green dress. The stitches in the shoulder gave way and Lyndsey hit the floor, pulling the dress with her.

There was no pain, not yet. Her stomach was frozen. Liquid continued to soak through her clothing, so much that she felt it drip to the floor. *An air rifle pellet shouldn't do so much damage*, her brain insisted. But apparently it had. Lyndsey tried to press her hand down on the wound, but her fingers flinched away from the cold wetness. She still couldn't feel anything. That had to be bad. She was so deep in shock already that her nerves had gone numb.

She curled on her side around her injury. The movement caused a scraping noise, like jagged bone shards. No, that couldn't be right, that couldn't be right at all. There was nothing but soft, squishy flesh around her abdomen. Nothing should make that noise.

Her searching fingers touched the front of her hoodie

again. Something shifted beneath her hand. It felt like broken glass.

The bottle in her front pocket. If there'd been any breath in her lungs, Lyndsey would've laughed with sheer relief. She'd been carrying the half-bottle of whisky around all afternoon, and had gotten so used to its weight that she'd forgotten it was there. She breathed in. The sharp stink of alcohol confirmed her suspicions.

She opened her eyes to find Amanda standing over her. The dropped headtorch cast a weak, fitful beam of light upwards at the pitted ceiling. As she watched, Amanda cracked open the air rifle and loaded another pellet, with an ease that suggested she'd done it many times before.

Get up. Quickly, before she's done reloading. But Lyndsey couldn't force herself to move. The shock of thinking she'd been shot, of thinking she was dying, had overloaded her brain. Right at that moment, she could do nothing but lie there, blinking stupidly.

'Is that your rifle?' Lyndsey said. She was surprised to find her voice sounded almost normal. 'Did you leave it in the shelter near the beach?'

'I needed to reconnoitre the island.' Amanda snapped the weapon closed. 'Setting up a cache seemed like a prudent idea, in case I needed to come back more than once.'

'Bet you weren't expecting the warden to come along and talk to you.'

Amanda grimaced. 'No. I could've done without that. It meant I couldn't risk her recognising me when we arrived this weekend.'

Marne was telling the truth. We should've listened to her. 'Is that why you faked your accident? So you could hide in your bunk all day?' It was the only explanation Lyndsey could think of for why Amanda was no longer limping. The accident hadn't been real.

'One of the reasons,' Amanda admitted. 'I also wanted to be left alone in the bunkhouse as much as possible. It gave me plenty of time to do my own thing.'

'I can't believe you would cut your own rope on an abseil. You could've died.'

Amanda's expression darkened. 'Yeah, well, there wouldn't have been any risk if Juliet had been holding the safety line properly, like she should've been. When the rope gave way, she should've caught me. We did dozens of climbs together when we were teenagers. I can't believe she would be so careless. Honestly, I expected the rope to give way while I was higher up. I'd cut almost all the way through it. I was looking for drama, not for Juliet to actually let me fall.'

Lyndsey shook her head in amazement. Now she knew she wasn't dying, she slid her fingers under the hem of her hoodie, searching for broken skin. She found a tender place where the pellet had struck her, but its force had been deflected by the glass bottle. By tomorrow, she would have a hefty bruise, but nothing worse.

The thought stopped her. She suddenly realised she might not be alive tomorrow to see the bruise appear.

She curled up tighter as fear pulled at all her muscles. With a jolt, she realised the green dress was puddled on the floor right next to her, half pinned down by her body. She instinctively flinched away from it. *Cherry's dress*. She was certain now that it was the same one Cherry had been wearing the night she died. It must've been given back to the family after the inquest. Of course, that raised the question of why Amanda had kept it, and why she'd brought it all the way out here to the island. The thought that it must've been in Amanda's bag all weekend, packed neatly in with her socks and T-shirts, gave Lyndsey a queasy sensation in her stomach.

She'd planned all this.

'Amanda,' Lyndsey asked, 'what happened to Bobbie?'

'There was poison in her water bottle. I filled it up for her before we left home, yesterday morning.'

The casual way she said it chilled Lyndsey to the bone. 'Why?'

'Why do you think?'

Lyndsey closed her eyes. She tried to muster her strength. Amanda was standing quite close, just a few feet away. Could Lyndsey move fast enough to disarm her? It was difficult to think when her mind was in a whirl. Lyndsey couldn't get past the simple, awful fact that Amanda had killed Bobbie, for no reason that she could possibly think of.

'I don't know,' Lyndsey said. 'I have literally no idea.'

'Yeah, you do.' Amanda stepped a little closer. 'Bobbie helped kill my sister.'

'Cherry's death was an accident.' Lyndsey felt an instinctive guilty flinch as she said it. She'd repeated those words to herself so many times over the years that it'd become an instinctive mantra. *It was an accident; just a tragic accident.*

'I spent ten years telling myself the same thing,' Amanda said. *'It was an accident. No one could've prevented it.* But I know the truth now. I found out earlier this year that it wasn't an accident at all.'

'Amanda, you weren't even there. You don't—'

'That's the point, isn't it? I had to go home early, but it was okay, because you lot promised you'd look after Cherry for me. You'd keep an eye on her and make sure she got home safe. Those were Bobbie's exact words. *We'll get her home safe.'*

Lyndsey shook her head carefully. The pool of alcohol around her lower half was cold, as was the concrete floor beneath her shoulder. The fabric of Cherry's dress was close enough to scratch her cheek. She couldn't keep lying there forever. Sooner or later, Amanda would catch on to the fact that Lyndsey wasn't actually injured. Lyndsey had to do something before then.

'You could've stopped Cherry from drinking at any time that night,' Amanda said. 'When you saw how drunk she was, you could've stopped her, put her in a taxi, and got her home, like you promised you would. You literally could've saved her life.'

Yes. Lyndsey knew it was true. She'd always known that Cherry's death had been a group act, a group failing, a group tragedy.

And they *had* tried, hadn't they? Lyndsey remembered Juliet in tears at the inquest as she described how they'd been thrown out of the nightclub because Cherry was too drunk and too disruptive. None of the taxis would take them. If they'd stayed out there on the street, trying and failing to convince a taxi to drive them home, the night would've ended with Cherry being arrested for, at the very least, being drunk and incapable. So, they'd made the decision to go somewhere quiet and give everyone time to cool down.

We didn't know what would happen. But that was an excuse that was only useful in hindsight.

'It was Bobbie's idea to go to the beach that night,' Amanda said. 'It was her fault that Cherry ended up there. Bobbie was the one who promised me she'd look after Cherry, and instead, she convinced you all to go the beach and keep drinking.'

Lyndsey remembered that detail coming out at the inquest, but honestly, she herself couldn't have sworn to it. A lot of that evening was mercifully lost to her.

'I suppose it weighed on Bobbie's conscience,' Amanda said. 'Just like it should've weighed on yours too. Ten years is a long time to carry that much guilt around.'

Carefully, Lyndsey rolled over a little, so she could see Amanda. It turned out to be a mistake, because it meant she could also see the air rifle. It was pointed at Lyndsey's eyes.

Amanda laughed. It was a high, brittle sound, and it put ice into Lyndsey's veins. *She sounds just like her sister.* Lyndsey had never heard Amanda laugh like that. Had she practised, alone and in private, attempting to recreate that one distinctive part of Cherry?

'It's not a great weapon, is it?' Amanda said, hefting the air rifle. 'I really hoped I could find something better. But it'll do the job, I think. It'll put a hole in a tin can at a distance of ten feet. It should be able to do the same to you, if I hit a tender spot, like the eyes or the roof of your mouth.'

Lyndsey clamped her mouth shut. The calculated note in Amanda's voice was chilling.

'What'll that achieve?' Lyndsey managed to ask. 'It's not going to bring Cherry back.'

'No, of course not. But I've been thinking about this, y'know, a lot. I've had plenty of time to consider it over the last few months, since I learned the truth. At first, I couldn't work out who I blamed most. Bobbie led my sister to the beach where she died. Sonia brought along the bottle of vodka that killed her. You kept pouring drink into her, even after she was down.'

Lyndsey froze. 'How did you—?' She couldn't finish her sentence.

It was one of few memories that'd survived that awful night. One she'd never mentioned to anyone.

'Why the hell am I even here with you lot?' Cherry had asked, for what might've been the second or third or twelfth time.

'Sit down, will ya?' Watching her stagger about was making Lyndsey dizzy. She looked behind her. Sonia was sitting with her back to a rock, eyes closed, a cigarette burning dangerously low to her fingers. Further up the beach, Bobbie and Juliet were huddled together, near the tiny fire they'd built, laughing about something or nothing. Val was perched on a rock next to Sonia, staring off at the sea as if entranced.

Cherry at last flopped down next to Lyndsey. 'I hate you all,' Cherry had said, but she'd laughed as she said it, so Lyndsey had

replied, 'Hate you too, bitch,' and that had sent them both into
giggles. They'd wound up lying on their backs, with pebbles
digging into their backs, giggling at the stars.

As it subsided, Lyndsey reached over Cherry's supine body to
grab the vodka bottle. It was nearly empty. She took a last swig,
then tipped the last couple of shots into Cherry's mouth, even
though she couldn't have been sure if Cherry was awake or not.

'Bobbie told me,' Amanda said.

Lyndsey could only blink stupidly at her. 'Bobbie—?'

'She contacted me in February and said she had to talk
to me about something. Apparently, Val had been raking
over the past with her, and it'd stirred up a lot of memories
that Bobbie wanted to *process*. She contacted me to air her
conscience. For her own sake, I'm sure, not mine.'

Lyndsey was still struggling to get her head around
everything. 'Bobbie didn't remember anything from that
night,' she said. 'She'd just been started on strong
antihistamines for her allergies, and she wasn't supposed to
be drinking. It took out whole chunks of her memories.'

'That's what she told the inquest, yeah. Turns out she
lied. Our dear, sweet Bobbie told a lie under oath, and stuck
with it. As it happens, she apparently remembered quite a
lot more than she told anyone. She just didn't want to make
it public, because she knew it'd point the finger of blame at
her friends. But the truth always comes out, doesn't it? She
contacted me, and told me everything, then begged for my
forgiveness.' Something flickered across Amanda's
expression. 'Ten years, you all kept the truth from me. You
all lied.'

'Amanda, I don't know what Bobbie said, but—'

'But I should've waited to hear everyone's side of the story first, right? That's the only reason why I agreed to come on this trip. To find out what you'd all kept from me.' Amanda shook her head angrily. 'Not only did you lie, you *conspired* not to tell me.'

'No, that's not—'

'Don't bother. Val confirmed it all.'

'Val?'

Amanda's mouth twisted. 'She's planning to write a book about it. Did you know that? A whole book about Cherry's last tragic night. She's put together a document full of character details about all of you. You were going to be characters in her new masterpiece, whether you liked it or not. She talked about it with Bobbie. Dragged up all the past. I guess Bobbie thought she ought to tell me the actual truth at last, before I found out about it second-hand. Eventually, I was able to confirm it from Val as well.' She grimaced. 'Of course, she *had* to write it all down, didn't she? Val was nothing if not thorough.'

Val's laptop. All her worldly work would've been on there, and Sonia had proved it was easy enough to look through the saved documents. Amanda had been alone in the bunkhouse all day. She would've had ample time to read anything she liked.

'It was a group effort that killed my sister,' Amanda said. 'None of you were innocent. But Bobbie was the only one who hated her. She never forgave Cherry for *stealing* Darren away from her in high school. I should've realised it was too stupidly convenient how Bobbie ended up getting together with him so soon after Cherry died.'

'Bobbie would've never—'

'Yes, she would. She admitted she hated Cherry. That's why she got you all to go out to that beach and keep drinking, even though Cherry could barely stand.' Amanda shifted her weight. 'I wanted Bobbie to be the first one to go. I'd hoped a couple more of you would've gone the same way, but you all got suspicious too fast. A suitable dose of poison in your alcohol seemed like a sure bet. Appropriate too.'

Lyndsey remembered the bottle Sonia had accidentally smashed on the kitchen floor. It made her sweat to think of how close she'd come. She balled up her fists, and the green fabric scrunched beneath her. 'Was it you I saw?' she asked, faintly. 'Were you up on the cliffs in this dress?'

'Ah, I'm glad you saw me. I've been following you idiots around the island all day, hoping you'd catch a glimpse of me. I wanted to prod your consciences.' Amanda's gaze switched to the crumpled dress. 'It seemed appropriate to bring it here. I've carried it everywhere with me for the last six months.'

'You were planning to kill us all,' Lyndsey said. The idea filled her brain, leaving no room for thought.

'Some, all, whatever.' Amanda lifted her shoulders in a shrug. 'I had no definite plan after Bobbie. I figured fate and improvisation would see me through. And it has. Did you manage to get Sonia out of the sea in time? Or is she long gone? How about Val? I saw you drag her out of the bunkhouse. Do you think she'll pull through?'

Neither of us know for sure. They could all be dead by now. Lyndsey tried to bury the thought. She let her lips curl in disgust at Amanda's tone. There wasn't an ounce of remorse there. Amanda genuinely would've been happy if they'd died.

'What about Juliet?' Lyndsey asked. 'What about me?'

'Juliet's doomed herself. She lied to get us all here, to an isolated spot where no one can help us, just because she was so, so desperate to fix everyone's problems and make us all be best friends again. She lied about her break-up and about the weather report. She was Bobbie's closest friend, the one she trusted most. She'll be the first one the police want to question.'

'You'll let them blame her for Bobbie's death?'

'I'm going to let it play out however it likes. Juliet's done a great job of setting herself up. And if there was any evidence to the contrary—' Another loose shrug. 'Well, it all inconveniently got destroyed in the fire at the bunkhouse.'

Lyndsey kept shaking her head, stubbornly. 'It'll be her word against yours.'

'And that's all it'll need to be. There's far more circumstantial evidence against her than me. At the very least, her life will be hell for the considerable future, as she gets dragged through the fallout from all this. Maybe then she'll know how I felt.'

'They'll never believe it. Juliet loved Bobbie.'

'You all loved Cherry, too, or at least you said you did, and you were still careless enough to kill her.'

Slowly, Lyndsey started to sit up. She kept one hand to her stomach to maintain the illusion that she was hurt. 'What about me?' Lyndsey was scared to ask. She thought she might know the answer.

'You and Juliet were in it together. We've all seen you whispering in secret this weekend. Not hard to believe you came up with a murder plot between you.' Amanda took a step back, putting herself out of Lyndsey's reach. 'Of course, you've probably guessed you won't be there in person to contradict my story.'

Lyndsey lashed out with her foot, aiming a kick at Amanda's shin. Amanda jumped back. The kick only skimmed her leg. Lyndsey surged to her feet.

There was another crack as the rifle went off. Something hit Lyndsey's cheekbone. This time she felt the pain – a hot sear of heat across her face. For a moment she was blinded. But she was already moving. She flung herself at Amanda.

Amanda tried to club her with the rifle. It struck Lyndsey's shoulder and glanced off. The blow didn't slow Lyndsey. She grabbed for the rifle with both hands.

Again, Amanda was slightly too fast for her. Lyndsey's left hand got hold of the barrel of the rifle but her right hand slipped as she tried to grab a fistful of Amanda's sleeve.

Rather than try to wrench the weapon away from her, Lyndsey shoved Amanda with all her strength. Taken by surprise, Amanda stumbled back. Glass snapped under their feet.

Lyndsey hooked a foot behind Amanda's ankle and they both fell. Lyndsey landed on top, Amanda letting out a yelp as the breath was forced from her lungs. The air rifle was pinned between them. Lyndsey couldn't give Amanda an opportunity to reload it. She struggled to her knees and grabbed the rifle. She tried to snatch it away, but Amanda clung on tightly.

Then, abruptly, Amanda let go. It was so sudden that Lyndsey fell backwards and sat down hard. Pain jolted up her spine. She was still half-blind, only able to see Amanda as a blur in the shadowy light, but she twisted away from her and scrabbled to her feet.

Lyndsey could barely see out of her right eye. Pain held it closed. When she forced it open, her vision was watery and vague. The pellet from the air rifle ... where had it hit her? Had it put out her eye?

Lyndsey reached a hand up to her face, as close as she dared to her blinded eye, and felt wetness on her cheek. She couldn't tell if it was blood or the contents of her eyeball leaking out. The pain flared outwards, spearing through her whole head. Was the pellet lodged in her skull? Had it poked a knitting-needle-sized hole into her brain? She didn't dare touch the wound itself, because she dreaded what her fingertips might find.

Lyndsey staggered towards the brightest part of the room. She knew that must be where the door to the balcony was. Through her blurred vision, she saw the doorway and aimed for it. Fresh air blew into her face.

As soon as she got close enough, she coiled her arm, then flung the air rifle outside. It clipped the doorframe and clattered across the balcony before it went spinning off the edge and vanished. She listened for the thump of it hitting the ground far below.

There. Relief flowed through Lyndsey. She'd eliminated the most dangerous element in the room. Now—

With a screech, Amanda flew at her and knocked her to the ground. Lyndsey couldn't react in time to catch herself. Her elbow and knee struck the floor hard. She tried to roll away but Amanda landed on her, crushing the air from her lungs.

Something bit into Lyndsey's waist, just above her hip, pain sharp enough to make her cry out. She lashed out with her numb arm. More by luck than judgement, the blade of her hand smacked Amanda across the bridge of the nose. Amanda jerked away from the blow. Lyndsey took advantage and shoved her off.

Get up. You're an easy target on the floor.

Some kind of deeply buried instinct pushed Lyndsey to her feet again. She had never been in a fight, not even at school, not even a play-fight. She had no idea what she was supposed to do or how to defend herself. All she could think to do was fling up her arms in case Amanda came at her again.

High above the lighthouse, lightning split the sky. It was so bright it burned out Lyndsey's vision for a moment. When she blinked, all she could see were dancing afterimages.

She put a hand to her side and felt warm wetness pulse beneath her fingers. It felt significantly different to when the bottle in her pocket had shattered.

'You stabbed me,' she said to Amanda. Sheer surprise pushed out every other emotion. 'You *stabbed* me.'

'Come over here,' Amanda said from somewhere in the shadows. 'I'll do it again.'

'Look, just – we can talk about this, okay? It'll be just like

377

you said. You can tell the police your side, and Juliet can tell them hers.' Lyndsey had to force the words out through the pain that was radiating up through her ribs and down into her hip. 'No one else has to get hurt.'

'I'm going to tell them you attacked me,' Amanda said. Where the hell was she? She must've known Lyndsey couldn't see properly. 'Everything I did here was in self-defence.'

'Fine. Let's go with that. I agree completely.'

Feeling faint, Lyndsey checked the injury to her flank. It'd cut through her hoodie and torn a deep gash in her flesh. A knife … where had Amanda got a knife from? There were none in the bunkhouse. With a lurch, Lyndsey realised Amanda must've had it on her this whole time. How else could she have cut through the abseiling rope yesterday?

The feel of warm blood against her gloved hands made her want to throw up. 'Like you say,' Lyndsey called, 'it's for the police to decide, right? So, let's just wait for them to get here, yeah?'

'They'll be here soon, you know. If you'd all been smart, you would've set fire to the bunkhouse hours ago.'

'What?'

'It's one giant beacon. People are going to see that fire for miles. And no one's going to mistake it for a bonfire or someone burning gorse. They will have raised the alarm as soon as they saw the flames.'

Lyndsey hadn't thought of that. 'None of us wanted to burn our stuff, Amanda.'

'Why not? It's just *stuff*. I thought everyone's lives were more important than that. You wouldn't even have had to burn the building. You could've just made a bonfire out in the field.'

'It's a little late in the day for you to suggest these things. If you wanted to raise the alarm, why didn't you help us?'

Amanda laughed again, that high, brittle laugh. The sound echoed through the empty space. Lyndsey was having a hard time pinpointing exactly where Amanda was in the room. She kept blinking in the hope her vision would clear. Her cheek and her flank needled her.

'I didn't want to help you,' Amanda said. 'I wanted to see how you all reacted when the pressure set in. Would you close ranks, like you did after you murdered Cherry? Or would you turn immediately on each other? I shouldn't have been surprised by the result. None of you wanted to help anyone else. Look at you – you can't even help yourself.'

Another roll of thunder concussed the room. Lyndsey still couldn't be entirely sure where Amanda was. The woman kept moving, and the sound of her feet was disguised by the noise of the storm.

One way to find out.

Lyndsey set off across the floor towards the exit. The sight in her right eye was still blurry; her left eye was clear but wouldn't stop watering. She could just make out the doorway that led to the stairs. It was a dark rectangle in front of her. She wished she still had her headtorch, but it was lost somewhere in the shadows.

As soon as she started moving, she heard Amanda's footsteps rushing at her. Lyndsey turned her head in time to see Amanda come charging out of the darkness. Her hand was raised, gripped around something that glinted in the meagre light – a sturdy lock-knife with a four-inch blade.

She saw all those details in the frozen instant. Amanda led with the weapon, bringing it across in a vicious slash that was aimed for Lyndsey's throat, but that meant Lyndsey was able to see it coming and dodge. She ducked under Amanda's swinging arm and sprinted for the door.

Halfway there, she realised her mistake. The long, winding stairs down to the exit were steep and treacherous, even at the best of times. If she tried to take them at a run, she'd almost certainly fall, and it was a long way down to the unforgiving floor at the bottom.

What other option do you have?

She grabbed the doorframe and used it to swing herself onto the stairs. Her other hand found the rusted railing.

There was hardly any light in there. Lyndsey couldn't see the steps in front of her. The centre of the lighthouse was a pitch-black hole that went down forever. Right at the bottom, so far away it made her sick, was the scrap of pale light that seeped in through the open door. The noise of the storm echoed through the space like a continuous roar.

You'll never make it. The thought froze Lyndsey to the spot. She knew she had to move but she *couldn't*. If she did, she would fall and die. The darkness below yawned like the depths of the sea, waiting for her.

Then Amanda crashed into her back. She hadn't expected Lyndsey to stop right there, right at the top of the stairs, and had run full tilt through the doorway.

The impact knocked Lyndsey forwards. She collided

with the railing, which shrieked its protest. For one horrifying instant, she thought it would give way. She pushed herself off it, her other arm striking the stone wall as she stumbled down the stairs.

Amanda was off-balance. She tried to swing the knife at Lyndsey but missed. The momentum caused her to trip on the dark steps.

Lyndsey had only just recovered her own balance when Amanda slammed into her for the second time. This time there was no way for her to stay on her feet. Lyndsey fell hard against the railing, clutching it with both hands, and felt it sag beneath her weight.

There was an instant of weightlessness. Of falling. With a scream of rusted metal, the railing gave way. Lyndsey pitched forwards into the darkness. She cried out as she fell.

It was only her death-grip on the metal railing that saved her. She swung out over the drop, her legs kicking wildly at empty air. Her arms were almost pulled from their sockets. The railing creaked and groaned, but it was still anchored somewhere above her. Flakes of rust pattered against her face.

The interior of the lighthouse echoed with a long, drawn-out wail. Lyndsey thought it was her. It was only when the sound cut off abruptly that she looked up and realised.

Through the dim light and her watering eyes, she could just see the steps leading up to the doorway. They were empty. Amanda wasn't there.

Chapter Thirty-Four

SATURDAY

8:15pm

Afterwards, Lyndsey would have no memory of how she hauled herself back up onto the stone steps. She would've sworn that she didn't have the strength in her body to do even a single pull-up. But adrenaline and abject terror apparently worked wonders. She managed to pull herself up high enough to swing her legs onto the stone steps and, from there, claw her way to safety.

The first clear memory she had was of lying on the steps with her cheek pressed to the cold stone. She was shuddering and crying. Each breath hitched in her chest. There were deep pools of hurt in her stomach, in the side of her face, all the way up both her arms, and throughout her lungs. It was easier to catalogue the bits of her that *didn't* hurt.

The noise of the storm outside seemed to match her heartbeat. A steady pulsing beat that made her head ache. She lay still, in the hope that it would fade, but if anything it seemed to be getting louder.

At length, she made herself move, just enough so she could peer down over the edge of the steps.

Far below her, just discernible in the last traces of daylight that edged through the open door down there, something lay on the floor. It might, with a little imagination, have been a person. The most visible part was the blonde hair, which was a smudge in the darkness. When Lyndsey saw that, she had to close her eyes until her dizziness passed.

She lay there for some time. The noise of the storm increased, still at that steady rhythm, until Lyndsey at last raised her head. The sound was too steady, too regular.

It wasn't just her imagination, or the pulse of blood in her head. Something else was producing that noise.

She couldn't find the strength to walk all the way down the steps, in the dark, knowing that she would have to step right past Amanda's shattered body in order to get out. The idea made her chest tighten to the point of panic. Instead, she slowly crawled upwards, one stone step at a time, her hands clinging for purchase like she was drowning.

At the top, she made herself stand, even though it felt like the floor was pitching like the deck of a ship. She limped across to the doorway that led to the concrete balcony. She was aware she'd left trails of blood droplets all across the floor.

As she stepped outside, wind and rain lashed her face. It felt almost comforting. She was glad she was alive to feel it. The thrumming noise reverberated through her chest.

Off to her left, a bright light speared through the twilight. It was pointed away from her, illuminating a chunk of land near the bunkhouse, dancing over the wind-tossed bracken. It came from the powerful searchlight of a helicopter. As Lyndsey watched, the helicopter descended, to make a delicate landing in one of the fields. The downdraft of its rotors flattened the grass.

Lyndsey shielded her eyes against the glare. She couldn't quite see the bunkhouse from that angle, but she saw the glow and flicker of the fire which was still burning fiercely. A figure ran across the grass towards the helicopter, stopping a safe distance from the rotors, waving their hands. It had to be Juliet.

Lyndsey sagged against the solid support of the doorframe. Juliet would tell them to pick up Sonia and Marne from the sea. That absolutely had to be their first priority. Lyndsey prayed that those two had been able to hang onto the rocks in the middle of the channel until now. The helicopter would airlift them out of the sea and take them to hospital. And Val as well, they'd get her to hospital. It was a flight of only a few minutes.

Within an hour, they'd all be back on the mainland.

'We're saved,' Lyndsey said aloud, to see what the words sounded like. She could barely hear them over the steady thrumming of the helicopter engine. 'We're safe.'

She realised she couldn't stay up there. After the helicopter rescued her friends, they would come looking for her. Since Juliet didn't know where Lyndsey had gone, it could be ages before they thought to look at the top the lighthouse. Lyndsey would have to go meet them. Even if that meant tackling the stairs and walking past Amanda's body.

She took one last look out over the storm-ruffled island, with the waves smashing themselves to pieces against its shore, then turned away to make the long, slow descent down the stairs to the exit.

Chapter Thirty-Five

SUNDAY 25TH AUGUST 2019

7:00pm

Furness General Hospital, Barrow-in-Furness

They had given Lyndsey a separate hospital room to herself, and all the blankets she wanted. She cocooned herself, wrapping them tightly around her body, until at last she managed to feel warm again. Even so, there was a chill right through to the marrow of her bones that she suspected would never leave. She would carry some of that coldness with her forever.

'Are you cleared to have visitors?' a voice asked from the doorway.

Lyndsey raised her head. 'You're alive,' she said in amazement.

'Of course I am. What made you think otherwise?'

Lyndsey didn't answer that. 'How come they're letting you wander around?' she asked instead. 'I thought we were supposed to stay in our beds.'

'Pfft,' Val said. 'If they wanted to enforce that, they should've kept the police officers here. Do you realise there are only two officers on the ward now? And they've got their hands full with Juliet.'

She came into Lyndsey's room and closed the door behind her. Although the police had taken away their clothing – forensics, they'd said – Val had managed to source a slightly unflattering tracksuit from somewhere. The graze on her face had been cleaned, but there was some ugly bruising all the way up that side of her face, disappearing into her hairline. Lyndsey blinked twice, just in case her mind was playing tricks on her. But no, Val was there, in person, alive. It felt like a miracle.

'What's wrong with Juliet?' Lyndsey asked.

'Nothing. She's just giving one hell of a statement. I could hear her shouting earlier. She's very angry about a lot of things.'

Lyndsey found it hard to picture Juliet being angry enough to shout at a police officer. 'So she's okay, then?'

'Sounds like it. Gary tried to get onto the ward earlier to see her, and when they said he wasn't allowed, he kicked off as well. That relationship seems to be ninety per cent based on drama. Hopefully, when they finally get a chance to talk, they'll do it without shouting. It sounds like they've got a few things to work through.'

'Speaking of communicating,' Lyndsey said, 'I'm pretty

sure we're not supposed to be talking to each other. The police said we shouldn't.'

Val waved it away. 'I've already given my statement. I assume you have as well, right? So it's a little late for us to do any collaborating, if that's what they're worried about.'

'Still.' Lyndsey shifted in her bed. She was aware how ridiculous she must've looked, mummified in her blankets, with only her face poking out. However, she wasn't going to unwrap herself, not for anyone. 'We shouldn't be talking.'

'You're no fun. Don't you want to compare notes?'

Val's voice was still scratchy and raw, deeper than usual, and she moved slowly as she pulled a chair up to Lyndsey's beside and collapsed into it with a sigh of relief.

'How're you feeling?' Lyndsey asked.

'Sore. Unhappy. They put me on oxygen and a drip for almost four hours. Look.' Val pushed up her sleeve to show off the crook of her elbow. A purplish bruise discoloured her skin. 'I told them that I bruise like a peach, but they cannulated me anyway. Bunch of sods.'

'They saved your life.'

Val's expression turned uncharacteristically serious. 'No, *you* did that. If you hadn't dragged me out of the bunkhouse, I'd be dead. No question about it.'

Lyndsey gave a crooked smile. 'Sorry I bashed up your face while doing it.'

'Think nothing of it. Gave the police an excuse to photograph my best side. Besides—' Val gestured at Lyndsey. 'Your face didn't escape unscathed either.'

The air gun pellet had torn a gouge right across Lyndsey's cheek, less than an inch below her right eye, but it'd been deflected by the bone. If Lyndsey's head hadn't been slightly turned away when the rifle went off, it might've been a different story. She could easily have lost an eye. Or ended up with the pellet lodged deep in her sinuses.

A bulky package of gauze now covered the injury. It was a constant blur in the bottom of Lyndsey's peripheral vision. One of the reasons she was keeping her hands inside her blanket-cocoon was so she didn't fidget with the bandage.

'You're going to have a great scar,' Val said. 'A real war wound.'

'Don't. The doctors keep talking about plastic surgery. I don't know how I feel about that.'

'Problems for another day.' Val settled down into the visitor's chair. It was the same chair that the police officer had sat in earlier that day, when Lyndsey had given her statement. 'Have you heard from any of the others?'

'Nobody will tell me anything,' Lyndsey said bitterly. 'The nurses, the police … they're all keeping quiet around me. I figure it must be because…' She braced herself. 'They're dead, aren't they? Sonia and Marne. They didn't make it.'

Val's eyes widened in surprise. 'No, no. They made it. The helicopter plucked them both out of the sea.'

'You know that for a fact, do you? You've seen them?'

'Not for myself, no, but the people are saying—'

'People are saying almost nothing. And when they do tell us something … I don't know whether we can believe them.'

About the only thing the police had confirmed to her

was that Amanda was dead. She'd died instantly from the fall. Lyndsey was not ready to start processing that just yet. The rescue helicopter had made a return trip to retrieve Amanda, and also pick up Bobbie from that ledge by the sea.

'I didn't trust them when they said you were fine either,' Lyndsey admitted. 'I thought maybe … I don't know. I thought they were telling me what I wanted to hear. I was scared it wasn't true.'

Part of her still wasn't ready to accept that her friends had survived. It felt too impossible. Lyndsey tried to focus on Val, who was definitely there, at her bedside. Lyndsey considered poking her with a finger to make sure she was real.

'This is why you should get up and wander the ward,' Val said. 'Make a nuisance of yourself. It's amazing what you find out.' She smiled. 'Marne's been discharged already. I don't know the full story, but it sounds like she's a bit battered and bruised, and had a touch of hypothermia, but that's it. Walking wounded.'

It still sounded like a lie to Lyndsey. After what Marne had gone through, would she really have been discharged so quickly? What was a *touch* of hypothermia, anyway? Surely hypothermia was an all-or-nothing condition. Val sounded certain, but maybe the police and the doctors had lied to her too.

We've got no way of contacting Marne or her family, Lyndsey realised suddenly. *We don't even know her full name.* There was a chance they would never run into each other again. If Marne didn't want to speak to them – and it seemed likely that she wouldn't, even if she was in fact alive and well – then Lyndsey would never get a chance to thank her for trying to save Sonia's life.

The police had refused to tell Lyndsey whether the fire had destroyed the bunkhouse and the observatory, or whether anything could be salvaged from it. Lyndsey could only hope Marne hadn't lost everything. Poor Marne, who had risked her life to save Sonia's and, in return, had lost her job and her livelihood. If she was alive, there was no way she'd be able to return to Shell Island this season. Lyndsey had no idea how long it'd take National Heritage to repair or rebuild the observatory … or whether they might decide it wasn't financially viable to do so.

The thought caused fresh tears to sting Lyndsey's eyes. Ever since she'd arrived at the hospital, she'd been constantly emotional. Every little thing made her cry.

'What about Sonia?' she asked.

'She's not on this ward. As far as I could find out, she's been transferred to Ward 4.'

'Ward 4. That's—?'

'Gynae. I don't know.' Val lifted her hands; let them fall. 'It could mean anything. I don't know for sure. The staff are *really* cagey up on that ward. Don't like answering questions at all.'

'You went there? We're not allowed to leave the ward. How—?'

'I didn't go anywhere. But I suppose I did use the phone at the nurses' station while no one was looking. They told me Sonia's still there, but I couldn't blag any other answers out of them. And then a nurse came by and told me off.'

Lyndsey laughed. It hurt, but she didn't care. She'd assumed she would never laugh again. 'How did you talk your way out of that one?'

'I told them I'd been trying to call my missus and couldn't figure out how to get an outside line. I'll try again after the shift changes.' Val cleared her throat. 'It, ah, it sounded to me like someone's there with Sonia. She's not on her own.'

Lyndsey's eyes widened. 'You don't think it's—?'

'It's not the guy that's caused all her troubles, no. He's in custody right now. Helping police with their enquiries.'

Lyndsey slumped back on her pillow. 'God. What a mess.'

'If I had to hazard a guess, I'd say it's Marne who's sitting with Sonia on the ward.'

'Marne? You think?'

'Intuition. Or maybe just hope.' Val folded her hands on her stomach. 'So, do you want to talk about things?'

'Not in the slightest.' Lyndsey sighed. 'But I'm betting that you do, yeah? Otherwise, you wouldn't be here.'

'Correct.' Val inched her chair closer to the bed. 'I told the police everything I knew, and everything I suspected, but obviously there are some gaps in my knowledge.'

'Wait, everything? Even about Sonia having an affair?'

'Well, no, not that.' Val wrinkled her nose. 'If Sonia wants to come clean, that's her business.'

Lyndsey smiled faintly. 'I didn't say anything either. Did you tell the police about Cherry?'

Val hesitated. 'In respect of what?'

'You were planning to write a story about her. You

talked about it with Bobbie. Who promptly went and told everything to Amanda.' Just speaking the names aloud made Lyndsey's chest hurt.

'Ah. Right. I wasn't sure if you knew about that.'

'Amanda told me. Val … do you realise how much this upset everyone? Amanda never knew the full story. Those details we kept from her… I guess we thought we were protecting her.' *Or protecting ourselves*, Lyndsey thought with a guilty twinge. 'When Bobbie decided to confess everything to Amanda this year … I think it tipped Amanda over the edge. She thought we'd all conspired to keep her in the dark. Worse, she thought we'd murdered Cherry, either deliberately or by our own dumb negligence, then lied to save ourselves. What were you thinking? Why did you have to drag everything up like that?'

Val's eyebrows went up. 'I only mentioned it to Bobbie as a hypothetical,' she objected. 'I'd been toying with the idea for a while, and I wanted to find out how closely her memories matched my own. At some point, I was going to speak to you all about it. I wanted to hold off putting anything in writing until I was sure everyone was comfortable with the idea. I get how that's important.'

'Except you didn't hold off, did you? You'd started writing it. There was some of it on your laptop, right?'

'Crap.' Val winced as she realised. '*Crap*. You think she read it?'

'I think you need to start password protecting your work. Or at least stop leaving it lying around where just anyone can read it.' Lyndsey felt anger flare inside her. If Val had just left well enough alone… 'Why on earth did you think it was a good idea to rake up the past like that? When you told Bobbie about possibly writing a book about Cherry, it stirred up all her memories and made her feel guilty all over again for something that was never her fault. She thought it'd make things better if she talked it out with Amanda.' Lyndsey thinned her lips. 'If you hadn't dug it all up, none of this would've happened.'

Val knotted her fingers together. Distress was stamped on her face. 'It was just an *idea*,' she said. 'I thought it'd make a good basis for a story. I was going to anonymise everyone's details and change the circumstances around enough so that it would only be *based* on the truth. Like, a fictionalised account. I only spoke to Bobbie about it because I wasn't sure how everyone would react. I never meant to upset anyone.'

Lyndsey closed her eyes. The anger still burned through her chest, but it was hard to direct it solely at Val. 'We're all to blame,' she muttered. 'We should never have kept anything from Amanda. She deserved to know the truth about her sister's death.'

'None of us deliberately lied to her,' Val said, quietly. 'We were all shocked by what happened to Cherry. None of us wanted to admit we'd played a part in it.'

'We should've admitted it.' Lyndsey sighed. 'It was the anniversary of Cherry's death this year, and we all forgot. Not one of us even checked in with Amanda to make sure she was okay.'

Val was quiet for a moment. 'Ten years. That's right. How could I forget? I've got all the dates written down. I can't believe it didn't click.'

They both fell silent. After a minute, Lyndsey said, 'Do you think the police will believe us?'

'Don't see why they wouldn't.'

'Amanda pointed out it was just our word against hers. I know she's not going to get a chance to tell whatever story she wanted to tell the police, but there's still no real evidence to back us up.' Lyndsey glanced moodily out of the window. From her angle in bed, all she could see were grey clouds and the raindrops on the glass. The storm still hadn't let up. 'Everything went up in smoke with the bunkhouse.'

Val slapped her thigh with the palm of her hand as if remembering something. 'That's what I forgot,' she said. 'You don't know why I went back to the bunkhouse, do you?'

'Went back? When?'

'When you were all off at the harbour, flashing your torches at the Sound Café. Juliet and Amanda were faster walkers than me, and I was pissed off with Juliet and her opinions, so they took off ahead of me. By the time I got halfway there, something suddenly clicked in my mind. I realised how the poison must've got into Bobbie's system.'

'It was in her purple water bottle.'

'It was – hey, how did you know that? Did you figure it out too?'

'Amanda told me.'

Val pursed her lips in annoyance. 'Well. I figured it out myself, at least. It was the best way of administering the poison that any of us could've managed – and, even better, it could've been set up *before* we ever got to the island.'

'Amanda refilled Bobbie's water bottle before they left to catch the boat. She put the poison in it then.'

'You are ruining all my revelations.'

'Sorry.'

'It's fine.' Val still looked irritated. 'Did you tell all of this to the police?'

'Yeah, but without the actual bottle itself, we've got no evidence.'

'And *that's* where you're wrong.' Val beamed at her. 'It's why I went back to the bunkhouse. I figured the bottle had to be important, so I went back and got it. I was going to put it in my bag, but seeing as at least two people had been poking through my stuff already that weekend, I stashed it in my jacket pocket instead.'

'You did?'

'Yep. Wrapped it in a plastic bag to keep it uncontaminated. Then I was going to come find you lot, but Amanda turned up at the bunkhouse. Said she needed to speak to me urgently about something. I don't—' Val frowned. Almost unconsciously, she reached to touch the back of her head, where a neat line of sutures closed the wound. 'I don't remember exactly what she was talking about. She was upset. I remember that. I turned my back on her for a second, and—' She let her hand fall. 'That's it. That's all I remember. They still don't know for sure what the hell she hit me with. A frying pan, maybe. I guess forensics will figure it out eventually. But, the good news is, when I woke up, the water bottle was still in my pocket. I kept telling the bods in the helicopter about it. One of them passed it to the police.'

'Do you think it'll be any use?'

Val shrugged. 'Well, it should be. None of us handled it except Bobbie and presumably Amanda. I wore gloves when I touched it.'

Lyndsey had a moment of true panic. She remembered seeing the water bottle in the bunkhouse and picking it up. Had she been wearing her gloves at the time? She tried to think, but couldn't be certain.

'So,' Val went on, oblivious, 'if there are any fingerprints to find, the police will get them. Plus, any residue that's left in the bottle.' She paused. 'I hope there's residue. Otherwise, we might never find out exactly what type of poison Amanda used. I mean, toxicology blood tests on Bobbie will give us a broad idea of what it *could* be, but I'd like to know for definite. Or else I'm going to wonder about it forever. Those exact symptoms, the confusion and disorientations, the hallucinations – auditory *and* visual, do you realise how particular that is? And everything else as well—'

Lyndsey nodded and tuned her out. She didn't want to think about any of this. If she'd had any choice in the matter, she would've gone back to sleep, and stayed asleep until everything had been resolved, one way or another.

My friends are dead. Bobbie and Amanda, two people whom Lyndsey had known for longer than she could remember, now both gone forever. Sonia was almost certainly gone as well, despite whatever Val thought she knew. And Marne as well … Marne, whom Lyndsey had barely got a chance to know. There was a deep pain in

Lyndsey's heart that she knew would never fade. *My friends are dead.*

Val cleared her throat. 'Once we're past all this,' she said, 'I was thinking of writing about it.'

'Val, no.'

'Just, like, a factual account. To make sure all of our stories are told correctly. There's going to be a lot of speculation, y'know.'

'Don't you dare. I mean it.'

Val pulled a face. 'Fine. I'll leave it for the moment. I guess no one will want to talk about it until we're all out of hospital, at the very least.'

'We need more time than that. I'm getting let out today.'

Val went quiet. 'Who told you that?'

'The doctors.'

'They said you'd be released today?'

'Well, y'know. They never say anything directly, do they?' Lyndsey turned her head towards Val, frowning. 'Why are you looking at me like that?'

'It just doesn't fit precisely with what I heard,' Val said carefully. 'It sounded to me like they wanted to keep an eye on you for a bit longer.'

'Yeah, they said that to me too,' Lyndsey admitted, 'but how can we trust anything they say? We don't even know if they're telling the truth about Sonia or Marne or anyone else. So how can I believe them when they say I need to stay here for longer so they can *assess my state of mind*, or whatever it is they want to do.' Lyndsey closed her eyes. 'I'm getting out of here as soon as I can.'

'There's nothing wrong with accepting a bit of help, Lynds.'

Lyndsey snorted. 'I'm doing just fine. Thank you for your concern.'

'If you reckon.'

Lyndsey leaned her head back into her nest of blankets, eyes still closed. She felt like the storm was still going on within the confines of her skull. How was she supposed to know what to believe? People kept telling her conflicting stories – about her friends, about her health, about everything. She didn't know who she could trust. She wasn't even sure she could trust her own mind.

She untangled her hand from the blankets and reached out for Val. Her searching fingers encountered only air.

'Val?'

Lyndsey raised her head. Val's chair was empty. The room was empty. She hadn't heard Val get up to leave. Maybe Lyndsey had lapsed into sleep for a few moments, and her friend had snuck out. It was difficult to be certain.

It was difficult to be certain of anything.

She lay back down and waited for the police to return and speak to her again.

Acknowledgments

I always promise myself I'll keep a proper list of everyone I need to thank in the acknowledgements, but, once again, Past-Rakie has let me down. So I apologise in advance to anyone I accidentally miss out. Just know that I really appreciate you all and you're great. Also your hair looks lovely.

Thank you to Charlotte Ledger, Bethan Morgan, Lok Yee Liu, Hannah Todd, and everyone at One More Chapter, who did such amazing work transforming this jumble of words into an actual physical object. I couldn't ask for a nicer bunch of people to work with.

Thank you to my fantastic agent Leslie Gardner, for always keeping me on track and for talking me down off the ceiling when necessary. And everyone at Artellus too, you folks are awesome.

Thank you to my family for supporting me always. I apologise for any mistakes in the climbing sections of this book – it's been a while since I last abseiled! This might also be a good time to apologise to my sister for fictionalising some of her travel anecdotes. Again.

Shell Island is a fictional place, but some of the names and history are based on the Calf of Man, which is a cute little island off the south coast of the Isle of Man. My thanks to the folks at Manx National Heritage for answering a whole load of daft questions from me. Apologies to you as well for the liberties I've taken with the geography of the island. (As a side note to readers, the actual bunkhouse on the Calf of Man is lovely and not at all like the one in this book. If you get a chance, you should definitely visit.)

Thank you to the various writing groups who've put up with me, especially Shut Up & Write, Manx Litfest Writers' Group, Happy People, and NaNoWriMo. I can assure you that the characters in this book are definitely not based on any of you. Not even Val.

Thank you to the Bridge Bookshop, Mobile Family Library, HBN Library, Women of Mann book group, Noir at the Bar, Manx Litfest, and everyone else for all your help and support and promotion.

Thank you to my husband for believing in me, making endless cups of coffee, and chasing me back to my laptop when I was procrastinating. Go Team Marriage!

Thank you to Jacob and Elliott for being awesome. Go Team Fam Squad!

A couple of sad thank yous to finish with: Thank you to the late, great Guy N Smith, for encouraging me to put words onto paper. You were always an inspiration. And thank you with all my heart to my mum-in-law, Helen, who sadly died just before completion of this book. I'm so sorry you didn't get a chance to read this one; I hope you would've liked it.